REBELS

ASSASSIN'S MAGIC
BOOK FIVE

EVERLY FROST

DISCOVER THE EVER REALMS

Seven series. One world.

Suggested Reading Order:

Bright Wicked
Storm Princess
Assassin's Magic
Soul Bitten Shifter
Supernatural Legacy
Dark Magic Shifters
Kingdom of Betrayal

A NOTE ON TIMELINES...

The events in this book cross over with the events in Assassin's
Maze.

That means you may see a character you weren't expecting
to see...

For the rebel in all of us.

1. PEYTON PRICE

My family escorts me like a small child through the wide wooden entrance to Bloodwing Academy.

My father grips my upper arm, ready to drag me if he has to. On my other side, my mother holds my hand, as if she can't bear to let me go, but her fingernails sink into my palm, prepared to draw blood if I try to pull away again.

I fought them the entire car trip here, my efforts earning me a cut above my left eye when my brother thumped me across the face. I guess he thought it would be like the movies where he'd knock me out and I'd stay unconscious for the rest of the trip—not the thirty seconds I was actually out.

His dark stare burns my back. Literally. A glance to the side tells me his eyes are glowing, the heat from his fire mage power causing sweat to pool uncomfortably between my shoulder blades.

It's a family affair today. They've brought me to Bloodwing to say goodbye and leave cold kisses on my cheek because this is the last time they'll see me alive.

People leave Bloodwing in body bags. My parents may as

well put a bullet in my head and throw me in a ditch. At least it would be quick.

The woman behind the mahogany front counter is dressed in a bright yellow suit that clashes with her lacquered black-and-orange striped fingernails. Her graying hair is short and permed and her eyes are washed out like they used to be brown but don't know what color to be anymore.

"Peyton Price?" she asks, directing her question to my father instead of me. Her disinterested gaze passes over the blood smearing my forehead.

"That's us," he says, drawing me to the counter, taking my right hand and pressing it, palm down, onto the countertop while his other arm encircles my back. Mom does the same with my left. It's so I don't try to escape.

The woman's name badge is bright yellow with black lettering: *Headmistress Osprey*. She picks up a pen before she pulls a file across the countertop, opening it. Running the pen down the page, she says, "Well, everything looks in order except..."

Here it comes. The question that will make my parents want to sink into the polished wooden floor.

Headmistress Osprey leans across the counter, ballpoint pen poised above the form. Behind her on the wall, a large wooden plaque embossed with gold lettering reads: *Bloodwing Academy for the Magically Repressed*.

She peers at us expectantly. "What is your daughter's magical repression?"

Mom shimmers at the edges as she tries to disappear, her power of invisibility momentarily out of her control.

Dad lets go of me to place a firm hand on her arm, reaching around behind my back, anchoring her but shoving me forward at the same time so my stomach presses into the ledge. Flames lick off his bare palm, his fire mage power jolting her back to herself.

The heat scorches my shoulder and makes me sweat even more.

To Headmistress Osprey, he says firmly, "We don't know."

She studies me for the first time, her lips pinched, her washed-out eyes narrowed into unwelcoming slits.

Hello. Hi there. I actually exist. I'm an actual person.

The expression on her face says otherwise.

She turns back to my parents, her gaze passing over my brother. It's impossible to miss the flicker of appreciation in her eyes. I picture his smug smile. Younger women, older women—it doesn't matter as long as they wear a skirt and aren't afraid to lift it.

Her brow arches. "You don't know? You mean to tell me that Peyton has never exhibited any magical manifestations in her entire life?"

Not once in all my twenty years. It would be better if I'd been born non-magical, but my heart skips every sixth beat like other supernaturals. Yet in all my time on this Earth, I've never revealed my magical ability. I don't know what it is. Nobody does.

Mom pulls herself together. "None."

"At all? Not even a flicker?"

Mom loses her cool, her power of invisibility out of control and her entire torso disappearing as she snaps, "That's what we said! Peyton is unknown."

Unknown.

When I was a baby it was okay. When I was a kid it was tolerable. When I was a teen, it was unbearable. And now…

Now my choices have been taken away from me.

Now I'm a walking corpse.

Headmistress Osprey sucks in a sharp, unhappy-sounding breath. "We'll have to house her in the attic. An Unknown is too dangerous to allow her to sleep with the others."

"She'll have her own room?" Mom asks, her body fully reappearing. "Is that safe?"

I don't kid myself that Mom means *safe for me*. She means *safe for everyone else*.

"Oh, don't worry. She'll be constantly monitored by her own personal guards. We assign two compliance officers to every student. Our staff is trained in all forms of magical restraint. Believe me, they will be able to handle her."

Headmistress Osprey bops the silver bell on the counter and on cue, two tall men appear at the entrance to the hall on the right. The entrance room is mostly empty—wooden floor, wood walls, and the counter—with a walkway on either side. It feels almost like a crossroads.

Both newcomers are dressed in navy blue uniforms that remind me of the human police force: button-down pockets on each side of a collared shirt, crisp navy trousers, and a wide ammunitions belt, except that they carry wands instead of guns.

Headmistress Osprey points them out in turn. "These are the compliance officers who will take care of Peyton: Collin and Colby. They will ensure she doesn't give us any trouble."

Most schools would be concerned about ensuring *my* safety. Definitely not this one.

"What about when she leaves?" Mom asks.

Headmistress Osprey looks surprised. "She won't leave. Not unless she's cured—no matter how long that takes. Don't worry, dear. By handing her over to us, you are no longer legally responsible for her actions."

"Good." Dad takes that as permission to let me go. His responsibility for me and my dangerously unknown supernatural powers is at an end. "You'll receive payment for her tuition every month for as long as she remains here." He adds, "With our gratitude."

Mom also relaxes, letting me go, as if she can't stand to touch me anymore. She exhales, sheer relief showing in her bright smile. "We'll leave you to it then."

They both spin on their heels, gathering my brother up with them as they pass by. He dumps my single duffel bag of belongings onto the floor and turns away with a final wicked smile cast in my direction.

No cold kisses after all.

Would it matter if I screamed at them? *I'm still a person. I have a heart and a mind. I'm not a monster!*

I still… *feel.*

Once my family disappears through the front door, Headmistress Osprey steps back from the counter, revealing her own weapons belt. She detaches her wand, a thick, curved one with thorns jutting from its surface, starting halfway along and extending all the way to the tip. She taps it in the air and the far doors seal behind my departing family with a bang that echoes through the silent halls.

"There," she says. "All done."

I take another quick look around. *Where are the other students?* So far, I haven't seen anyone other than Headmistress Osprey and the two guards. It's so quiet, I can hear my heartbeat rapidly increasing.

The older lady smiles at me for so long that it makes me uncomfortable.

It's her mouth that's smiling, not her eyes.

"You're wondering where everyone is?" she asks, reading my mind so accurately that I wonder if she's telepathic. I deliberately test that theory by thinking loud, unflattering thoughts about her yellow suit.

Her expression doesn't change, so either she has a poker face, or my telepathy theory is bogus.

"The entire school is on lockdown for your arrival," she says. "We don't expose our current students to a newcomer until we've verified the true nature of their condition. It's time to find out if your parents were telling the truth."

She puts her wand down on the counter and props her elbows on the tabletop, casually resting her head in her hands as if she's about to watch a show. "Over to you, gentlemen. Let's see if Peyton really is Unknown."

The two men separate, one remaining on my right while the other walks to my left, locating themselves between me and each hallway. Both are giving me a once over, head to toes.

I fold my arms across my chest, wishing I were wearing more than a thin sweater and skinny jeans. Maybe a puffer jacket. Or a suit of armor.

It's difficult to find a supernatural who isn't good-looking. Power tends to lend itself to eye colors that are brighter, deeper, lips that are perfectly shaped, and skin that is somehow lustrous. Don't even get me started on hair. Supernatural women don't need styling products to look amazing every day.

But these guys come close to regular scary, crack-your-skull, don't-bump-into-them-in-dark-alleys guys. They are both broad-shouldered, tattoos peeking from under their long shirt sleeves.

One of them—the one whose name is apparently Collin— has pale blue irises that make his eyes look creepily white and he's missing a little chunk out of the top of his left ear. His gaze lingers on my breasts in a way that makes me want to gouge his face.

The other one—Colby—has tattoos peeking from beneath his cuffs and above his collar. He watches my feet, then my hands, then the press of my lips, studying me in a way that tells me he's waiting for me to run.

Maybe a lot of newcomers do.

Colby inclines his head at the exit. "The door's right there. You can leave if you really want to."

Come to think of it, it's odd that they've blocked off the hallways into the school but not the door to the outside. Something tells me it's not going to be that easy. "It doesn't look that way to me."

"Reveal your power, control it, and you can leave," he says.

Reveal, control, leave. Sounds stupidly easy. Also out of my reach.

Also a lie. No student has ever walked out of Bloodwing. Not that I've heard of anyway.

"I can't control something I don't have," I say.

His eyebrows arch. "You don't believe you have magical powers?"

I shrug. I lost count of all the doctor's visits. The supernatural community doesn't use human doctors—it's too dangerous because medical tests could reveal our magical anomalies, especially our heartbeats. Mom took me to so many different supernatural doctors that it felt like it became her hobby.

They'd listen to my heart and it would pound:

Ba-bam, ba-bam, ba—

Nothing. No *bam.*

Damn missing sixth beat.

I grit my teeth. "I guess that's what I'll find out."

If I try to run right now, it will be so much worse for me. I need to accept that my life is going to be hell for a while, but I won't accept my fate. I'm going to bide my time. Plan. Proceed carefully. I won't die here.

Colby taps his wand against his leg, tilting his head and studying my hands again. I've heard that magical manifestations start with the hands, so if I'm going to reveal anything, it will begin with my fingertips.

The other guy, Collin, wears a growing smile that sets my teeth on edge. "Go hard?" he asks Colby.

Colby shrugs. "Why not?"

I press up against the counter, discovering that I've slowly backed into it. I unfold my arms to brace my sweaty palms against the wooden paneling. I'm not sure when I'll next get the chance to breathe, so I take a deep one—

They flick their wands so fast that I'm still mid-breath. Pulsing blue light spears at me from each side, a wide circular wash like two sides of a sphere that rapidly elongates to my size and height and seals around me. I wobble and drop to my knees inside the large bubble, my hands tingling when they brush against it.

I recognize the energy now surrounding me. It's a magical poultice. A massive one. Designed to draw out any power inside me like a splinter out of a fingertip. I've only had little ones applied in the past—a moist blob attached to my shoulder or my stomach. Once a doctor put one on my cheek. That hurt. This one is full body and it—

I groan, doubling over, pressing down across my knees, squeezing my eyes shut.

A gnawing pain fills my stomach like a drill digging beneath the surface. A low moan thrums at the back of my throat as I try to vocalize the pain, humming it out.

I grip my knees, pressing my fingernails into my jeans, the heels of my boots digging into the backs of my thighs. Uncomfortable. Uncaring.

Make it stop.

It won't stop until these men see a hint of my power.

The poultice thickens around me, the air stinging as I draw it in and out of my lungs. I force my eyes open, stretching my hands out from my knees, my torso pressed flat against my thighs.

I arch my fingers back. *Please manifest.*

It could be a transformation of my fingertips or a tiny flame. Even a moment of invisibility, something that indicates what my power is, whether I'm a shifter, a witch, a mage, or something else.

My power could be anything.

Magically repressed supernaturals don't follow their family's genetics. We're genetic throwbacks. Like strange supernatural mutants.

We also don't have magical auras like other supernaturals that indicate what sort of supernatural we are.

But when our power explodes, it's called a flicker fit. It's a sort of aura explosion that's too strong to distinguish our unique abilities.

That's when we're dangerous.

There's not a lot of research on the magically repressed, since we're few and far between, but what I could dig up in books indicates that we never live long before we have a flicker fit, kill everyone around us, and are put to death for it.

I won't manifest.

I know I won't.

The drilling sensation inside my stomach deepens, spreading up through my chest, the pain intensifying.

Humming isn't working anymore. *Oh, please.* I rock against my knees, dragging the heels of my palms against the inside of the poultice, its energy crackling through me.

Tears stream down my cheeks, making it difficult to see.

Outside the bubble, the compliance officers are bracing, wands outstretched, lines of energy flowing from their wands' tips into the poultice. Deep concentration forms creases in their foreheads, the ligaments at the sides of their necks bulging, the only signs of strain.

I drop my head, unable to hold it up. My forehead hits the floor with a *smack*.

The poultice breaks, disintegrating into misty liquid. A single drop, unexpectedly cold, splashes the back of my neck where my long brown hair has parted and falls down on both sides of my face.

A horrible scream echoes around the entrance room, beating back and forth from wall to wall, making me shudder until it finally fades.

Was that me? Was I screaming?

I slump and roll onto my side, my knees still pulled to my chest, slowly unfurling.

I don't care about my dignity right now. I need to breathe.

Headmistress Osprey's heels clack angrily across the wooden floor and stop at my eye level. I raise my eyes to see her plant her hands firmly on her hips above me.

Collin and Colby appear above me too—blurry, navy silhouettes—as my tears fall across my vision. It's hard to tell the men apart through the water filling my eyes.

With a disgruntled huff, one of them says, "That always works."

"Not always," Headmistress Osprey snaps. "Get her up."

I scoot away from them, thumping the first hand that reaches for me. "Get off me!"

I press back against the first solid surface I can find and slide up the counter paneling until I bump my head on the overhanging ledge.

Rubbing my smarting scalp with one hand, I swipe my tears with the other, dragging my sweatshirt sleeve across my streaming nose. I'm a revolting mess, but my appearance is the last thing I care about right now. I don't take my eyes off the wands the compliance twins point at me.

Headmistress Osprey's lips are tightly pinched. "You really do belong in the attic."

She gives the compliance twins a sharp nod. "Bring her things."

I only came with one bag containing a few jeans, sweatshirt, T-shirts, nightclothes, all my underwear, and some basic toiletries. I don't have a cell phone. No books. No trinkets. Apparently the Academy supplies everything, including uniforms, but I wasn't going to take the chance with underwear.

Colby picks up my lone bag and strides ahead of us while Headmistress Osprey grabs my arm and propels me along the hallway to the left. Collin brings up the rear, his wand still out.

"This is the west wing," Headmistress Osprey says, "Students sleep on this side. Classes are given in the east wing. The food hall is also in the east wing on the first floor."

We climb a set of stairs that opens onto the next level. She describes this floor with a clipped: "Staff sleeping quarters."

She continues to push me up the next flight of stairs to the next floor, which apparently belongs to "Female students. Not you."

The next is for the males.

Finally, the stairs let out onto a fourth floor, but this one is nowhere near as big.

A wall blocks off the left side and the walkway on the right extends for only fifty or so paces. Wall-to-ceiling windows fill the length of the corridor's left side.

A couple of steps closer to them and my vertigo goes haywire. I can finally see how high up we are, but I don't venture close enough to see outside. It's high enough to fall to my death and that glass looks far too flimsy to me.

Headmistress Osprey shoves me along the corridor and I resolutely pin my gaze to the floor.

"Scared of heights?" Collin's snicker makes me jump as he leans in close to me.

I resist the urge to give him a bloody nose. The internet was great for learning self-defense moves, which I needed for school on a daily basis. I'm used to being shoved around—but not always good at judging when to hit back. I somehow always managed to do it when a teacher was looking.

The wand Collin waggles at me keeps me in line for now.

We approach the first door, but I'm surprised when we keep walking. It's ajar. Just enough to glimpse a bedroom with distinctly male décor.

"Does someone else sleep up here? I thought you said I'd be alone."

I'd rather be alone than share a floor with a guy. There'd better be a lock on my door. My experiences with guys have not been positive.

Headmistress Osprey gives my arm a yank. She shoves me toward the next door, which is also ajar.

Inside, the bedroom is nearly empty. I take stock of the nothingness: bed, closet, annoyingly loud ticking clock on the wall. No curtains. No rug on the floor. Nothing else on the walls. Not even a desk and chair. At least the bed has a pillow and blankets, all prison gray. A pile of folded towels on the end of the bed indicates there's a shower somewhere.

It doesn't look anything like the bedroom next door, which had a desk, multi-colored pillows, and pictures on the wall.

"Bathroom?" I ask.

"At the end of the hall," Headmistress Osprey replies.

Colby dumps my bag next to the towels while Collin stands in the doorway, guarding it.

Finally released from Headmistress Osprey's claw-like fingers, I put as much distance between myself and her as I can, heading straight for the window despite my hatred of heights. This one sits at waist height, extends nearly to the arched ceiling, and looks over the front of the Academy.

The garden is immaculately sculpted, dotted with neat red rose bushes. At the entrance, the wrought-iron gate is firmly closed, a stone raven sitting on top of each pillar at its side. The fence around the Academy is made of the same iron bars as the gate, ten feet high, too tall to scale.

There's so much security around this place that nobody in the supernatural community knows its location—only that it exists. My parents were told to drive. At random intervals, they received a phone call giving them the next set of directions.

When we finally pulled up outside the gate after a long trip, a security guard in uniform placed a delayed memory wipe on us to slowly obliterate the memory of the way here.

It must be kicking in because I can't remember much now, not which way we drove or what I saw along the way.

I don't know where we are. Somewhere in the western United States, I think.

My lingering glance out of the window gave Headmistress Osprey the chance to prowl up behind me. *Damn.* I can't turn my back on this woman.

She shoves me hard up against the glass. A shriek dies in my throat as I discover that it's sturdy enough to hold my weight, even though she's pressing my face against the lowest pane firmly enough to squish my cheek.

"The fence is electrified," she says, lowering her mouth to my ear as if she thinks I won't hear her otherwise.

Her breath smells of cigarettes and mint gum. I struggle to get away from her, only to discover she's hooked her leg around my ankle, causing me to stumble harder forward.

"If you try to escape, that fence will send enough volts into your body to knock you out cold. Trust me, we tested it. A fun little test. We made the students choose which one of them would touch it. You'd be surprised how quickly friends turn on each other when they want to avoid pain."

I sigh against the glass, my breath misting it.

As the mist clears, a figure moves in the grounds below, a guy dressed in gray gym pants and a short-sleeved T-shirt that hugs his chest and biceps. He doesn't look as small as I expected from this high up, which would make him taller and bigger than average.

He's running the perimeter close to the fence, a steady jog, arms pumping, feet kicking up the turf. Within moments, he passes the front gate and disappears around the other side.

He looks like he's not much older than me, mid-twenties at most, but he must be a teacher since Headmistress Osprey said the students are all on lockdown for my arrival.

My voice is muffled against the glass, but I'm hoping I can distract her from her torturous grip on my hair. My eyes water as I ask, "Who is that?"

A slow smile crosses her face, her lips close enough to my face for me to see the snarky curve. "That's Striker Draven."

Draven... Why does that name sound familiar?

She eases up on me, so I ask her another question, hoping she'll let me go altogether. "What class does he teach?"

She scoffs. "Striker isn't a teacher. He's a student."

My forehead creases with confusion. "I thought you said the other students needed to be—"

"Oh, no, my dear." She snickers. "Striker Draven is the only student who doesn't need protection from you."

She leans in close again and whispers, "You'll need protection from him."

With a pleased smile that makes my heart sink, she finally lets me go. "Get yourself settled. Dinner is downstairs at 6 o'clock sharp."

I glance at the clock. That's only half an hour away.

"Your uniform is in the closet. Your books are in the bottom of your closet along with your class timetable. Don't be tardy. The last student to class is always punished."

As she makes her way to the door, Colby asks her, "Do you want us to guard her room?"

"Whenever Draven isn't around, yes. Otherwise, you can leave her to him."

I guess that means they won't always watch me in class.

Osprey whirls back at the last moment. "Oh, by the way, there's no infirmary. If you get hurt, you'll have to deal with it."

With that, she and the men file out of the room. I hear Collin and Colby take up position outside my door while Headmistress Osprey's footfalls retreat.

Alone in my room, I slump against the window. My neck aches and so does my forehead. It's stopped bleeding, but I don't have a mirror to check how badly it's cut.

I hope there's a mirror in the bathroom because otherwise, my hair will be a mess each day. My parents wouldn't let me near scissors—they equated me with a serial killer in the making—and hairdressing trips were out of the question, so my tangled, brown hair is an unruly length.

Down below, Striker passes around the perimeter again. Assuming he traveled the full perimeter, it tells me that the grounds aren't all that large.

From this high up, he doesn't look so scary. If I press my thumb against the glass, I can imagine squishing him.

Wait a minute...

I remove my thumb and crane forward. He's moving much faster this time around, rapidly picking up speed and heading in a straight line instead of curving at the same angle as the fence. If he doesn't veer away, he'll run straight into it.

What is he doing—?

At the last moment, his muscles bunch, he turns his shoulder, and his feet leave the ground. But he doesn't leap in the safe direction.

He throws himself at the fence.

I cry out in shock before I clamp my hand over my mouth in case the noise invites the compliance officers back into my room.

Down below, light sparks as Striker's body jolts rapidly. He shudders and rolls to the side across the fence before he drops forward onto the grass.

My heart is in my throat as I wait for him to get up.

Is he hurt? Is he dead? Why the hell would he do that?

I'm still in shock when he pushes up onto all fours. I can't tell if he's making any sounds. He could be shouting for all I know.

I jump as he punches the ground with his right fist, driving his knuckles into it. He rises to his feet, draws himself upright and lifts his head high, standing very still for a moment.

He isn't shouting. I can't really tell, but I think his eyes are closed. I can't see his expression, but I can sense his tension.

Without warning, he throws himself at the fence again. This time, he pushes his back up against it, digging his heels in to the grass, his whole body jolting with the electrical shocks.

He thumps his fists back against the fence posts, smoke rising where he connects.

I want to cover my eyes.

This is… I can't even… He's inviting the pain. *What the hell is wrong with him?*

The only reason I don't race down there and yell at him to stop is the possibility that his actions have something to do with his power. Maybe it's electrical and this is all part of a normal day for him.

Some freaking crazy aggressive part of his day.

He finally lurches forward, falling to the ground, his shirt burned apart at the back. I can't see if his back is burned too. He rips off the scorched material as he lifts himself upright once more, his bare chest rising and falling, sculpted muscles shifting with every breath he takes before he stretches his neck side to side, appearing weirdly relaxed. As if he didn't just electrocute himself.

I rub my eyes in disbelief and when I look again, he's gone.

My thoughts churn as I sink to my bed. Headmistress Osprey wasn't exaggerating. Striker Draven is dangerous.

My first goal—in fact my daily goal—is going to be avoiding him at all costs.

I clasp my hands in my lap, taking a moment to center

myself, telling myself to take it step by step. I've made it through the first hour. I'm still alive and *mostly* unharmed. Now I need to make it through my first night. And the next. And however many nights it takes.

Reform academy. Prison. It's all the same.

No student has ever escaped from Bloodwing.

I intend to be the first.

2. STRIKER DRAVEN

air rakes into my lungs as my feet pound the grass, my speed increasing around the Academy's perimeter.

The sickly scent of roses invades every breath I take.

The perfume might be soothing if it didn't remind me of the woman who put me here—a woman whose appearance is so sweetly innocent, nobody would ever suspect her of being a mass murderer, the leader of an underground that trades in lives, both human and supernatural.

I can't do anything about her while I'm trapped here.

I focus on the cut of the grass—every sharp blade—the gleaming iron bars that form the cage around me, and the sizzle of electricity that warns me every time I get too close to the fence. I focus on my feet, each breath dragging in and out of my lungs, but it's no use.

I can't block out the echoes from within the Academy's walls.

The new girl is screaming.

It's nothing new. Pain is the melody of my life. I live and breathe by its rhythm. But her voice carries an edge that I've never heard from any newcomer to this hellhole. Most cry in fear and pain, but her screams carry anger, a deep fury that hits a nerve inside me.

I have to escape it. I won't be fooled by a girl again. If I could close my ears, I would.

I refuse to care.

Her scream deepens, a moan that tears into me like claws ripping at my heart.

Impossible. I don't have a heart anymore.

I force my feet to move faster, sprinting as rapidly as I can around the perimeter. Sweat builds on my chest and back, soaking into my shirt. My breath tears out of my throat.

The rest of the school is on lockdown, but the Headmistress doesn't treat me like I'm a student anymore.

I'm a fixture in this place, hated by both students and guards alike. I move around as I please. As long as I don't try to leave the grounds, Headmistress Osprey doesn't care.

I arrived when the Academy first opened three years ago and I'm bound to be the last to leave—in a coffin inevitably, but I'm determined to stave off that day as long as I can.

The new girl's screams finally stop.

The silence is a sudden weight dropped on me and I misjudge my footing, stumbling enough to throw myself off course, veering toward the fence. I pull to a stop right in front of it, inches from connecting with the electricity surging through it.

I resist the urge to wrap my hands around the bars. My breathing's too rapid. I need to calm down before I take on the voltage coursing through the iron poles.

Taking off again, I slow my pace, fill my lungs with the scent of roses, and empty my mind of the new girl's furious screams. With every step, the squeezing sensation in my chest eases, the claws retracting from the cold organ that used to be my heart. It's a muscle, that's all, pumping blood around my body. Nothing more.

Fifteen minutes later, I'm calm again, my mind at ease. I'm prepared for my daily ritual.

I empty myself of all thoughts as I increase speed around the back of the Academy. Headmistress Osprey pays no attention to my movements anymore—my reckless aggression. I can get away with anything. If I hurt someone while I'm at it, it's all the better with her. Her delight in my hostility certainly makes it easy to hide my true motives.

I charge in a straight line toward the fence, throwing up a mental shield around my mind, anticipating the pain.

Air whooshes across my chest and legs as I launch myself at the fence, turning my shoulder to connect with its surface.

Electricity sparks at the corners of my vision, pain screaming through my shoulder and down my back, a gripping, tearing agony.

With it comes energy, a deep, surging power that feeds my body. It's an excruciating contradiction to the biting pain tearing at my flesh.

I shudder and drop to the grass, hitting it on hands and knees.

The electricity I absorbed is not enough for what I need.

Dammit. I punch the grass, feeding my frustration into my fist, telling myself I can go again.

Forcing myself upright, I take a deep breath, close my eyes, and clear my mind again. I fight the urge to step back into the fence before I'm ready, fight the pull, the need for its energy.

My mind is empty again.

I throw myself backward, digging in my heels this time, jamming myself against its deadly surface.

Pain sears my back. The scent of burning material, burning skin, makes me want to hurl up everything I ate today, but I need the burn. I need the spark, the flame. I need it like I need air.

I smack my fists back against the bars. Once. Twice.

I hold on just a little too long.

But I'm okay now.

The fire inside me is fed.

I slump forward, finally dropping away from the fence. My back is in agony, but my mind is calm. I'm in control again.

I rip off my burned shirt as I rise to my feet. I normally take it off first, but I forgot today.

Damn the new girl. She threw me off routine. She's already a distraction I don't need. Burning through another shirt is going to annoy the Headmistress and I don't want her asking questions.

I jog inside the building through the back entrance—a wide wooden door—and head for the stairs.

Rounding the corner to the central staircase, I jolt to a stop as the Headmistress comes down them. I quickly scrunch the ruined material in my fist and position it behind my back.

"Draven," she says, casting a haughty look down her nose at me. She loves to play like she's in control, but I know who her boss is. Osprey doesn't control a damn thing.

She declares, "Our new student is verified as an Unknown."

I consider her with disinterest, but inside, I'm suddenly anything but calm. *Furious* doesn't even begin to describe the fiery feeling in the pit of my stomach.

Unknowns are too rare to be true.

The new girl is either a magnificent liar or Osprey is losing her touch. No doubt she left the verification to Colby and Collin. Those two brainless brutes wouldn't know their right hands from their left. I ignore the dissenting voice in the back of my mind reminding me that the newcomer screamed like she was being ripped apart.

There's also a third option—in addition to liar and incompetence—but I'm not ready to consider it yet.

Headmistress Osprey's heels click on the wooden floor as

she maneuvers around me. "Due to her status, she will sleep in the attic."

"What?" My objection is sharp. The attic is my space. The compliance officers don't venture up there anymore, but if the new girl is housed there, they'll swarm all over it again. "Like hell she will."

Osprey arches an eyebrow at me. "Unknowns must be kept apart from the other students. You know that, Draven. Otherwise, you would sleep on the fourth floor with the other male students."

She takes a step forward, her hand hovering around her curved wand, a clear threat.

I ignore it. She's forgotten that I don't fear her magic.

"Peyton Price will sleep in the room next to yours," she says, her tone allowing no further objection.

Fucking third option confirmed. They're using the new girl to get to me. It isn't the first time they've used another student to mess with me, and it probably won't be the last. I've held out, never revealed my power. For all intents and purposes, I don't know what I am. This is yet another complicated ploy to force my hand.

I grit my teeth and lean forward with a growl. "Well, she'd better be prepared for hell, then."

Osprey gives me a broad smile that would chill anyone else to the bone. "I'm counting on it, Draven."

Her response should worry me, but I've given up trying to interpret her intentions. She's a practiced liar. I take the stairs two at a time, pausing on the landing when a shout rings out below.

I lean back around the corner of the staircase to see what's going on just as one of the other compliance officers races up to Osprey.

"There's a problem in the pit," he says. "The beast broke the gate. We need reinforcements."

A scowl darkens her face. "Call the officers from the dining room."

"But the students—"

"They will behave. We can't let the creature escape."

Osprey hurries away with the officer.

Ignoring the shouts from below, then the bang of a door that leaves the building in silence again, I head for the bathroom at the end of the fourth-floor corridor instead of the one in the attic, intent on a quick shower.

The other students are being held in the dining room so I won't be disturbed. If I go up to the attic right now, I'll just as likely throw the new girl through the glass windows as anything else.

I need to cool down.

A sarcastic laugh builds inside my chest. For me, cooling down is impossible. Just like escaping from this place.

3. PEYTON PRICE

I exit my room cautiously on my way to the bathroom before dinner, surprised to find the compliance twins gone.

I listen for a moment, but the silence tells me I'm alone.

Not sure if I should be worried about that, I hurry to the bathroom, determined to assess the damage to my forehead.

I'm dismayed to find that there isn't a mirror. Just a shower, toilet, and sink. The door doesn't lock, either, just like my bedroom. There's no guarantee of privacy.

An oversized towel takes up the entire towel rack, making me wonder where I'll hang mine. I quickly wash my hands and use the washcloth I was given to gently prod my forehead, feeling for the wound my brother gave me, trying to figure out how bad it is. It has to be superficial or I wouldn't have stopped bleeding, even if it hurts like hell now.

Pain never makes me angry. Only sad. I cry when I'm in pain, no matter how hard I try not to. My tear ducts open up and pour like I'm a damn rainmaker. It's a weakness I'll have to conquer in this place.

It feels strange to change into my uniform to eat dinner so I remain in my jeans and sweatshirt. I finish washing up and hurry downstairs, my stomach rumbling.

I look left and right at each floor, checking out the lower levels. Still no students. No other compliance officers, either. Maybe they're all at dinner.

I take a moment to peer down the hallway on each level, making mental notes about the locations of the rooms along each.

On the lowest level, the sign on the half-open door tells me that the first room on the right belongs to Bloodwing's Founder. There's no name badge. Her name is kept secret. All I know is that she's female.

Curious, I peek inside her room. A vase filled with red roses sits on top of an otherwise empty desk. A painting hangs on the wall. It must be her, but she looks younger than I would have expected.

With radiant hazel eyes and masses of chocolate brown hair cascading across her shoulders, she wears a faint smile on her lips as if she's pleased about something. An insignia is painted in delicate, flowing letters across the bottom right corner of the painting: *Avery.*

It's probably the name of the painter, but it's reminiscent of an aviary—a bird cage. Maybe the Founder is obsessed with birds. It would certainly explain why she chose to name this place "Bloodwing."

The whole room feels vacant, not lived in. I assume I'll meet her at some point, but obviously not today.

When I veer toward the front door, I find the entrance is empty too. The magic sealing it pushes me away like a physical force. I press a little into it, testing its strength and finding it solid. Every chance I get, I plan to test the security at Bloodwing.

Headmistress Osprey said the food hall was on this level, so I continue down the hallway, passing another staircase and a number of closed doors along the way.

At the end of the hall is a door with *Dining Room* written in elaborate gold text on a wooden plaque, similar to the one in the entrance.

The whole place looks old world, almost quaint, but the silence is confusing.

I push on the door. Again, nothing decorates the walls except a lone clock. Wooden chairs. Clean, wooden floor. Nothing metallic as far as I can see. A corridor of sorts extends down the middle of the room, dividing six elegant mahogany tables into groups of three.

About thirty young men and women sit around the room, their plastic plates and cutlery a distinct contrast to the earthy surroundings.

As soon as I step into the room, they turn to look at me.

The minimum age for attendance at Bloodwing is twenty years. I couldn't find an explanation why. It drove my parents nuts that they had to wait two years after I finished high school.

They wanted to send me here as soon as they heard Bloodwing existed. Most of the students in the room look a little older than me, but not by much. I guess they don't live long after they arrive.

Girls sit silently at the tables on the left. Guys sit on the right. They're all dressed in neat uniforms—white collared shirts and black pants for the guys, red plaid skirts for the girls. Everyone wears a black tie.

An older woman stands behind a counter to the right, her wand raised. I expected to see some sort of kitchen, a buffet of sorts, pots of goopy cafeteria-style food at minimum. Every student has food on their plate already but I don't see where it came from.

"Peyton Price is late," the woman snaps. "You may all begin eating now."

They were waiting for me? That might explain the death stares I'm getting.

The woman has the reddest hair I've ever seen, definitely dyed that color, not natural. It washes out her pale features and makes the creases around her mouth more pronounced as she descends upon me.

A glance at the clock tells me it's not 6 o'clock yet.

"I thought I was early." *Oh, my big mouth.*

The redhead sucks in an angry breath. The nearest female student—the one sitting at the corner of the table on my left—drops her plastic fork on the floor. Her jaw drops with it.

Talking back on my first day must be unexpected.

I stand my ground as Redhead storms toward me, her heels beating the floor. She stops within arm's reach of me. "Are you hungry, Peyton Price?"

I return her stare. My tears will only start if she hurts me. Until then, I'm determined to remain as emotionless as stone. "I've gone without dinner before. Feel free to starve me."

Her lips pinch. I wonder if she's Headmistress Osprey's little sister. Their mouths react in the same way. I check her name badge: Ms. Sparrow.

She taps her wand against her open palm as if it's a cane and she can't decide where to beat me with it first. I prepare for a lashing and the pain that will come with it. Bring on the waterworks and my tough act will become a farce. Until then, I'll maintain it to the bitter end.

Her eyes narrow and it's the only warning I get before a sudden wind whooshes around her body and a plastic plate zooms around her out of nowhere, sailing straight into my surprised hands.

She taps the plate's edge with her wand and I'm startled when sausages and mashed potatoes appear on it. Peas roll around at the edges, threatening to tip right off as I try to hold it horizontal. *Damn bendy plastic.*

"I leave the dining room at 6 o'clock each evening," she says with a glare. "If I'm not here to feed you, you *will* starve."

With that, she hurries away as if there's somewhere she needs to be, her shoes clacking away.

The door closes behind her and I'm alone with twenty-eight students.

What? No supervision? The compliance twins aren't anywhere in sight. Headmistress Osprey said there were two compliance officers for each student, so where are they?

The four guys at the table on my right are all different shapes and sizes. So are the girls on my left and throughout the room. I guess magical repression doesn't discriminate on the base of gender or physical appearance.

Hmm. Except for the table at the back.

Three guys sit there who look like they're compliance-officers-in-training: muscled, tall, broad-shouldered. The guy at the end of the table has messy, dark blond hair with a sweep in it and surprisingly intelligent-looking hazel eyes. Only the plastic forks in their hands indicate they're students.

Their cold, hard stares tell me to stay away.

I quickly check to make sure I'm not misreading anyone's body language, hoping to see a hint of something less than immediate hatred.

My stomach sinks.

Once again, I am a pariah. All of them have had at least some magical manifestation. They know what their powers are; they just can't call their power at will or control it.

Really, they're not much less dangerous than me or they wouldn't be here, but I guess they don't see it that way. Even among them, I am different. I can't deny that their reaction stings.

I had hoped they wouldn't all hate me on sight.

Well, I'm not a shrinking violet.

I force myself to focus on the air above their heads as I

speak. "I thought I'd be welcomed by my own kind. I guess not. Whoever doesn't want to get dead when I spontaneously combust had better vacate a table so I can sit alone."

The girls at the table nearest me on the left immediately stand up, juggling their plastic plates and dispersing themselves through the room without a backward glance. One of them drops a trail of peas when her plate bends, but she doesn't look back.

The girl at the corner stands, too, but she shuffles a couple of chairs across, inclining her head at the chair she vacated.

I hate sitting in warm chairs, but I won't snub her gesture since it's the first welcome I've had. She has long, straight caramel-brown hair, and warm, brown eyes. She isn't exactly smiling, but she isn't glaring, either.

"I'm Lucinda," she says.

If she was listening to Redhead, then she already knows my name, but I introduce myself anyway. "I'm—"

A flash of light ripples through the air, a short burst.

I blink rapidly, not sure what's happening. Uncertainty makes me freeze to the spot as I try to clear my vision of the bright spots in it.

Lucinda's eyes pop wide and her focus shifts to the back table. One of the big guys at the back—the one with the messy, blond hair—stands up so suddenly that his chair tips back with a loud *bang* that makes me jump.

He grips the table, shuddering so hard, he knocks his plate across its surface. The whole lot flies into the guy opposite him, who is too busy shielding his eyes to react to the splatter of food across his chest.

Lucinda jumps out of her seat, her face draining pale. "Oh, no. Joseph's having a flicker fit."

Another flash of light bursts through the room, emitting from Joseph's entire body—head, shoulders, torso, arms, and legs—the brightest burst I've ever seen. It's like fireworks, but at close range.

Lucinda drops into her seat and clutches her head as if she's about to have a breakdown, curling down over her knees. "Oh, no, no, *no*!"

I've never seen a flicker fit.

Never felt its effects.

Every student in the room is doubled over, covering their eyes. I should be in pain too, and I don't know why I'm not. The light is bright, but it doesn't hurt.

The third burst of light is sharper than the first two, making the guys at Joseph's table jolt back in their seats, shouting as they scramble to get away from him.

One of them yells through gritted teeth. "Joseph! You gotta stop, man, or they'll come in here and kill you!"

"I… can't…" He's gripping the table so hard, he lifts it off the floor on that side, tipping it upward.

The light bursts more rapidly. Not fireworks anymore but like a strobe.

Now that the initial blindness has worn off, every burst makes the room clearer for me, as if the shadows are gone and everything is bright.

I take a step forward. A stupid moth-to-the-flame move.

I bump right into a warm body that wasn't there a second ago.

A deep, angry voice burns into me. "Get out of my way."

I catch sight of startling amber eyes and black-as-night hair before two big hands shove me to the side, thumping my plastic plate right into my chest.

Food smooshes across my stomach as I crash into the corner of the table.

Pain explodes through my hip, shooting down my leg. I bounce, hit nothing but air, then smack into the side of the chair. It topples as I fall to the floor, landing on my tailbone with a full view of the walkway between the tables.

My surprised shout is a vague echo as I try to figure out which way is up.

I hit so many objects on my way to the floor that I'm struggling to center myself. Pain spirals through me, but shock is my biggest enemy right now. I can't seem to move, and I have a feeling I really need to get up.

The newcomer charges toward the back table, causing the guys near it to scatter.

His naked back is burned.

A red welt extends down each side.

It must be Striker Draven.

Droplets of water splatter down his back, as if he recently got out of the shower.

He doesn't stop, doesn't pause, barreling into Joseph so hard that the table bucks and tips.

Joseph clutches it so tightly that he drags it for a full two feet before he finally lets it go. It thuds onto its side, cracking against the floor.

Striker drives Joseph into the back wall with enough force to make Joseph's head bounce. Striker's fist follows, exploding into Joseph's cheek with a brutality that makes me gasp.

A second fist cracks into Joseph's temple. He slumps, dropping across Striker's waiting shoulder.

Striker hefts Joseph up and deposits him into the nearest chair, sitting him upright. Then his angry glare lands on me.

He takes a step toward me, his fists clenched.

Oh, no.

I don't need another fist in my face today. My brother's was enough. I certainly don't need one that has the power to knock a big guy like Joseph out cold. I've met enough guys like Striker to know that a perceived slight like simply getting in his way results in a disproportionately violent retaliation.

He stops when the doors burst open at both ends of the dining room. Compliance officers stream into the room with Headmistress Osprey at their head. They quickly line the walls, their wands out.

Striker immediately relaxes as if nothing happened, settling into the spot where he stands.

Nobody moves.

Headmistress Osprey takes one look at the upturned table and me sitting on the floor, food scattered around me. Her shrill voice cuts through my hearing. "What is the meaning of this?"

Get up, Peyton. I scramble to obey my mental command, but a boot descends over my outstretched thigh and a fist grips my hair.

Collin's pale eyes enter my field of view, his breath an unwanted tickle across my cheek. He wrenches my head back so hard, I think he tore out some hair.

I can't stop my cry of pain before I clamp my lips together and squeeze shut my eyes. Why do scalps have to be so sensitive?

I didn't cry when I hit the ground, but it's impossible not to now. A sob tears out of me as pain shoots through my head.

Damn. There goes my tough act.

"Peyton Price," Headmistress Osprey says, standing over me. "Explain yourself."

Indignation rises like a tidal wave. "It wasn't me. I didn't—"

It was Joseph. He had a flicker fit. But the other guy's shout still echoes in my ears: *You gotta stop, man, or they'll kill you.*

Flicker fits are a precursor to an uncontrollable surge of power—the whole reason this place exists. They're unpredictable and completely random. Minor flicker fits can stop after a single short burst, but big ones—ones like Joseph just had that make others double over in pain—end with a powerful explosion that kills everyone within a quarter mile radius.

Someone put Joseph in this Academy because they're afraid he'll do exactly what he just did.

If I tell Headmistress Osprey what happened... she will kill him.

I can't see Lucinda, but I can hear her. It sounds like her head is still in her hands and she's whispering, *"No, no, no."*

I swallow. Think hard. Through my blurry tears, Striker Draven's expression—even from a distance—tells me he's going to kill me slowly, maybe rip my arms out first and break my legs second.

I grind my teeth. Suck in a breath. Taking the fall for the mess suddenly seems like a wise thing to do. "It was my fault."

In the distance, Striker's expression shifts, more of a dangerous look than a murderous one.

Headmistress Osprey doesn't ask for details, which is good because I'm not sure how I'll explain how I tipped over a table twice my size from halfway across the room while I was sitting on my butt in mashed potatoes.

"That's what I thought." She spins to Collin. "Get her up. She's going to the pit."

Audible gasps echo out around the room. Even the girls who vacated the front table look shocked, their faces pale and drawn as they watch me go.

With tears streaming down my cheeks and a fist against my lower back, I shuffle toward the door.

Collin finally eases up on my hair as we wait for five other officers to proceed ahead of us. Five more take up position behind me, the others remaining in the room.

A final green pea drops from my tangled shirt and rolls across the floor. The bald officer behind me squishes it beneath his boot, giving me a grin that reveals a missing tooth.

The pause at the door is long enough for me to see Lucinda fly to the back of the room and hit Striker in the arm.

She's even littler than she looked sitting down, barely reaching his shoulders.

He bats at her, grabs her hand when she tries to hit him again, and effortlessly spins her away, giving her a dismissive push in the direction of her chair.

I guess she's mad about him hitting Joseph, but his violence worked. Joseph's flicker fit stopped.

Outside the dining room, Headmistress Osprey draws level with me. "It normally takes students a month to be wicked enough to visit the pit. Whatever you did to cause that disturbance, this is a very bad beginning for you."

I can't help myself. "If my compliance officers were doing their jobs, I wouldn't have been making such a mess."

She glances at Collin and Colby. "We were unexpectedly detained."

I give her a disinterested shrug, blithely asking, "What could be more important than torturing me?"

Her mouth splits into a cruel grin. "There was a problem in the pit that required all hands on deck. You'll soon see for yourself."

The dining room suddenly seems like a safe haven.

They push me along the corridor back to the entrance room. Headmistress Osprey taps a panel at the side that is located behind the front desk. *Well, what do you know?* It's only a few steps from the entrance of this place to the entrance to the pit. A mere stroll, in fact.

We descend into a dark stairwell, flaming torches popping alive as Headmistress Osprey taps her wand against the wall. The stairwell descends but veers to the right.

"The pit is located beneath the combat zone outside, not under the building," she says. "It's a magical cavity dug out of the rock beneath our feet and lined in iron to prevent any unexpected magical outbursts from doing any damage. Which is why we have no concerns leaving you in here."

Magical outbursts are the least of my concerns. The air grows colder the deeper we go. I rub my arms, shivering. The hairs on the back of my neck rise as the air—and the smells inside the stairwell—grow thick with...

I shudder.

Fear.

I've always believed that rooms and walls absorb the unhappiness of those who live within them, that those emotions live on in a place.

The fear and desperation of the pit's former occupants is like a physical force screaming at me to run.

We stop at the bottom of the stairwell in front of a locked iron gate. Headmistress Osprey produces the key and removes the padlock, swinging the gate open wide. "In you go. We'll be back in the morning to collect you."

"Or your bones," Collin adds. The other officers snicker as he pushes me inside.

The gate clangs before Headmistress Osprey locks it again.

She turns away without another word.

Their boots recede.

The light winks out.

I'm left in darkness with the scent of fear and my own pounding heart.

4. STRIKER DRAVEN

The flash of power from beneath the dining room door is the last thing I want to see tonight.

Water drips down my back from my towel-dried hair. I didn't bother getting a new shirt and now I'm glad I didn't delay.

I was already preparing myself to lay eyes on the new girl, but now my focus shifts entirely. Whoever's having a flicker fit, I have to get in there and stop it before the compliance officers return from the pit.

Bursting through the door, I locate the source of the power coming from the back table.

Damn, it's Joseph. It's his second fit this month.

The first time, he was in the hallway and I could get to him fast, shove him into a spare room, and knock him unconscious before anyone noticed. He's lucky the guards aren't in the room right now or he'd already be dead.

He's gripping the table harder with every flicker, his body awash with light that pops so rapidly now, it's like an old-fashioned camera on speed.

Half out of their chairs, arms flung over their eyes, Ryan and Lachlan—the two guys at his table—shout at Joseph to stop.

No damn chance of that.

The table starts to tip, telling me he's lost all control. He's seconds away from a major outburst that will strip the paint from the walls, not to mention the skin from our bones.

I power forward, registering the female silhouette in my way.

I nearly pull up sharp. Unlike everyone else, she's facing directly forward, her head slightly tilted, her hair a messy dark cascade down her back.

Her back is to me, but the way she's standing—no hand over her eyes—indicates she doesn't have her eyes closed.

Every burst of light illuminates her body.

The flickers lose their white glow and turn scarlet as they pulse around her head, shoulders, narrow waist, curvy hips, all the way down her long legs.

Fuck. She's perfect.

If she had wings, I'd believe she was some sort of fire angel.

To my shock, she steps toward the light, not away from it.

She'll be the first to die.

My instincts kick in. I'm beside her in a mere second, using all my speed to step into her path before her foot lowers.

She thuds into me and jolts in surprise, her dark lashes turning up to me, revealing surprisingly guarded brown eyes. Some people flee from danger. She's definitely a fighter.

My heart thuds—a single powerful beat—as the energy I sense from her rages through my hip and chest where we connected, a sharp, dangerous contrast to the soft, harmless perfection she portrayed in the light.

Anger spirals through me. I don't have time for girls pretending to be angels. My focus now is on survival. I have to get to Joseph. "Get out of the way."

I shove her out of my path harder than I intended,

registering the plate my hands smack into, the whoosh of air out of her lungs as she crashes into the table.

Thud-thud-smack. Her shout reaches me from a distance, but I don't have time to stop.

I charge toward Joseph.

Ryan and Lachlan hear me coming and scramble to get out of my way. I thunder into Joseph, knocking into him so hard that he drags the table with us for several paces before it tips and cracks against the floor.

His body is like a dead weight. His mind is gone. *Damn*.

I can't be too late. I can't be…

Panic and fear rise inside me for the first time in years.

Fuck panic.

I throw him against the wall and slam into him at the same time, my shoulder against his chest, not caring about the cracks I make in the plaster.

His head bounces—right into my oncoming fist. I hold back enough that I don't shatter his cheekbone, the shock of the hit stopping the next flicker fit in its tracks.

I'm not done yet. I can't take the chance it will start up again.

I throw another fist at his temple, desperate this time. If I don't knock him out, the next flash could be the last. The impact jars through my arm and down my spine.

Joseph's eyes roll back and he finally slumps across my shoulder.

The flicker fit stops.

Deathly silence follows. I take a moment to catch my breath before I lift him up, pull out the nearest chair with my foot, and slide him into it.

We're safe, but I'm not done.

I turn back to the new girl. *Peyton*. She's sitting on her butt in the middle of the aisle between the tables, mashed potatoes and peas spilled across her shirt, her legs stretched out in front of her.

I take in her full features for the first time: sexy, messy hair like she just got out of bed, rumpled clothing, and sharp, brown eyes that tell me I'd better not mess with her.

Damn they chose her well. *Pretty* doesn't come close. She's gorgeous.

There's no way in hell I'm letting her get under my skin.

The doors on both sides of the room burst open and guards swarm in with Headmistress Osprey at their head.

I relax, unclench my fists, and place one hand on the chair Joseph's slumped in. He'll come to at any moment and I want to make sure he doesn't give himself away when he does.

If I have to physically gag him, I will.

The advantage of my reputation is that I don't have to explain any sudden aggressive outbursts to anyone.

Headmistress Osprey shrieks when she sees the mess. "What is the meaning of this?"

Peyton twitches as if she's about to jump to her feet. She needs to if she's going to avoid a beating. She doesn't see Collin sneaking up behind her until his boot traps her leg and he fists her hair, pulling her head back in a savage jolt that makes every girl in the room wince.

She cries out—that same angry cry—but quickly shuts her mouth and squeezes her eyes closed. Silent tears spill down her cheeks, but I've got to hand it to her—she doesn't whimper.

Headmistress Osprey towers over her. "Explain yourself, Peyton."

Tears release when Peyton opens her eyes. She gasps, "It wasn't me. I didn't—"

She stops, but I know she's going to spill the truth.

As soon as she tells them it was Joseph, he's dead. I don't have friends here anymore, but I won't let him die because some newcomer points the finger at him.

I consider how fast I can get to her to keep her quiet. I

recount the steps between me and her. Too many but I'm sure I could make it in time.

Pain makes people shut up and I'm very good at causing it.

She sucks in a shaky breath as her eyes meet mine. The fight is back in her expression, displaying a fierce determination she has no business showing me.

Her voice rings out clear. "It was my fault."

What the hell?

She has no motive for taking the fall. None that I can see. For the first time, I question my assumptions about why she's here. Is it possible she's for real?

I mentally shake my head at myself. Another Unknown like me? Impossible.

Osprey snaps. "Get her up. She's going to the pit."

Lucinda gasps. Even the guys stare, shell-shocked. Joseph hasn't woken up yet, but he won't be happy when he finds out someone went down because of him.

Osprey usually reserves the pit for the worst offenders. I know because I've spent many nights in there. Not recently, though. My visits to the pit stopped a year ago.

I shake off the memories I refuse to revisit: the night that changed everything for me...

I've obliterated the memory of it the same way I've obliterated weak emotions like love and happiness.

Peyton hobbles to the door with Collin's fist shoved against her lower back, dropping chunks of food from her clothing as she goes. She's surrounded by more compliance officers than I was expecting.

I could almost believe they were scared of her, but I can't see why.

She glances back and the look in her eyes claws at my chest again. It tells me she expects to get hurt, but she'll fight them anyway, even if it makes things worse.

I shake off my thoughts. I won't accept that I'm wrong about her.

She's a device, a ploy. As soon as they leave the room, they'll ease up on her. She'll straighten her clothes. They'll probably even splash her with some blood to make her night in the pit look real.

Lucinda breaks my thoughts when she suddenly flies at me, too little and too light to do any damage as she hits me on the chest and arms.

"It's your fault she's going to the pit!" Her eyes flash with accusation as her fists connect. "Damn you, Striker. You didn't have to knock her over."

I don't answer, easily evading Lucinda's next hit, taking her hands and spinning her so she's facing away from me.

I nudge her in the direction of her chair.

She needs to sit or the guards will target her next. She stumbles away from me, casting a glare that I shrug off.

I have thick skin, and nothing is going to change that.

Nobody is going to claw their way into my life again.

5. PEYTON PRICE

I press against the bars until my eyes adjust to the dark.

I count my heartbeats, trying to stay calm. It's just a dark, cold cavern. It's meant to scare me, but I can't let it.

A creature scuffles to my right, something small. A rat probably. Just a rat.

I press against the bars, deciding to stay right where I am. I can make it through this. I just have to count the seconds until I return to the light. I tell myself it's not worse than being locked in my room at home.

What home?

Home is for other people. I lived in a house, a place with four walls and a roof. I was allowed to go to school, but I was required to come straight home afterward. The one time I disobeyed, my father beat me within an inch of my life with his belt.

How could I be so selfish that I would jeopardize my family? Didn't I know he would have to pay compensation to the Magical Magnate if I killed someone? Was I so selfish that I would risk bankrupting him?

I didn't date, but who would date me? Guys would show off

how tough they were by shoving me, daring me to have a flicker fit. Girls would whisper behind my back and post all sorts of shit about me on their social media accounts.

Over time, I learned to recognize the fear in their eyes.

A low moan resonates throughout the darkness. Not my own.

A flutter of wings makes me shiver.

Silence resumes, but I know I'm not alone. I can sense another presence in the shifting air.

As I edge along the wall, the cavity opens up ahead of me, large rock pillars rising upward, dark caverns in the distance that could hide anything. If I stay here and something attacks me, I'll be trapped in this narrow corridor. I resolve to move and find a better place to hide.

Just as I step forward, a shape shrieks toward me through the dark. It's large, humanoid, but not human. I catch a glimpse of ragged feathers, wings, a feathered body before bright silver talons rip through the air toward me.

I don't have time to scream, barely ducking. One of the talons slices across my shoulder as I dive to the ground. The creature hits the gate, its talons closing around the bars.

I jump to my feet and run.

"Oh, come back," a female voice croons, a sibilant whisper behind me. "I want to play with you."

It talks! What the hell?

I don't stop, stumbling through the dark, running toward the nearest pillar and sliding behind it. I can't see well enough to know what I'm running into, so I don't dare go much farther.

The flutter of wings tells me she has moved closer. "Will your flesh taste as good as the last one?" she asks. "Those men. They like to hurt me. So I hurt them back. They are very tasty."

Assuming she's talking about the compliance officers, we have our hatred of them in common. Except the bit about successfully hurting them back. I'm determined to do that one day. Once I figure out how.

I crouch low to the ground, trying to catch a glimpse of her through the gloom. Her talons glint as she moves and her wings are ragged but large. She doesn't have feet. No arms, either.

But she has a female body covered in feathers from her ankles to her stomach and across her breasts. Her long hair is wild and matted, but her tiny nose and mouth remind me of a doll, strangely perfect.

"What are you?" I ask.

She jolts to a stop, her mouth dropping open. I wrench myself back into the darkness, pressing against the pillar, regretting my question.

"You don't know?" she whispers.

I kick myself. The location of my voice will give me away. I should avoid speaking again.

She pauses and the silence stretches. "I'm a harpy."

Her wings beat, but the sound heads in the other direction, indicating she's moving away from me. She's either toying with me or she doesn't know where I am yet.

"I don't belong here," she says, her voice soft. "I nearly escaped when they came to feed me tonight, but they called in reinforcements."

I guess that explains why the building was so deserted when I came down to dinner.

"I'm a prisoner like you," she says.

She sounds so reasonable. I could almost like her, but I consider what I know about the mythology of harpies.

They are said to torture their prey while they transport them to hell. Which is pretty much where I am. They're smart, they regenerate if hurt, and they're stronger than most supernaturals.

We studied them briefly in biology class at high school. Harpies are a Class B monster to be avoided at all costs.

My inner thoughts take a sarcastic turn. At least she's not a Class A monster like a Valkyrie or a Keres. They are indistinguishable from humans and supernaturals alike.

They wouldn't stop to talk. They'd kill me swiftly.

I cast around for something to defend myself, trying not to make a sound as I pat the ground. Even a rock would help.

My fingertips touch a hard object—long, sturdy—a piece of wood maybe. Gripping it with one hand, I run my other hand over it, checking its size. It has a knob at one end that will make a nice dent in her skull if I need to defend myself.

Her voice is far too close to me now. A whisper. "You must have surprised them with unexpectedly bad behavior. They wouldn't have fed me if they planned to bring you here tonight." She pauses, crooning. "I do like the badly behaved. They are much more fun to hurt—"

In a sudden whoosh, she flies around the pillar at me, her talons outstretched.

I swing my wooden weapon, managing to hit her shins with a *crack*. She screeches, sweeps her wings back, and makes another grab at me.

I grip the weapon, swinging it again, but this time I duck under her wings, ramming it into her stomach. As I slip past her wings, I catch sight of more talons where her fingers should be, but in the next moment, her feathers rake across my face.

I swallow a scream.

I thought they'd be soft.

My face stings. I don't have time to check, but I'm sure I have scratches down my cheeks now. I have to stay away from her talons and her feathers or I'll end up more cut up than I already am.

She drops to the ground and doubles over, heaving a racking cough that turns into a laugh as she swings in my direction. "Oh, you're fun. Most students cower and tremble, waiting for me to pick at their bodies. They give in so I don't kill them. They let me play with them. I give them little cuts, little nibbles. I like your fight. It will be so much more satisfying when I taste your blood."

I wield the weapon, holding it aloft. She scratches her talon nails across the pillar as she takes slow, clacking steps toward me, sounds that grate in my ears.

How am I going to hold her off all night?

It isn't in my nature to submit. I won't let her nibble me. I will fight her, and she will kill me.

I'm going to die here.

As I step back, taking paces to maintain distance between her and me, I stumble across another hard object on the floor. It scrapes along my leg, ripping through my jeans, and then snags.

I crouch down to release my jeans, finding myself surrounded by multiple slender, white, curved objects rising up at regular intervals around me. I've backed into a…

Shock rivets me to the spot.

I'm standing in a ribcage.

An enormous ribcage. It can't be human. It's too big.

A scream of horror tears out of me. "What died here?"

She cackles as she slips closer to me, taking her time. "The beast that used to torture students until it was killed. A beast stronger than you."

Without taking my eyes off her silhouette in the gloom, I reach down to free my jeans, my hand closing around one of the ribs. It snagged my jeans because it's sharp at one end, pointed enough that I could use it as a dagger.

I leave my current weapon on the ground—what I now realize is another bone—and wrench the new one upward.

I slowly feel my way out of the skeleton and into clear ground again. If they'd left me with some sort of light, this would have been so much easier. As it is, I'm fumbling in the dark.

But then, so is she.

If it weren't for the darkness, I have no doubt she would be upon me already.

"Come on, then," I say, sounding much braver than I feel.

She launches forward, talon-fingers and toes outstretched to grab me. If she gets her talons around me, she won't let go, but the only way to her chest is through them. The only way to beat her is to do what she doesn't expect.

She expects me to run.

I turn my shoulder and charge toward her. Her talons bite me, grip my upper arm, and pull me closer.

She laughs and says that she has me now, her mouth opening, revealing sharp incisors as she bends to sink her teeth into my neck.

I shove the bone into her stomach as hard as I can, breaking skin, sensing it sink deep. It's sickening, but my survival instincts are in full swing.

She screams, a shocked wail that echoes around the room. She doesn't let go of my arm, her talons ripping through my skin.

Sobbing out the pain, I push the bone with all my strength, propelling her backward. Her talons rake down my back, finally releasing me.

Up close, her eyes are open wide as she flops to the ground. She has no hands to pull the bone out of herself, her finger-talons sliding across it.

She tries to grab it with her toes instead, clawing at it.

My stomach turns, but if she gets it out, she'll regenerate.

"How did you do this?" she shrieks.

It takes me four steps to race back to the skeleton, wrench out two more rib bones and return to her. She's too fixated on sliding out the first one to see me coming.

I try not to think.

With a scream, I drive the next one through her throat,

finding out just how close to the pillar we are when it clunks into it. My hands judder under the impact.

She doesn't make a sound, but her talons finally stop scrabbling at the bone jutting from her stomach.

Silence falls and all I can do is stand there, another scream shrieking out of me.

I just wanted her to stop—to leave me alone. I knew she could regenerate so I knew I had to strike hard. But what I've done...

I've never killed anything. Maybe spiders. Insects. Never something breathing and cognizant like her. I don't even know if I killed her for good. I have no way of knowing.

The final bone I'm still holding shakes against the floor, making me realize I'm going into shock, trembling so hard, I can't control it.

Soon, I won't be able to think clearly.

I curl down over my knees, wrapping my arms around them, but my head stays raised. I can't take my eyes off her, no matter what happens. If she moves, I have this third bone ready.

If she moves.

She. Not it.

Oh, dear ancients. They put me in this place because they think I'm going to be a killer one day.

Now I am one.

This time when the tears come, I'm not afraid to let them flow.

6. PEYTON PRICE

"*What have you done?*" Headmistress Osprey's shriek breaks through the haze in my mind.

The light from her thorny wand illuminates the space around me, casting shadows across the dead harpy's features.

I shrink back from the death in front of me, unable to look at it for another second.

I don't know what hour it is, but it's been a long time since I killed the harpy. Long enough for the blood to dry on my face and shirt—mine and hers.

"I killed her." I stare up into Headmistress Osprey's furious eyes.

For a dangerous second, I consider ramming the third bone I still hold into her soft belly, but that will only get me a place in a real prison.

She straightens and takes a quick step back, her wand ready. I'm clutching the bone like a weapon and pointing it at her after all. I'm sure my violent intent was loud and clear.

Compliance officers file in around us, but it's difficult to see their expressions. I'm sure Collin and Colby are among them.

"But, how?" Headmistress Osprey's wand shakes, wobbling in the air as she stares at the bone I'm holding.

The light from her wand flickers to the dead creature whose rib I took. It looks like some kind of enormous dog, but there are boulders where its head would be—or is that a skull? I'm not sure.

I carefully place the bone on the ground, unfurling and rising to my feet.

I'm starving, tired, and unsteady on my feet. "I'd like to leave now."

One of the compliance officers scoffs as he leans around the corner. His eyes widen when they land on the dead harpy. He curses and then quickly retreats when Headmistress Osprey gives him a glare filled with daggers.

Her wand twitches in the direction of the open gate—my only invitation to leave—and the officers part to let me through.

We file up the staircase in silence broken only by their boots and Headmistress Osprey's clacking heels. Today, she's wearing a bright pink suit, but her lipstick is orange. Someone needs to get her a color wheel.

Bloodwing is staffed by witches and wizards. Other supernaturals like shifters would make better guards, but witches and wizards are more disciplined, less likely to make decisions based on their baser instincts.

They can use their magic without their wands, but they're much more powerful using the wand as a conduit. I've heard of rare witches who control instinctive magic not connected to wands or words, but I suspect they are a myth.

I gulp fresh air inside the entrance room, only now realizing how accustomed I'd become to the scent of sausages, mashed potatoes, and blood.

I need to shower. I need to wash off the horror and somehow partition my memories so I can move past what I did.

Unlike last night, the halls are busy with students.

I squint into the light streaming through the windows set high on the wall behind the front desk. "Is it morning?"

"You have an hour to get ready for class," Headmistress Osprey snaps, straightening her suit.

The compliance officers part for me again, but Colby and Collin dog my steps as I make my way along the corridor. My legs wobble, but I refuse to show any weakness as I climb each laborious step to the attic.

I'm too tired to care about heights this time, ignoring the wide windows, but as soon as I see who's standing in the hallway, I take a sharp breath and stop so suddenly that Colby bumps into me.

Striker stands in the hallway ahead, holding a pile of books and dressed in his uniform, his white sleeves rolled up to his biceps, black pants hugging his thighs.

His presence confirms that he's the other Unknown.

My first goal is out the proverbial window: there will be no avoiding Striker Draven.

He is expressionless this morning. His gaze flickers across my cheek and down to my shoulder. I haven't had a chance to check my wounds yet, but I'm covered in dried blood.

At least I'm not crying this time.

The walkway is only just wide enough for me to stride resolutely past him.

I pause as I pass his room. It looks like he's an Unknown with special treatment—he has a wide desk, pictures on the walls, and a high-backed leather chair. His room even has a sound system.

I can't help the reckless laugh that rises into my throat. I'm not afraid to poke the beast.

Hell, I just killed a harpy. I'm a little high on wild right now.

I spin and call after him, "You'd better have good taste in music, Draven."

He takes a beat, drops his books with a clunk, and strides back to me, a dangerous smile curving his lips.

My taunt was meant to be a throwaway line, not the start of a confrontation. I backpedal, but he grabs my injured shoulder in one big hand, sending shockwaves of pain through my torso.

"You'd better not get too comfortable in your bed, Price."

I swallow, but I think I'm going to throw up. The harpy's claws dug deep and now that he's pressing the wounds, the pain is making me dizzy.

"Would you mind grabbing my other shoulder?" I ask, sarcasm dripping from every syllable. "My *other* shoulder is the one that gets off on being grabbed by assholes."

No amount of silver-tongued bravado can hide the fact that my eyes are filling with tears.

"Are you crying?" It's an accusation, not a sympathetic question.

"No."

His eyes narrow.

I swipe my cheek with my free hand. The tears are loosening the blood and it smears all over the back of my hand. It's probably smearing across my face too. Good old tear ducts.

I lean into him, more because I can't stay upright than because I'm trying to be provocative.

I tip my head back. My voice lowers, soft, a gentle threat. "If you don't let me go, I'll gore you like I gored that harpy."

His eyes meet mine and for a very small, infinitesimal moment, I catch a flicker of surprise. *Yes, asshole. I guess you didn't hear. I killed the harpy.*

I reach up on tiptoes as he becomes very still, my chest brushing his in a way that is not only extremely provocative but will also leave flecks of dried blood on his clean shirt.

I whisper, "But with you, I'll make it slow."

He's a blank slate again. His fingers uncurl from my shoulder one by one. I don't move until he turns away and strides back down the corridor, picking up his stack of books, which somehow managed not to spill all the way across the hall. Even his aggression is precise.

Colby and Collin stare at me like I'm suicidal, but since Striker is on his way out, they remain where they are. Their orders are only to leave me alone when he's around.

I stumble into my room, grab my towel, fresh underwear, bag of toiletries, and my uniform, and make my way to the bathroom.

I lean over the sink, bracing myself for the task of peeling my clothing off myself. My first attempt makes me retch. The blood has dried the material onto my wounds, so I'll have to soak it off.

Turning on the shower, I get in fully clothed, slowly and surely detaching my clothing from my body.

Then I stand under the spray, letting it wash away my anger.

I don't remember when I became so defensive. There was no turning point, no life-changing experience. It was slow, like a snake that's basked in the sun for too long. It was born from a few too many snide comments, a few too many "accidental" bumps and shoves at school, just a few too many weeks spent alone while my family went on vacation without me.

I had to work at creating a shield around myself, learning how to deliver a quick verbal comeback and to cultivate thick skin.

I forced myself to harden up.

Ten years ago, I would have asked Striker Draven why he was being so mean. I would have asked him to stop. I would have even said "please." These days, I know better, but the hurt is the same.

When the water finally runs clear again, I step out of the shower to dry myself, patting over the wounds. I curse the absence of a mirror. I need to see the cuts down the side of my face from the harpy's feathers. I also need to check the puncture wounds across the back of my shoulder.

The front isn't so bad, but the back really hurts. The cut on my leg from where I bumped into the bones needs bandaging too.

I check the wounds the best I can without a mirror. The punctures across my shoulder are the most concerning. I'm lucky the harpy missed severing any tendons because I still have full use of my arm, but blood trickles from each of the four punctures at the front.

It's slow blood loss, but if it continues for too long, it will become dangerous.

I need padding and something to adhere it to my skin to keep the pressure on. Absorbent padding is easy—I'm a girl with plenty of sanitary items—but I don't have tape.

I test my hair tie but it springs off as soon as I move my arm. I try my black school tie next. It's clumsy and only keeps the padding tight against three of the punctures, but it's better than nothing.

Too bad about my leg. I don't have a spare tie to deal with it.

I swallow an agitated laugh at the idea of wearing a sanitary pad tied to my leg all day where everyone can see it.

With a sigh, I brush my hair and pull it into a tight ponytail, then pull on my white collared shirt and red plaid skirt. The tie around my shoulder is visible through the thin shirt and blood seeps through it immediately, but I can't allow myself to care about how I look.

My goal will be to look for tape—any kind of tape—today so I can dress the wounds properly tonight.

Returning to my room, I glance at the clock before I pick up my class timetable: Magical History first, followed by gym.

My forehead creases as I study the timetable. There's a lot of gym. It makes me wonder if it isn't a euphemism for put-the-students-in-life-threatening-situations-and-see-whose-power-reveals-itself class.

Also, a class called "School Maintenance" every afternoon. No guesses what that's about—cleaning toilets probably.

I'm late for Magical History already, but I was prepared to be the last student to arrive. I consult the rudimentary map that came with the timetable, which shows the location of the class on the second floor in the east wing.

My stomach rumbles loudly as I pick up my stride down the stairs. I tell myself the cut on my leg is nothing.

I don't need sleep.

I don't need bandages.

I don't need food.

I am totally fine.

The compliance twins peel themselves off the wall and follow me all the way to the second level, where I find my class.

A brief glance tells me all of the students from last night are here, including Striker, who lounges with his feet up on the desk at the back. I guess if there are only thirty students, then it stands to reason we take classes together.

Once again, girls sit on the left and guys sit on the right.

Lucinda is located toward the back, but there are no spare seats anywhere near her.

The only spare seat is next to Striker.

The teacher turns from writing on the whiteboard as I try to creep in. He wears a moustache and his hair looks prematurely gray for someone who appears to be in his early thirties. His collared shirt is crumpled but his long pants have neat creases down the front, an odd combination.

"You," he says.

I freeze. Sigh. Turn. "I know," I say. "I'm last to class." I blink hard, trying to alleviate my fatigue as I lift my head. "What's my punishment?"

He considers me for a moment. "Well, I might consider

sending you to the pit." He chews his words. "But apparently, we're down a harpy." He hands me the cup of coffee off his desk. It has his name stenciled on the side: Mr. Mallard. "This will have to be torture enough."

I stare at the creamy caramel liquid inside the mug. "Sir?"

"Bloodwing coffee. It's punishment enough."

My eyebrows draw down. My lips compress. Is he making a joke? Is he one of those bully teachers who offers me a drink, pretending to be nice, but next he's going to accidentally knock the liquid all over me and say, "Oops, sorry"?

He takes a step back, his palms up. "It's yours if you want it. Take it to your desk."

Maybe it contains a substance that will make me sick.

I scowl into the cup, carry it to the only vacant desk next to Striker, and place it deliberately as far away from myself as I can.

As soon as I put it down, Striker moves. He's so fast, I hardly follow it. His foot kicks across the distance, hooks around the coffee cup, and slips it right off the desk.

Despite being the one to knock it off, he lurches forward and catches it in one hand, cradling it in his palm.

It all happened so fast, I'm still processing when he turns his gaze up to me, his amber eyes glinting. "Let's put this somewhere safer."

He deposits the cup on the other side of his desk, far away from me.

I turn back to the front of the class. I'm too tired to react. I wasn't going to drink it anyway.

A little wad of paper lands on my desk. My head jolts, seeking the source, my defenses kicking in again.

Lucinda gives me a discreet wave, but it's an attention-seeking wave, not a greeting. Her wide-eyed stare is pointed as she mouths, *Are you okay?*

I nod once. *Yes.*

I've told a lot of lies today, but that's the biggest. I can't remember the last time someone asked me if I'm okay. I want to tell the truth, but it won't do me any good. Striker's gaze is burning my neck, making me wonder if I'm cut across it. The feathers scratched me all over my arms too.

Mr. Mallard leans on his desk. "For the sake of our new student, I'm going to repeat what you already know: Everything here at Bloodwing is designed to encourage your power to more fully reveal itself. Once you understand the nature of your power, you must learn to control it."

He peers at me as if that might be news to me, but it isn't. It's the reason I haven't asked for help with my wounds. There's no infirmary. The staff will deliberately leave my health to worsen because illness is more likely to force my body's natural instincts to take over and result in a magical manifestation.

I know this, because my parents tried it.

The philosophy here is: Danger invites reaction.

He continues. "However, this class is not concerned with compelling your magic to manifest. It's about enabling you to understand where your magic comes from so you can better consider how to access it.

"As we've been discussing, all magical power originates from the ancient gods in one way or another. Last week, we looked at how shifters originated primarily from the Egyptian gods, in particular Anubis, the first wolf shifter. This week, we're turning to the Greek gods. And where else to start but with Zeus..."

For the next hour, Mr. Mallard talks about the magic of the Greek gods, how fire mages are descended from Apollo, the god of the sun, and invisibility is a power derived from Hades, god of the underworld. I take most of it with a grain of salt, even though it's fitting that my mother's power originates from the god of hell.

Despite the ache in my stomach, it's the most peaceful hour

I've ever spent in a school environment. It occurs to me that it might be the most peace anyone here experiences. Even Striker is quiet. I guess that's why Mr. Mallard has such a captive audience. When he says that our time is up, everyone is slow to rise.

"Time for morning tea." He beams. "Don't forget to receive your food before gym class."

It's a weird way to talk about food, but my attention remains on Striker. I quickly gather up my books, amazed at the number of notes I took, aiming to get out of his way before he has a chance to push past me. The only place I'm not hurt right now is my ribs. I don't want to end up rammed against the edge of a desk while I'm getting up.

I slip into the aisle and away, hurrying past Lucinda who tries to catch up to me before I reach the door. I appreciate her concern, but I don't know if I can handle her asking me if I'm okay without breaking down. I can't do that in front of everyone.

Outside in the corridor, I realize that I don't know where gym class is. It isn't listed on the stupid map they gave me. It can't be on the lower level—there isn't a room big enough—and it wouldn't make sense for it to be on a higher level.

Now I regret not stopping for Lucinda. Other than her, the other students are still avoiding me. A quick glance back tells me that Mr. Mallard stopped her before she left the room.

"You lost, Price?"

Striker Draven's voice holds a hint of derision. He hovers at my shoulder, one step behind me so I can't see his face without turning and giving him my full attention.

I squeeze my eyes closed for a second but don't move. "I'm fine, thanks."

I pause long enough to take my cue from the direction the other students are walking. They're all facing forward, heading toward the stairwell, which means they're probably going down to the first level.

Up ahead, Ms. Sparrow suddenly appears at the juncture at the top of the stairs, her red hair unmistakable. "Food!" she shouts.

Around me, all of the students tuck their books under their arms and hold out both hands, palms up. A pear appears in one of their hands and a cookie in the other.

Wait... what?

My books are only halfway under my arm when a large cookie appears in my left hand and a pear drops out of midair into the space where my right hand should have been. It splats onto the floor, too ripe to hold its shape.

A second later, Striker's large boot presses down on it, squishing it into the floor.

I stare at the crushed food, my left hand closing over the cookie, instinctively gripping it tightly. I can't let him take it from me. I'm starving and I need to eat.

I breathe out my rage, fueled by intense hunger. "You... asshole..."

Before I can make a run for it with my precious cookie, his big hand snaps out, grabs my left wrist, and squeezes. He dodges the useless fist I aim at his chest, sidestepping it. It's too late anyway because my left hand snaps open out of reflex and the cookie drops to the floor, rolling neatly under his boot.

I stare down as his shoe annihilates the doughy substance, turning it into sludge on the wooden floor.

He pauses—I guess it's for effect—before he leans down close, still holding my wrist, daring me to look at him. "No tears this time? I thought you said you'd gore me slowly."

My blood boils as I stare at the floor. If I had power, I would use it now. I would make him hurt and crush him slowly... piece by piece... but instead... he's the one crushing me.

He has all the power and I have none.

I'm so hungry. I don't remember the last thing I ate. Maybe dinner the night before my parents dragged me into the car to bring me here.

I'm too hungry.

The fight drains out of me.

I focus on his shoulder, hardly moving at all. "Let me go."

There's a pause. Silence.

I wait, remaining right where I am, unmoving, not caring about whatever cruel smile he's giving me right now. Not caring about whatever he does next.

His fingers slowly unfurl from my wrist one at a time, the pressure easing in increments. His thumb grazes my palm as he slides his hand away from mine, a confusingly soft touch for what began as such an aggressive gesture.

As soon as he releases me, I step back, avoiding looking at him, discovering that everyone is watching us. Not only the other students, but also the compliance officers, who stand at intervals along the hallway, smirking at the way he's treating me.

It might have been better if I'd fought Striker harder, made it look like I still had fight in me, but I need to conserve my energy.

The next time I see Ms. Sparrow, I'll make certain I'm ready for whatever food she gives me.

Until then, I swerve toward the water fountain and take a long drink. For whatever reason, Striker lets me consume it. I guess he's not going to kill me by dehydration—only starvation.

Lucinda hurries up to me, catching my arm, creating a visual distraction between me and him.

I wince because she grabbed a sore spot, and she immediately lets go, hovering at my side and keeping her voice to a whisper. "You're not okay. Nobody spends a night in the pit and comes out okay." She air quotes around "okay" before she asks, "What happened down there?"

I press my lips together. "I really don't want to talk about it."

"They said you killed the harpy. Like actually *killed it dead.*"

There's a question in her voice, but I don't answer her.

I feel bad that she's not getting anything out of me, especially because she seems to care, but I... can't relive it. I've put up a partition in my mind, carving the memory off like so many bad memories before. I won't climb over that partition ever again. The harpy is gone. Only the physical wounds remain.

Her tone is accusing. "You're all cut up across your face and you're bleeding all over your shirt. Everyone can see it."

I finally arc up, raising myself in defiance. "I'm sorry my appearance is so offensive."

"That's not what I meant." She stares at me as if she expects something. The moment stretches. Her eyes widen. "When are you going to ask for help?"

"I'm not."

She peers at me, her surprised expression fading, a deep furrow forming in her brow. "Oh, hell. You're really not." She sighs. "Well, I'd give you my food, but Striker will just swat it. He's really not happy you're here."

I laugh, but it has no humor in it. "Tell me something I don't know."

The man in question strides past at that point and once he's well into the distance, Lucinda and I follow the other students.

I'm not sure where we're going until we descend the stairs and exit the building by the back door.

I could tell myself the day can't get any worse, but I know that's a lie.

7. PEYTON PRICE

The pebbled pathway outside the main building leads directly to a large, raised platform.

It looks like a massive boxing ring without the ropes around the outside. Wooden training posts are positioned on each side of it—the kind that look like they're from a martial arts movie.

A woman stands on the platform, her wand already out and ready. It's a crooked wand with a vine wound around it. She's taller than any woman I've seen before, possibly mid-thirties with black hair cascading down her back that matches her tight black pants and shirt. Her eyes are a bright blue as she surveys us.

"That's Ms. Hawk," Lucinda explains in a whisper at my side. "Don't be fooled by her beauty. She's cruel. Do whatever she says without question."

Ms. Hawk doesn't wait for us to gather round. "You know the rules! Combat is the fastest conduit to your power. You will all take turns in the ring. Show me your power and you can leave. Until you do, you will continue to fight."

I swallow hard. *Show her my power. I'll be here until sundown.* But then... so will Striker since he's also Unknown.

Lucinda throws me a sympathetic glance as she bends to remove her shoes. All of the students are doing the same, but they don't stop there, removing their outer clothing, revealing tight black workout clothing underneath.

I take off my shoes, but I can't strip beyond that because I didn't know I was supposed to come prepared. I didn't even notice gym clothes in my closet.

"Price!" Ms. Hawk screams at me. "Uniform off."

I lift my head. "I don't have gym clothes on underneath."

She storms toward me, her wand raised, shouting as she moves. "Then we'll get a peep show. Get your uniform off or I'll strip you myself."

I expect to hear snickers, but none of the students makes a sound. Not even the girls.

A glance tells me the guys have fixed their gaze on the fighting ring, rather than on me. I'm surprised. I assumed they'd be assholes and gawk at me.

I'm confused when Striker steps up between them and me. The moment Joseph glances in my direction, Striker steps across and takes a swipe at him—a light tap on his cheek that makes him look away.

What… is he seriously defending my honor right now?

Or… is it a possessive move?

My heart sinks. That's bad. Really bad.

If he's claiming turf around me then I'll not only be his target but I'll be well and truly isolated. Plenty of assholes don't like someone else playing with their prey. I wasn't expecting to progress to that level so quickly.

Just when I think I've got him pegged as a complete brute, he turns his back to me.

It's more privacy than I thought I'd get.

Thank the ancients I'm wearing black underwear, including boyshorts. Delaying the inevitable, I turn my back on the other students as I shimmy out of my skirt and unbutton my shirt.

I curse beneath my breath when my makeshift wound dressing slides off with the shirt. It turns out my tie wasn't really holding it on after all. A trickle of blood slides down my back while I fold up my shirt and place it on the ground.

There are gasps and murmurs behind me.

I take a deep breath before I turn around. My body is a bit of a mess. Thin lines of blood slide from the punctures in my right shoulder, soaking into my bra. Two trickles make it all the way to my stomach, sinking into the top of my panties.

It could be worse. I'm not falling over and that's what matters.

To be honest, I'm not sure how I'm still standing. I should probably be on an intravenous drip by now.

Maybe that's my superpower—to keep taking hits and not collapse. Maybe I have extra blood supply or something that means I can bleed out for an extended period of time before I pass out.

Someone's stare is burning me like I'm in hell. Feigning nonchalance, I consider the open mouths and shocked eyes of the girls, especially Lucinda, as they gape at my wounds.

I casually pass over their faces to Striker.

He looks angry as all hell. I can't for the life of me figure out why. It can't be on my behalf. Maybe the harpy was a friend of his and he's mad she's dead.

He swings to Ms. Hawk, his jaw tense. "There are finally two of us. Let's get this over with."

She smiles. "Price and Draven. In the ring. The rest of you to your practice stations."

As the other students move to the training posts, an unsettled laugh rises inside me.

Of course. The two Unknowns. I should have predicted it.

No wonder Striker wants to keep me unfed and weak. Fighting me each day will be like crushing a ladybug over and over again. Or stepping on a ripe pear.

Aside from self-defense videos on the internet, I have no idea how to fight. I don't even know where to begin. Eyes, throat, groin. That's all I've got.

Oh, and in the case of harpies, sacrifice my shoulder to get in close enough to kill with a makeshift sword made from a dead animal's ribs.

Striker ambles up to the ring, pulling off his shirt at the same time and throwing it on the ground. The burn marks down his back have faded. Up close his back is… muscles in all the right places, perfectly sculpted like some sort of sun god.

It's completely wrong that such a beautiful body belongs to such an asshole.

I follow him onto the platform, but he doesn't give me time to find the middle. He swings a fist at my face.

I dodge it on sheer reflex alone, adrenaline spiking through me. He comes after me, his fists like swinging rocks, swipe after swipe so savage that the air shifts around me. I narrowly avoid each one, barely inhaling as I jump and sidestep.

I can't believe I'm still upright.

I've only been in the ring for ten seconds, but I didn't expect to make it this long.

If his expression is any indication, he's just as surprised as I am. It only seems to make him more determined to knock me out.

His forehead creases deeply before he takes another swing.

I duck and slide beneath his arcing arm. His stomach is exposed and it seems entirely logical to jab him as I pass by. My fist connects, his bare skin on mine. I sense the air leave his lungs, his jolt backward, a split second after energy tingles through my fist.

It was hardly a graceful maneuver and I smeared blood all over the platform when I slid across it, but the stains on it tell me mine is not the first.

He follows my movements with his eyes, his body half-turned, his shoulders squared. I didn't hurt him. Not even close.

I jump to my feet behind him, clutching my hand where I made contact. *What the hell?* I'm tingling all over. I shake out my shoulders, trying to rid myself of the odd prickling from my hand up my arm.

Dancing backward, I inhale air, my nerves sizzling, as if I'm more alive than I was before.

Energy spikes through me. It must be adrenaline. Whatever it is, I like it. My wounds suddenly don't hurt. My head is clear. And I somehow know that his left arm is weaker than his right, he exposes his right side when he hits out, and it will hurt most if I hit the location of the burns on his back.

How I know any of that is beyond me, but I'm not about to ignore this new knowledge.

A smile breaks across my face and a breeze brushes the back of my neck as I rise up to face him again.

He launches forward, but this time the gap between his arms seems wide open. My bare feet won't make much impact, but I switch weight and kick straight at his stomach before he can get close. His own momentum adds to the hit.

Energy shoots through my foot up my leg, directly from his stomach.

He dances away from me. The fact that he doesn't stumble is an indication of the lack of power in my kick, but it was enough to make him think twice about coming at me so fast again.

He jiggles his shoulders, stepping across the pavement, giving me wary looks before he stops moving altogether, studying me carefully.

This time, he approaches me step by careful step. He stops close enough so that he could grab me, so I take a cautious step back, aware that I'm standing at the edge of the platform.

"You fight by instinct, but your technique is off." He holds out his hand. "Give me your fist."

"Why?"

"You can give me your fist or we can go back to fighting. I'm not going to ask twice."

I remain unemotional. I may as well be stating facts like talking about the weather. "You're going to hurt me."

"You're already hurt. Very badly, as far as I can see." He's blank. No hint of sympathy. He, too, is stating facts. "You're right to distrust my motives."

I raise my eyebrows. "Then...?"

"You're forming your fists wrong," he says.

I glance at Ms. Hawk. Her arms are folded across her chest as she stands watching us, but she doesn't object to Striker's quieter actions.

That alone should scare me.

Holding my breath, I take a reckless step forward and place my hand in his, ready to escape if I need to. He closes my fingers over my palm, tucking my thumb at the side, enclosing my fist in his big hand.

I don't like the way my entire hand disappears inside his palm. I feel too small. Too weak.

At his touch, I nearly expected to feel the energy that shot through me when we fought, but I don't. Instead, his hand is warm and strong.

"Like that," he says. "Now your feet."

He taps my feet with his own until I shift them into the position he wants. "Balance your weight. Harness your core. Now relax into it."

He pulls my fist toward his chest, where it connects gently with his upper ribs. "Hit me here and it will hurt most. Go on."

I hesitate. He's lying. It won't hurt most to hit him there. It will hurt most if I hit him on his back where his burns are still healing.

My fist slowly unfurls, my fingers escaping his as I flatten my palm against his ribs, sensing his quick inhale. I tell myself that I'm preparing to shove him aside, but I linger just a moment too long.

His arm slips around my waist, drawing me closer. His free hand rises to the back of my neck, gently cradling my head. A shiver runs down my spine, confusing me because I'm not afraid.

His lips hover above mine.

He whispers, "*Now* I'm going to hurt you."

"What—?"

My reflexes aren't quick enough.

His thumb runs down the side of my neck, a raking burn. The air stops in my lungs. A scream forms in my windpipe and then it stops.

My body ceases to respond to my internal commands. My arms and legs go limp.

I slump in his arms, sense myself slipping to the ground as he lays me down. His figure blurs as consciousness fades.

His lips press to my ear as he whispers, "Goodnight, Peyton."

Everything goes dark.

8. STRIKER DRAVEN

ater and electricity are a bad mix, but I deserve every agonizing shot of pain I'm experiencing.

I press back against the fence, rain pouring down my back, the excruciating burn ripping through my chest.

I grip the bars harder, my fingers curled tightly around them, refusing to let go even when my head spins and my stomach turns. It's been hours since I ate, but my body doesn't care, trying to make me hurl up my long-ago lunch.

When afternoon classes finished, I ran for two hours around the perimeter, circling the fighting ring again and again, watching and waiting for Peyton to wake up, but she's still out cold.

Every time I circle the ring, I peer at her to see if her chest still rises and falls—that she's still breathing.

The nerve-pinch I delivered was supposed to knock her out for an hour—just long enough for Ms. Hawk to lose interest and leave her alone.

I tried to knock her unconscious the moment she stepped into the ring so she wouldn't have to face the remainder of the class, but she surprised me with her determination to fight back.

She shouldn't have remained unconscious this long.

The afternoon has stretched into the evening and now it's dark, well past dinner time. Worse, storm clouds have gathered and the sky opened up.

Now the rain beats at her unconscious body and the combat mat runs red with her blood.

She's still bleeding out.

Her wounds are real. They're actually real.

I didn't believe that the blood all over her this morning meant she was hurt. Even the scratches across her face looked like they could have been deliberately made—an elaborate hoax, but it wouldn't be the first.

I tried to discover if her shoulder wound was genuine when I grabbed her outside my room, but it was impossible to tell. Especially when she got up in my face with her throaty threats and get-the-hell-away-from-me eyes and her body pressed against mine in a way that nearly drove me insane.

I didn't believe she killed the harpy. I didn't believe she was wounded. I didn't believe how pale she was. I didn't even believe the way she gave up fighting me in the hallway when I stomped on her food.

I didn't believe anything about her… until she took off her shirt.

The foundations shifted beneath me when I saw the deep claw marks across her shoulder, the thin trickles of blood running down her back and chest.

Now I shout into the wind and rain, cursing every step I've taken since she arrived. Her screams, her flickering silhouette when she stepped toward Joseph, the way she took the fall for him…

She's an Unknown, brought here to die, and I've treated her like trash.

If she dies tonight, I'll be lucky to salvage what's left of my charred conscience.

Finally letting go of the fence, I drop to my hands and knees in the mud, gripping the sodden mounds of grass, my fingers pressing into it.

I want to scoop her up in my arms and take her inside, but the outcome will be much worse for her if I do. The Headmistress made it very clear that anyone who tries to help Peyton right now will be punished. I don't care about myself, but I do care that they'll throw her in the pit overnight if she doesn't wake up on her own.

Even without the harpy, she won't survive if she spends the night down there. She needs fluids and blood, neither of which she'll get if she's locked up.

I try to shake off the memory of the way her palm flattened against my stomach when she was supposed to hit me, the smallest flicker of trust in her eyes when her head fit perfectly into my hand, her messy hair tangling between my fingers.

The way she let me hold her when she shouldn't have.

The way my senses filled with her nearness in a way I've never experienced before.

I tell myself my reaction in that moment was purely physical. I've been in this place too long. Been without sex for too long.

Lights flicker high up in the attic and the silhouettes of two men become apparent, backlit as they stand surveying the yard and everything in it through the wide windows.

They don't care that I throw myself against the fence each day. The voltage is set to stun, not kill. They think I'm trying to prove my strength. But they will care if they see me worry about Peyton.

If I stay here, hovering over her, I'll make things worse.

I pull to my feet, forcing myself to move, pretending I don't care that she's dying twenty feet from me as I jog away from her.

I don't look back, but my chest hurts with every jarring step I take.

9. PEYTON PRICE

It's raining.

A shudder racks my body as I force my eyes open, blinking through the downpour.

I'm alone on the platform, lying here in my underwear, my head resting on my arm. The sunlight's long gone. My saturated uniform lies in a pile beside me.

Storm clouds obscure the sky and lightning streaks above me in short, sharp bursts that remind me of Joseph's flicker fit.

They left me here. The teachers, the students, Striker.

I don't know for how long.

I try to push up with my arms, easing out my stiff neck, but my muscles are weak and my limbs wobble. My shoulder aches so bad, but I'm beyond screaming. The rain is like icicles and I'm numb inside and out.

They left me here to bleed out, but they'll be watching me. I cast my gaze around the deserted grounds and then higher.

Way up on the fifth floor, two figures stand at the floor-to-ceiling windows along the corridor outside my bedroom, their silhouettes illuminated by the dim light: my compliance officers.

The fact that they don't bother to stand closer guard tells me they don't believe I'll make a run for it. In my weakened state, taking on the electrified fence would be suicide. I have nowhere to go. I'll be lucky to make it back inside the building.

I check my fingers in case being near death has caused my power to surface. I could fantasize for a moment that the storm raging above me is my own creation, but my fingers are pale, numb—no manifestation, no power, not even the faintest flicker.

Another shudder shakes me so hard that I struggle to close my fist around my uniform, dragging it beside me as I crawl to the edge of the platform.

I manage to get my feet under myself before I roll off the raised surface. Trying to find my balance, I stumble to the back door, gratefully leaning against it when I finally reach it.

I'm freezing. My only hope is to curl up under a warm shower, try to beat the threatening hypothermia and figure out a way to...

What, Peyton? Die peacefully?

I breathe out. Shaky breaths. Pressing against the door, I feel the rain beating at my back. I don't know how much blood I've lost now. I'd planned to find a way to dress my wounds, but instead I was lying on a hard surface with my wounds exposed for hours.

Standing under a shower probably isn't the smartest thing I could do, but I have no other way to get warm and right now, that's all I can think about.

I push open the door and stumble to the steps, pressing against the walls at intervals. The hallway is silent. So is the second floor. It must be way past dinnertime. Way past bedtime.

What the hell did Striker do to knock me out that long?

And dear ancients, how am I going to climb another flight of stairs? My feet are heavier with every step, my knees buckling on the final three steps. I fall to my hands and knees and pull myself onto the fifth floor.

The compliance twins step out of the shadows the moment I appear.

"Look who finally woke up." Collin smirks. "We got tired of standing in the rain. We watched you just fine from up here."

I don't have the energy for a retort. Placing one foot in front of the other is all I can do.

I make it past Striker's open door before I veer to the wall and press my way along it. He stops mid-pushup as I pass, jumping to his feet, his chest gleaming with sweat.

He looks warm and I need to be warm. I fight the reckless urge to stumble back to his room, press against him, and steal his body heat.

I must be delirious. In fact, I probably am. Blood loss and hyperthermia. I'm not thinking straight.

Asking Striker Draven for help will earn me a punch in the face. He's the reason I'm in trouble to begin with.

I stumble to the bathroom door, sensing movement behind me.

Striker's confident statement follows me inside the room. "I can take it from here."

The compliance twins laugh. "She's all yours."

The thud of their boots fades and then cuts off as the door closes behind me.

I don't care what Striker plans to do. I'm beyond fear right now. My instinct is basic: survive.

I turn on the shower and have the presence of mind to make sure it's not too hot before I collapse to my hands and knees and crawl inside it. The warm water eases my frozen limbs, driving warmth across my head as I curl up under the spray, my eyes closing.

I exhale a sigh of relief. Finally, I feel warm.

I can rest now.

My breathing slows. Calm now. Quiet and soft.

"Get up."

Striker's order reaches me from far away, washing over me like a breeze before it fades into nothing, means nothing.

His hand curls around my shoulder, grabbing me hard, but it doesn't hurt. I don't feel it at all. I probably should. Maybe I should be worried about that, but I'm beyond caring.

"Peyton?"

His voice sounds different, urgent, worried.

My head tips back. He tilts me across his arm in the water, giving me a fierce look. His face, his amber eyes, are a distant blur, becoming more distant by the second as I close my eyes again.

"Fuck."

The water stops. A towel scoops around me and the room shifts. He just took away the warm water, the one thing I needed.

Damn him. I struggle against him, wanting my cocoon of warmth again, but my efforts don't do me any good. My arms won't move. My legs aren't responding.

Let me go, damn you.

He grips me tightly, one arm braced across my shoulders and supporting my head, the other under my knees.

Within moments, we pass my room and enter his. I can't fight him as he lays me on his bed, turning me onto my stomach, my head facing the wall, my wet hair splattering his pillow.

I shiver when he unclasps the back of my bra and pushes my bra strap off my right shoulder, but my awareness of his actions is patchy, fading in and out.

I'm confused when his footsteps hurry away from me and there's a *clunk* like shifting wood cracking against itself before he returns. Within seconds, cold liquid burns across my shoulder.

I exhale a moan at the sudden pain, wanting to sink into numbness again.

He presses his palm against my back. "Lie still."

Something soft presses against my wound. A tearing sound scratches my hearing before the pressure against my shoulder increases, but it's a soothing pressure.

Is he… dressing my wound? He can't be. I must be hallucinating. Why would he do that? And where did he get the supplies?

I fight my disbelief as he takes hold of my left shoulder and hip and turns me over. My bra slips farther down my chest, barely concealing my breasts, but it's difficult to care when I can't even move.

His focus doesn't descend below my right shoulder, which is now closest to the wall, as he quickly straddles me so he can reach that side and presses a medical patch over my wounds at the front. Duct tape scrapes my hearing again as he pulls and cuts it, pressing firmly across the patch to keep it in place.

He checks my neck, running his fingers across my skin before he slides them down my torso, across my stomach and hip, all the way to my leg, leaving a burning trail of tingles all through me. The sensation is like a last living lifeline as darkness threatens to engulf me again.

The tape screeches.

A patch presses against my leg.

Then his weight lifts off the bed and a blanket settles over me.

His chair scrapes across the floor before he pulls my left arm out from beneath the blanket.

"This is going to hurt." There isn't a shred of apology in his voice as a sharp object pierces my skin. Tape descends over the object he stuck into me and then there's a moment of silence.

My eyes fly open when I hear him take a sharp breath. It sounded like pain.

I fight to focus on him, my vision blurred.

He's sitting in a chair beside me, his teeth gritted, a plastic line dangling between us, running from his arm to mine. Crimson liquid spears through it toward me.

A breathy sound escapes my lips. "Wha—?"

"You need blood. Mine's your only option."

Humans give blood all the time, but Striker is Unknown and so am I. There are so many things that could go wrong right now.

Blood of a different species could kill me. We have no way of knowing what the outcome will be—

His blood hits my vein.

Oh, fiery gods of hell.

A scream builds inside my lungs and my back arches as liquid magma surges through my arm, striking through my shoulder with every heartbeat drawing it in. I thrash, but he lurches across the space between us, spreading the fingers of his free hand across my chest, pushing me back to the bed.

I moan out the pain as scorching heat spreads through my torso. I'm barely able to distinguish between the heat from his blood and the warmth from his hand.

The blanket slips with my sudden movement, the heel of his palm pressed against the top of one of my breasts, his fingers splayed against the other, tangling in my bra.

His command breaks through the intense fire licking through my stomach and traveling down my frozen legs.

"Be still."

The first coherent response I can make tears from my lips. "I can't."

"You can."

I shake my head as heat pulses up my neck, filling my head with—

I gasp, my chest rising again, but not with pain, not fear, not hatred, not anger.

Pure, blissful warmth.

It fills my mind, spreading outward, downward, finally relaxing my tense muscles, washing through my arms and torso and my legs.

A deep blush spreads across my cheeks as the heat washes past the apex between my legs, triggering an intense sensation I'm not remotely familiar with. Definitely not painful.

The torturous warmth reaches my toes, making them curl as the initial burning heat fades to a soothing sensation and I settle back onto the bed.

Touch has always been a negative experience for me. The back of a hand, a fist, always severe, never gentle, never wanted.

Whatever magic courses through Striker's blood, it's making me wish he wasn't my enemy. I can't even begin to imagine what it would be like if he stroked my hair, maybe even hugged me in a way that made me feel as comforted as I feel right now.

His gaze meets mine, a fierce crease between his eyebrows, his eyes startlingly bright.

For a second, I find myself imagining that the fire I felt in his blood is reflected in his eyes, a dark, volcanic flame, but when I blink, the reflection is gone.

He seems to suddenly become aware of his hand still pressing across my breast. He hurries to remove it, but his fingers are tangled in my bra. He only makes things worse when he accidentally wrenches the material with him.

He freezes with my bra pulled partly across my chest and barely covering the important parts. Lowering his hand before he rips my bra off completely, he stops very still.

He firmly fixes his gaze on the window at the other side of the room. "A little help?"

The warmth filling my body is making me much less inhibited than I would normally be. If something like this had happened this morning, I'd gouge out his eyes. Instead... I almost feel sorry for him.

I almost don't want him to move away.

It's that damn warm feeling muddling my emotions.

Sliding my free arm over my chest, I trap my bra against my breasts, obscuring them, so he can untangle his fingers and carefully remove his hand.

With an exhalation, he sits back in his chair, his focus turning to the closed door. The medical line hangs between us in the silence, his blood continuing to revive me.

There are a thousand snide comments I could make right now about his idea of medical help. I hope the needle is clean. He'd better not give me any diseases. But all of them are born of the protective mechanisms I've developed over the years to put up prickly barriers between myself and others.

I remind myself that he's an asshole and a danger to me, but for now, all I want is truth. "Why are you doing this?"

He's silent. Fixated on a spot on the door. A photo is taped there that is only visible once the door is closed. It looks like a young Striker—maybe only ten years old—standing beside an older girl with black hair. She could be an older sister, but other than the color of her hair, I don't see much resemblance to Striker in her face or eyes, so maybe she's a nanny.

I try again. "Why are you suddenly helping me?"

His gaze snaps to mine, anger making his tone sharp. "Suddenly? I've been helping you since you got here."

I stare at him, wishing I had the strength to push up on the bed so I could see him better. "Are you kidding me? You've shoved me, grabbed me, stolen my food, and knocked me out. You call that helping?"

His jaw clenches so hard, I can see the muscles in his face shift in the lamplight. "Okay, first of all, nobody walks toward a flicker fit and walks away again unscathed—"

He must be referring to the way I stepped toward Joseph last night, right before Striker shoved me out of the way. Interrupting him, I argue, "*You* did. You ran straight toward him."

"Because I'm the only one who can."

Without giving me time to think about that, he plows on. "Second, if I hadn't knocked you out this morning, you would have ended up with a broken arm."

My retort is scathing. "You wouldn't have gotten close enough to break my arm if you hadn't pretended to teach me—"

"I'm not talking about me. I'm talking about Ms. Hawk. Nobody walks away from the ring on their first day without her breaking a bone. If you're lucky, it's just a finger. If you're unlucky, it's your leg."

My stomach sinks. "She does that? Lucinda warned me about her, but—"

"Third, they poison your food for the first twenty-four hours."

"What?" A shudder runs through me. He destroyed my dinner last night by smooshing it all over my shirt. He stole the coffee Mr. Mallard offered me this morning and then he decorated the floor with my morning tea.

He leans forward, his hands gripping the armrest. "The first twenty-four hours determine whether you live or die. They break you, beat you, and make you puke your guts up. It's a perfect trifecta of pain, dehydration, and fear that works every time. All newcomers reveal their power."

I stare at the ceiling. "Not every time. Nothing works for me."

"You would have died." He turns away, quiet again, resting back in his chair. He's quiet for so long, I wish I could read his thoughts.

I dare to ask, "Did they do it to you?"

He breathes out an exhale. "The Headmistress made an exception for me."

I consider his room and all its extras. Leather desk chair, metal workout bar attached to the ceiling, large desk, lots of books, sound system.

My gaze narrows on the electronics and the insignia: *Draven Industries*.

Of course, that's why his name is familiar.

His family owns and runs an electronics company, but sound systems aren't anywhere near their biggest game. They're one of the largest military contractors for weapons production: guns, ammunition, bombs, whatever humans want so they can kill each other.

I can't keep the scathing tone from my voice. "I take it Daddy made a sizeable donation to the Academy."

He shakes his head. "Not money. Weapons."

A confused expression spreads across my face. "Why does the Academy want weapons when they have wands?"

"Not the Academy. The Founder. They call her Lady Tirelli. She runs the underground mob in multiple cities. A lot of humans work for her, so she wants weapons for them. This academy is a blip in her life. She's never here."

That would explain why Headmistress Osprey is so drunk on her own power.

My voice sounds too small. "If you weren't trying to hurt me... why didn't you just tell me? Give me a warning, you know. I could have played along—"

He's up and out of his chair in a flash, dragging the line with him. I grab hold of my arm, pressing on the needle's entry point in case he rips it out.

He leans down over me, one fist on either side of my head, his eyes blazing into mine. "Let's get something straight, Price. We are not friends. We will never be friends. I might kick you a favor every now and then so I can stick it to this institution, but don't think for one second I won't kill you myself if I'm in the mood."

His gaze is cold and hard, not a flicker of a lie in it.

He means it. He will kill me. There isn't a shred of doubt in my mind.

My pulse is suddenly hammering, fear striking through me, my chest rising and falling as I suck in air.

It has the unwanted effect of shooting his blood around my body far too rapidly and the burning tingles intensify so fast that I jolt.

He's leaning down so close to me, my chest presses against his for the tiny second that I arch up and the brief contact sends all the wrong signals to my core.

Holy hell, what is his power? Is he some kind of sex god?

I need him gone, away from me, or I'll do something stupid like kiss him after he threatened to hurt me. I am not that girl. I don't care that his magic is practically orgasmic.

When... *if...* the day comes that I sleep with someone, it will not be with an aggressive brute like Striker Draven.

I shove him away from me, both palms pressed to his broad chest as I sit up, a movement that forces him to step back.

The fact that I can move again is a good sign. I grab the line in my fist, my teeth clenched as I command him: "Get this out of me. Right now."

"Gladly," he snarls. His gaze flashes over me and then quickly returns to the line as he works to remove the needle from his arm.

Damn. My bra. Unclasped, it may as well be flapping in the breeze. I don't have the largest bust in the world, but I'm busty enough that I need coverage.

In this case, survival trumps decorum, so I ignore the fact that he's getting an eyeful right now. Well, he would be if he looked. He's violent and unpredictable, but he seems to draw the line at disrespecting my body.

When he reaches for my arm, I give him all of two seconds to remove the line and tape over the wound. As fast as I can, I grab his blanket and drag it with me, awkwardly clambering to the base of his bed while I wrap the material around myself.

I only pause when I spy a roll of duct tape and a pair of scissors wedged at the end of the bed. I snatch them both before he can stop me, trying not to trip on the blanket while I grab the door handle and wrench it open.

Cold air rushes into the room, making me realize how hot it is in here. A brief glance back reveals a first-aid kit sitting on the floor and an open panel in the far wall where he must hide the kit in the wall cavity—that would have been the *clunk* I heard when he retrieved it.

I want to ask him where he got it, but the sooner I leave, the better.

Striker stands with his arms folded across his broad chest, watching me go. "One more thing, Price."

"What?"

"They've been known to enroll fake students."

My brow furrows as I remain poised in the doorway. "What do you mean?"

He doesn't answer. He presses his lips together and steps back into the shadows of his room.

"You can have your blanket back in the morning," I call as I fully exit the room. "Mine isn't warm enough." I don't know it for a fact since I haven't slept in my bed yet, but the blanket they left me looked far too thin for what I need tonight.

I'm still shaky. I need to rest.

I hurry to my room and close the door, leaning back against it while I rub my eyes. Despite his deadly intent, he didn't let me die tonight. His motives are confusing in the extreme.

What I do know, though, is that when he targets me, there could be a secondary purpose. Poisoned food. Teachers who break arms. Even when he grabbed my shoulder after I killed the harpy…

His comment about fake students is alarming. Did his fingertips move along my wound this morning as if he was checking that it was real? Did he suspect that the blood and the story about the harpy was all fake? But for what purpose? To get him—everyone—to trust me? Or feel sorry for me?

It would certainly explain why the other students gave me a cold welcome if they think I'm here to spy on them. Maybe the idea of another Unknown is too farfetched to be believed.

I shake my head as I cross the floor to my bed. Trying to decipher Striker's intentions is going to drive me to the brink of despair. I have to keep him firmly in the enemy box. I have to keep everyone in the enemy box.

They all left me out there in the rain tonight.

My room is much brighter than Striker's because there aren't any curtains. Faint flickers of lightning pulse in the distance as I towel dry my hair and pull on clean underwear and pajamas.

I hide the duct tape and scissors in the bottom of the closet under my books. The storm is passing and soon the moonlight will stream across my bed.

A sickening, drawing sensation pulls at me as soon as I lie down in it. My stomach squirms as I stare up at the ceiling directly above my bed. A rune has been painted on it in ink that lights up with every lightning strike.

It's another poultice. A fixed one.

I tip my head over the side of the bed, attempting to see the floor beneath it.

Dammit. A second rune is painted on the floor, directly below the one on the ceiling. I guess it's supposed to work while I sleep, drawing my power out, but there's no way I can sleep under it with the crawling sensation it causes under my skin.

A quick scan tells me the bed is bolted to the floor so I can't shift it away from the runes.

I drag myself, both blankets, and my pillow to the far corner of the room where I curl up on the floor beneath the window.

Striker's blanket smells like him—a mix of cedarwood and balsam, oddly calming. He might be dangerous, but the thick blanket is a lifesaver on the hard floor.

I fall asleep, resolving that I'm not giving it back after all.

10. STRIKER DRAVEN

As soon as Peyton leaves, wrapped up in my blanket clutched across her nearly naked chest, I pace my room like a caged animal.

The beast inside me—the one I keep hidden—thrums and claws at my insides, wanting to be released.

Growls hum at the back of my throat, my basic instincts nearly overcoming rational thought.

Peyton doesn't know what her power is. I don't either, but I know she's like a flame drawing me closer. Except I won't be the one who gets burned.

I make it as far as my door before I stop myself.

What am I thinking?

I drop my forehead against the doorframe. I'm thinking about the way she arched her back beneath my palm, the way she didn't care that her bra was all over the place, the way she planted her hands against my chest and gave me orders.

She was so angry with me.

A sudden smile curves my lips. Nobody's ever dared to be that righteously furious with me before. I've experienced aggression, abuse, cruelty, sure, but nobody has ever been so justified in their feelings as she is.

I've only known her for two days and already I've run the gambit of emotions around her: hate, distrust, apathy, empathy, fear, worry, *lust*.

The burn behind my eyes tells me that my beast likes her. A little too much.

I'm going to have to be careful. The last time I got close to someone, it ended in bloodshed.

The beast's feelings are expressed as a deep growl in the back of my mind. A smug thought on its part: *That situation in your past was different than this. That other girl was not your equal.*

That other girl. I stop myself before I think her name—the girl who ripped everything apart and shredded what was left of my heart. The one who proved that loving someone is never worth it. *Never.*

My fingers curl into fists.

I can't sleep now.

Throwing on a shirt, I exit my room. I fight the urge to turn in Peyton's direction, to find an excuse to argue with her again, make her hate me a little more so I can see the fire in her eyes one more time before I fall asleep.

Prowling down the corridor in the opposite direction, I take the stairs quietly in my bare feet.

My intention is to roam the perimeter. Now that the storm has abated, the air outside will be fresh and cool; the wild scent of the forest will reach the enclosed space around us and remind me what freedom smells like.

I make it as far as the bottom step on the ground floor before I jolt to a stop.

Quiet voices float from the room directly around the corner —the Founder's room—which is unusual in itself. That room is always empty.

An all-too familiar female voice reaches me through the

partially open door. Her voice is soft and gentle—too gentle—in the way that a predator coaxes its prey into a trap.

Lady Tirelli says, "You nearly killed Peyton today, Isadora."

Headmistress Osprey's response is a strained appeasement. "We wouldn't have let her die, I promise. We were just about to bring her in from the rain—"

"Don't lie to me!" Lady Tirelli snaps, the anger in her voice like a whiplash. "Or it will be the last thing you do."

There's silence inside the room and I picture Headmistress Osprey's alarmed expression, the flutter of her gaudy fingertips as she folds her arms across her chest, pretending that she's still in control of this situation.

She clears her throat a couple of times, but her voice wobbles when she speaks. "Peyton Price is Unknown. There's no telling whether she's even worth our time—"

"The Unknowns are the strongest. Do not underestimate the power they can control."

Osprey's response is incredulous. "How do you know that? We don't even know what they are."

Lady Tirelli's voice lowers, soft and deadly now. "Because I sense their power, Isadora. They are as dangerous as I am. You would do well to remember that."

I've never been sure whether Lady Tirelli was human or supernatural. It doesn't seem to matter. Both races are terrified of her and for good reasons. Anyone who stands in her way—in fact anyone who dares to bother her at all—ends up dead. Usually in a gruesome way.

Headmistress Osprey gulps so loudly that I hear it even from this distance. I picture the nervous sweat breaking across her brow.

She's wise to be afraid.

Lady Tirelli's voice becomes gentler, but again, she's like a predator soothing her startled prey. "I can't afford to lose any more students. Especially not to flicker fits."

Osprey's voice is strained. "We do everything we can to make sure they don't flicker: strenuous daily exercise, continuous spikes in adrenaline, poultices above their beds to absorb sudden power surges while they sleep. We make sure they're in a constant state of fear. We lost many in the beginning because we were still figuring out what would work. We won't lose any more."

"Keeping them alive is only the first half of the equation. They need to control their power." Lady Tirelli's response holds hints of frustration. "I want them at their peak, Isadora. They were meant to be my soldiers. I want my army!"

Osprey is quiet for a moment. "Why them? You have hundreds of humans and supernaturals at your beck and call."

"Because they're dangerous, but more importantly, they're expendable. Nobody cares if they die. What's more, they'll do anything to survive."

The Headmistress's voice is a hoarse whisper. "What do you want me to do?"

"Focus on Striker. I want to know what his power is."

I sense the slow shake of Osprey's head. "We've tried everything with Striker."

"You haven't."

Now Osprey sounds confused. "But… we've beaten him, hurt him, crowded him, left him alone, given him something to fight for, ripped it away again. Nothing works."

"Are you sure it hasn't?"

I fight my flight instinct, jolting with shock. My beast suddenly whispers warnings inside my mind: *She knows about me. She knows what we are.*

No. I shake my head, trying to convince myself and my beast. *She's asking, not saying.*

"He hasn't flickered," Osprey says. "We've seen no signs. Except…"

"Except what?"

"He likes the electric fence."

Again, I tense. My daily dose of electricity is the only way I control the beast and keep him from revealing himself. They think I'm just batshit aggressive. I'm in trouble if they figure it out.

"Interesting," Lady Tirelli murmurs. "He doesn't black out?"

"No."

"Then it's a compulsion. A clue to his power. Get Mallard onto it. Find out which powers could be connected to a hunger for electricity. Storm power, maybe. And watch Striker more carefully. The moment you see a hint that might reveal the nature of his power, I want to be informed."

"What about Peyton?"

"As I said, you haven't tried everything. I'll be sending The Specialist as soon as he's finished his current work for me."

I've heard of The Specialist. He's particularly violent, but I don't know much about him other than that.

Osprey's tone of voice tells me she isn't happy about this. "Are you sure? His methods are extreme. Dangerous… even for us. If you want Peyton alive—"

"Are you afraid?" Lady Tirelli's response is scathing. "If you're too scared to do your job, I'll replace you with Hadrix."

"No!" Osprey is indignant. "My work here is far superior to anything Hadrix could have achieved."

Hadrix is a new name to me. I filter through my memories, trying to remember if my father ever mentioned him, but I come up blank.

"Then you won't object to enhancing your options," Lady Tirelli replies smoothly. "The Specialist will arrive as soon as he's available. In the meantime, continue with your current methods." There's a pause and I sense a shift in the room, hear the swish of a skirt as if Lady Tirelli just stepped up into Osprey's face. *Don't. Kill. Peyton Price.*

"I-I won't. I promise."

"Good. I don't need to tell you how important it is that I have my army. I *want* their powers, Isadora."

"You will have them. Soon. I promise."

Footsteps approach the door. I step back into the darkness as Lady Tirelli emerges dressed in black leather pants and a low-cut top that reveals more of her curves than it hides. Masses of dark brown hair sweep down her back, wisps resting next to her pale cheeks. Her hazel eyes glow in the moonlight streaming from the high windows.

She pauses, her head raised, twisting a little to peer into the shadowy corner where I hide. She won't see me. My beast has already taken control and hidden me from sight. I'm nothing more than a shadow right now.

Lady Tirelli gives herself a shake. Her quick steps take her to the wide doors, her hips swaying as she pushes on them and descends the staircase, disappearing into the dark. She leaves behind a cloying scent of roses that fades into an odd scent of decay.

There's a whoosh of rapid movement, and then she's gone, leaving me with a sense of dread.

I've been a student at Bloodwing for three years now. In that time, I've been ripped apart body and soul and somehow pieced myself back together again.

But what I put back together... I'm not sure what I am. Not human. Not even supernatural.

I'm a monster.

My beast growls. *Don't fear for your safety. I can kill them all.*

I know it can. I know *I* can.

I've lain awake night after night wondering what would happen if I tried to escape. Whether I'd make it out alive.

I've fantasized about pulling apart those fence bars with my beast hands and walking out of here. But the other students would get caught in the crossfire.

I've closed off my heart, killed nearly every emotion, but

there must be some last small shred of decency left in me because I refuse to let any more of them die.

I don't care about them. If we ever get out of here, I won't think about them again. But as long as we're here, whatever it takes, I'll keep them alive.

My beast is accusing: *You do care.*

No, I tell it. *It's about power. If I can stop anyone else dying, it means I'm in control.*

It's a lie I'm willing to believe.

11. PEYTON PRICE

The next morning, I wake up feeling like I've chugged several cans of energy drink.

I'm surprisingly alert despite the crick in my neck from sleeping at an awkward angle.

A quick check of the clock tells me it's only half past five. I'm not sure if breakfast is as strictly regimented as dinner, but I'm not taking any chances.

Striker said they poison the food for the first day. I can't be sure they won't still try, but I'm starving despite the energy tingling through my body.

A search through my closet reveals the elusive gym clothes I missed yesterday, tucked in behind multiple skirts. Not taking any chances, I pull on the workout shorts and tight tank top beneath my uniform and quickly visit the bathroom to wash my face.

Once there, I pry open the front patch on my shoulder, relieved to see the wounds have started to heal over, before I press it back into place.

I'm determined not to run into Striker and I manage to sail past his room just as he steps out from within it with a towel slung over his shoulder. The dark circles under his eyes are a surprise. He either didn't sleep well or giving me blood didn't agree with him.

I miss a step. I was too out of it last night to consider that giving blood can be dangerous for the giver.

I shouldn't care but I swing back to him, attempting to see if he's okay. He's already striding away down the hall. The bathroom door clicks closed behind him.

I chew on my lip for a moment before Collin's snide voice cuts into my thoughts.

"Morning, Price. Still alive, I see."

I spin to him and Colby. "No thanks to you."

"Aww, she's all cut up about it." Collin smirks, his pale eyes glistening.

I wait for them to move out of my way, worried for a moment when they stay where they are.

Colby taps his wand against his palm. Even though Collin is the one who makes the snide comments and grabs me more often, Colby seems to call the magical shots. His shirt sleeves are rolled up, revealing tattooed scales up his arms. After another beat, he inclines his head and Collin moves out of my way.

I skirt them as widely as I can before hurrying away, knowing they won't be far behind.

Entering the dining room to find half of the students there already, I'm completely prepared for another frosty welcome. Compliance officers line the room and I'm beginning to recognize some of them, although I haven't linked them with the specific students they guard yet.

Lucinda sits at the front table like yesterday, but this time she's facing in my direction. Her head is down and she grips a handkerchief in her fist, which rests on the table. The girls on either side of her sit with their arms around her, leaning in.

I catch the end of her conversation.

"You can't know that," the girl hugging Lucinda says. She has long, straight blonde hair, luminous green eyes, and I think her name is Ashley.

"Her body was gone." Lucinda sobs. "They took it away."

The guys on the other side of the room notice me, call out to Lucinda, and the room falls silent.

Lucinda's head snaps up. Her mouth drops open. A dark bruise covers her left cheekbone. Her bottom lip is split. Her eyes are red and her cheeks blotchy. She's not a pretty crier, but then, neither am I.

Ignoring the compliance twins, who take up position against the wall, never taking their eyes off me, I head in Lucinda's direction, eyeing her wounds as I get closer.

I stop at the table as the other students continue to stare at me.

"What happened to your face?" I don't mean to sound so blunt but she wasn't beaten up yesterday and I want to know why.

They all blink at me, a heavy silence settling around us. I eye the compliance officers. One of them steps farther forward than the others, making me suspect he's Lucinda's guard.

Lucinda stammers. "You... It wasn't... I don't..." She takes a deep breath and speaks on an exhale. "You're alive. We thought..."

They thought I died.

I can't seriously believe she's crying about it.

I find myself switching gears. They didn't know I survived until I walked into this room. The looks on their faces indicate that they didn't think I would.

I don't tell them it's only because of Striker. "I guess I got lucky."

She meets my eyes. "We didn't help you."

It's probably the closest to an apology I'll get, but all it does is make me angry. Mostly at myself. For a second there, I was worried about Lucinda. I forgot they all left me out in the rain to die.

I take a step back, unable to push away my anger fast enough. The last thing I want is to cause a scene that might jeopardize my now-critical need for food. "Okay, you know what, if you're not going to tell me what happened, I'm just going to get my breakfast and eat it… uh… over there."

I point at the empty table on the guy's side of the room. Ms. Sparrow hasn't arrived yet, so nobody's eating. I'll just have to sit and wait.

I'm halfway across the room before Ashley stands up so suddenly that her chair falls over. The bang makes me whirl in her direction.

I pause, my eyes narrowed, not trusting a single move she makes. She twitches as the falling chair's echo rings out in the silence. She brushes the hair out of her eyes, revealing a cut across her forehead.

A second compliance officer steps forward, his wand pointed in her direction, a dangerous scowl on his face. This guy must be Ashley's guard.

I quickly scan the faces of the other students. Many of them are cut up, bruised in ways they weren't yesterday, which makes the hairs on the back of my neck prickle.

Something's going on here and I can't put my finger on what exactly it is.

Ashley gulps as I cast a wary glance her way. She hesitates too long. Just as I'm about to turn away, she speaks in a rush. "Lucinda tried to bring you in."

I only half turn back. I'm not sure I heard her correctly. "What?"

"Lucinda's hurt because she tried to bring you in yesterday."

Ashley's gaze flicks to the compliance officers. Several of them have now peeled themselves off the wall and the others have all removed their wands from their belts, gripping them tightly.

There's suddenly an unexpected charge in the air. The compliance officers are tense and alert, the students are sitting taller than before. The girls at the back table slowly push back their chairs and the guys on the other side of the room cast sideways glances at each other, the kind that indicates silent communication.

I inhale a slow breath. My understanding of what happened yesterday afternoon is suddenly set on fire, exploded into shattered pieces.

I picture myself lying in the rain, oblivious to the chaos around me... Lucinda trying to grab me, Ashley trying to pull her clear, the compliance officers lashing out, their magic knocking Lucinda in the face, cutting across Ashley, slicing into Joseph's arm, piercing the darkness around me, electricity splitting the air, cutting the students down before they could pick me up...

Then darkness as they scatter...

What the hell?

This isn't possible. It has to be a lie. I hate lies more than I hate loneliness. "Why the hell would you help me?"

Ashley recoils. "Because you're..."

I raise an eyebrow, waiting for her to go on, filling in the blanks when she doesn't. "Because I'm like you? Really?"

Another quick glance at the compliance officers tells me how this is going to go down right now. Ashley's guard will grab her first. The girls at the back table are ready to lurch forward, but the guards will hurt them too. The guys at the back probably have a small chance of fighting, but it will be mere seconds before they're subdued.

If I light the spark, a fight will break out. How I respond will determine whether or not this morning goes to hell.

I relax my shoulders, then lift them in a shrug. I paste a

bored expression on my face. "I'm not like you and never will be."

She looks confused. "But… we…"

I see the entire room with an awful clarity right now. Every student in this place is hurt, has been knocked around, and they're angry. They want a reason to fight back.

I can't be that reason.

The fact that I was left out in the rain to die can't be that reason.

"Get over it, Ashley." I give her my best uncaring, deliberately fake smile. "Sorry about Lucinda's face, but she really shouldn't have bothered."

I stride over to the empty table and sit down, fixing my gaze on the spot where Ms. Sparrow stood the day before, pretending that she's going to materialize any second. As soon as my butt touches the seat, the compliance officers relax, slowly putting away their wands one by one.

I just gave up my chance at friendship, but if I'd taken it…

That road doesn't end in roses and rainbows.

When Striker's hand grips my shoulder a few moments later, I'm already so emotionally numb, I hardly feel it.

I know he heard everything when his deep voice murmurs in my ear. "Now you're learning, Price."

His fiery eyes meet mine for a second and I suddenly hear him the night before louder and clearer than I've ever heard anything before.

We are not friends. We will never be friends.

Friends get hurt.

"Okay, Draven," I whisper, fixated on the table while he hovers close to me. "I'll play your game. Just know that I'll play it well."

A slow smile breaks across his face. "I wouldn't expect anything less."

12. PEYTON PRICE

The first class of the day is Magical Instruments.

Ms. Sparrow places a wand on the desk in front of each of us and leaves it there.

She tucks her fake red hair behind her ear as she pauses in front of my desk, placing a long, thin wand in front of me. She positions a white crystal ornament beside it and throws me a challenging look.

I glance at the other students to see what they're doing, hesitating to touch either of the objects.

When I look up at Ms. Sparrow, she says, "These wands are restricted to basic, harmless magic. Your task is to simply change the color of the crystal." She leans down with a patronizing gleam in her eye. "We wouldn't give you a weapon now, would we?"

What a shame.

As it is in every class, the only spare seat is beside Striker. I'm not sure if it's deliberate, but it hasn't escaped my notice that there are exactly an even number of girls and guys at the Academy—fifteen of each.

Somehow, two desks are always placed at the back of the

class, side-by-side for Striker and me, so I have no choice but to sit next to him.

"Pick up your wands!" Ms. Sparrow's voice could not be more shrill. I press a hand to my ear, still studying the wand.

She orders, "Repeat the words of the color-change spell: Pretty pink perfection."

Once the students obey her, lifting their wands and murmuring the spell, Ms. Sparrow shrieks, "Lucinda! I expect more from you today. As the only repressed witch, you should be far more progressed with wand magic."

Lucinda's shoulders slump.

Now that the teacher's back is turned, Striker's glare is burning me again. I'm not sure how he manages to so effectively make me feel like I've dived into a molten pit of lava every time he glowers at me.

I ignore him as I hover my hand over the wand.

Nobody's ever given me one to use before. I'm not sure what will happen—or if I want to find out.

When Ms. Sparrow casts a commanding scowl around the room, I decide there's only one move I can make: pick up the wand.

I lower a single fingertip to prod it.

On contact, a jolt passes through me, like a shot of electricity. I quickly withdraw, assessing the prickly sensation echoing through my arm. It circles around my forearm, back down through my wrist, and into my palm. I wasn't expecting any reaction. Certainly not such an instant one.

Maybe this means I'm a witch.

It would be a relief to finally know what I am. But what I felt wasn't magic. It didn't feel like power or even pain, more a sense of... *revulsion. Dislike.*

I shake my head because that doesn't make any sense. It isn't possible to dislike a wand. I mean, really?

A few rows in front of me, Lucinda's wand changes color,

not the crystal. The wand is now hot pink. Ms. Sparrow slaps her over the head. "Useless!"

I tense, telling myself not to get involved, channeling my anger into the task at hand. *Pick up the damn wand, Peyton.*

My hand closes around it, fingers curled tightly, pulling it firmly upward. A flash of electricity passes up my arm, shoots across my shoulder, and passes straight into my heart.

My heartbeat slows, every thud like a deep drum driving a shock of electricity through my body.

Emotions stab me. Deceitful, cold, calculating thoughts flow with them—thoughts that aren't my own. My blood runs cold as they pass through my mind. *I'll make him hurt. I'll keep pretending. He doesn't suspect a thing. He'll do anything for me...*

Images whoosh through my mind like a visual flicker fit that makes me want to hurl. Pinpricks of blood, a shimmer of magic, a vase of sickly sweet-smelling red roses, the fighting ring, blood splattering across its surface, a shout of agony echoing up the dark stairway to the pit—someone else's cry of pain.

My stomach turns. It's like I'm inside the head of the person who last held this wand, like I'm seeing what she saw, tapping into her memories. But I don't want to, because she's so full of lies it makes me sick.

I'll make him love me. I'll make him trust me. Then I'll hurt him.

The rush of images slows, dragging me into a single moment. Striker's bedroom—I recognize the chair and the blanket I stole—and a warm, male body pressed against mine on the bed. A kiss presses to the back of my neck and an arm encircles my waist, sliding beneath my shirt to graze across my bare stomach, the gentlest touch, the sort of touch I've never experienced—

He loves me. He doesn't suspect a thing.

I drop the wand with a gasp, dragging fresh air into my lungs, my chest heaving. I cough, clutch my stomach, and try not to dry retch across the floor as the deceitful thoughts finally… *finally*… leave my mind.

The wand clatters across the table, coming to rest against the crystal, stopping the wand from rolling off the table altogether.

My voice grates in my throat, a revolted growl. "This wand belonged to a liar."

Releasing my stomach, I curl my fingers around the edge of my desk, trying to get rid of the crawling sensation beneath my skin.

Ms. Sparrow enters my field of view. "What did you say?"

I grit my teeth, anger burning inside me as my voice rises. "*I said* that the last person who used this wand was a liar."

There's a sharp *snap* nearby, but I don't have time to see what it was before the entire class suddenly becomes silent and still.

The other students stop waving their wands around, stop repeating the useless chant, to stare at me. Lucinda casts a glance from me to the wand. When she sees it, her eyes widen in a way that tells me she recognizes it.

I'm too focused on Ms. Sparrow to look across to Striker, but I sense his stillness.

Ms. Sparrow's eyes also widen. "How did you know…?" She blinks rapidly, rallying quickly. "Pick it up."

"I'm not touching it again. It disgusts me. Whoever it belonged to, *she* disgusts me."

Ms. Sparrow's eyes turn into wide pools. She takes a step toward me, screaming, "You will not disobey me. Pick it up, Price!"

Her voice is so shrill, I'm surprised she isn't a banshee. I stand and raise myself to my full height, my fists sliding from the table, balling at my sides. "No."

Magic sizzles through her wand. "Curse cut clean!"

The breath stops in my lungs. Pain slices across my arms and cheeks. Neat cuts blossom along my skin as if invisible blades sliced across me.

I swallow a cry and bury a sob as blood slides down my arms.

I raise my eyes to hers, squeezing my own clear of tears. "You can cut me all day," I say. "I won't touch that wand again."

Ms. Sparrow gasps.

I brace for more pain as she raises her wand.

Lucinda's sudden shout breaks through the heavy silence. "Disarm!"

Her pink wand shoots through the air, targeting Ms. Sparrow's like some sort of homing beacon.

Ms. Sparrow jolts, shouts, and turns her wand on Lucinda, but in the next instant Lucinda's wand splits down the middle like a tuning fork, neatly colliding with Ms. Sparrow's and collecting it before changing course completely. It zooms upward and lodges in the ceiling. Ms. Sparrow's wand ends up pressed against the ceiling between the two prongs of Lucinda's.

The teacher gapes, her mouth dropping open before her face turns red with rage. She screams for the guards. "Compliance!"

Lucinda shrugs as the sound of running boots meets my ears. "You wanted me to improve, Ms. Sparrow."

The teacher points at the ceiling. "That is not improvement! That's insolence."

Lucinda's lips twitch into a smile. "I think that's subjective."

Compliance officers swarm the room and Lucinda's compliance officer grabs her, but she relaxes into his hold, allowing him to pull her arms back without breaking them.

He drags her away from her desk and forces her to the floor into a kneeling position, his wand pressed against her bruised cheek. He looks to Ms. Sparrow for instructions.

Before she can speak, Lucinda suggests, "You can throw me in the pit if you want. I wouldn't mind the peace and quiet."

Does she have a death wish?

Ms. Sparrow's jaw clenches. She presses her lips together in anger. "This class is over. You can go to gym early. That should be punishment enough."

She snatches up the wand on my desk, glaring at me before she waves it at the two wands stuck to the ceiling and speaks a command. "Return!"

The now two-pronged pink wand wobbles, refusing to unstick. Ms. Sparrow repeats the command. "Untie unstick!"

Finally, the pink wand slides from the ceiling, both wands falling to Ms. Sparrow's waiting open palm. She calls all the wands to her and they coast through the air behind her in a bundle as she storms from the room.

Lucinda's guard releases her with a shove that forces her into the floor. She quickly rolls clear of his descending boot before jumping to her feet.

I release the breath I was holding. She's okay. I check my cuts and discover that they're no worse than papercuts. They sting like hell, but they should heal quickly.

A burning sensation tells me that Striker is still staring at me. When I cast my gaze in his direction, pasting a nonchalant expression on my face, I'm shocked to see pain etched across his features, his face pale, his forehead creased, lips pressed tight.

A muscle ticks at the side of his jaw. His hands are clenched around… something… I can't see what it is.

Whoever the girl is that the wand belonged to, she did what she set out to do. She hurt him. Badly.

She could still be here. She could be one of the girls in this room, but I don't think so. The sense I got from her… I would know it if I felt it again.

His expression hardens, closing off, but his movements are slower as he presses two jagged pieces of wood onto his desk and leaves the room.

It's his wand. What remains of it, anyway.

I think back, remembering the *snap*. He must have broken it in two when I first called the wand's owner a liar.

I'm the last to leave class. I'll be the last to arrive at gym if I don't hurry. I break into a quick stride and then a jog, darting around the other students, even sprinting past Striker, to take the stairs quickly and exit the building.

The warm morning air fills my lungs as I rip off my uniform and ascend to the ring, arching an eyebrow at Striker when he arrives after me.

Ms. Hawk already stands next to one of the practicing posts, leaning against it with her arms folded, eyeing me. She's probably heard about my display in Magical Instruments and is prepared to deal with my insolent behavior.

Striker keeps me in his sights while he pulls off his uniform and follows me up onto the ring. He doesn't take an immediate swipe at me like he did yesterday, keeping his distance instead.

It's impossible to miss the quick assessment he gives my new wounds. I'm bleeding, but I'm okay.

I wait another beat for Ms. Hawk to be distracted by the arriving students before I take quick strides to breach the distance between Striker and me.

Up close, I'm hit with the scent of cedarwood. Damn, he has the best scent in the world. I keep my voice low. "Teach me how to fight."

The crease in his forehead deepens to a scowl. "You're not worth my time."

Oomph. I mimic a dagger to my heart with an exaggerated wince and pout. "Ouch, Draven. You really hurt my feelings."

Without giving him time to respond, I drop the act and glare at him. "Like I haven't heard that a thousand times before. Now, teach me how to fight."

He doesn't budge, his eyes narrowing. His chiseled bare chest is a little too distracting in the sunlight. All that gleaming skin. I keep my focus on his face as I circle him, giving him a chance to think.

"I don't care how you teach me," I say. "Beat me up for all I care. As long as I learn something along the way, it's all the same to me."

There's a tic in the muscle in his jaw. Without warning, he twists, and his rock of a fist strikes toward me.

I dart to the left, barely managing to avoid it.

He watches my movements, dropping his arm and standing back. "Your reflexes are good, but you need to think about your next move. Avoiding a hit is only one part of the equation. You need a follow-up."

I dance backward before I force myself to stop and plant my feet. "Okay, then. Hit me."

The corner of his mouth tugs up. He paces toward me, surprising me by using his left hand instead of his right. I don't have time to avoid it. His fist clocks me smack on my cheek.

Thud.

The world spins and I kiss the ground. *Hot damn.* That hurt.

I take a deep breath and squeeze my eyes closed before I press up on my hands, telling myself it's all good. I'm totally fine. Ms. Hawk was starting to look at us and now she's turned away again. Watching me get beat up is obviously not very interesting to her.

I draw up to my feet as Striker towers over me. I grit my teeth, bracing, determined that I'm ready for anything this time. "Again."

He gives me a look like I've lost it. He aims another hit for exactly the same spot on my cheek, this time with his right fist.

I duck but miss the fact that he's following up with his left, which slams into my shoulder so hard that I spin before I hit the ground, landing on my stomach.

So much for being ready for anything.

I tell myself to keep moving—lying on my stomach is one of

the most vulnerable positions I can be in—but damn, I'm in pain. I swallow a sob as I roll to avoid the kick he aims at my ribs, shouting out my frustration that I'm crying right now. "Fucking tears!"

He glares down at me. "You've got a mouth on you today, Price."

"Fuck you." I jump to my feet, my head swimming, my balance shaky. This time I don't plant my feet. I keep moving. Mostly because my balance is pulling me in wonky directions that I can't control. "Again."

I don't focus on any part of him. My only goal is to get in a hit of my own. Yesterday when I connected, it was like a trigger for my senses, some sort of clarity-inducing rage.

I need to feel that again.

I watch for the openings in his movements, the gaps between his arms, the spaces where his body isn't protected.

When his right fist shoots toward me, his left shoulder is exposed. My fist crunches into him so hard that I barely feel the impact of his hit on my own shoulder. Energy rages through me on impact, a violent, searing thrill.

We hurtle away from each other, our hits propelling us in opposite directions. I tumble before ending up in a half-kneeling crouch, both hands planted on the ground.

I can't help but smile at the way heat surges up my arm, the power flowing through me despite the pain in my left shoulder. It occurs to me that he had the decency to target my unhurt shoulder, not the one that he bandaged.

Still, I don't hesitate, sprinting toward him before he has time to fully stand, my energy levels heightened.

I throw my body, feet first across the distance, landing a hard hit into his chest, forcing him flat onto his back. I land on my side, grazing my elbows, one leg landing on his chest. I hurry to use his body as a platform, planting my foot against his ribs and attempting to propel myself back to my feet.

Oomph. I sense the air leave his lungs as my foot connects, but before I can complete my getaway, he grabs my ankle, yanking me to the ground.

I twist just in time so I don't fall on my side, using my stomach muscles to throw myself upright, ending up partially straddling him. He grips one foot in his hands, holding it high against his shoulder while my other leg is bent awkwardly on his other side.

Plan my next move, huh? Well, that didn't go so well.

Energy still rages through both my legs from the connection I made. I'm breathing hard, but my arms are completely free and he's lying on his back, trying to stop me freeing my leg again.

I could easily punch him in his beautiful face.

I lean forward, flexing over my leg to plant a fist on the mat next to his cheek. "What move would you make right now if you were me, Draven?"

He surprises me by grinning, a disarming gleam in his eyes. "I'd knock your lights out."

"Okay, then."

I raise my fist to take a swing, but—*damn him*—he used my hesitation to shift his legs. He harnesses his stomach muscles in a way I never expected and lifts me up still straddling him.

Without supporting my back.

He shoves my foot away from his body and flips me backward. I shriek. There's nothing to stop my fall as I tip back. It's too late to get my feet under me.

I crunch gracelessly onto my shoulder, narrowly avoiding landing on my head, rolling quickly to avoid his stomping feet aimed at my torso and then my legs.

I barely get to my feet in time to face him again.

His eyes are blank, expressionless, a cold glint in them. "Never stop to talk, Price. It gives your opponent time to think."

Lesson learned. That time, I fell on my wounded shoulder and I'm sure I ripped open some of the cuts.

I inhale a calming breath, but it's no use.

Now I'm mad.

I lift my eyes to his and let go of all planning whatsoever.

I just want to hurt him back. *That is all.*

Taking a deep breath, I launch forward, swinging at Striker's head, feinting left when he blocks my fist. I connect with his side instead and follow up—finally—with a punch to his lower back. I sense his inhale, the tensing of his muscles, the heat raging through my hands, up into my head.

When he swings toward me, I throw another fist at his chin. His head snaps back, but I don't stop there, following up with my left fist crunching against his shoulder and a hard knee to his stomach.

He flies back, landing on his butt several paces away.

I can't believe I put him there. I'm as shocked as he appears to be.

Standing with my fists clenched at my sides, I wait for him to get to his feet and fight me again.

He rises, a cautious angle to his body as he rubs his chin, a surprising worry entering his expression as his gaze descends to my feet.

I follow his line of sight and for a second… it looks like my feet aren't touching the ground.

Am I levitating? That's not possible… unless I actually do have powers. The idea is so startling to me that I gasp.

Ms. Hawk swivels in my direction.

Just before her gaze lands on me, Striker's body barrels into mine, forcing the air out of my lungs as he wraps both arms around my waist in a tackle that carries us out of the ring.

We fly backward, hit the grass, and narrowly miss cracking our heads on the practicing posts on that side of the ring.

Lachlan and Ryan jump out of the way on either side of us.

I roll to a stop several paces from Striker, groaning out the pain. The impact of our fall is still reverberating through my chest and legs. I'm hurt everywhere now. There's not a single part of me that doesn't ache. *Oh, give me painkillers.*

When Striker jumps to his feet before I can, I throw up my hands in defeat. The fall took the wind out of my sails. He ignores my upraised hands, grabbing the back of my shirt and dragging me away from the ring.

Ms. Hawk casts a bored glance in our direction before returning to the other students. I guess she assumes he's determined to get revenge because I beat him just now—and that seems fine with her.

"Hey!" I thump Striker's hand as he continues to pull me away—all the way to the neat rows of rose bushes at the back of the grounds. "Let me go!"

He dumps me on the grass and rounds on me, his voice a low growl. "That was stupid, Price!"

A merciless laugh tears out of me. "Which part? Wanting to learn how to fight or kicking your butt?"

He leans down to grab my shoulders, surprising me when he eases up on my hurt shoulder. "The part where you rose off the ground."

I can't stop my sudden excitement, the strangest feeling when I'm otherwise in horrible pain. "I did? That really happened?"

His face crinkles in disgust. "Don't play dumb. You know exactly what you did. You accessed your power. You showed increased agility, strength, and a sudden burst of speed. It's how you beat me."

I replay my actions in my mind—the force behind my fists, the way I dodged his attack, rounded on him faster than I thought possible, and thrust him across the combat mat.

None of it was conscious on my part. I was aware of my energy—I was drawing on it like sucking down on ice on a blistering summer day—but I didn't willfully know what I was doing.

I search his eyes for a sign that he believes me when I say, "I'm not pretending, Draven. That's never happened to me before."

I'm not sure if I should tell Striker that I think it has something to do with him. My brother used his fire mage power on me all the time—burning my hair, making me break out in heat sweats at awkward moments, forcing me to dodge him, only to step into the path of someone I really didn't want to bump into.

But I never felt the surge of energy that I feel when I connect with Striker's body.

His scowl deepens. He casts a wary glance back at the class. He doesn't relax even when it's clear Ms. Hawk isn't paying attention to us. The compliance officers have left us alone so far too. When I'm with Striker, they seem to take the attitude that I'm in enough danger already.

When he turns back to me, he doesn't have to speak. The scathing glint in his eyes tells me he doesn't believe me.

"I'm not lying," I persist. "I hate lies."

His grip eases, a new caution in his eyes. "You made that clear in Magical Instruments."

"I don't know what I am," I whisper. "If I can levitate, I could be any number of things. A witch… a winged shifter… Did you see if I have wings? I didn't have time to look—"

"Stop!" He shakes me hard again. If I didn't know better, I'd think he looks worried. "The moment they know what species of supernatural you are, they'll start phase two on you. You don't want that."

"Phase two?"

"The phase where they bombard you with targeted attacks that trigger flicker fits. If you can't control the fits, they'll kill you."

I ease out a shaky breath. "Joseph's in stage two, isn't he?"

Striker gives me a short, affirmative nod. "They think he's a shifter. Ashley's in phase two as well. They thought she was an ice mage because she could make things freeze, but now they think she's telekinetic."

"What about Lucinda?"

"She just finished phase two. It goes on as long they want—a year even."

Again, I search his eyes. "Why are you warning me about this? You said you'd never help me."

His expression hardens. He said we weren't friends and he wasn't lying. I'm still figuring out what sort of relationship he has with the other students, but other than helping Joseph the other night—with a fist in his face, no less—I haven't seen Striker interact with them in any positive or friendly way. I don't understand why he's helping me now.

Unless… he's not.

Oh. Right. He's helping himself.

I swallow, breathing quietly. "You need them to believe that the power of an Unknown can never be known. If I show signs of my power so quickly, they'll restart their efforts on you."

His only reaction is a narrowing of his fiery eyes. "They've already tried and failed."

Failed? Now I know he's lying to me. The flame I thought I saw in his eyes the other night was real. I take a deep breath, challenging him with my suspicions. "You know what you are, don't you, Draven?"

His grip tightens again, his eyes blazing and this time, I know I'm not imagining the fire that flickers in his gaze.

His mouth forms a threatening line. "If you tell anyone, I will kill you, you hear me?"

I stare at him in shock. He knows what he is. He really knows. His death threat is a mere wash of sound—his admission of knowledge is more shocking to me.

He snarls. "Do you hear me?"

I nod. *Loud and clear.*

13. STRIKER DRAVEN

I try to calm myself as I stride away from Peyton.

Fighting her is dangerous. Touching her is dangerous. She brings out my beast and that's the last thing I need. Damn her. She brings out the worst in me.

She brings out the best in you.

I ignore the stirring beast and its unwanted contribution to my inner turmoil. I fed him so much electricity yesterday he should be in a slumbering stupor right now.

Instead, he woke up the moment Peyton's fist connected with my shoulder.

At the most basic level, I could conclude that her use of force triggered my beast as a protective mechanism, but it was more than that. It was as if her emotions transferred to me and I *felt* what she felt.

But it wasn't what I expected.

I expected anger, the need to survive fueling a desire to hurt me. I didn't expect to feel hunger, a fiery need to connect underpinned by curiosity. Her touch was seeking, questioning, demanding to know who I am.

The impact of her touch made me feel... *hell... more* powerful, not less.

But what really scares me is that I transferred emotions back to her. The power she stirred inside me bounced right back to her. She must have felt it, because after that she moved differently in the combat ring. The final hit to my lower back actually hurt, but it made my inner beast buzz like a happy puppy.

You could teach her how to fight. Like she wants you to. My beast is dangerously alert now and I need him to sleep. I can't afford to lose control of him in front of a crowd of students and compliance officers.

No, I reply. *It's too dangerous.*

She might not give you a choice. His response is a rebuke. I hate it when he forces me to face the truth.

I like her, my beast continues. *She speaks to me with the fire in her heart. I want to listen—*

Shut up.

My response is dominant enough to make my beast back down. Peyton knows far too much about me. Admitting that I know what I am is the most reckless thing I've done all year.

I try to decide if I believe Peyton's assertion that she doesn't know her own power. The look on her face when she realized she was levitating couldn't be faked. She was genuinely surprised—excited even.

I don't think she's a witch, unless she's an extremely powerful one. Her power is fundamentally raw and emotional. Her ability to identify and call out a liar tells me that. She's also profoundly angry, although that could be a result of our surroundings. I wish I could have observed her in a normal environment.

Hah, normal. I don't know what normal looks like.

There's no figuring her out.

As I approach a practicing post and lay into it hard enough

to tear the skin across my knuckles, I force my beast to back down, blocking out his impulses and thoughts. I can't afford to let Peyton trigger him again. Ever.

I need to not only put her out of my mind, but to put as much distance between her and me as possible.

It's going to be nearly impossible.

I may as well try not to breathe.

14. PEYTON PRICE

The compliance officers won't let me sit here on my butt for long, but I need to think.

I just had my first magical manifestation and I don't know how to feel about it. It isn't like a first kiss, or getting first place in a sprint, or winning a poetry competition. It isn't an achievement I can celebrate. My survival depends on it.

I want—*need*—to know what I am but if what Striker said is true, I have to be careful not to let anyone else know. Levitating is hardly a definitive answer about my powers. I might be a witch or I could have some sort of angelic powers. I could even be a bird shifter.

Most supernaturals would laugh that I'm even considering the possibility that I'm a shifter since my mother has the power of invisibility and my father and brother are fire mages. There are no shifters in my immediate family and shifters are always born to other shifters—except in the case of the magically repressed.

If I ask Lucinda what her parents are, she's bound to tell me that there's never been a witch in her family.

If Striker knows what his power is, then he must have

learned how to control it. That's the only way he can still keep it a secret. I have to find out how he's doing it.

As I pick myself up off the grass, I take advantage of these last few seconds of being alone to survey the security at the back of the Academy.

The tall electrified fence extends unbroken around the perimeter, telling me that the front gate is the only way in or out. There's no garden apart from the rose bushes. No trees, sheds, or other visual obstructions. Nothing to hide behind.

In contrast, beyond the fence line, a forest obscures the rest of the world. It's impossible to tell how far the forest extends in any direction. Every way I turn, all I see is trees.

I make a mental note to get over my fear of heights and check out the landscape from the attic tonight.

Returning to the class, I also study the other students. There are too many for them to each get a practicing post of their own, so they're sharing them—one on each side. What they're doing looks more like physical punishment than any sort of combat training. Kicking and hitting a wooden post is a great way to make your knuckles and feet bleed.

On this side of the two practicing posts that I'm approaching, Joseph is kicking his post hard while Lachlan alternates between kicks and punches.

I catch sight of Lucinda on the other side of Lachlan's post and Ashley's long, blonde hair flying behind Joseph's.

Farther behind them, two students whose names I don't know grapple each other in the ring, but neither of them has Striker's skill. They're trying their hardest, though.

As I draw nearer, I can see that Ashley's whacking her post as if she doesn't feel the impact, but she's leaving bloody smears all over it.

On the other hand, Lucinda's pulling her punches as if she doesn't want to connect. I hear her muttering with every hit, "Sorry, sorry, *sorry...*"

I don't know what she's apologizing for. The post can't feel pain.

Just when I spy the only free practicing post and head toward it, Ms. Hawk's shout pierces the air. "What a sorry bunch of losers! You're all useless today. I'd keep you here until you were covered in blood, but the Headmistress insists on Academy Maintenance today." She swings in my direction with a glare. "Since we had to skip it yesterday."

I bite my tongue before I tell her I'm sorry my near death caused so much inconvenience.

"Get out of my sight! Bring your game tomorrow or I'll switch up the rules again."

The murmurs around me tell me changing the rules is a bad thing. I quickly grab my uniform and pull it on before I head to the dining room for lunch, sitting alone at what is now my table.

I'm intensely aware that I'm sitting on the guys' side of the room and that by me taking up a table of my own, they're cramming themselves around the other two. The gender segregation seems strict and almost pointed.

When Lachlan approaches me with a determined expression, saying, "We need the table, Price," I glare daggers at him.

"Walk away," I say, twisting my plastic fork in the air as if it's a deadly weapon. "Or you'll end up like the harpy."

With a flicker of annoyance, he turns away again, leaving me to eat in peace.

After lunch, Ms. Sparrow's shrill voice announces that it's time for Academy Maintenance. She swiftly assigns us to various tasks. The guys get the lucky job of cleaning toilets and washing floors. The girls get yard cleanup, which apparently involves cutting grass and pruning rose bushes.

Three of the girls end up behind push mowers. They quickly

strip off their uniforms again, sweating in the sun as they push the noisy mowers around the yard.

Ms. Sparrow hands me a pair of pruning shears and a basket. "For cutting fresh flowers."

I guess I'll go skipping through the meadow while I'm at it. I already know there's a bad wolf waiting for me at the end of this task.

When I test the weight of the shears in my hand, she gives me a patronizing look again. "They're spelled to only cut wood. You can't use them as a weapon."

"I guess I'll cut up some wands then," I murmur, but only after she's walked away. I consider the shears carefully as I approach the first rose bush, choosing one that's farthest from the other girls.

There has to be a way around the spell cast on the shears. All spells have limitations, parameters that can be breached. Only instinctive magic is unbeatable.

I head into the corridor between rose bushes and kneel on the grass, hoping ants don't crawl up my pants while I'm sitting here. I know enough about rose bushes to know there's an art to pruning them. I'm clueless what the technique is, though.

Why would anybody ever need this many rose bushes in the first place? I consider myself lucky I'm not pushing a mower, but I'm sure my time will come.

Taking glances at the other girls, I note how they're carefully thinning out the leaves, cutting only the roses that are in full bloom. I reach for the first flower just as Lucinda takes a seat on the other side of the grassy corridor, her back to me.

She doesn't acknowledge me, and I don't acknowledge her.

I snip the first rose, prune off the excess leaves, and place it carefully in my basket. For the next ten minutes, we sit in silence, broken only by the *snip-snip* of shears.

Silence doesn't normally bother me, but she nearly got

herself hurt this morning when she disarmed Ms. Sparrow. That's on top of yesterday's attempt to help me.

I don't know if she'll hear me when I whisper at the rose bush in front of me. "Thank you for trying to help me yesterday."

There's silence behind me. I guess she didn't hear me. That's probably just as well...

Her incredulous whisper reaches me. "I thought you didn't care."

I should say that I don't. That I never will. Instead I remain silent as I carefully prune a wayward leaf from a rose stem.

When I glance Lucinda's way, I find her studying me with a furious crease in her forehead. I quickly turn back to my task, angle the gardening sheers, and carefully cut a rose, placing it in the basket at my side. It gives me an excuse to turn toward her again. "You didn't freeze me out like the others when I first arrived. Why was that?"

She levels her gaze with mine. "A fake would never scream like you did."

I freeze. She must be talking about the magical poultice the compliance officers subjected me to on my first day.

It hurt. A lot. But I didn't know I'd been screaming until it was over.

My voice sounds strained to my own ears when I say, "You all thought I was a fake student."

She turns back to her roses, her whispers remaining quiet. "The chances of another Unknown are a million to one, so we thought it had to be a trick. Especially when we heard you were going to sleep in the attic. We thought it was a ploy to get under Striker's skin."

I try to keep my tone even. "There was a pretend student before?"

Lucinda's fingertips hover around the rose stem she's pruning. "About a year ago. I'd been here for a few months when this girl, Kaitlyn, arrived. She was supposedly a repressed witch like me. She had these amazing brown eyes that sucked you in, you know. She was one of those chicks who guys can't help wanting to protect."

"What happened?"

"Striker fell hard."

I jolt a little, piercing my finger on a thorn. Sucking on the wound, I murmur, "I'm having trouble imagining that."

Lucinda twists, places a rose in her basket, and gives me a wide-eyed look that says I'd better believe it. "Every time one of the teachers hurt Kaitlyn, he was there, getting in their way, defending her. He spent more nights in the pit than ever before. He came out every morning bloody and cut up. That was the first beast—the one before the harpy."

"What was it?" I whisper.

"It was an Orthrus—a two-headed dog." She shivers. "That dog was a nightmare. It would..." She takes a deep breath. "It would sink its teeth into one of your limbs—arm or leg—but never deep enough to make you bleed out. It would drag you around for hours, just playing with you, you know."

She shakes her head as if she's shaking off terrible memories. "What Striker didn't know... what none of us knew at the time... was that Kaitlyn was a spy. Her sole purpose was to cause Striker so much pain that he would have a flicker fit and finally reveal his power. Nothing they tried before had worked, you see."

The fingertips she rests against the roses in her basket grip the stems suddenly, a reflexive action. "He came across her one night casting a beautification spell on herself—to make herself prettier. Those big, brown eyes weren't natural after all. But beautification spells are complicated. If she really was repressed, there's no way she could control that kind of magic."

Lucinda shudders. A thorn pricks her fingers, a thin trickle of blood spilling from her hand, but she doesn't seem to notice.

"Striker went berserk. He nearly killed her. Nearly killed his compliance officers. They had to lock him in the pit. That was the night he killed the Orthrus."

She grimaces. "That dog was supposedly unkillable—just like the harpy. You Unknowns sure have a way of shaking things up."

I swallow. "What happened to Kaitlyn?"

Lucinda sighs. "She waited for Striker to come out of the pit. He was all covered in blood and gore from ripping the Orthrus apart." She shudders. "Kaitlyn laughed in his face and then she left. She was scared of him, though. We could all see it. His compliance officers were taken away—probably to a healer—and they never came back. Nobody was assigned to guard him after that."

Before she falls silent, she says, "Striker wasn't the same after that night. Now he only speaks with his fists."

I stare at the rose I'm still clutching in my hand. "He thought I was another Kaitlyn, didn't he?"

"Yes."

I ask the question I need to know. "Was that her wand this morning?"

"It was." Lucinda sounds far too casual when she asks, "How did you know Kaitlyn was a liar?"

"I felt it as soon as I picked up her wand." I don't want to tell Lucinda that I saw snatches of Kaitlyn's memories: moments of Striker's pain, his shouts from the pit, his body taking hits as he stood in front of her and made himself a physical shield, and then... moments of impossible tenderness that I struggle to reconcile with the Striker I know.

I quickly change the course of the conversation. "I guess they gave me her wand to play with his mind."

Her shears snip. "No," she says, shocking me with the certainty in her voice. "They gave it to you because he sees her when he looks at you. He's taking out all his hate on you,

Peyton. All the hate he couldn't take out on her. If you'd unwittingly used her wand this morning, it would have made you an even greater target."

I pause, but my hands are suddenly shaking. The Headmistress placed me in the room right next to his. The teachers make me sit next to him in every class. I have to share a bathroom. "So it's about me."

"The Headmistress gave up trying to make Draven reveal his power a year ago," Lucinda says. "He may as well be one of the guards now. You're their focus." She turns to me, her lips pressing into a sad line. "I get that you were trying to protect us this morning, but you need friends, Peyton. I wouldn't have survived the last year without Ashley and Joseph. Even Lachlan and Ryan have helped me get through stuff. You don't have to push us away. There's nothing that hasn't already been done to us, nothing that we haven't survived already."

She fixes her gaze on me, her bruised cheek dark and blotchy in the sunlight, a wry smile on her lips. "Besides, if there's a good time to rebel a little, it's now. Before they get a new beast for the pit."

She holds out the rose she just cut, as if she wants me to take it. "Come sit with us at dinner."

There's a question in her voice.

I consider the flower. She's right. I'm not going to survive on my own. The more I observe the Academy and its teachers, the more I realize that I'll need help if I'm ever going to get out of here.

And maybe… some of the other students will come with me.

I reach out and grasp the flower.

It's time to take a chance on friendship.

15. PEYTON PRICE

That night at dinner, I casually walk to Lucinda's table and take a seat beside her.

She doesn't make a big deal out of it, which I appreciate, but when she hands me a cloth filled with ice, I annihilate my tough act by laugh-sobbing. "I don't know where to use this first."

An ice pack is like gold to me right now. Unexpected pain relief.

"Try your face," she says, holding it up to my cheek.

"Where did you get it?" I ask, taking deep breaths to calm my emotions as the soothing cold seeps through my bruised skin.

"There's an ice chest on our floor. You can get ice from there any time, but I guess they didn't tell you that."

I give a shake of my head. "They wouldn't want to appear that caring."

She introduces me to the other girl at the table along with Ashley. "This is Bree. She's a repressed water mage. Bree has been here longer than me and Ashley."

Bree gives me a smile. She has light brown hair and soft aquamarine eyes. "I'm all that's left of the first intake." She clears her throat. "Other than Striker, I mean. He was the first student here."

She leans forward. "His father set up Bloodwing with our elusive Founder. Until this academy was established, the magically repressed were kept isolated in their own homes. Sometimes they 'disappeared' or 'ran away.'" She air quotes the events that often led to a magically repressed person's demise.

Ashley shivers. "As much as I hate this place, the alternative is worse. A few years ago, in a couple of towns over from mine, a magically repressed girl was murdered and her killer walked free because the Magical Magnate determined that it was an act of pre-emptive self-defense. Her parents left the house unlocked so her killer could walk right in."

I shudder. I hadn't heard that story before, although I'd heard others where the killer was never identified.

"They say humans fear what they don't understand," Lucinda interjects. "But supernaturals do too."

Striker arrives moments before Ms. Sparrow. He heads to the back table without looking in my direction, but I catch the swing of his gaze from where I was sitting solo this morning to where I'm located now. I don't expect my move to go unnoticed, but he doesn't stop or miss a beat.

Ms. Sparrow waves her wand, muttering a spell, after which food and cutlery promptly appear on plastic plates on the table in front of us. She stalks out again, leaving us with the compliance officers.

I find it oddly disturbing that I've stopped noticing the guards as much as I did when I first arrived. They're becoming a bit like a knife lying on a kitchen bench—a potential threat, but part of the furniture. I can't live my life in continual fear, so I'm blocking them out.

I do, however, take note of their positions. Just like the students who sit at the same tables for every meal, the officers stand in the same positions around the room. Predictability is good. It will let me plan.

I reluctantly put down the ice pack to pick up my cutlery and begin eating. I have so many questions I want to ask Lucinda, Ashley and Bree—how did they find out about their powers, and have they ever tried to escape?—but I need to take it slow.

"Did your families bring you here?" I ask, trying not to sound too nosy.

Bree gives me a sad smile. "My parents tried to keep me with them, but the Magnate wouldn't let them. Believe it or not, my family didn't hate or fear me, but I'm in the minority."

"My father was an alcoholic," Ashley says, her face carefully blank, as if she doesn't care. "He started drinking after Mom left. He used to beat on me every day. Coming here is no different for me."

I cast a questioning glance at Lucinda. She's quiet for a moment before she says, "Mom tried to hide me, but Dad found out and brought me here. They're both wolf shifters, so you can imagine the fights they got into over me. Mom told Dad she'd kill him if he betrayed me. None of us has any contact with our families, so I don't know what happened between them after I got here." She shrugs her shoulders—a brave show of nonchalance, but it's obvious her family's history hurts her.

Ashley's emerald eyes glisten. I imagine in a normal world, the girls would hug each other right now, but displays of physical affection are rare here. Heightened emotions from the students attracts violent reactions from the compliance officers.

Ashley quickly deflects the conversation away from Lucinda, who is quiet after revealing so much about her parents. "What about you, Peyton?"

"My parents and my brother brought me here. They couldn't wait to be rid of me." I point to the cut above my forehead. I don't know what it looks like now, but it still hurts. "My brother did this on the way here. I used to want their love, but now I'm just angry at them. Pretty much all the time. I'm hoping for the day my anger becomes indifference. I'd prefer not to care."

My declaration falls into silence.

A deeper silence than I was expecting.

Bree and Ashley are suddenly tense and focused on something above my left shoulder. I half-turn to find Striker paused behind me. He's carrying his empty plastic plate. It looks like he was on the way out. He must have inhaled his food to finish eating so fast.

I can't read his expression when he says, "Your brother hit you?"

I narrow my eyes at him. "Don't tell me you care, Draven."

The corner of his mouth twitches up. "Not at all. I was just marveling at the fact that he must have the weakest right hook in the world."

Placing his empty plate on the table, he leans down, both hands planted on either side of me so that he traps me against the edge of the table.

My instinct is to lean away from him, press farther into the table's edge and keep a scant inch of open space between us, but I don't budge.

If he wants to menace me, he can damn well make contact.

"I never pictured you with such a lame-ass brother," he says.

I give him a quizzical smile. "Well, since I'm glad he didn't do more damage, I'm not sorry my brother's right hook is a disappointment to you, Draven."

He considers the cut above my eye. "Put some ice on that, Price."

He removes his hands and straightens, scooping up his plate and pitching it into the trash can at the side of the room before he leaves.

Normal conversation resumes around us.

I shrug and turn back to the girls. They release a breath and give me surprised looks.

"What?" I ask.

They glance at each other before Lucinda says, "You go head to head with Draven even when you should be afraid."

"Maybe I am... afraid." I consider my half-eaten food, suddenly not very hungry. "But if I'm going to die here, I may as well fight back while I can."

I raise my eyes to theirs. They don't contradict me. We're all on borrowed time.

Lucinda is the first to confirm it. "We're all waiting for the flicker fit that finishes us. If I could control my power..." She folds her hands on the table after she shrugs.

"What makes you think you can't?" I ask.

She stares at me. "Because I can't."

A surge of annoyance flows through me and I'm worried I'm channeling Striker's aggression, but I have to challenge her beliefs. I keep my voice low. "You threw a wand today and it disarmed a teacher. You must have done something to make that happen."

"I..." She looks helplessly at the other two girls, as if they can help her, but they rapidly shake their heads. "I don't know. I just wanted it to happen."

"You wanted to create a pitchfork that would trap her wand?"

"Yeah."

"And it did."

"Okay." She's still staring at me. "What are you trying to say?"

I eyeball her, leaning forward. "Maybe that's all it takes. You want it to happen, so it happens. That's instinctive magic, isn't it? Only the most powerful witches can access it."

"But I..." She swallows. "I'm not powerful. If I were powerful, I wouldn't be trapped here."

I give her a fierce glare. "Why were you apologizing to the practicing post today?"

"What?" Her question is a sharp whisper.

The other girls lean in, but their foreheads are creased, as if they're confused, especially Ashley. She was standing the closest to Lucinda today, but I can't be the only one who heard it.

"Today, when you hit the post, you kept saying *sorry* over and over. Why?"

Lucinda's mouth drops open. "I wasn't."

"You were. I heard you."

She's suddenly pale, her voice lowering to a bare whisper. "I wasn't saying it aloud."

Wait... what? Now I'm confused. I lean away from her, trying to gather my thoughts. Was I mistaken? I remember thinking it was a really strange thing to say and do. Maybe I took too many hits to my head and got muddled. My thoughts were in turmoil after my conversation with Striker...

I begin to protest. "But—"

Lucinda's hand darts out to grab my arm. She gives me a firm shake of her head. Her brown eyes fill with worry. It takes me a moment to realize she's worried for me, not herself. "We can't have this conversation here."

My gaze shifts to the compliance officers. The noise of the students around us is loud enough that I don't think the officers can hear us, but they're certainly watching carefully. Ashley's guard leans toward us in a way that shows he's interested in our conversation, which makes me nervous.

"I've eaten enough anyway," Lucinda says, a little more loudly. "We should show you around the girls' floor."

Bree and Ashley nod, their chairs scraping back as they gather up their nearly empty plates and dump them into the trash. The number of disposable plates that pile up after every meal makes me cringe, but the teachers don't give us reusable options.

I follow Lucinda while Ashley and Bree bring up the rear. Four compliance officers peel off the wall and follow us, including pale-eyed Collin.

We climb the stairs to the third floor in silence and then Lucinda leads me along the corridor. Each door opens to bedrooms on the left and right sides of the corridor.

"There are ten rooms on each side," she explains. "Twenty in total, although there are only fourteen of us right now. Mine is three doors down." She taps the ice chest positioned close to the front of the corridor and points to the small linen cupboard on the wall above it. "You can find cloths up there and ice in here. Ladies?"

They each retrieve a cloth and pack it full of ice, holding their bundles to various parts of their bodies. Ashley simply fists hers, her palms red from pummeling the practicing post today.

"Sometimes we fall asleep with ice packs all over us," Lucinda continues. "I don't think you would have met the working staff yet—there's a cook and two other women who do the laundry."

"I thought Ms. Sparrow magicked the food."

"Hah! It looks that way, doesn't it? She likes to take credit for work that isn't her own, but she's just the delivery service."

Lucinda's room is sparsely furnished like mine, but she's taped various colorful hand-drawn pictures to the walls. "I can't draw to save myself, but it helps make this room feel like home," she says when she catches me looking at them.

"You're right, they're terrible," I say, widening my eyes at her in an exaggerated gesture.

She laughs. "You don't pull your punches, do you? No wonder you give back as good as you get when Draven gets in your face."

I haven't forgotten why we came up here. I raise an eyebrow at her. She inclines her head at the door to her room and scoops up the freshly folded towel at the base of her bed along with some clothing. "This way."

Outside, I find Bree and Ashley waiting for us. They're also carrying towels and pajamas. They set off quietly for the bathroom at the end of the corridor, gathering me up and taking me with them.

I'm not sure what to expect when we enter the communal shower room. There's a small entrance first with a second door leading into a changing room. The girls dump their clothing on the benches that line the room but hang their towels on hooks just inside the third room. It's wide open with showerheads positioned at intervals around all three sides opposite.

I thought I was badly off with a bathroom that doesn't lock. The other girls have to share. At least the compliance officers didn't follow us in here.

I hover in the opening between the change and shower rooms. Lucinda places a finger to her lips and then turns on several of the showers before drawing me into the center of the tiled area. "This is the only place we aren't followed. The white noise drowns out our voices and should stop them using magic to overhear us."

"*Should*," Bree emphasizes. "As in, we hope it does."

"So far, it seems to," Ashley adds.

Bree laughs. "You'd think they'd be smart enough to employ female compliance officers. The guys leave us alone in here, but apparently, they walk right into the guys' bathroom." She shudders visibly.

It just highlights to me the privilege of Striker's existence.

Before I can think any more about Striker, Lucinda pins me in her gaze. "Explain to me how you can hear my thoughts."

I give Lucinda the only honest answer I can. "I don't know. I honestly thought you were talking aloud."

The look she gives me conveys her disbelief.

I try again. "I think I made it clear that I hate liars. I'm not making this up."

"Oh, I know you're not," she says. "But I wasn't talking aloud."

I chew hard on my lip, feeling like we're going around in circles. "Maybe it would help if you told me why?" I ask. "You hated hitting that post and it wasn't because it hurts your hands."

Lucinda glances at the others. She looks worried that they'll judge her, but both have open expressions. It makes me wonder how many times they actually talk to each other about their powers, whether there are things they're afraid to admit to each other and speak aloud.

"It wasn't that I hated hitting the post," Lucinda says. "I wasn't even thinking loud thoughts about it. It was just... a *feeling*."

"What feeling?"

"I hate it when wood breaks."

I eye her carefully. "But you broke your wand this morning."

"I didn't break it," she protests. "I changed it. And it was willing. I didn't force it to become anything it didn't want to be."

Her hands fly to her face, pressing to her temples. "Oh... I'm talking about wood as if it has feelings. I must be losing it." She wobbles a little side to side. "I've finally lost it."

"No." I shake my head. "I don't think you have."

Water rushes around our bare feet into the drain at the center of the room. With the amount of time we spend in gym class, our feet are bare more often than we wear shoes. It's a wild feeling to have the water rush around my toes and head in all sorts of chaotic directions. The white noise is calming to my mind in ways I haven't felt for a while.

Actually... their company is calming to me. I've spent my life either alone or surrounded by people who actively hate me.

Suddenly, I'm surrounded by people like me who, even if they aren't exactly my friends, don't wish me dead.

"My father and brother are fire mages," I say. "They can sense a hot day coming from the moment dawn breaks. They can sit in front of a camp fire for hours watching the flames burn, coaxing the fire across their arms like putty in their palms. Putting out the flames makes them uncomfortable just like abusing wood makes you uncomfortable."

"What are you saying?" Lucinda asks, the crease in her forehead deepening.

I study her eyes, the nearly imperceptible rings inside her brown irises, so many rings that they blur unless I'm looking for them. They're just like the rings inside a tree trunk that form as it ages, influenced by events in its life.

"I'm saying that maybe the teachers got it wrong. Maybe you're not a witch. What you feel would make complete sense if you were an earth mage. Or something even more powerful… like… a dryad."

I watch her reaction carefully. Her forehead creases at the suggestion of an earth mage, but her expression lifts when I mention a dryad.

"A tree spirit?" she asks. "They're incredibly rare."

I nod. "But it would explain why you turned your wand pink and how you manipulated it to trap Ms. Sparrow's wand. It would also explain why it hurts you that we punch practicing posts made from tree trunks. You're—"

"Remembering when they were alive." She gasps. "This changes everything. If I'm a dryad, I've been doing everything all wrong. The wrong magic, the wrong techniques, the wrong lessons."

The corner of my mouth twitches. "Lucinda, you don't need someone to teach you who you are."

"I need to test this." She nods to herself and then to me. "I'm going to figure this out. I'll go out early tomorrow morning and see if I can… I don't know… talk to the forest or… something."

She blushes and presses her hands to her cheeks before she reaches for my hands, grasping them in hers. It's the most startling contact, her hands clasping mine in a way that seeks my reassurance.

"Will you come with me?" she asks, her expression hopeful.

"Sure," I say, trying not to react to the painful trust in her eyes. "You'll need my protection from Draven. He goes for a run every morning. I'll make sure he doesn't disturb you."

"You won't be able to avoid your compliance officers," Bree says with a grimace.

"Then we'll pretend to be out for a run too," I say. "They'll most likely stand around watching us. Draven can't be the only student allowed to jog in the mornings."

Lucinda gives me wide eyes. "Don't expect me to do more than a lap. I'm not a runner."

"Neither am I." I shrug. "But I plan to become one."

I plan to run out of here as far and fast as I can one day. If I can… I'll take Ashley, Bree, and Lucinda with me.

The far door opens and several other girls appear in the entrance. I step back from Lucinda. The other girls will think it's weird that we're all standing around in here so it's time to go. "See you tomorrow morning. I'll be near the combat ring at five o'clock."

I spin in the water without waiting for an acknowledgement. It won't bother me if she doesn't end up showing in the morning. Well, maybe it will a little. It's nice to feel like I have friends.

I stride from the bathroom, pick up another cloth full of ice, and head back upstairs, resolutely ignoring the fact that I still don't know how I sensed Lucinda's thoughts.

16. STRIKER DRAVEN

Peyton doesn't return to her room for a long time. I finish working out and then shower, slinging a towel around my waist before I exit into the corridor.

If she's not back in her room by now, it's time to worry.

I'm grateful my beast has gone back to sleep or he'd choke on his own self-righteous laughter right now. I'd have to tell him to shut up again.

I'm not worried about her. I'm not going soft. I don't care if she's dead. I just don't want my sleep interrupted if there's some drama tonight, that's all.

I stop short in the corridor when she appears at the end of it.

Her hair is some sort of bird's nest now and her long legs are splattered with water, her bare feet padding along the wooden floor. She's clutching an ice pack pressed to her cheek. It's the spot where my left hook caught her unawares.

A burn starts deep in my chest.

I find myself asking a question I don't want to answer.

If someone hurt my sister like I hurt Peyton…?

Yeah, I'd fucking kill him.

Collin follows close behind her but gives me a nod when he

sees me before he heads away again. I've proven I can be trusted to beat her up and push her around, so they'll leave her with me. No matter what Lady Tirelli says.

Although I'm focused on her, Peyton is fixated on the windows. She veers toward them, peering into the dark before quickly swerving back into the center of the walkway.

Her rapid swing away from the edge makes me wonder if she's afraid of heights. It would make levitating more alarming to her. Still, there's nothing to see but endless trees out there. We're in the middle of a forest that stretches for miles with no end in sight. Lady Tirelli wouldn't be so reckless as to build this place within running distance of civilization.

Peyton casts a glance in my direction, making me aware she wasn't so oblivious to my presence as I thought. Those long legs that wrapped around me on the combat mat today carry her right past me and to the bathroom without a word from her lips.

She closes the door and the shower turns on.

I head back into my room, get dressed, and pace back and forth twice before I retrieve the medical kit from its hidden location in the wall.

I'm the only student allowed family visits—only because my father has some control over this institution and my sister insists on visiting me. If Zara were younger than me, she'd have no sway, but she's older, a woman in her own right and proving to be a thorn in Dad's side.

Even so, she can only visit once a year, but each time she brings me precious medical supplies—magically enhanced healing gels, antiseptics, and antibiotics, along with tape and bandages. She gets the healing gels from an apothecary in Boston that she swears is the best in the country.

Despite the power I keep hidden, I can't heal my own wounds. I can accelerate my healing if I allow my power to flow, but I'm not strong enough to heal broken skin or bones. My power is destructive to its core.

I pull out the tube of healing gel. It's rolled up nearly to the end since I've squeezed every little smear from it. There's only enough left for a few more applications, but if I don't treat the scratches on Peyton's face, they're going to scar. Not that I care. I don't.

When I hear her bedroom door open and close, I cease my indecisive tapping of the tube against my palm, make my way to her bedroom, and pause in front of it with my hand raised to knock.

Knocking is what polite people do.

I'm not a polite person. I never learned how to be, and my stepfather sure as hell wasn't any sort of role model.

I shove on the door and stride right in, inviting a dramatic response. I brace for her to leap out of the darkness beside the door and aim a fist at my face. Or for her to scream bloody murder at me. Or to throw something. Not that there's much to throw in here, not even a chair.

I never bothered to care how bare this room was before, but it hits me like the slap in the face I was expecting from her. A slap that's conspicuously absent.

I find her standing perfectly still at her window, her back to me, her head slightly tilted, as if she's considering something intently.

Without turning, she says, "Nobody taught you how to knock, huh, Draven?"

"That would be correct."

She gives a self-satisfied "hmm" but falls silent. Her only movement is the slow tap of her forefinger against her thigh. She's wearing a white T-shirt that barely covers her backside, black underwear peeking out from the bottom of it. Her curvy silhouette is highlighted in the moonlight shining around her.

She isn't wearing a bra and her legs go on for miles until they reach the floor.

She drips with snark as she asks, "Did you want something?"

Hell, yes. Wrap those legs around me again and I promise to make up for that underhanded maneuver on the combat mat today.

I stop my thoughts in their tracks. "What are you looking at?"

"Have you ever noticed that the sky here is wrong?"

What the hell is she talking about? I approach cautiously, wary that she could turn at any moment and clobber me in the face—a more expected reaction than the one I get.

She turns, but only slightly, a bare indication that she's aware of my approach. I can't get too close to her because of the narrow space between the bed and the closet.

A glance down tells me she's standing on my blanket, which is spread out along the floor with a pillow at its head. The dark rune on the ceiling explains her sleeping arrangement. I sense its sickening pull the closer I get.

"What makes you think the sky is wrong?"

She points. "See the glimmer across it? Stars don't shine like that. Neither does the moon." She pauses as if she's trying to find the words. "It's thick, not crisp."

I squint, cautious about getting too close to her, but I don't think I'll see what she sees unless I'm standing right where she is.

I push forward. "May I?"

She turns fully this time, arching an eyebrow at me. "Was that a polite request?"

"Hell, no," I reply, annoyed at myself. "Get out of the way."

She steps aside, but she's not in any hurry to do so, annoying me even more. She leans up against her closet door, an odd smile on her lips as she turns her full attention from the sky to me, staring at me as I peer at the sky.

Her shirt is way too see-through to maintain my concentration.

I wrench my gaze from her body back to the window with a growl. "If you want me to see what you see, stop distracting me."

"I'm not doing anything. Do you see it or not?"

I see… curves and legs, lips that snap at me, and eyes that promise she'll kill me in my sleep. I see a woman who guards her boundaries and isn't afraid to tell me to get fucked.

Only my last shred of common sense stops me from asking her for permission to kiss her. I might be a completely aggressive asshole, but consent is non-negotiable. I've never crossed that line and never will.

I force myself to focus on the sky. Stars. Moon. Deep blue night. Also… a sheen across it that doesn't spring from any of the natural light sources.

I move to the left a little and tilt my head. The deep blue is too luminescent. It's like looking through another transparent layer. "It must be the window. Imperfections in the glass."

She sounds certain. "It isn't."

Pulling away from the closet, she dares to move up close, pointing. "See that ripple? That's not in the glass."

"Then what is it?"

She looks up at me. "I was hoping you would know."

I shrug, even though the answer is disturbing. "Some sort of cage, most likely. In case one of us learns how to fly out of here. Or levitate," I add pointedly.

She lowers her arm, but her weight shifts enough that her bicep brushes mine. The hairs on the back of my neck shoot up, as if she's an electric fence and she just jolted me. Her power… whatever it is… she just transferred it to me again.

She gives me a startled look, making me realize that I just growled at her.

"What?" she asks.

Damn. The beast must have woken up. I wait for its latest snarky comment, but it's completely silent.

I guess that was all me, then.

I clear my throat. Up close, consent becomes a clearer necessity. My focus remains on her face and doesn't descend no matter how much I want to take in the sight of her gorgeous curves.

Lifting the tube, I keep my tone even. "I need to take care of your face." I cringe. That came out wrong. I don't *need* to take care of anything...

She eyes the tube before she takes a step back. "What is that stuff?"

"The same sort of medicine I put on your back. I just need to put a little on your—"

"You mean the stuff that stung like hell? No, thank you."

Annoyance floods me. "You're going to scar. All over your face."

"Oh, and you need to stop that from happening? You're my hero, Draven. Thank you for worrying about whether or not other people can look at me without disgust. I'm used to that already, thanks."

She takes another step back, but she quickly bumps against the closet. Whatever languid pose she took up before, it's long gone now. She is all tension and anger. Her gaze darts around the moonlight-flooded room, but she has nothing to throw at me or fight me with.

I exhale in frustration, reaching for her. "It won't sting. Just let me—"

"No." Her chest rises and falls rapidly as she drags air into her lungs, watching my lowering hand, as if it's full of claws. "Just leave the medicine and I'll do it myself."

I try to remain patient. "You can't see the wounds yourself and there isn't enough gel left to get it wrong."

Her voice rises. "I can do it myself!"

My fist closes around the tube as I study her. Her breathing is too rapid. Her hands press flat against the closet door.

The tension in her shoulders, in the way she presses her head back as far from me as she can get it, is palpable. Sweat forms on her forehead before she wipes it away with shaking hands.

I've never seen her panic, but she's close to panicking now.

I don't understand it. She stood in the combat ring with me today and took multiple hits and yet... *now* she's panicking. "What are you afraid of?"

"Are you freaking serious right now?" A little of the fire returns to her eyes. "You actually think I'll ever invite you to touch me?"

She wrenches herself away from the closet, taking rapid steps toward me, but it's the kind of move a cornered animal makes, retaliation on instinct alone. "We fight because we have to. I let you hit me because I have to. Last night, I had no choice but to accept your blood into my body. But this?" She shoves my hand away. "I don't have to do this. This is where I get to choose."

I take a step back, ending up hard up against the edge of her bed. The poultice painted on the ceiling is stronger than any I've felt before. It pulls at me so hard that I have to slide away from it—and away from her. No wonder she sleeps on the floor.

My gaze lands on her blanket. It's a bargaining chip and I'm not ready to give up yet.

"If I swap rooms with you tonight, will you let me put this on your face?"

She startles a little. "What?"

"That blanket can't be comfortable. If I give you my bed tonight, will you let me help you? I'll sleep in here."

"No."

I peer at her. Stare at the tube. Replay her words in my mind. She said she will never invite me to touch her. Invitation implies willing participation. It implies consent. Everything that's happened since she arrived has been against her will. Including me and all my bullshit behavior.

I ask the question with the answer I don't want to know. "Has anyone ever touched you in a way that wasn't hurtful?"

She recoils. Her mental defenses are so strong that it's like a physical push.

I thought Lady Tirelli could speak like a whiplash, but she's got nothing on Peyton. "What do you think?"

"Is that a *no*?"

"Go to hell, Draven." She glares at me, her gaze so sharp, it could be a blade in my chest. "Along with the rest of the world."

I stare at the floor, remembering the conversations we had today. She asked me to train her and I told her…

Oh, hell. I told her she wasn't worth my time.

And she said… *Like I haven't heard that a hundred times before.*

Lucinda asked Peyton when she was going to ask for help and Peyton said… *I'm not.* Peyton wasn't kidding.

Making a decision, I point to the corner of the room behind the door. "I'll wait as long as it takes, Peyton. But I'm not leaving this room until you let me touch your face."

"You won't make it to class tomorrow then," she retorts.

I shrug. "If that's how long it takes."

Dragging the old, scratchy blanket off her bed, I pull it around my shoulders and settle into the corner beside the door, closing my eyes against the moonlight. I'm surprised she can sleep at all with all the light pouring into her room.

My choices are limited right now. I can walk out of here with the medicine she needs and be the true asshole that I am. Alternatively, I can leave the gel with her, knowing she'll be lucky to get enough out of the tube if she misses a spot—that's assuming she can place it where it's needed to begin with.

I'm surprised her whole face doesn't feel like it's on fire right now. Or maybe it does and she's hiding it well.

Third option: I can grab her, pin her arms and legs, and force her to accept it. Again, like the asshole that I am.

Use of force is what she knows and expects, so she's probably ready for me to do just that.

Or... I can wait and see if she changes her mind and gives me permission.

I've never been the patient type. I act in the moment and deal with the consequences after. My emotions have always been a livewire. The beast is my excuse, but I can't blame him for all of it.

Tonight, I'll wait.

I tell myself that if she doesn't give me permission, I can always try the third option while she's sleeping. It won't be difficult to subdue her.

My decision to wait doesn't mean she's got under my skin. Nope. She's the last thing I care about. She's an annoyance. She... and her gorgeous curves and her go-to-hell eyes and her fierce spirit. I can deal with all of it.

With that thought firmly in mind, I close my eyes and try to sleep.

17. PEYTON PRICE

Over in the corner of my room, Striker's breathing becomes deep, but my own is still erratic.

I crawl into my blanket—the one that used to be Striker's—and press up against the wall, not taking my eyes off him. The last time he pretended to help me, I ended up bleeding to death in the rain.

The moment I close my eyes, he'll jump up and grab me. I know he will. I'd kick him out of my room right now, but I don't have the combat skills to take him on yet.

Yet.

That's something I'm determined to change.

I have no choice but to accept that he can barge into my room any time whether I'm dressed or not. In fact, I expect him to do it. I was ready for it. But I wasn't ready for his offer of help.

I pull the blanket to my chin and sit like that for the next hour, unable to sleep. The strange gleam in the sky is the last thing on my mind now.

Hating on Striker allows me to avoid the real problem.

My face really hurts. It's been getting worse all day. I thought maybe his blood was the reason my back felt so good—I convinced myself my face would feel better soon too—but now I know it must have been the medicine he smeared over me last night.

I need that tube, need the treatment inside it, but he's right. I can't see the wounds. I'd have to apply it all over my face and judging by the rolled-up state of the tube, there isn't enough left to waste any.

But I can't trust this guy.

I can't trust anyone. Well, maybe Lucinda, Bree, and Ashley but I'm still figuring that out.

If I walk on over to Striker and give him permission to touch me, I'll be giving away the last bit of control I have over anything. I can't escape the physical force that has been used on me my whole life by my parents, my brother, kids at school, and even teachers on occasion.

The last thing I control is consent.

To give Striker consent to do anything feels like giving away everything.

Pain strikes through my chest. My hands are shaking. I'm more afraid than I am when I know there's a punch coming my way.

One irrefutable fact remains: I can't do this alone.

I rise to my feet, my blanket pulled tightly around me like a protective shield and force myself to cross the distance. He leans into the corner, his eyes closed, his head tilted away to that side, his blanket slipped low across his chest, which rises and falls in an even rhythm.

He doesn't awaken when I lower myself to my knees beside him, his breathing remaining deep. The fact that he fell asleep at all tells me he doesn't fear me anywhere near as much as I fear him.

I hate the way my hand shakes when I push it out of the blanket to gently nudge his shoulder. "Striker?"

He inhales, his eyes opening slowly, but his body remains still. He makes no sudden movements other than to raise his head. "Peyton?"

My mouth is completely dry, my voice catching. "Okay."

He takes a moment, his gaze running across my face, before he quietly and carefully shifts his arms out of his blanket and repositions himself so he's facing me, also kneeling.

He doesn't ask me why I changed my mind or say anything else about it. One of his hands still grips the tube. The other reaches for my face.

I flinch away from him but force myself to stop.

He retracts his hand, saying, "I need to use two hands for this. Is that okay?"

I swallow hard. "Yes."

He nods and shuffles all the way out of his blanket. "You need to face the light."

He slips to the side, staying within my sight as I turn to face the window, before he returns to his knees, studying my face again. "The slashes on the right side of your face are the worst, so I'll start there. The cut above your eyebrow where your brother hit you is next. Then I'll treat the scrapes on your left cheek. Okay?"

He waits for me to answer. I try to breathe out some of my tension. "Yes."

Opening the tube, he places the merest blob onto his forefinger before he leans in and cups my chin with his left hand.

I squeeze my eyes closed. His left hand is warm, gentle, but firm. All business. His right hand is feather-light, breezing down my face. I was worried it would sting, but it soothes instantly, the pain disappearing.

He lets go of my face.

My eyes fly open to see what he's doing, but he's simply looking down, portioning out another blob onto his finger before he reaches for me again. This time I welcome his touch and the absence of pain that comes with it.

After three gentle swipes down my right cheek, the tension drains out of me. When his forefinger grazes the cut above my left eye, I nearly moan with relief, swallowing the sound before I can make it.

I refuse to let him know how much I needed this. Pain makes me cry, but the absence of pain is making me want to weep. It's completely unfair that he's the reason I feel so much better right now.

His serious eyes meet mine. "There's enough for the rest of your face, so I'm going to use it up. But if I do, you can't get cut up again, okay?"

"That's up to you," I whisper. I don't only mean whether he uses it up or not. He's bound to be the reason I'll end up wounded again.

He considers the tube, studies the left side of my face, and eventually shakes his head. "It won't heal on its own."

He sets to work and I close my eyes again. His movements become slower toward the end, his fingertip grazing down my left cheek.

This time, the way he cups my chin softens and the entire palm of his right hand settles against my face. His fingers splay out, the lightest touch brushing my jaw and earlobe in a way that makes me shiver. He's close enough that the slightest lean forward would close the gap between us.

His hand tugs, nearly imperceptible, but I sense it, urging me toward him. I open my eyes to find his gaze shifting from my cheek to my lips. Every harsh line of his face has softened, but the amber of his eyes is more crimson... as if the moon were suddenly firelit. Mesmerizing. Confusing.

Dangerous.

The last time he cupped my head so gently, I ended up in severe pain.

He starts to speak, but my survival instincts kick in and I jolt away from him, breaking the connection. "You're done?"

He nods, his expression hardening again, suddenly unreadable. "Don't wash your face in the morning. The wounds should be healed by tomorrow evening, but you're better off protecting your face for the next two days."

"From you," I say.

He nods. "I won't hit your face."

"Thanks, Draven." Sarcasm drips from my tongue. "It's really kind of you to make that concession."

He doesn't miss a beat. "Why do you want to learn how to fight?"

"Because I refuse to die here."

He opens his mouth but seems to rethink it. He leans around me to pick up the scratchy blanket from the floor, rolling it up and pitching it onto the bed. "You need to increase your fitness first. I go for a run every morning and evening. If you want to learn, meet me outside at 5 A.M."

"I'll be there. Lucinda will too."

He pauses in the act of stepping toward the door. "Why Lucinda?"

"She needs to figure something out. Don't worry. She won't get in your way."

He continues to the door, opens it, but pauses. "If I stop pushing you around, the compliance officers will notice and they'll beat on you themselves. You don't want that."

"So you're going to do me a favor and keep hating on me then?"

He doesn't acknowledge my retort. "Be prepared for me to treat you like rubbish, but I won't touch you again. It's safer for both of us if we engage in as little physical contact as possible."

My forehead creases as he disappears into the corridor.

His final statement is confusing. *Safer for him?* I'm not sure what he could possibly be afraid of.

18. PEYTON PRICE

The morning sunlight wakes me well before five o'clock.

I hurry to dress in gym clothes, running to the bathroom to brush my teeth, but I avoid splashing water on my face. I dash out of the bathroom just in time before Striker emerges from his bedroom looking half awake.

He scowls at me as I pass by.

"You should try leaving your curtains open," I say. "You'll wake up earlier."

Yeah, I'm poking that beast again.

He grunts an unintelligible response that sounds like a string of curse words as he heads to the bathroom and closes the door.

I'm early, but I head downstairs anyway, startling Collin and Colby, who wait at the bottom of the attic stairs. They follow me all the way to the first floor.

Along the way, we pass two groups of compliance officers—those waiting for the guys to wake up and those waiting for the girls.

I think I've caught them in the middle of a shift change because some of the officers are arriving and others are leaving.

Nobody has clarified this for me, but even though every student has two compliance officers, there appears to be one present in the day and another at night. I'm the only student with two officers during the day but I think that's because they assume Striker is my guard at night—a role he's obviously willing to play.

I head out the back exit into the fresh morning air to wait for Lucinda. I attempt to stretch my legs, but I'm not really sure what I'm doing. Collin and Colby don't seem to know either, giving each other quizzical glances as they watch me awkwardly attempting to lunge. *Yeah, that's not working.*

I give up and wait beside the nearest practicing post instead.

When Striker bursts through the back door dressed in workout gear, water dripping from his hair, his eyes bright again, Collin and Colby raise eyebrows at each other before taking up position against the back wall to observe us closely.

Ignoring them, Striker points to the grassy area at the side of the combat ring and starts a series of warm-up exercises that I attempt to follow before he sets off at a slow jog around the perimeter.

I try to keep up before I decide it's impossible and set an even slower pace for myself, ignoring the smug smile he throws my way when he laps me.

Rounding the corner of the building again, I find Lucinda dressed in gym clothes and waiting at the combat ring. Her gaze fixes on Striker as he jogs ahead of me.

I wave her over to me and she falls in with my slow jog, keeping pace beside me.

"Your wounds look much better today," she says as she runs. "I was getting worried."

"Thanks," I manage. "I don't suppose you have a mirror?"

"Not a hope. Mirrors can be smashed and turned into weapons."

I snort. "How do you manage to look so good, then?"

"We do each other's hair."

I miss a stride. "Wait… really?"

"Yes, really. Now look, don't get the wrong idea. It isn't all girly sleepovers on our floor. We don't always get along and there's no hope that we can protect each other from anything. But we have some basic rules that we never break: we do each other's hair and we never stab each other in the back."

"That sounds nice." I try to ignore the odd pain in my chest over the fact that I'm not part of it. I cover my emotions with a scornful smile. "Maybe I could ask Striker to braid my hair for me."

She gives me a smile. "I can fix your hair if you'd like. After our run. Braiding really helps with the tangles." She points to her own.

"Yeah," I say, trying not to make a big deal out of it. My ponytail is hiding one hell of a bird's nest and I haven't been able to untangle it. "I'd appreciate that."

I sense Striker's approach behind us, not sure what to expect now that Lucinda has joined us.

"Morning, Adams," Striker says as he laps us.

Lucinda startles. I suspect it's his cordial tone that surprised her.

"Morning, Draven," she manages, but he's already too far ahead to hear her.

She changes the subject. "I mentioned I'm not a runner, right?"

"Me, neither," I respond, with a genuine wheeze. "But I'm determined to give it a shot."

A glance back tells me that Lucinda's compliance officer has joined Collin and Colby at the side of the building.

"That's Cameron," Lucinda says, not yet out of breath. "My night guard is Christopher."

"What's with the 'C' names?"

She shrugs. "They all have them: Curtis, Chad, Craig. One of

Ashley's officers is called 'Charleston.' They're all aliases. It's the same with the teacher's names. Bird types to match the Academy name."

"Yeah, I figured that was deliberate." My breath is failing me now. Talking and running is going to kill me. "Let's not talk… Just do what you need."

I wave my hand around, hoping she knows I mean the trees. My legs are already wobbly and my breath is wheezing audibly now. I'm pretty sure I might be dying. It's one thing to throw myself around the combat ring for a few minutes. It's another to sustain a run.

Lucinda quiets beside me. She relaxes into the jog. Her gaze flicks to the trees every now and then. Despite her assertion that she isn't a runner, it doesn't take her long to fall into a steady rhythm.

"It's nice out here in the morning," she says, her breathing annoyingly even. "I should come out here more often."

I focus on not falling over. "Yeah. Sure."

We run on. Five minutes later, I'm ready to drop and I have no idea whether being out here has helped Lucinda even the slightest. She does seem at peace, though, her features relaxed and her breathing even. Her random glances at the trees have stopped and instead she focuses on the curve of the fence.

Striker laps us for what feels like the thousandth time, but this time, he falls in beside Lucinda. In stark contrast to his polite demeanor before, now he resembles an impending storm, his eyebrows drawn down, his glare at a thousand percent.

She glances up in alarm. "Draven?"

His response is low and dangerous. "You'd better stop, Adams. Or they're going to notice."

She gives him a confused look. "What are you talking about?"

"The trees, Lucinda. If you haven't stopped whatever the hell it is you're doing by the time I lap you again, I'm going to throw you against the fucking fence. Do you understand me?"

"Y-Yeah. I got it."

He tears away from us. Judging by his sudden speed, Lucinda's only got thirty seconds before he carries out this threat.

She picks up her pace. "What was he talking about?"

"I don't know, but let's get away from the fence. Striker doesn't make idle threats." I grab her arm, pulling her away from the perimeter.

Just as she takes a step back, she gasps, jolts out of my hold, and then stumbles on nothing, falling hard onto her bottom.

I drop to my knees beside her, taking wary glances at the guards. "Lucinda?"

"I just realized what he's talking about. Don't look. I mean… Do look. Don't make it obvious."

I stand and turn, not sure what I'm supposed to be looking for. Rose bushes, combat ring, practicing posts, compliance officers, ugly building, stretch of grass, fence… trees…

Trees! They're bending in a way that trees shouldn't bend. Each tree outside the perimeter sways inward, straining toward Lucinda's location, branches reaching toward the fence like she's some sort of magnet. The effect must have been behind us so we couldn't see it, but Striker could because he ran up on us.

Now that we've stopped moving, I give the officers five seconds before they focus beyond the fence and realize that the trees aren't simply moving in the spring breeze.

"I can't stop it!" she whispers, panic filling her face as she fists the grass, fixated on the tree line. "I don't know how."

What's worse, her skin is transforming before my eyes, a hazel sheen forming across it, her fingers shifting on the grass, all visible skin taking on a luminescent mottled appearance of…

Bark. Just like a tree.

The sound of Striker's pounding feet meets my ears.

He knows how to make it stop. The same way he stops a flicker fit.

I spin to him, stepping in front of her. "No!"

He darts around me and scoops her up as if she weighs nothing, throwing her over his shoulder. She screams, flails, and kicks her legs.

I lurch for him but he's too agile, skimming my reach by an inch. Despite his threat to throw her against the fence, he runs her to the combat ring instead. If I weren't so mad at him, I'd appreciate that he drew the officer's attention away from the tree line.

I race after him, a shot of adrenaline overcoming my lame jogging fatigue. I sprint as fast as I can. There has to be a better way for her to control her power than a punch to the face.

He drops her against a practicing post, making her yelp and wince when her shoulder hits it first. He pulls his fist back, preparing to thump her beautiful, transforming face, but I ram into him and grab his elbow to annihilate his aim.

I barely make an impact, but it gives Lucinda a precious split second to lean left.

Striker's fist hits the post where her head used to be.

His knuckles crunch. Blood splatters the wood.

Lucinda loses her balance and falls to the side and back onto her hands, staring at the bloody smear Striker left on the post.

He raises his fist over her again, blood spraying across her face with the suddenness of his movement.

I prepare to jump onto his back, anything to make him leave her alone, but she gives a sudden inhale and a wide-eyed smile before he can let fly.

The growing texture disappears from her face, instantly transforming back into her usual skin.

"I stopped, Draven," she says.

His aim wavers, his hand clenched above her face, his other

hand fisting the front of her shirt, half-lifting her off the ground.

She whispers, "I just needed to connect with the wood." She pats the post beside her. "I controlled it. I know what I am now."

A quick glance at the trees confirms it. They're back to normal, leaves blowing in the breeze in all directions like ordinary trees do.

Striker doesn't move, but his chest rises and falls rapidly. I'm standing behind him and can't see his expression. I want to know what he's thinking, but I don't want to trigger an aggressive response. I hold my breath, waiting for his next move.

Finally, his fingers unfurl from her shirt. "They won't hear about it from me."

He gives her a little shove away from him before letting her go. Turning to me, his jaw clenches as if he's grinding away at his thoughts and everything he wants to say to me. "She needed to figure something out, huh?"

I raise my chin at him. "That's what I said. That's what she did."

Without a backward glance, he takes off toward the building, jogging past the officers who relax against the wall again. I guess as far as they can see, Striker's back to his normal hateful self. It's probably more expected than the possibility that we were all out for a happy jog together.

I help Lucinda stand. She presses her palm against the practicing post. "Now that I know... I'll find ways to practice without giving it away."

"You could leave," I say. "Reveal your power, control it, and you can leave. That's what they said."

She shakes her head, searching my face. "Peyton, no. Nobody ever leaves. We've seen what goes on in this place. The only way they're letting us go is in a coffin. Even then, they'll dig a hole in the forest and throw us in. There's no walking out of Bloodwing alive."

"But you're not a threat anymore. You won't flicker."

"It doesn't matter."

"How do you know?" I sound desperate and I know it. I still had hope that there was another way to get out of here other than escape.

She pries my fingers from her arm, squeezing my hand tightly in hers. Her casual glance beyond me tells me she's checking that the officers are still standing at a distance. "After being here for a while, you get to hear things. Snatches of conversations, whispers behind closed doors, things you aren't meant to hear. The woman who runs this place… She didn't start Bloodwing out of the goodness of her heart. She wants to use us. I've even heard the teachers talk about us as if we're supposed to be her soldiers."

"What?" My response is too sharp. I try to calm down. "There's no freaking way I would ever willingly do anything for the person who controls this place."

"We might not have a choice. But we have to be smart. For now, I plan on learning everything I can about myself until I'm strong enough to fight back."

I manage a smile. "If she wants soldiers, I'm happy to be one. I just won't fight for her."

Lucinda gives me a sudden grin. "We'll figure out your power next."

"We'll see."

Lucinda's reluctance to reveal her power explains why Striker is so determined to keep his a secret. He and Lucinda are the first two students I'm aware of who control their magically repressed abilities—whatever Striker's actually is.

I don't hold out much hope that I'll discover mine, but it doesn't matter.

Lucinda's plan aligns with mine now: grow stronger, no matter what it takes, and escape.

19. PEYTON PRICE

I survive my first week at Bloodwing Academy and it feels like a small miracle.

Striker delivers on his promise not to touch me again. He picks random fights with the other guys before gym class and ends up on the combat mat with them.

Another time, he shoves one of the girls, who stumbles into me, pitching me into a practicing post, where I start working out before the chaos clears and Ms. Hawk can order me onto the mat.

Every morning, I drag myself around the perimeter, eating Striker's dust and resisting the urge to stick out my foot and trip him when he laps me. I'm smart enough to know that I shouldn't willingly break the no-touching rule.

As the days pass, I find I can run farther without wheezing and my fitness is improving each day.

Every afternoon, I leave him alone on his run. There's no way I want to watch him electrocute himself. It was bad enough the first time I saw it. I'm certain it has something to do with his power, but I can't figure out what.

Ms. Sparrow doesn't try to make me use Kaitlyn's wand

again, giving me a plain white wand instead. I can't do any magic with it and she likes to give me paper cuts on my arms every time I fail. They sting, but they always heal.

I make it through my first Magical Biology lesson taught by a sweet-looking old witch named Ms. Vulture, who blinks rapidly every time she looks at us over her glasses.

I find myself studying her carefully—the faded blonde color of her hair and her pale, blue eyes. When she steps into the sunlight streaming through the side window, she looks younger than her wrinkles would imply.

I quickly abandon my close study when she begins describing in great detail all the stages of shift that a shifter goes through. Except that her point is to describe all the gory ways in which a shifter can be killed at those various points of shift—when the eyes are vulnerable as opposed to the throat or the stomach.

My own stomach turns while her sweet little old lady voice croons on about how easily the skin can be pierced at different points of the body.

Finally dismissed, I stumble from the classroom, whispering to Lucinda. "What was that?"

She looks as green as I feel. "I have several theories: currently, psychological trauma is winning over desensitization to violence."

"Oh, good." I laugh. "I was worried she was trying to turn us into killers."

"Well, last week she told us how to defang a vampire."

"What the hell? Is that even possible?"

"Apparently. Funnily enough, she never tells us how to kill a witch."

By the end of the week, I've settled into a cautious daily routine that always ends with me leaning over the ice chest, scooping the soothing cubes into as many cloths as I can get my hands on.

I constantly soak Striker's blanket with melting ice packs jammed against my knuckles. I have no idea how the other students pummel the wooden practicing posts every day. I have blisters on top of blisters now. Lucinda promises I'll develop callouses soon but I'm not so sure.

At the beginning of my second week, Striker prowls up to the post I share with Ashley, leaning against the free patch of wood between us and staring at me, his arms folded across his chest. I ignore him for all of five seconds before I stop my aimless exercise.

I arch my eyebrow at him.

"Feet," he says, scowling.

I glance down. "What about my feet?"

He rolls his eyes. "Take a look at Ashley's."

With that, he turns and walks away, taking a random swipe at Lachlan, who deftly dodges Striker's blow and swings back with a punch that clips Striker's shoulder. The two of them muscle up at each other and Ms. Hawk screams at them to get on the mat.

Ashley leans around the post with a surprised expression lighting up her emerald eyes, mouthing: *What was that about?*

I shrug but study the position of her feet when she resumes her exercise, mimicking her stance before I lay into my post again. I'm surprised to find it gives me better balance.

As soon as I ease up to give my hands a break, Ms. Hawk appears at my shoulder, tapping me with her wand. The electrical shock makes me yelp.

"You will not rest in my class, Price."

I respond by whacking the post, imagining it's her face.

"Better," she snarls before she walks away, shouting orders at Lucinda, who is visibly avoiding hitting her post.

The next day, Striker approaches my position again. Lucinda is opposite me this time. He catches her hand mid-motion, gripping tight even though she jolts and struggles to free herself. "Hey! Striker, what the hell?"

I lurch to the side to see her, ready to throw myself at him if he hurts her. He takes a firm hold of her waist with his free hand and pulls her arm back in an arc. She resists until he growls at her, "Relax."

He guides her hand toward the post in a perfect swing. I consider the motion and the way Striker's gaze meets mine. Without another word, he releases Lucinda and stalks away, this time shoving Joseph along the way.

Lucinda gapes after him, but then eases her arm back and forth at the angle he demonstrated. When she taps the wood, she gives an intrigued, "Hmm."

I study the angle of her arm and torso, mimic it, and follow through with a much stronger hit to my side of the post. It hurts my hand like hell, but the motion is a lot smoother.

On the following day, Striker grabs Bree's leg, giving her the same treatment he gave Lucinda. She attempts to balance mid-kick while he supports her back. Again, he waits until I'm watching before he guides her body in the direction he wants it to go—a perfect kick. He lets her go and walks away.

Bree glares at his back before she swings to me, planting her hands on her hips. "Spill it, Price. Yesterday it was Lucinda. The day before it was Ashley. Whoever takes a post with you gets groped by Draven. What's going on?"

I chew my lip thoughtfully. Speaking aloud my quiet truce with Striker feels dangerous. He said he wouldn't touch me, but he also agreed to teach me how to fight. It looks like he's found a way to do both.

"How did that kick feel?" I ask.

She continues to glare at me as she tests it out. A curious crease settles on her forehead. "Better. Easier."

"Well, then, what's the problem?"

She purses her lips, scowling, but lets it go.

At the end of my second week at Bloodwing, Lucinda takes up position opposite me again, but she's quiet and still. I can see her leg and arm from where I stand, but not her face—the post is too wide and too high. She doesn't move and worry settles in the pit of my stomach. If we don't start working out, Ms. Hawk will storm over and zap us.

I start in on the post with my open palms, trying to develop callouses on them and give my knuckles a break. I use the movement to peek around the post at the same time.

Lucinda's right palm presses against it for a moment. Then she lets go. Her arm moves like normal after that and the smacking sound I expected to hear resumes opposite me.

I close my fist and revert to a punch. My knuckles hit the wood… but this time the impact doesn't hurt.

My eyes widen. I inhale a surprised breath.

Trying not to draw attention, I press gently against the wood. It's softer. Not like a cushion, but like a squishy punching bag. It has the give it needs to provide a proper surface for a workout.

When I hit it again, my fist is cushioned, the wood bending and fitting to the contours of my hand before it springs back.

Lucinda did it. She's manipulating the wood.

Relief and happiness flow through me. Controlling living trees is one thing—the fact that she can now control dead wood tells me how powerful she's becoming. I'm happy for her and, admittedly, for myself. These posts are a nightmare.

I find an excuse to bend, rub my foot, and lean around the post to take a glance at her.

She casts me a secretive, self-satisfied smile, but neither of us says anything.

That night at dinner, she nudges me while Bree and Ashley are deep in conversation opposite us. "I'll do it to the others tomorrow."

I assume she means the other practicing posts. I cast a

casual glance around the room to make sure the compliance officers aren't listening. "Thank you. It makes a big difference."

She nods, the light in her brown eyes glowing brighter. For a second, a ripple flows through the tiny rings within her eyes. Her power is subtle but unmistakable now that I know what I'm looking at.

"I finally found a way to make peace with what we're forced to do," she says. "The earth and wood are willing when the motivation is right."

For the next two months, Lucinda keeps up her magic on the posts and Striker maintains his arm's-length method of teaching me how to fight. Any time he doesn't like my technique, he targets whoever stands opposite me, waiting until I'm watching before he manipulates their bodies in the way he wants me to move.

Ms. Hawk doesn't seem to mind since he's rough with the girls and he always sprinkles his attention between menacing me and picking fights with the other guys.

After that initial brief conversation with Bree, nobody questions why he does it, and to my surprise, the other girls relax into it.

Some of them even race to choose the other side of my post so they're on the receiving end of Striker's instructions. At first, I'm cynical. I mean, seriously, are they that desperate to be groped?

Then I realize... they're learning too. Combined with Lucinda's effect on the practicing posts, all of the girls are becoming stronger and faster.

So much so that the guys are starting to take notice.

Lucinda softened their practicing posts, too, and every time Striker picks a fight with one of them, they hit back hard. But I notice that they watch the way he moves. It's as subtle as the rings in Lucinda's eyes, but a few days after, I'll see them try out

Striker's moves on each other, practicing over and over until they get it right.

They're not fighting anymore. They're training.

I nearly wish Striker would pick a fight with me. I'm stronger and faster than I believed possible after only three months at the Academy, my hits on the post making so much impact that it sometimes wobbles and I have to ease up before Ms. Hawk notices.

The speed with which I'm becoming stronger tells me I'm built for something more.

I'm approaching a place in my development where I need to practice on someone I'm not afraid of hurting, but asking Striker to fight me will only break our careful truce.

Ashley is the only one who isn't improving. She tries hard at the post, but her movements are clunky and graceless. She's quiet at every meal, the dark rings under her eyes growing darker, and her blonde hair is loose and becoming matted.

Lucinda starts sitting close beside her at mealtime, trying to encourage her to eat. She also takes up position on the other side of Ashley's practicing post every day, but Ashley barely communicates anymore.

Most alarming, her green eyes lose their luminosity, becoming dull. Even the guys start to notice.

Lachlan most of all hovers over her, walking beside her, picking up things she drops because her hands are shaking, giving her his snack food because she can't hold out her hands to catch her own anymore. The fact that she barely notices tells me how bad her situation is getting.

By the end of my fourth month, my focus shifts from my own survival to Ashley's. It's hard to find places to talk, but I drag Lucinda aside after dinner one night. "We need to help her or she's not going to make it."

"It's phase two," she says, frustration showing in her tense shoulders and the way she rubs her eyes. "They've painted her room with runes. She can't sleep. She's nauseous all the time. Her mind is breaking."

"Can't you do something about that? The walls are wooden, aren't they?"

Lucinda's eyes fill with frustrated tears. "I've tried already, but the magic they use... It's... I don't know how to describe it... It's sticky. I can't peel it back or remove it. I'm trying really hard." Her voice rises and she gulps, taking a deep breath before anyone hears us. "I'm trying, but I'm scared. Another week like this and she won't survive."

I clench my teeth as Ashley stumbles past us, her head down, her hair falling across her eyes. She barely ate two mouthfuls at dinner.

"We won't let that happen."

Lucinda peers at me. "It sounds an awful lot like you care, Peyton."

I ignore the truth in her statement. "What if you stop focusing on the runes and start focusing on the ceiling and walls? Can you turn the panels around?"

She blinks at me. "I'm sorry, what?"

"Turn the wood panels around and mix them up so the runes are broken."

"You're talking about changing the structure of her bedroom without everything collapsing around her." Lucinda stares are me, incredulous. "I'm not that powerful."

"Really?" I cast her a challenging glare. "Do I have to pull a Striker on you and smack some belief into you?"

She gives a little laugh, but it sounds like a shriek. I suddenly realize that I'm menacing over her the way that Striker does, fists clenched, too close for comfort.

Damn, he's rubbing off on me.

She gasps. "Not necessary. I'll try."

"Do more than try, Lucinda," I threaten. "I'll give you one night. If it doesn't work, I'll break into Ashley's room and get us both committed to the pit for the night. She'll sleep better there anyway."

Lucinda nods with wide eyes. "I'll do it."

I stride away from her, heading to the attic to shower, passing Striker on the way. His eyes are narrowed at me, but I push past, running up the stairs two at a time. I'm not even out of breath when I reach the top.

The next morning marks the beginning of my fifth month at Bloodwing. For the first time, Striker doesn't lap me on my morning run. He can't. Every time I hear his footsteps behind me, I respond by increasing my own speed, keeping him at a distance. He's eating my dust for the first time and I can't help enjoying it.

After half an hour, he finally heads inside before I do, casting an unreadable look back at me while I continue around the perimeter. The compliance officers have become tired of my daily routine. They watch me for the first few laps before they get bored and disappear inside again.

I sprint the final lap and when I finish, I'm still not tired. My breathing is easy. If it weren't for the whole levitating thing, I might wonder if I'm a panther shifter. They're incredibly fast and don't tire easily.

Alone out here for the first time in a long time without Striker, I take a moment to study the tree line beyond the fence.

Out at the back, there's a brighter spot within the forest, what I imagine is a track. I stroll casually past it, taking glances between the thick trees, trying to see where the path leads, but it's impossible to figure it out.

Trees for miles. That's all there is. My surveillance of the Academy over the last months has, frustratingly, revealed no chinks in the security around this place. I thought I had the compliance officers' routines figured out, but then they went and switched them up.

Over time, I've come to recognize the way they operate.

They're all wizards, carrying wands, but definitely ex-military. The fence around the perimeter keeps us penned in and the strange glimmer across the sky tells me I'll be dead if I ever try levitating over the top of it. I can see the shimmer in the day now, a fake sheen like a plastic bubble stretched out high above us. It descends into the forest, a wider perimeter than the Academy grounds.

Finally heading inside for breakfast, I find Lucinda sitting with Ashley, and I'm relieved to see color in Ashley's cheeks. She's inhaling her food like nobody's business.

I take two bites of my toast before I hand Ashley the rest of mine. "Knock yourself out."

She sweeps her hair out of her face, her eyes a little lighter today, a hint of determination returned to them. "Thanks, Peyton."

Lucinda gives me a nod and I return it with a haughty I-told-you-so glare that makes her roll her eyes.

Lachlan passes us, stops, and presses his hand to Ashley's shoulder. "You okay, Ashley?"

Despite his attempts to help her over the past weeks, it's the first time I've seen him speak with her—or touch her, for that matter.

She looks up at him between the strands of her hair. The faint smile she gives him seems to be enough of an answer. He nods and strides away.

Joseph is close behind him, giving Lucinda an equally careful nod.

Striker is the last to leave as the other students file out to gym class.

I flick my braid over my shoulder, already dressed in gym clothes. I practically live in them now, at ease with my body and the muscles developing in my legs, arms, and stomach.

I catch the sudden flare of heat behind Striker's eyes as his gaze travels the length of my body to my bare toes but he doesn't make a move toward me before I head out to class.

20. STRIKER DRAVEN

*P*eyton gives me a self-assured smile before she stalks out ahead of me.

It's hard to look at her without remembering the way her pajama shirt clung to her curves on the night she told me the sky was wrong.

She was vulnerable that night. Since then, a confident air has grown around her, a defiance in her eyes and posture. Damn, she draws me like wildfire.

Trying to catch up to her this morning was like trying to catch a flame speeding along a trail of dynamite.

Still, I've kept my word. I've stayed away from her. Every day, the distrust in her eyes lessens.

Actually… the longer I stay away from her, the more like me she becomes. Watching her threaten Lucinda yesterday was like looking in a mirror.

When did violence become a virtue?

It shouldn't be like this, but this place skews everything. I can't tell what's normal anymore.

I follow her out, captivated by the way her long legs glide across the ground. Her grace and agility have increased with her strength. The other day, I was worried she was going to smash her practicing post but she eased off just in time.

She was gorgeous when she first arrived. Now she's mesmerizing.

Once outside, I prowl around the practicing posts, not sure what I'll teach Peyton today. Short of getting on the mat with her, I'm reaching the limit of what I can show her.

She needs to practice against someone. I consider whether I could wrangle a fight between her and one of the guys, maybe Joseph since he owes her for the night that she took the fall for his flicker fit. He'd approach her more carefully than the others would.

Although… Lachlan hasn't ignored the fact that Peyton has been watching over Ashley. He'd be another good choice.

Lachlan has already taken up a spot past the far side of the combat mat—at the same post that Ashley is standing at. She's hitting her post with an energy she hasn't had for weeks.

Peyton's headed in their direction, her purposeful steps indicating she'll choose the post next to theirs, still watching over Ashley like a hawk.

I decide to veer around the combat mat and approach from the other side. That way I'll reach Lachlan without walking past Peyton. I can shove him directly into Peyton and get them on the mat together.

I'm five paces away from Lachlan's post when a flash of light catches my eye. I tell myself it's just the sunlight glinting off a compliance officer's belt buckle, but my inner senses sizzle and my stomach sinks.

It's a flicker fit.

But whose?

My beast wakes up, triggered by the surge of fear inside me, but I shove him down. I can't allow him to show up right now. I need to act fast, but not draw attention. This whole area is surrounded by compliance officers. If I run or do anything sudden, they'll know there's a problem.

Whoever's in trouble, the bright sunlight is camouflaging them for now, but it won't be long before Ms. Hawk notices. I have precious seconds to figure out who it is before another flash of light will catch her eye. Then whoever's fitting is going to have a very bad day.

My gaze quickly rakes over the students directly ahead since that's the direction it came from.

Peyton has reached her post. It could be her, but her steps are too smooth and steady. Flicker fits make people twitch. She would have frozen up by now.

Joseph is also directly in my eyeline. He's standing at the post on my left, before Ashley and Lachlan's post. Joseph was the last to have a flicker fit. It has to be him.

I take two steps toward him before the light flashes again, this time from the next post.

Fuck. It's Ashley.

She suddenly grabs her practicing post, both hands pressed against the wood, her fingernails digging into it as if she wants to gouge its surface.

At the next post past her—the one Peyton just took up position at—Lucinda's head suddenly snaps up, a pained gasp on her lips. She clutches her chest, her eyes widening with pain as she focuses on Ashley.

Ashley twitches, seeming unaware of everything around her. Panic floods her expression as she stares at the post. She's facing outward and Lachlan is directly in her line of sight.

Such pure fear for her fills his eyes that it makes my head spin. Dammit. He can't be in love with her. Love can't survive in this place. He knows Ms. Hawk will kill Ashley.

Lachlan spins, a shout dying on his lips when he sees me coming already. The guys hate me, but they know I'm the only one who can save them.

I tell myself to be calm. I know what to do.

The second flicker is as unobtrusive as the first, a quick glimmer and only visible if seen from the right angle. Ms. Hawk's back is turned. She's focused on the students on the combat mat, but the compliance officer nearest to Ashley's post squints in her direction.

It's time for me to be aggressive, unpredictable Draven once again and knock Ashley out cold.

Hell, I'll say she looked at me wrong. I'll say Peyton pissed me off and I wanted to hit somebody, didn't care who. I'll tell them I don't need a fucking reason.

I'm one pace away when Ashley gives another, stronger flash. Bright light flickers in a stream around her head and shoulders. For a second, her face changes, her skin becomes as luminescent as her bright eyes, and her hair...

Her hair...

I nearly don't hit her because she's—

I shake my head. Blink hard. I block out what I can't explain.

The compliance officer turns in her direction.

She's out of time.

I raise my fist and swing it as hard as I can.

21. PEYTON PRICE

I've just taken up position at my post when a flash of light on my left catches my eye.

It came from Lachlan and Ashley's post, but I'm sure it was a glint of sunlight, nothing more.

I settle my weight, concentrate on my swing and get in a good few hits before the light catches my eye again. I cast a sideways glance at Ashley. She's hitting her post so hard that her knuckles leave bloody smears on it despite Lucinda's magic.

Ashley's face is a picture of concentration, fixated on the same spot. Every time she smacks the post, her body shimmers at the edges in a way that makes the air sizzle.

She must be accessing her magic, but it's like nothing I've felt before. It's sharp and dangerous and makes me feel like my feet are made of stone, rooted to the spot. Lucinda told me Ashley can freeze objects, stop things from moving, and that's what this feels like—like I'm not in control of my body anymore.

A sudden small flash emits from her back and her face drains as pale as death, even though her eyes remain brighter than they should be. She lurches forward, her hands gripping the practicing post in a way that tells me she can't let go, just like when Joseph gripped the wooden table on my first night at Bloodwing.

It's the first flicker fit anyone's had since then.

I try not to make any sudden moves—if I do, I'll draw Ms. Hawk's attention. I casually shift from my post, although my heart rate speeds up.

A glance past Ashley tells me Striker is heading straight for her. I'm closer, but I don't have his strength yet. I can't knock her out like he can. I should back away, but I... can't...

My feet carry me to her side.

I reach her just as another stronger flash fills the space around her head and neck, but this one is slow, delayed, spreading out into space like it's transcending through time. I'm close enough to feel it, close enough that it reaches out to strike my cheeks and my chest.

Ashley's eyes meet mine. Hers are lit up, glittering like gems, and her skin has become translucent, the veins in her cheeks and neck twisting like delicate emerald threads beneath the surface of her skin. The golden strands of her hair begin clumping together, her tresses thickening and entwining, rising from her back as if they're alive.

Her lips part and I hear her silent scream.

We're caught in her flicker, but this moment won't last forever and as soon as it ends, Ms. Hawk will kill her.

I sense Striker's movement behind her, the swing of his arm, the perfectly aimed thump that will drive her head into the post and knock her out to stop her flicker fit in its tracks.

I know he can take care of it, but her eyes...

They're far too bright, far too deadly, and far too afraid. Within their depths, emerald threads writhe and sway. Unlike Lucinda's eyes, which are ringed like the trunk of a tree, the shifting tones of Ashley's irises swarm like a nest of vipers.

Her power is definitely more than telekinesis. It must be connected to her eyes, just like Lucinda's comes from her heart.

I move in a flash, pressing my hand over Ashley's face. "Close your eyes. Be calm. Control it."

She inhales. Calms. The flicker stops instantly.

Her knees wobble before she drops to the grass, her hands flying up to cover her eyes as she slips out of my hold.

Everything speeds up again.

Ashley hits the ground, curled up tight, but I'm located higher than she is and—

Smack.

Striker's fist cuts clean across the empty space, knocking me against the post.

Pain explodes across my jaw. I sense my lip split. He was angling for the back of Ashley's head, but his fist caught me right in the middle of my face.

I bounce off the post and land on my backside with a roar of pain.

If I could bottle the look of horror that passes across Striker's face, I'd sip happily from it for the rest of my damn life.

I've never seen him look so sorry about anything.

Ms. Hawk spins to us, but the compliance officer is still staring at Ashley, which tells me we need a major diversion right now.

"Draven!" I shout. "You fucking asshole!"

I launch to my feet, leap over Ashley, and shove him with both hands, driving him back into the compliance officer, who takes a tumble.

Striker's elbow happens to jam into the guy's face as he regains his balance, making the officer bellow with rage. Striker rounds on him with a glare, as if the compliance officer got in his way and not the other way around.

Ms. Hawk's dark hair flies out behind her as she races toward us, screeching, "Both of you! On to the mat. Now!"

I'm not waiting for the mat. Covering for Ashley, who remains curled up on the ground with her head tucked under her arms, I take a step toward Striker, landing a perfect punch on his chin.

His head snaps back and he reacts on instinct, his fist shooting back at me but I dodge it, dancing out of his way before I dart in and clip his temple hard enough to draw blood.

He retaliates with a roar and another fist, which I also dodge.

Everyone around us scatters. Lucinda reacts just like I hoped she would—dragging Ashley out of the way. The other students follow but it's clear from their confused faces and shouts that they don't know what's going on. The confusion will give Ashley the precious moments she needs to regain full control.

There's no time right now to consider her power further. I'm flat-out avoiding a pummeling.

The compliance officers don't care about the other students anymore. They're focused on Striker and me. Especially since we disobeyed a direct order. Wands out, they're clearly pausing for a command from Ms. Hawk, but a glance in her direction tells me she's been waiting for Striker and me to go head to head again.

The cruel smile she gives me tells me she's happy to get her wish.

Striker gives up trying to land a blow and tackles me, lifting me off my feet and throwing me across his shoulder. I'm ready for that move, closing my fists together and ramming them down on his shoulder. I follow up with an elbow to his face, but —*dammit*—he still doesn't release me.

I prepare for him to throw me across the mat, ready my body to tumble and roll, relaxing into it. He hits the edge of the raised combat platform. The jolt is all I need. I push backward, neatly planting my hands in a backward handstand, kicking his face as I go.

He roars at me again as I flip to my feet.

I shake my head at him, enjoying the rare height advantage I have from up here. "C'mon, Draven. Is that all you've got?"

He storms up the platform and neatly dodges my next fist. Capturing my hand, he shocks me when he leans in with a cool gleam in his eye that tells me his rage is all for show.

Beneath the diversionary façade, he's as cold as ice. "When this is over, just remember that you asked me to touch you, Price."

A shiver runs down my spine. I guess this means the no-touching truce is over.

He blocks the next fist I throw, grabs my wrist, and drags his hand down my arm. His touch is firm but not hurtful, his fingers sliding across my skin. I raise my knee to aim a kick at his stomach at close quarters, but he deflects that too, hooking his arm under my thigh, his hand splaying across the sensitive skin at the top and back of my leg in a way that sends all the wrong signals through my body.

He hoists me up off the ground, nearly straddling him, one arm under my backside, pulling me close.

The last time we were in this position, he dropped me on my head. I'm not going to fall so easily this time.

I plunge my weight to one side, leaning so far and so fast that it pulls him off-balance, but he swings with it, dropping to his knee. I end up straddling his upraised knee instead, trapped in the circle of his arms. One hand grips my right hip, and the other strokes up my back to my shoulder in a very confusing way.

All I can do is look for an escape. I lean back and roll, arching over his arm, but to my shock, he drags his free hand all the way from my hip up my chest between my breasts to my neck, following the curve of my chest as I arch.

I gasp. *What the hell is he doing?*

This isn't fighting.

His amber eyes are backlit with flame but anyone else would think it's the bright sunlight glinting off his eyes.

My body laps up his touch, but my thoughts are in a spin.

Dear ancients, what did he say to me moments ago? *Remember that you asked me to touch you.*

Not like this. I wasn't expecting this.

I drop to the mat and barely make it to my feet, backing away before he comes after me again.

He reaches for my waist, deflecting my fist when I try to strike him, stroking down my arm in a way that makes me shiver.

I try to hit him with my other hand, but he grabs it too. Before I know it, his palms graze all the way down my arms and chest, curling around my hips again.

He leans in close and whispers, "I could touch you all day, Peyton, but we need to end this. You ready?"

The silence around us is thick. I'm aware of Ms. Hawk's narrowed eyes, but there's a cruel twist to her lips. The last time Striker lured me into a false sense of security, he knocked me out for hours. She will be expecting the same now.

He steps back and swings at me, quick and sharp, but my skills have improved a thousand times after daily practice for the last five months. I evade the blow and follow up with a kick that he also avoids. His fist jabs again, but I block, quickly retaliating.

For the next two minutes, we trade blows, each one fiercer than the last, each one deflected. Our fists blur, faster and faster, neither one of us doing any damage, until we both finally land a hit at the same time, the impact spinning us away from each other.

We rise to our feet, paces apart.

Both our chests are heaving.

I swipe at the blood trickling from my split lip.

He drags at the blood dripping from his temple.

With a smile, I realize that he didn't hold back just now. His breathing is as rapid as mine. We circle each other, but even Ms. Hawk seems to realize that Striker and I are too evenly matched. There is no victory for her today.

She stares at us with wide eyes before she shakes herself, her blue eyes blazing as she screams, "Get off the mat! Everyone back to your posts."

With a last cautious look at Striker, I head back to my place, casually checking over Ashley and Lucinda.

Ashley's in control again, a calm expression on her face, but Lucinda glances at me in a way that tells me we need to have another shower conversation.

On the other side of her, Bree looks as confused as everyone else. Striker and I haven't voluntarily fought for a long time and as far as they could see, he picked a fight out of the blue.

His gaze burns my back when I leave gym class to follow Lucinda, Ashley, and Bree straight to the girls' floor. I grab a pack of ice for my lip on the way.

When we reach the shower, Ashley is subdued, but Bree demands to know what's going on. She plants her hands on her hips. "You took a swipe at Striker like you have a death wish. What the hell, Peyton?"

Lucinda turns on all the shower faucets, filling the room with white noise before she says, "Ashley had a flicker fit."

Bree's face falls. She curses. "No, Ashley! Are you okay?"

Ashley nods. "Only because of Peyton." She turns to me. "How did you know I should close my eyes?"

I take a deep breath. "I'm going to tell you what I saw and then you can draw whatever conclusions you want."

She nods cautiously.

I chew over my words. "Your eyes were lit up emerald and the light shifted inside them as if they were made up of threads. Your skin was pale, the veins in your face ran green, and your hair… was turning into…" I close my eyes, trying to hide my disbelief. "Your hair was becoming snakes."

Ashley recoils. "Snakes!"

I nod. "I know what I saw."

Ashley spins to Lucinda. "Did you see it, too?"

Lucinda shakes her head. "I can't see through flicker fits. They're too bright."

The girls stare at me again, but I pin Ashley with my own glare. "You need to acknowledge what you are. Then you'll understand why you had to close your eyes."

She's paler than before. Her hands shake as she presses them to her mouth. "But it's not possible. I can't be…"

I step up to her. "The teachers think you have the power to freeze things. What you really have… is the power to turn living things to stone."

She stumbles backward but Lucinda catches her, holding Ashley tightly before whirling toward me. "A gorgon? Are you serious?"

"One of the deadliest creatures," I say. "A power like no other."

Ashley shakes her head in denial. "But I don't want to hurt anyone."

"I know you don't." I sigh. Ashley is one of the gentlest girls at the Academy, even more so than Lucinda. The day she stood up to tell me that they tried to bring me in from the rain took a lot of guts on her part. "Tell me what happened when you closed your eyes."

Her lip quivers. "Um… I…" Her forehead suddenly creases. "I could still see everything, but my vision was bright, like all the shapes around me glimmered at the edges."

"Then you're only deadly if you open your eyes."

She lets out a laugh, nearing on panic. "I need a really good pair of sunglasses."

I take her hands, forcing her to look at me. "You'll learn to control it, just like Lucinda has."

Lucinda nods rapidly. "I'll help you. We can go outside in the mornings and practice on those awful rose bushes. I might be a dryad, but those plants aren't natural. I'd like to see some of them turned to stone."

A tear slides down Ashley's cheek. "How did this happen? Why am I like this?"

Lucinda shakes her head. "How am I a dryad when I have wolf shifter parents? Our genetics are completely messed up."

I sigh. "Or perfectly aligned."

Bree arches her eyebrows at me. "What do you mean?"

"The original gorgons..." I say. "There were three of them, right? Sisters? People were terrified of them because they didn't look human—they couldn't hide their power. But you can, Ashley. You can transform from human to gorgon."

I swing to Lucinda. "Lucinda, you're a dryad. If you accessed your full power, I bet your hair would turn to vines and your legs into tree roots. But you walk around like everybody else. And Bree..." I shake my head at her. "There's no way you're a simple water mage."

Bree has remained quiet for the last minute. "I feel close to the water. I like being near it, but I can't control it. The teachers were wrong about Ashley and Lucinda, so maybe they're wrong about me too."

Lucinda draws Bree into a hug, dragging her and Ashley close. "We'll figure it out."

They look at me, and Lucinda reaches for me past Ashley's shoulder, as if she wants me to join their hug. I take a deep breath and step into it, worried I'll feel awkward, but they're all quiet and unassuming. I'm not used to hugs, don't really know where to start, but here seems like a good place.

I don't speak aloud my deeper fears. There's a general belief among the supernatural community that the magically repressed have the power of other mainstream supernatural races, but Lucinda and Ashley have proven they have rare and unique abilities. They aren't a repressed witch and a repressed telekinetic. Not even close.

They're something else.

I have to face the question that could be the key to understanding our true nature: What if the magically repressed aren't repressed at all?

What if we're a different class of supernatural altogether?

A class of supernatural with no aura who appear human... A perfectly lethal type of supernatural.

The Founder wants us to be her soldiers. What if she suspects that we have these abilities and wants to use them for her own means?

I shudder. As far as I know, only the Valkyrie and Keres were able to appear completely human—before they became extinct that is. They had no aura and could transform at will. They could walk among supernaturals without detection, which made them deadly. It was only because they went to war with each other that they died out.

Yet here we are. Magically repressed students with no aura who can transform into...

I shy away from thinking of myself as a potential monster. I don't know what I am yet. And there's no way I think of Ashley that way. She's one of the sweetest people I know.

Striker, on the other hand, fits that description perfectly. The chances of him being a fire mage are getting slimmer by the second. The power that simmers behind his eyes is far greater than the power I ever sensed from my father and brother.

It's lethal. And so is he.

That night, Headmistress Osprey marches into the dining room with extra compliance officers in tow.

From where she sits next to me, Ashley nudges me with her foot. "The last time this happened, she told us you were coming."

"Students!" Osprey demands our attention, her thorny wand resting in her hand. Tonight, she's wearing a fuchsia pink pants suit and her nails are lacquered solid yellow.

"Starting tomorrow, we're introducing a new subject into the curriculum. We're calling it Magical Pathways." She gives us a cold smile, her mouth stretching up at the corners while her eyes remain deadpan, washed-out brown. "It will be taught by a new teacher."

She pauses, but nobody reacts. I'm not sure if a new teacher is a good thing or bad. I maintain a blank expression. Bree, Ashley, and Lucinda give no hint of their feelings.

"His name is Professor Raptor, and he will teach the class with each of you individually. Your new timetables will be distributed to you." Her smile broadens. "We hope to encourage you to get in touch with your inner selves."

Her focus lands on me. "Price, after the stunt you pulled today in gym class, I've decided you will be first. Present yourself to the east wing, third floor, immediately after breakfast tomorrow."

Within seconds of Osprey's departure, a male hand lands on the table beside me and Striker's shadow looms over me. "Watch yourself, Price."

That's all he says before he walks away, leaving me with a sort of anticlimactic feeling.

I was expecting more now that we're touching again. A threat, a taunt, an insult, a shove…

Lucinda's serious eyes meet mine across the table. She murmurs, "He's worried. We all should be."

Okay, so maybe I should be too.

22. PEYTON PRICE

The next morning, I hurry out for a run before breakfast, nervous energy making me more hasty than usual.

I'm surprised to find Striker out there already. It looks like he barely slept, his shirt a crumpled heap on the grass, his bare chest gleaming.

When I appear, he surprises me by slowing down until I catch up to him. Then he paces himself beside me for a full ten seconds without saying anything. I count every step until he drops behind me.

After a minute, he catches up to me again, but he still doesn't say anything.

I scowl at him as he drops back again.

When he does it a third time, I'm ready to demand answers. "Spit it out, Draven."

He's surly. "What?"

"Whatever you want to say."

"There's nothing to say."

I huff out an annoyed breath. My fitness levels have

improved to the point where I can carry on an entire conversation while running without bursting a lung.

"I heard you last night," I say. "I'll be careful this morning. I won't say anything about… well… anything. About you. If that's what you're worried about."

"I'm not worried about that."

"What then?"

"They've gone easy on us for the last few months."

I arch a disbelieving eyebrow at him. "Vomit-inducing shifter dissections aren't awful enough for you?" Ms. Vulture's biology classes have been nothing short of colorful in the worst possible way.

"They were waiting for Raptor to arrive," he says. "Things are going to change."

Aside from the surprising realization that Striker and I are having a nearly-normal conversation, the tone of Striker's voice is also a little unnerving. He *does* sound worried. "What makes you think they were waiting for Raptor?"

"A while ago, I overheard something I shouldn't have. Raptor's dangerous in the worst possible way."

I want to retort that so is Striker, but he steals the wind out of my sails by sounding genuinely concerned. "Be careful in there, Peyton."

He pulls away again, but this time, he jogs to the building and heads inside.

Striker telling me to be careful makes me even more worried.

I run another few laps before I return to the attic, get dressed for the day, and try to settle myself during breakfast. The other girls don't have to ask me for me to say, "I'll tell you what happens."

Not knowing what to expect, I head for the third-floor in the east wing. The fourth door is open, and I stop outside it.

Bright sunlight fills the space inside it, but it's empty of furniture other than a chair and a table. And Headmistress Osprey. She stares back at me from her perch on the chair before her gaze flicks to her left.

The hairs on the back of my neck prickle a second before a disarmingly pleasant male voice says, "You can come in."

A guy not much older than me appears in the doorway inside the room, leaning against the doorframe in a way that completely blocks the entrance despite his invitation to enter.

He's dressed in a black T-shirt that hugs his muscular biceps, distressed jeans that cling to his thighs, and black military-style boots. Strands of blond hair fall around his face and across his pale green eyes. Right now, he's hitting a disconcerting spot between military commander and surfer dude.

I narrow my eyes at him. "You're not old enough to be a professor."

He arches an eyebrow at me before casting a disapproving glance back at Osprey. "Is that what they're calling me? I thought 'Raptor' was a bit much, but 'Professor'? That's going too far."

When I scowl at him, he steps out of the way, gesturing. "After you."

I step carefully into the room, keeping my distance from both of them. Raptor extends his hand as if he wants to shake mine. I stare at it before I take a step backward. He may as well offer me poison.

"O-kay," he says, as if I'm the weird one. "Doesn't like physical contact. Duly noted."

Osprey rises to her feet and addresses Raptor. "Well, she's here. Remember what we talked about."

He grins. "I know the limitations. Don't worry."

"Then I'll leave you to it."

With a haughty glance at me, she glides to the door and closes it behind her.

Raptor gives me a smile that doesn't reach his eyes. It's just like Osprey. I'm quickly learning that people who smile with their mouths and not their eyes can't be trusted.

"The Headmistress and I had a small wager," he says. "She bet that you wouldn't come to this class of your own volition. I disagreed. I think you're smart enough to know that disobeying me would be painful."

He paces to the chair Osprey vacated, takes a seat, and rests his elbows on his knees in a casual gesture. "She also told me I'm not allowed to kill you. Apparently, Lady Tirelli will swoop down from on high and end me if you die."

I'm surprised by his admission. Many students have died here—nearly half, from what Bree told me. I don't see why I would be any sort of exception.

He shrugs, confirming my thoughts. "Osprey's wrong. Our Lady has much bigger problems right now. She won't be coming back anytime soon. So, I think I'll do whatever I want."

He leans forward. "Do you dislike physical touch more or less than you fear heights?"

I'm not surprised he knows about my fear of high places. Collin and Colby noticed it on my first day and no doubt wrote it down in a file somewhere. So far, none of the teachers has tried to use it against me.

I remain where I am, not answering him, checking out our surroundings now that I'm inside the room: bare window, bare table, one chair.

Then I notice something else. "You don't carry a wand."

"Doesn't like to answer questions," he says, studying me.

I persist. "All of the teachers carry wands."

"Because they're witches and wizards. I'm something else. When they don't call me 'Raptor,' they call me 'The Specialist.'" He stands, fixating on my face as he approaches. "Recently healed wounds. The cut on your lip was a blow to the face, but you've also been scratched at some point. Maybe by claws."

I scoff. The damage from the harpy's feathers is long healed.

He must think that his deductions will impress me. "They told you I spent a night in the pit with a harpy."

"They told me nothing. I'm observant."

I eye him as he begins to circle me. I'm not sure how… but I'm certain he just told me a lie. "What am I doing here?"

He looks me up and down as he moves, making me feel less like a person and a lot like a specimen.

"I have a particular skillset the Academy needs," he says.

"And what's that?"

"The ability to extract information from even the most unwilling participant."

I hide the shudder that threatens to topple me. He's some sort of interrogator.

Get in touch with your inner selves, Headmistress Osprey said. No wonder Striker was worried. This guy is here to seek out every secret—including the powers some students are hiding.

I paste a smile on my face. "I'm an open book. Ask me anything."

"How about telling me about the night your brother pushed you down the stairs?"

I snatch a breath, my palms suddenly clammy. Raptor is an outright liar. He may be observant, but they've told him everything. There's no way he knows about my brother's murderous act of aggression without talking to someone or reading some sort of file on me—my medical records or even my elementary school history.

"Tell me how it felt when his hands connected with your lower back." He suddenly pushes both hands firmly against either side of my spine.

I jolt away from him, but his arm snakes around my waist so hard that the air whooshes out of me, pinning my back to his front.

His arm is like a vise, forcing me to stay still while his other hand remains pressed against my spine and his lower half presses against my backside. Dear ancients, he's totally getting off on my position right now.

Before I can ram an elbow into his stomach, Raptor whispers into my ear, "How did it feel when you teetered for the smallest moment—a beat—at the top of the stairs? Just long enough to realize how far it was to the bottom? How did it feel to hit each step one by one, to be so out of control that you couldn't even breath? Hearing, *feeling* the crunch when your wrist broke and you prayed nothing else would."

I inhale a deep breath and close my eyes, the memory suddenly threatening to overwhelm me.

I'm not there. I'm not falling. I'm here. I've put the memory behind me. It isn't happening and… I've moved past it.

"You haven't conquered the fear," he says. "You're still afraid of heights."

I open my eyes. Focus on my breathing. I'm stronger than this. I've faced Striker in a combat ring, for heaven's sake. I've killed a harpy. I've climbed five damn sets of stairs when I was literally dying.

The fact that Raptor's grabbed me in a way that makes me vulnerable… hell, who hasn't?

"I'm still afraid of heights," I say, owning it. "I'll always be afraid of heights." I focus on the sunlight streaming into the room, my hand closing over his arm, preparing to remove it. "What are you afraid of, Professor Raptor?"

He releases me as suddenly as he grabbed me—so suddenly, I stumble a little, righting myself in time for him to round on me again, folding his arms across his chest. "Now we've got up close and personal, you should call me 'Jake.'"

"No."

He grins. "Osprey told me you don't obey commands."

"That would be correct."

He gestures to the chair. "Take a seat."

I eye it for less than a second. "No."

"Sit on the floor then."

"I'll stand, thank you."

He walks to the table, bends to his boot, and pulls out a gleaming silver blade from inside it.

Very carefully, he lays it on the table, as if it's precious. Leaving it there, he returns to my position, standing exactly opposite me. He points to the weapon without taking his eyes from me. "Pick up the dagger."

I can't help my surprised exclamation. "What?"

He's offering me a weapon? I haven't trained with weapons, but I'm prepared to learn quickly. Still, there's no such thing as a free ride in this place. Picking up that dagger is going to come with a catch.

"If you reach it before I do, I'll let you leave this lesson," he says. "If you reach it after me, I'll cut you slowly for the next hour."

What the hell? He's officially more of a psycho than Ms. Hawk.

"You're trying to decide if I mean it," he says, studying me as I remain silent. "Will I really spend an hour torturing you? I assure you, I'm good at it." His expression doesn't change. "It's why I was excommunicated from the last institution I joined. I was too extreme even for a clandestine group of assassins."

A chill passes through me. If he's telling the truth, then I'm in trouble.

My brother was obsessed with the assassins growing up. The supernatural community fears them—even the Magical Magnate doesn't mess with them.

There are three Factions of assassins in the United States: the Legion based in Boston, the Dominion in Portland, and the Horde in Austin. Each assassin is an elite warrior who moves in the shadows, expert killers who have no mercy for their targets. They're all human but control magical rings that give them superhuman strength and agility.

Despite their ferocity, they live by a very particular code of honor that requires clean kills and restricts who they're allowed to target.

My brother wanted to grow up to be an assassin before he found out he wouldn't be allowed to kill whomever he wanted.

If Raptor trained with the assassins… that makes him very dangerous. At least he doesn't still have an assassin's ring—his fingers are bare.

"Which Faction?" I demand to know, testing the truth of Raptor's story. "Legion or Dominion? You don't have a Southern accent to be Horde."

He looks surprised. "You know the Factions." He tilts his head to the side. "I was Legion."

I shake my head. He's lying again. I can't pinpoint how I know. A glint in his eyes maybe. A twist of his mouth. A flicker of his gaze. "You were Dominion."

"What makes you say that?"

"The Legion is most ruthless, most likely to bend the rules. They wouldn't excommunicate you for being aggressive."

He tilts his head in an acknowledging gesture. "I guess I joined the wrong Faction then. You've got three seconds, Price."

He means the dagger. His changes of subject are abrupt, but I was anticipating he wouldn't let it go.

I glance at the weapon, calculating the distance to reach it. Only four quick steps, but if he's trained as an assassin, there's no way I'll get to the dagger before him.

I won't have a chance of fighting him, either. He will have trained for years, whereas I've only been training for a few months.

"No," I say.

"No?"

"I'm not racing you to the dagger."

"Wrong choice, Price." He gives a heavy sigh. "Never mind. I can do just as much damage with my fists."

I grit my teeth. "Go on, then. Get on with it."

He arches his eyebrow at me, his voice clinical. "High fear threshold. Ability to compartmentalize memories." He circles me again. "Welcomes pain."

I jolt when he runs a finger across the side of my neck.

"But hates gentle touch. What are you, Peyton Price? A witch? A shifter? With eyes like yours, you must be something other than what you appear."

I'm genuinely curious. "What about my eyes?"

A smile glimmers around his mouth. "Take the dagger and I'll tell you."

Without another thought, I dart to my right as quickly as I can.

He's a step behind me, but my target isn't the dagger—it's the table. It's a flimsy wooden one, not anchored to the floor. Ramming into its side, I flip it, a split second before his fingers would have closed around the weapon.

The force sends the knife flying toward the wall.

My hand is already on the table's edge. I vault it, throw myself toward the dagger and slide across the floor, hitting the wall. My shoulder collides first and then my head.

Raptor lands at a crouch opposite me, but I'm a second ahead of him.

My hand closes around the fallen dagger's handle.

For a second, I'm afraid I've grabbed its blade—cut my fingers—because pain strikes through me, shooting through my hand and up my arm.

Suddenly, I can't breathe. Images race through my mind. The slash of the dagger across a man's throat, striking into another's chest, then another... too many... too many deaths...

It's just like when I picked up Kaitlyn's wand, except that her thoughts were calculating and cruel, but Raptor's are...

Horror fills me and my stomach turns.

A scream builds inside me, but it's trapped in a cage of silent images that suddenly burst into sound. A woman crying, a child screaming…

Raptor's memories are cold, unemotional, and analytical. *He doesn't care…*

I need to drop the knife. Need to escape Raptor's memories, but I'm not fast enough.

His fist cracks against my cheek, his other hand grabs the wrist of my hand holding the dagger—the same one that broke when I fell down the stairs—and twists.

Finally, my scream reaches my lips, peeling into the air around us as I let go of the weapon before he can break my bones.

He deftly catches the knife, plucking it out of the air as it falls, his movements faster than I can anticipate.

I jolt back against the wall, the force of his punch casting me there, my scream dying in my throat as he thrusts the dagger toward my face.

He stops its downward thrust right before the tip would pierce my left eye. Grabbing my shoulder, he pulls me upright while I try to wrench away from him.

Keeping the dagger pointed at my face, he pushes me around the fallen table toward the window. I can't fight him or I'll impale myself.

"I promised you I'd tell you about your eyes," he says, forcing me up against the window pane. The wooden surround digs into my back and my fear of heights rears its ugly head when Bloodwing's garden comes into view far below me.

If I fall through this window, I'll land in a grave of red roses.

He grabs my chin, forcing my face into the light.

"Your pupils dilate when they should constrict," he says. "Right now, your pupils should be pinpoints in the sunlight. Instead, they're widening, taking in more light. So much light, you shouldn't be able to focus on me. Yet you can see me, can't you, Price?"

I can.

I don't want to.

"You killed innocent people," I say. "People you weren't given permission to kill."

He gives me a quizzical look. "Now, how could you possibly know that?" He nods to himself without easing up on me. "Possible psychic capability. Interesting."

When I don't respond, he grabs my hair and bashes my head against the wooden window surround.

His movement is so sudden, so unpredictable, that I don't have a hope of protecting myself. The *thud* reverberates in my hearing. My vision blurs, my stomach turns, and everything goes black for a second.

I fight the darkness, coming back to find he's running the dagger's tip down the front of my shirt, leaving a thin red line from my neck to my bra line. He's already cut through my tie and discarded it on the floor.

The blade barely breaks skin but stings like hell.

I struggle against his hold, kicking against his legs, but my hits barely have an impact. He quickly uses his weight to immobilize my lower half against the windowsill. Gripping my jaw in his free hand, he ignores the extra blows I land on his chest. My hands are free, but fighting back isn't making any difference.

Oh, ancients. This isn't good. He broke his word about letting me go if I picked up the knife, but I guess he never intended to let me leave.

He pushes harder against me and—

Pop. The knife slices through the threads holding the buttons onto my shirt.

They hit the floor one by one, rolling away across the room.

"Don't worry. I'll figure you out," he says with a smile that chills me to the bone. "Let's see if we can break those barriers you've built around yourself."

23. STRIKER DRAVEN

The seat beside me remains empty all through Magical History.

Mr. Mallard drones on about Zeus and the power of lightning, how it manifests in today's storm mages but no known supernatural has power over all of the storm's elements.

It would be nice to believe that we are all somehow descended from the gods, but I don't buy it for a millisecond. As far as I'm concerned, it's a theory that's been invented by the Magical Magnate to make mediocre supernaturals feel self-important.

My greater concern right now is Peyton. She doesn't show for the entire lesson.

When gym class begins, I expect her to appear at the back of the building, but she doesn't.

Dread creeps into my chest, heavy on my mind. The conversation I overheard between Osprey and Lady Tirelli tells me that Raptor is The Specialist that Lady Tirelli was talking about. Even Osprey considered him dangerous in the extreme.

I end up on the combat mat with Joseph, but I'm distracted, taking glances at the back of the building whenever I can.

Peyton's going to appear at any moment. She has to, or I'm going to lose it.

Joseph thumps my face several times before he finally tackles me, clips me across the forehead with a savage right hook that gets my attention, and snarls, "We're all worried about her. You're the only one who can find out what the hell is going on, so do it already, Draven."

He releases me and I jump to my feet, striding from the mat without a backward glance. I should have left class half an hour ago to find her.

"Draven! Where are you going?" Ms. Hawk screams at me, but I'm already disappearing into the building at a run. "Come back or I'll—"

The slamming door cuts off whatever she says. I'll deal with the consequences later.

Peyton was told to go to the east wing, third floor so that's where I run first. I take the stairs two at a time, my feet flying along the corridor to the only open door.

The room is empty.

A bloody towel lies scrunched on the table.

Dread claws inside me. Why the hell did I let her come to this class alone? I should have stalked her, made it look like I was here to torment her, but protected her somehow.

I run farther along the corridor, opening every door in case she's in another room. Empty classrooms, all of them.

Racing back to the stairs, I have a decision to make. Up or down? There are so many rooms in this place. She could be anywhere.

Panic strikes through me. There was too much blood on that towel. I need to find her fast.

Beast!

My blood sizzles as he roars to the surface. *I'm here.*

Where is she?

As soon as I ask the question, my senses expand. Power

floods my mind and I fight to make sure it doesn't take over. I inhale the air, seeking Peyton's scent, a scent I've avoided naming because it's too complicated even for the beast to separate its layers. She isn't roses and flowers, not artificial sweetness, but something far more powerful.

Upstairs.

I burst into movement, taking the stairs all the way to the top, colliding with Collin and Colby. It's dangerous for me to show real emotion in front of them, so I grab Collin by the scruff of his neck.

They expect angry, so that's what I give them. "Where the hell is she? If she thinks she can avoid me on the combat mat today, she's got another think coming."

"Your timing is cold, Draven," Colby says, but he doesn't get in my way. "She's already beaten up, but, sure… Go ahead. She's in her room. We'll be downstairs if you need us."

He and Collin move out of my way, their boots clumping on the stairs as they descend. I pace my steps along the corridor to Peyton's room until I'm sure they're gone.

Then I run again, skidding to a halt outside her door.

The sun has ascended over the building, leaving her room in greater darkness. My heightened senses draw me to her location.

She's curled up in the far corner, wrapped in her blanket in a way that tells me her knees are drawn to her chest beneath it. I can't see her face. It's turned away, resting on her knees, her hair cascading down her side outside of the blanket.

The coppery scent of blood is so thick in the air, I nearly lose my mind.

Fighting my raging instincts, I approach carefully, quietly, listening to her shaky breaths, the way her breathing drags as she inhales and exhales. "I'm not falling. I'm not… falling…"

She's shaking, but she's wrapped up so tightly, I can't see where she's hurt and it's driving me crazy with panic.

Every instinct tells me to pick her up but grabbing her is only going to startle her and make things worse. I force myself to kneel beside her without reaching out. "Peyton?"

She doesn't lift her head. Her voice is muffled. A bare whisper. "You only call me 'Peyton' when you think I'm dying."

The need to pull her into my arms is growing more intense. Every sound out of my mouth is forced. "I need to know if you're okay."

Her breath catches. "Don't pretend to care, Striker."

Annoying, stubborn... "I know you're hurt. Tell me where so I can do something about it. I need to..." Blood drips down my palms and I realize I'm digging my fingernails into them so hard that I'm cutting skin. Clawed fingernails.

If I don't figure out what's wrong with her, I'm going to transform into full beast mode and so help me if I do.

I grit my teeth, then force myself to speak coherently. "I need to do something about it."

Her speech is slow and labored. "I don't want your help, Striker. I can handle it. Just leave me alone."

That's it. I'm done being patient. I can either pick her up now while I'm still all me or I can pick her up while I'm full-on beast. Of the two, being me will be less shocking for her.

My voice is a low growl, not my own. "No."

I scoop her up, sliding my arms all the way around her, but she stiffens, crying out and arching her back. "No, please, don't touch—"

Her cry descends into a low moan that drags at my chest like a knife.

I loosen my arms, but she's already close enough to me that when I lower her down again, she settles onto my lap, curled up on the top of my thighs.

The most shocking thing is... she doesn't fight me or try to push me away. She maintains her tight curl, her face turned toward me but covered by her hair, her right shoulder pressing against my chest.

Resting back against her closet doors, I carefully sweep her hair aside so I can see her face. Her forehead is clammy, her eyes are closed, and her hair is clumped with blood. The only relief is that her face isn't bleeding.

I ease the blanket open, coaxing her fingers to relax so I can draw it away from her shoulders. Her tie is missing and her shirt is covered in blood all over her back, telling me she's wounded, but there are no slits in the material, nothing ripped.

That means... she wasn't wearing her shirt when she was hurt.

Focusing hard to control my anger, I pry the blanket away from her knees and nudge her legs away from her chest. Her shirt gapes open at the front, every button missing. Cuts crisscross her chest above her bra line. One bra strap is cut clean through across the shoulder, the straight edge of elastic telling me it was a sharp knife.

Each cut is an act of precision. Not too deep. Just deep enough.

Rage spirals through me. "What the hell?"

I quickly scan her legs. As far as I can see, there are no cuts beneath her waist and her skirt isn't damaged, still zipped up. The damage is only waist up.

She opens her eyes, lifting her head, her hair falling across her eyes again. "Why so shocked, Draven?" she asks, an edge of defiance in her voice even though her cheeks are pale. "Are you angry that he did your work for you?"

I don't know how to feel about the fact that she thinks I could ever do something like this.

I'm callous, uncaring, and aggressive but *this*... "I'll kill that sadistic bastard."

Ignoring her defiant stare, I ease her shirt away from her

shoulders, one sleeve at a time, drawing the material carefully down her back.

It's worse than her front.

She continues to surprise me by not fighting me. Instead, she winces, inhales, and squeezes her eyes closed before she drops her head to her knees again.

"He asked me questions," she whispers. "Every question came with a cut. He asked me about everyone, even you. I didn't tell him anything."

I need the medical kit. I don't have any healing gel left but I do have antiseptic and bandages. I could bring it to her or I could take her to my room—that's safest in case someone interrupts us since there's nowhere to hide the kit in here. However, it's going to be hard to carry her without hurting her. "Can you walk?"

"Where, Striker?"

"To my room."

"Why? So you can heal me? They'll break me again tomorrow."

They won't. She's too tough for that. Before I think about what I'm doing, I press my lips to her forehead, the lightest kiss before I murmur, "They'll never break you, Peyton."

She shivers in my arms, her lips parting as she sucks in a sudden inhale. A faint crease appears between her brows.

In contrast to the suddenness of her breathing, she opens her eyes slowly, her gaze meeting mine. Her lips purse as if she's puzzled, mystified by something. I have no idea what she's thinking, but for the first time, her eyes don't tell me to go to hell.

She doesn't recoil like I thought she might. Like she should. Hell, she should run for her life right now.

I force myself to resume breathing, cupping the back of her head to support her, avoiding touching her back as I press my other hand to her arm, preparing to help her stand.

She startles me by leaning in, her lips close to mine. "Striker would you… do something for me?"

I cease moving, taken by surprise. I've mostly pushed the beast away but my power simmers beneath the surface. Her sudden nearness is like a spark, drawing me closer to her, but I fight its effects, determined to remain still.

Her eyes don't leave mine. "Would you… kiss me again? Properly this time?"

I'm sure I didn't hear her correctly. She swore she would never give me permission to touch her and I promised her that I wouldn't.

I've already broken that promise but only to protect Ashley, and I'm determined to keep my hands to myself as much as I can. Although… fighting her yesterday… I couldn't help myself.

"I don't think that's a good idea," I say, intensely confused by her request.

She doesn't contradict me. "I know it isn't, but… I think you can help me."

I shake my head, firmly focusing on her eyes. The moment my gaze lowers to her lips, I won't be able to stop thinking about kissing her.

I remind myself that she needs medical attention, and she needs it now. She's in shock and we shouldn't be wasting time. "I can help you by getting you to my room and treating these wounds."

The openness in her expression closes off and it's like watching a light die out.

"Of course." She rises slowly to her feet and the blanket falls away. Her broken bra strap flops to her lower back as she turns in my arms. "Not worth your time."

Oh, hell.

"That's not what I said." I flounder. *Damn, damn, damn.* "I mean… it *is* what I said. But you can't… You don't really want to… You can't make decisions like that right now…"

Dear ancients, I've never been this tongue-tied before.

Her eyes grow wider with every word I speak.

A fierce crease forms on her forehead as I give her a gruff order. "You're hurt and you're coming with me."

I scoop one arm under her backside and the other across her upper shoulders, avoiding pressing against the worst of the cuts on her back. I hold her out from me as much as I can, careful not to press her chest against mine in a way that will hurt her.

"Okay," she says, tucking her head against my chest and sliding her arms around me.

I nearly miss a step before I decide that she really is in shock. I quickly step over her ruined shirt and carry her to my room, placing her down on my bed so she can see the room and everything in it—including me—before I pull the blanket to her waist and close the door.

I retrieve the medical kit, pull up a chair, moisten a swab with antiseptic, and apologize. "This is going to hurt."

She bites her lip and squeezes her eyes closed as I set to work cleaning the cuts. I move around her as I go, propping my knee on the side of the bed for balance. I wasn't wrong about Raptor's precision. None of the wounds need stitches, but they're deep enough—and there are enough of them—to traumatize even someone as steel-hearted as Peyton.

There must be thirty cuts on her back and front. She said he gave her one cut for every question he asked. It's nearly impossible to bandage them all. I need a patch large enough to extend across her entire back or else I'll end up taping across the cuts and that will hurt more.

"Damn." I sift through the meager contents of the medical kit, trying to figure out a solution. For now, I'm avoiding the possibility that Raptor will cause every student the same pain. Ms. Sparrow's paper cuts suddenly look like child's play compared to this.

Peyton's touch on my hand interrupts my thoughts.

"Striker?" She leans across the bed, meeting my eyes. "There's nothing more you can do."

"There's always something more." I push around the medical patches in their sterilized packets. Maybe I can put them side by side and tape over the top of them, make a larger patch that way.

Her grip tightens, her fingertips closing over mine. "You've done enough." She slides her legs over the edge of the bed with a surprising certainty.

I'm not prepared to let her leave until I'm sure she's okay.

I grip her hand, trying to figure out a way to ask her to stay without it sounding like I'll force her.

To my surprise, she grips my hand right back, rises up off the edge of the bed, and plants a kiss on my cheek.

My heart thuds as her lips linger against my jaw, the softest, most hesitant touch.

She begins to speak. "I'm going to—"

"No." My beast roars to the surface. He won't let her leave.

Hell, it's time for me to face the fact that *I* don't want her to leave. Even though I have no right feeling that way, I don't want her to walk out that door.

She pulls back a little. "Striker, you don't—"

"No." My arm circles her waist, low to avoid her wounds as I pull her close.

The heat from her stomach and thighs seeps through my clothing. She's much warmer than I was expecting.

Sudden color blushes through her cheeks. "Striker, I—"

"No."

She breaks into a dazzling smile that lights up her eyes. Their chocolate depths suddenly dance with a fragile sort of vulnerability.

I've never seen her smile before and it's like the cage around my chest just cracked open and my heart started beating again.

It's painful, it hurts too much, but I'm struck senseless, too mesmerized to interrupt her when she asks, "Will you let me finish?"

I can't tear my gaze away from the smile in her eyes. "Maybe."

Her left hand brushes my jaw, fingertips trailing across my neck. She speaks softly. "I'm going to…"

She pauses. Glances up at me. Looks pleased when I don't stop her.

"I'm going to kiss you now, Striker Draven," she says. "Is that okay with you?"

Hell, yes.

I dip my head to hers, sensing her quick inhale before my lips touch hers. I want to claim her mouth but I force myself to go slow. Her kiss, her quick breath, is hesitant, seeking to explore the shape of my mouth, as if she's fitting herself to me.

I sense her shiver. I soak up the way she presses forward, her chest connecting with mine. She shouldn't be doing that. She'll hurt herself… but kissing her is like inhaling flames and they're only getting higher, a wave that's about to crash down on me.

She slides her hand around the back of my neck, moans against my mouth, and I'm drowning.

I'm fucking drowning.

24. PEYTON PRICE

Striker's blanket is the only thing keeping me grounded as I huddle beneath the window inside my room, the faint scent of cedarwood and balsam comforting me in a way that the man himself never will.

My only goal right now is to get my breathing under control.

Every time Raptor cut me, he told me I was falling. Even though I knew it was a strategy to rekindle my fears, I couldn't stop the effect it had on me.

The cuts themselves I could handle. I'm accustomed to pain and I left him with a few bruises he didn't expect. I don't think his crown jewels will function well any time soon.

But the mind games Raptor played with me... the height of the window... the way he was always in control...

I press my face to my knees, reminding myself, "I'm not falling. I'm not... falling..."

The scent of cedarwood grows stronger. I sense movement outside of the mental bubble I've created to protect myself.

I know the sound of Striker's footsteps now. Because I sleep on the floor, I hear his footfalls every morning as he strides down the corridor to the shower. I listen to them every night before I go to sleep while he paces his room back and forth.

I don't know why he does it, but I find the soft vibrations of his feet calming.

"Peyton?"

I don't move, can't see his face, but he sounds… agitated, angry even. I haven't seen him since our jog this morning, so I'm struggling to imagine why he's angry with me. More confusing is his use of my first name. "You only call me 'Peyton' when you think I'm dying."

"I need to know if you're okay," he says.

Oh. So maybe he's worried. I quickly banish that possibility. This is Striker. He doesn't worry. Certainly not about me. "Don't pretend to care, Striker."

It sounds like he's gritting his teeth. "I know you're hurt. I need to…" He exhales. It's a sharp sound, angrier still. "I need to do something about it."

I smother a sigh. He left me alone for a really long time and I'm grateful for it, but accepting his help puts me in an even more vulnerable position.

Not to mention, I can't bear to be touched right now. Raptor's focus remained above my waist, but every now and then his palm shifted to my hip. The only time I feared rape was when a guy at school cornered me in the bathroom and shoved his tongue down my throat while he ruffled my skirt. It didn't go any further because a group of girls came in and told him to mess with me somewhere else. He lost his nerve and ran out.

Technically, that was my first and only kiss, but I decided long ago it didn't count.

"I don't want your help, Striker. Just leave me alone."

The silence beside me suddenly fills with tension. The air warms in a way that makes me tense up.

He growls a response and it doesn't sound like his voice anymore. "No."

I lift my head, trying to see his face. I catch a glimpse of eyes flickering with flames just as his arms swoop around me. But he can't see the cuts, and the extra pressure around my back is too much.

I can't stop my urgent cry. "No, please, don't touch—"

Pain strikes through me. I thought I was dealing with it. I thought I was blocking it out, but it turns out I was failing the whole time. My back is on fire and there isn't a damn thing I can do about it.

I arch against the pain, a moan escapes my lips, and I have no choice but to give in to it.

I'm done. I can't fight the pain and I can't fight him.

His arms immediately loosen and he lowers me down. I end up curled up on his lap, my face to my knees again, facing him this time. I'm surprised he let me go so quickly.

Between the strands of my matted hair, I can finally see his expression. So unexpected is the strain around his eyes, the way his lips press together and his forehead creases.

He looks… broken. Even the fire in his eyes is a faint, distant glimmer.

I don't understand it. Why is he looking at me like that?

I close my eyes as he carefully brushes my hair aside, his fingers sweeping through the sweat that broke out on my forehead, disentangling from my hair without pulling it.

He tugs on the blanket, easing it from my frozen fingers, pulling it open at the back first and then finally the front. My buttonless shirt gapes when he nudges my knees. My bra is padded, so it remains in place despite the broken strap across my right shoulder, but it's hanging on by mere threads at the back.

I'm not sure if Raptor intended to break my bra. He was

asking me questions about Striker and all I would tell him, over and over, was:

"Striker Draven is the scariest asshole you will ever meet, so you'd better not make him mad. I don't care what sort of hotshot assassin you are. Striker will annihilate you."

Oh, boy. Raptor did not like that. He showed me how much with his knife.

"What the hell?"

My eyes fly open at Striker's outburst. He's scanning my legs now. I lift my head, my hair falling over my face again before he raises his eyes to mine. The tension in his face has increased a thousand percent.

He has no right being worried about me.

"Why so shocked, Draven?" I ask him. "Are you angry that Raptor did your work for you?"

Fire roars to life in his eyes again. It's so sudden that it takes my breath away.

"I'll kill that sadistic bastard," he says.

His reaction is much bigger than I was expecting, much more volatile. A promise of violence and he means it. But it can't be because of me... surely?

Without another word, he draws my shirt over my shoulders and I'm so dumbfounded that I don't object, but his focus is on my back, which stings when the air hits it. I drop my head to my knees, giving in to the pain again, closing my eyes as I tell him, "Raptor asked me questions and every question earned a cut, no matter how I answered it. He asked me about everyone, even you, but I didn't tell him anything."

There's a moment of silence before Striker asks, "Can you walk?"

I'm confused. "Where to?"

"My room."

"Why? So you can heal me?" I sigh against my knees. He

healed me once, saved my life, but here I am again. It will never stop in this place. "They'll break me again tomorrow."

There's another pause before his breath tickles my forehead and his lips brush my temple, the lightest kiss. "They'll never break you, Peyton."

I nearly scream. His voice is soft, his touch is soft, but the impact of both is like ripples of flame through my mind and body, all the way to my toes.

I try to catch my breath, trying to process the fact that he kissed my forehead, trying to process the fact that... it felt more than good.

For a second, it chased away my pain.

I don't know if he's aware that his eyes are so full of power, it's in full view. When he touched his lips to my face just now, I felt my power burst to life. Just like when we fight, but so much stronger despite how brief and light his kiss was.

I shiver.

Does he have the power, somehow, to heal me?

A muscle in his jaw clenches, but he moves very carefully, as if he's afraid I'll break. Or maybe run. He cups the back of my head and I know he's simply repositioning himself to help me up, but the shiver still running through me is overwhelming.

I need more of him.

His eyes widen when I lean closer. "Striker would you... do something for me?"

He freezes as if he doesn't want to move.

I can't believe what I'm asking him when I say, "Would you... kiss me... properly this time?"

My heart is in my throat. I've never asked a guy to kiss me before. Never wanted to kiss a guy before. Never thought I'd ask Striker Draven, of all people.

His forehead puckers. "I don't think that's a good idea."

He's right, but I need to know if what I felt was real, if it was the spark that I think it could be. "I know it isn't but I think you can help me."

He shakes his head, a firm *no*. "I can help you by getting you to my room and treating these wounds."

"Of course." What the hell was I thinking? He's probably regretting kissing me to begin with. I rise, not caring that the blanket falls away from me, exposing me and all my wounds. "I'm not worth your time."

His response is sharp. "That's not what I said."

My forehead creases. I'm surprised by his instant denial.

He hurries to speak. "I mean... it *is* what I said. But you can't... You can't make decisions like that right now..."

I stare at him. He's flustered. Really flustered. It's entirely unexpected unless... He wants to kiss me but doesn't think he should.

I consider how carefully he's avoided me, the lengths he's gone to so that he didn't break his promise.

What if... he actually cares?

It's a possibility that is shocking, striking, and... may the ancients help me... I want it so badly.

He is fierce, taking control again. "You're hurt and you're coming with me."

He scoops me up in a way that doesn't hurt me and for the first time, I allow myself to relax into it, taking warmth from the physical connection as I tuck my head to his chest and slide my arms around him.

He carries me to his room and places me on his bed, gently covering me with the blanket before he busies himself with the medical kit, apologizing before he cleans the cuts on my chest and back.

It stings like hell, but I take the pain, watching his every move. Every gentle touch. Especially the way he focuses on the task at hand, as if his life depends on it.

I didn't lie to Raptor. Raptor is the most sadistic man I've ever come across, but Striker is a fury I've never beheld.

Yet, here he is, fussing over me, trying to figure out how to treat my wounds when he has nothing left in the kit to help me. He sifts through the box as if he's hoping something will magically appear.

I reach out to stop him, touching his hand. "Striker? There's nothing more you can do."

He doesn't push me away, his fingers flexing around mine as he jostles the kit's contents with his other hand. His touch on my hand is warm… comforting…

"You've done enough," I whisper, sliding out of the blanket.

There's only one thing I want, and I have to be brave enough to ask for it. Or maybe I'll just tell him I'm going to do it.

Before he can react, I lift myself up off the edge of the bed, lean across the short distance where he sits in the chair, and press a kiss to his cheek. Touching him like this makes my heart race, but in a good way.

I nearly lose my nerve, but the way his breath catches when my lips brush the corner of his mouth gives me hope.

I whisper, "I'm going to—" *Kiss you.*

"No." The flame in his eyes, his power, roars to life. His hand closes around mine. He can't know what I was going to say. The quick look he gives the door tells me he thinks I'm asking to leave.

I allow myself to believe that he doesn't want me to go. He fought so hard to bring me to his room.

I pull back a little. "Striker, you don't—"

"No." His arm circles my waist, capturing me and pulling me close. Whatever his power is, it's like fury consuming him, a powerful instinct. Even so, he only pulls my lower half close against his, his arm across the top of my hips avoiding my wounds.

He doesn't want me to go.

He doesn't want to hurt me.

But judging from the press of our lower halves, he definitely wants to do something else.

My cheeks flame. "Striker, I—"

"No."

Oh, dear ancients, I've never had sex, don't even know where to start, but all I can think about is wrapping my legs around him.

Searching his fiery amber eyes, I allow myself to recognize the look he's giving me.

Dear gods of hell, he's promising me the world.

He has no idea I want to take it all.

I can't help the smile that breaks across my face. "Will you let me finish?"

His gaze narrows, his chest thrumming as he growls, "Maybe."

I dare to brush his jaw with my fingertips, testing whether he'll let me get that close. When his gaze softens, I try again, "I'm going to..."

I glance up at him, wait for him to interrupt me again. When he doesn't, I take a deep breath. "I'm going to kiss you now, Striker Draven. Is that okay with you?"

The fire in his eyes leaps seconds before he tilts his head to mine, his lips like a brand.

I inhale the warmth of his mouth, drown in the shape of his lips, fitting my own to his. The energy coursing from him to me is like a livewire.

The pain in my chest eases, the sting in my back soothes, but my wounds are the last thing on my mind right now.

I sense his restraint—the care he's taking not to overwhelm me—and it drives me mad. I press up against him, wanting more from his kiss and not knowing how to ask, my fingers finding the back of his neck and curling into his hair.

Maybe I make a sound, I don't know, but he suddenly shifts,

his kiss deepening, coaxing my lips apart, his tongue finding mine in a way that makes my legs wobble.

A moan thrums in the back of my throat. Energy courses through me, stronger and brighter than any I felt when we fought each other. The fury of his kiss strikes a match inside me and my body responds, heat washing through my arms and legs, my chest, my head.

My breathing is rapid, my hands seeking his back, tugging at his workout shirt, finding the bare skin beneath it.

Striker lifts me up against him, his fingers stroking up my spine, his palms a burning brand. I arch into his touch, drawing more from his kiss than I ever dreamed possible. An intense need builds inside me as his fingertips skip up across my shoulders and down again and then—

The back of my bra snaps and we both startle.

Striker draws back as if he's shocked. "I didn't do that, I promise you."

I know he didn't. The damn thing was cut to pieces at the back, holding on by threads.

But the moment he draws his chest away from mine, the only pressure keeping my broken bra cup upright is gone. It slips to the side, completely exposing my breast.

With a flicker of the muscle in his jaw, he fixes his gaze firmly on my face. His voice is husky, barely controlled. "Kissing you is one thing. Going further is not wise."

He strokes my back as he speaks, his thumbs grazing my skin. Despite his shift away from me, he hasn't moved far.

I can barely form coherent thoughts, let alone speech. Carefully pulling my broken bra from my shoulders, I cast it aside without moving from the circle of his arms.

Making my movements slow, I slide his shirt from the front of his shorts. The material is smeared with my blood now, so I pull it carefully up his chest before pressing my bare torso to his and wrapping my arms around him.

I sigh against his skin, inhaling sweat and cedarwood, an intoxicating mix. The touch of his skin against mine is feeding a deep need inside me.

I need to connect with him.

His heart thuds in my ear. *Ba-bam, ba-bam, Ba—*

Silence.

And then it resumes.

He folds his arms around me, dropping his chin to the top of my head, but he's tense and I'm not sure why until he asks, "Why isn't this hurting you?"

I don't understand it yet—I want answers too—but all I know is that I've healed.

A challenge enters my voice. I tilt my head back to meet his eyes. "Why don't you take a look and see?"

The crease in his forehead deepens. "You're inviting me to look at you."

I've never been so sure of anything in my life. "I am."

He pulls back to cup my face in his hands, our lower halves still plastered against each other's, his gaze burning mine, but not lowering. "You're playing with fire, Peyton."

I can't help the challenging smile crossing my lips. "I'm aware."

A slow smile eases the tension in his eyes. His fingertips graze my chin and then my neck, sliding down to my shoulders, his thumbs extending to play across my collarbones, all the while maintaining eye contact, but his expression becomes perplexed.

His gaze lowers and his focus is not on my naked breasts. In fact, the way he's holding his hands—out and parallel to my body—is deliberately shielding them from his view.

His forehead creases. "What happened to your wounds?"

The edges of his pinky fingers ease across the top of my breasts, his expression telling me he's completely baffled. I am too. All I know is that kissing him triggered something powerful inside me.

"You've healed," he says, pulling me close to lean over my shoulder and see my back, his touch shifting to my shoulder blades as he checks me over. "You're all healed, but how?"

He returns to my front, still searching for the wounds that were there moments ago. When his thumbs graze down the side of my chest, I sigh and close my eyes. "You can check me over as long as you like, Striker. The cuts aren't coming back."

He suddenly growls, making my eyes fly open. "Answers can wait."

I guess he wasn't as distracted as I thought.

"Peyton," he says, leveling his gaze with mine, his palms resting resolutely on my waist. "I'm done being a gentleman. You either want more or you don't, but I need to know which."

A shiver races through my body, making my toes curl. It's probably the worst decision of my life, but I do want more.

We're terrible for each other, we make each other mad, but when I'm in danger, he's there, ready to fight with me when I need him to. Ready to be a despicable jerk when it helps me. Ready to pick me up and take care of me when I'm too proud and stubborn to ask for help.

I didn't think I'd survive five months at Bloodwing.

Now that Raptor's here, I might not survive another. I don't want to waste another day pushing away moments of happiness because I'm afraid of making myself vulnerable to someone.

I can tell myself it's lust. Striker told me I'm playing with fire and, so help me, I want all the fire he's offering.

I step up to him, raise myself onto tiptoes, and join my mouth to his.

He responds with a groan, wrapping his arms around me and hoisting me up against him, drawing my legs around his hips. The heat from his chest and arms burns across my torso and back as his fingers splay across my skin.

Instead of returning me to the bed, he turns, nudges his chair out of the way, and strides to his desk, sitting me on its edge as he continues to kiss me.

His lips are warm and tantalizing, drawing across my cheeks and chin and down my neck as his fingertips play across my back, exploring the shape of my spine and shoulder blades, the curve at the base of my neck, then my collarbone and the space between my breasts.

I gasp as his lips follow his hands, dropping kisses all the way to my stomach, but he avoids my most sensitive places as he takes his time exploring my stomach and the tops of my hips, his hands finally finding the hem of my skirt and sliding along the tops of my thighs before descending all the way to my ankles.

His fingertips skip along my calves and curl around my ankles before he positions my legs around his waist again. He presses closer, his lips returning to mine.

I draw on every shred of my sanity when he unzips my skirt but leaves it in place.

An intense need grows in my center, only getting stronger the longer he avoids touching me. I drag at his shirt, breaking our kiss to pull it all the way over his head this time, trying to get what I need from pressing against him, naked skin on naked skin.

He draws back to meet my eyes for a beat. I thought he was in control, but the wild flames in his amber eyes tells me he isn't.

When I press my hand to his chest, his heartbeat is wild and erratic, thudding hard.

Running my hands through his dark hair, I search his eyes for a reason. I remember the way he picked me up when he brought me into his room, the power he keeps under control, the way his eyes promise me a sort of wild freedom.

I whisper against his lips, "Stop holding back, Striker."

For a second, fear strikes through his expression, shocking me with its intensity.

Striker Draven is never afraid. Why now?

He dips his head and his kiss changes. Intensely hungry. His hands grip my hips, dragging me hard up against him as his tongue finds mine, tasting every part of my mouth and sending my head into a spin.

When his palms drag across my ribs to stroke my breasts, my body responds with a fury of its own. I arch against his hands, wanting more, wanting everything, a moan growing in the back of my throat.

The heat from his body increases, a fiery edge that scorches my hands as I flex my palms against his back. I press against him, trying to remove my underwear at the same time, but it's impossible.

He smiles against my mouth, one hand leaving my breast and descending to halt my struggle. His forefinger hooks over the top of my underpants.

There's a snap, a rip, and the material separates. I don't know how he did it and I don't care. All I know is that I must be lost because I don't want to slow down.

When his hand slides between us and his thumb brushes across my sensitive center, I shiver so hard that I rock against him.

With another fiery kiss planted on my lips, he reaches for his shorts, swaying back from me to remove them and kick them to the side. I drag his hips forward in the same way he gripped mine, growling against his mouth when I can't tug down his underpants because...

Because... *What the hell?*

I swallow a shriek. He jolts, his reflexes kick in, and he grabs my hand—the one that just scratched him.

He wrenches my hand into view and we both freeze.

Sharp claws extend from each of my fingers. My fingernails

have turned crimson and sharp. My breathing becomes wild for all the wrong reasons.

I have claws!

I try to pull away from him, but he won't let me go.

His voice is a husky growl. "Your power is manifesting."

My breathing is rapid. I'm starting to panic, but a shockingly fierce smile grows on his lips.

He elongates his fingers next to mine, easing up his grip. "Look, Peyton."

I gasp as his fingernails extend into claws, blackening and sharpening like mine.

Panic flips to excitement, thrumming through me. "Are we the same?" I search his face for answers. "Am I like you?"

His smile becomes intense. "There's only one way to find out."

I've heard of supernaturals who experience significant shifts in their development when they have sex. Some supernaturals bond with their partners. Others discover greater power.

Intense physical contact with Striker has triggered my power in many ways ever since I got here—from giving me speed and strength to causing me to levitate to healing me—and now I have claws.

I'm terrified of what I'll find out the further we go, but I'm ready for it.

He draws my wrist to his cheek, nuzzling the sensitive skin of my palm before trailing kisses all the way down my arm. I arch against his mouth, drawing him back to me.

Hooking my fingernail across the band of his underpants, I bite my lip with a smile and prepare to tear them just like he tore mine.

He growls against my mouth, snaking his arm around my backside and drawing me closer, an invitation that I can't ignore. As soon as the material parts, there will be nothing between us.

Just as I move, he suddenly tenses. His hand closes over mine, stopping me. He draws back to see my face, his breathing barely under control, but his eyes are suddenly narrowed.

"Wait… Wait…" He shakes his head as if he's trying to think. "You're manifesting."

I smile, attempting to ignore the sudden worry springing to life inside me. "We already determined that."

"Yes, but you're manifesting *now*." He grips my upper arms before he slides his hands firmly to mine, holding my fingers up again, forcing my claws to splay between us. "Why are you manifesting now?"

"I don't… I don't know. Does it matter?"

"Yes! It matters." His voice is a growl, but not a husky growl. An angry one. "Is it me? Or is it sex?" He searches my eyes. "If it were me, you would have manifested like this before now. So it has to be sex. But you're Unknown. You've never manifested before, so…"

My cheeks flame. *Damn*. Here comes the virgin talk I wanted to avoid.

He'll get to the truth one way or another, so I take a deep breath. "I've never done this before."

The stillness that descends over him makes my heart sink. I know that humans count their first time as a big event.

Actually, most supernaturals do too, but I hate that he's looking at me like I'm a completely different person now. As if it means he has to treat me like I'm made of porcelain. Like he can't touch me the way he wants to. Like he shouldn't have touched me the way he did.

He pulls away from me, but I grab his hand. "It doesn't change anything. It doesn't change what I want."

He whirls back to me, prying my hand from his. His accusation hits me hard. "You should have told me."

"Why does it matter?" I respond to his anger with my own. "I could have had sex a hundred times before. This would still be the first time with you."

"It matters because you shouldn't be messing with me your first time. You shouldn't be fucking on a desk your first time." He runs his hand through his hair. "How the hell is this possible?"

I stare at him. Is he seriously asking me why I've never had sex? "Guys weren't exactly lining up to date me, Striker."

"Yeah, well, they were smart."

I inhale a breath, but it's all I can do. I try to process his sudden rejection, but I'm numb and just as suddenly incoherent. "I thought… maybe… you…"

His eyes narrow to dangerous slits. "What, Peyton? You thought there was something between us?"

A storm grows inside me. I know what I felt. I know what I saw in his eyes. There's a connection and it's more than lust. "I know what I feel."

My declaration makes him freeze like stone. His silence scares me. His cold, indrawn breath scares me more. "Don't get attached to me, Price."

The way he calls me by my last name makes me shiver. I fight the moan building in my throat. He shouldn't be able to make me feel so bad. I should be tougher, but he may as well have sliced my heart in half.

Unexpected physical pain claws through my chest. It makes my head ache and my eyes fill with tears I don't want him to see.

He doesn't have to say anything else—I'm already hurting, already pulling away—but he goes on. "We can fuck, but that's all this is."

I was sure there was more between us just now, a spark of something good. I thought I saw it when he picked me up in my room. I was sure I heard it in his voice when he told me they'd never break me, when he flipped through the medical kit searching for something to help me, when he touched me and his palms softened against my skin.

But maybe helping me was obligation and touching me was lust… and caring about me never came into it.

My hair falls over my eyes as my shoulders slump, the long strands tracking across my naked chest. All I see now are the claws on my hands.

They manifested when I felt the connection between us, but they haven't gone away. Actually… my claws are stronger, as if the more harshly he treats me, the more furious my power grows.

I'm such an idiot. This is Striker Draven. He never lied to me about his intentions or who he is. I'm the one who was lying to myself. He's an asshole and I dreamed up a different Striker for all of two seconds.

Well, that's over now.

A deep cold seeps into my arms and legs, a growing numbness. My arms drop to my sides, as if I don't care anymore. I slide off the desk. My skirt falls back around my thighs as I zip it up. The movement releases my torn underpants, which slip off the desk and hit the floor at my feet. I leave them where they lay.

Striker stands his ground as I take a step toward him, my head held high.

He isn't afraid of me—he's never afraid of me—not even when I tap my sharp foreclaw against his chest and line up my other claws around the location of his heart.

A wary light enters his eyes. He tenses, ready to act, but he still isn't afraid.

"One day, I will rip out your heart, Striker Draven," I whisper. "I'm sure you'll survive without it since you already do."

I drag my claws across his chest hard enough to scratch him

as I spin and stride from his room, pulling the door open without pausing.

I'm still naked from the waist up, but I only care to cover up my claws, folding them inside my fists.

I needn't have worried. Collin and Colby are nowhere to be seen.

Covering the distance to my room, I set my mind on finding a new uniform and taking a shower before afternoon classes.

I need to wash off the reminder of Striker's hands and how far I nearly went.

How far I can't go again.

25. STRIKER DRAVEN

*P*eyton's claws leave deep red welts across my chest as she stalks from my room, but nothing compares to the painful roar inside my mind.

My beast shouts at me, his rage like a hot lash. *What the hell did you do?*

I clench and unclench my fists, digging my claws into my palms until they bleed. My shoulders slump. *This isn't love.*

Like hell it isn't, my beast roars. *Kaitlyn messed you up so badly, you can't tell the difference between love and lust anymore.*

I shout back inside my mind. *I don't love Peyton!*

His growl is deep and raw. *She offered you more than anyone ever will, and you threw it back in her face. You hurt her.*

My heart is beating too fast. My body is out of my control. Peyton's underwear is scattered around my room—her bra on my bed, her underpants on the floor. Both items of clothing are torn up, like the look on her face when I told her she meant nothing to me.

I couldn't take her to the bed because that's where Kaitlyn always wanted to go. I held back when I touched Peyton because that's how Kaitlyn liked to be touched.

But Peyton... she wanted all of me—all the fire and rage— and the look in her eyes and the heat from her body told me she would give me back the same.

That doesn't mean she's my match. My beast is wrong. He's wrong about Peyton and how I feel about her.

I have to run, hit something, bloody myself up.

I grab a pair of track pants and pull them on at a run before I charge down the corridor. The other students will be at lunch now. The garden and the electric fence will be all mine.

Hurling myself down stairs, I burst through the back exit and pull up sharp.

A guy my age stands in the middle of the combat mat, his arms folded across his chest, his head tilted back so he's looking upward. His gaze is firmly fixed on the wide windows that line the floor of the attic. The very transparent windows.

Damn. He would have seen Peyton leave my room. He would have seen that she wasn't wearing much, but unless he has eagle eyes, he wouldn't have seen her claws.

He's wearing a black T-shirt with jeans and boots. He's not quite as tall as me, but it's obvious he works out. It's also obvious he hasn't bothered to change since he took his knife to Peyton. Her blood splatters his jeans. I can smell it from here.

Perfect. I need someone to fight.

Pale green eyes glitter at me between the strands of his blond hair as he lowers his line of sight.

He sizes me up as I plow toward him. I take the steps up to the platform and find a position far enough away from him that he won't be able to make any sudden moves, but close enough that I can smash his face in if I want to.

Hell, I didn't hold back when I last fought Peyton but for this guy, I'll let everything loose.

"Striker Draven," he says. "I've heard a lot about you."

The corners of my lips twitch upward. "It's all true."

He raises an eyebrow. "Huh. So 'fucking brutal' is an

accurate description? That's what the compliance officers say about you. Peyton said something similar, except maybe she meant the *fucking* part differently."

He's trying to bait me, but it won't work. "Professor Raptor," I say, making my own assessment. "Likes to cut up defenseless students."

"But I'm not the only one," he replies, circling me. "The cuts I make are visible. The cuts you make aren't."

I hate the accuracy in his statement.

I move while he does, keeping him in my sights at all times. I've lived on this mat for three years. I'm familiar with all its imperfections. I don't even need to look to know that he's about to hit an uneven part of it. Whether or not he loses his balance will tell me how skilled he is.

His foot falls right into the dent and he doesn't flinch, rebalancing as if the indentation isn't there.

I can't help the smile growing on my face. This just gets better. I might actually enjoy this fight.

"How does it feel to be the heir to a fortune you can't touch?" Raptor asks, switching gears. Again, he's trying to throw me, but he has no idea whom he's dealing with.

I shrug, stepping lightly. "My mother's money is in good hands."

He is visibly surprised. "You think your stepdaddy is doing a good job of running the company that should be yours?"

I scoff. "My stepfather? No. My stepsister? Yes."

"Ah, Zara Draven. I met her once. Headstrong. Needs a strong man to handle her. Has a beautiful neck I'd like to wrap my fist around."

He pauses. Again waiting for me to take the bait.

When I don't, he continues. "It's funny how your stepdad took your mother's name when they married and not the other way around. Most people think he's your biological father, but he and your stepsister have no more Draven blood than I do. It makes me wonder… Did he decide to kill your mother before or after they were married?"

Raptor watches me carefully, but I don't flinch.

Dear Daddy told me what he did on the day he had me committed to this place. The day I should have taken control of the Draven fortune—the fortune he held in trust for me until I turned twenty.

My magical repression gave him the excuse he needed to trigger the incapacity clause. Until I'm "cured," I'm legally denied the right to control my own inheritance. Meanwhile, he can do whatever he wants with it.

I was three years old when Mom married him. I gained a sister I love but lost my mother a year later in a freak car accident that was supposed to kill us both.

I survived. Mom didn't.

That's how I know that I will never leave Bloodwing alive.

My stepfather sent me here to die so he can finally seize control of the Draven empire. He didn't expect me to live this long and I'm certain he's becoming impatient about it.

I switch gears as quickly as Raptor did. "What about you Professor? They call you The Specialist out in the real world, don't they?"

A disgruntled crease forms on his forehead. I guess I stole his thunder.

"I'm sorry," I say. "Were you building up to a big reveal? I already know you're an ex-assassin." I switch direction and circle toward him, throwing him off-track. "Most assassins don't last long once they're excommunicated. Without Lady Tirelli's protection, you're a dead man."

The flare of anger in his eyes tells me I've hit a nerve.

"That's all you are," I say. "A man."

He narrows his eyes at me. "And what are you, Draven?"

He stops stepping around the mat, relaxing his shoulders in a way that tells me he's nearly done talking. "Trained in martial arts and boxing, but not football because they wouldn't let you on the field. You took to cage fighting for two years after high school. You learned how to fight dirty. Hurt or be hurt. So, which are you: monster or man?"

I smile. "How about both?"

I dart inward and clip his chin. He barely winces, but I didn't expect him to. My goal is to figure out how he likes to fight and to test his strength, but more than that, I need to get myself thrown in the pit.

I can't sleep near Peyton tonight.

He retaliates with an angry punch to my cheek and another to my side, throwing both with enough effort to hurt me. I exhale the air from my lungs as if he winded me worse than he actually did before I let him follow up with a kick to my chest.

I fake a backward stumble that makes him snarl.

"Not so tough," he says, looming over me as I drop to my knee, clutching my chest.

His knee collides with my face, busting my lip, and his fist rapidly collides with my temple, splitting skin as I fly backward.

Blood spills down my face. I taste copper in my mouth, spitting it out as I attempt to rise up on my hands and knees.

The vicious kick he lands in my side with his boot knocks my ribs around. It hurts, but I welcome the pain.

I want blood. I'm happy to see it drip onto the mat.

I'm vaguely aware of figures running toward us as I push up onto my knees, my torso rising just in time for Raptor's boot to cut across my shoulder, kicking me flat on my back, my legs twisted at an awkward angle.

Lucinda rushes to the side of the mat. "Striker!"

But Joseph's close behind her, shouting at her while he drags her away, hustling Bree with her. Lachlan grabs Ashley, who is turning pale before my eyes. That same strange glow is starting around her hair as if she's preparing to launch herself at Raptor and fight him herself.

Are they actually trying to come to my defense right now?

I came out here to beat myself up. I'm happy that Raptor's doing it for me.

But I won't have anyone else get hurt on my account. I've got enough red in my ledger already.

I raise my eyes to Lucinda's as she struggles against Joseph's hold. He's tense, worried, even more so when Raptor wraps his hand around my throat and lifts me up by my chin. The other students aren't used to seeing someone beat me.

Raptor leans in close. "You know, I have a new theory about what Peyton is. If I'm right, you just messed up your only chance to be with her. She'll only give her heart once. Come to think of it… maybe I'll give it a shot. She's the embodiment of violence. And she's got legs that could straddle me for days."

He knocks his knuckles against the same split above my eye and I don't fight back when he drops me to the mat with a disgusted grunt.

He's right that I blew it with Peyton.

If she's smart, she'll never give me a second chance. But he's an idiot if he thinks she won't kill him if he touches her that way.

A laugh bubbles through my lips and a smile grows on my face as I draw to my feet. I can't imagine how fucked-up scary I look right now, blood running down my face, seeping between my teeth, one eye shut.

But, hey, I only need one eye to see and the other works just fine.

Raptor stares at me, pausing as I grin at him.

I choke on my own blood, spitting it out at my side. "Fucking brutal, huh? Did you think they were exaggerating?"

Alarm shoots across his face, but he's too slow.

I fought in cages for two years, learned every trick in the book and then some. I move at full speed, putting all my strength behind my fists.

Crack. One fist to his face, the second to his shoulder, the third an uppercut to his jaw. My foot smashes into his chest and he flies backward, airborne and spinning until he hits the ground.

Blood streams down his face as he glares up at me from hands and knees.

I don't give him time to get up, barreling into him, lifting and throwing him against the nearest practicing post. His back hits it with a nasty *crack.*

He drops to the ground, but I'm already leaping from the mat, covering the distance as he throws his hands up to defend himself. He eats a barrage of fists as I smash his hands, his head, his shoulders against the post, a roar screaming from my throat.

Angry shouts from behind me don't even register, but the lashes around my hands do. A stream of magic suddenly hits me from all sides as compliance officers rush to take up position and Headmistress Osprey shrieks orders, her wand raised, an unbreakable chain of magic slapping around my arms and chest, dragging my hands behind my back.

"Draven!" she screams.

I struggle against the chains, but I don't call for the beast because this is what I wanted. Now they'll send me to the pit and I can sleep as far from Peyton as possible.

Osprey continues to scream at me so loudly, I can't distinguish what she's saying until finally I separate the words I want to hear. "Take him to the pit!"

But Raptor lifts his hand, spitting blood as he speaks. "No! Send him back to the attic. Let him sleep in the room next to Peyton's. Striker Draven will torment himself enough."

Osprey looks confused—it's hardly a punishment in her eyes.

"No." My objection betrays me more than anything else I could have said.

Osprey's eyebrows rise. "No?" She looks perplexed, but as long as she thinks it hurts me it will be good enough for her. "Very well. Take him back to his room."

Raptor smiles through the blood on his face, gripping the post to help himself stand. "Then let's see about getting another beast for the pit. One Striker can't kill."

The compliance officers drag me past the other students while my hands are still bound. I'm relieved to see that Lucinda and Ashley have stayed well away.

I allow the officers to shove me inside the building and force me up the stairs.

When we reach the attic, Peyton emerges from the bathroom at the end of the hall, her hair dripping down the front of her fresh shirt. Her quick gaze takes in the blood covering one side of my face, my shut eye, my split lip, and the blood splatter across my bare chest, but she doesn't react as the officers push me into the room.

Releasing me from the magical bindings, Collin shouts in my face, "Stay here until the morning!"

He slams the door behind me, leaving me in silence.

Stumbling to the door, I'm careful not to leave a bloody handprint across the picture of Zara and me when we were kids as I slide to the floor.

I listen for Peyton's soft footfalls, the smallest vibrations in the wooden floor. She doesn't return to her room, pausing outside my door instead.

I want her to knock.

I'll tell her to come in.

I want to tell her... I don't know. Tell her that I'm sorry. Tell her she shouldn't get mixed up with me. Tell her to walk away. Tell her she doesn't need my shit in her life.

Her footsteps move on and I'm grateful. And angry. Both.

My beast growls an unwanted opinion. *Fuck your self-destruction.*

I push him away, push harder than I have before.

Am I a monster or a man?

This time, I don't have an answer.

26. PEYTON PRICE

I pace back and forth outside Striker's door.

Despite the rough way they handled him, the compliance officers leave the floor.

What on Earth did Striker do while I was in the shower?

I veer toward the wide windows to take a quick glance below in case I can see anything. On the ground, a ring of teachers surrounds Raptor, who slumps on the grass next to the combat mat. His face and body are covered in blood, but it looks like the teachers are healing him, their spells making him glow.

Striker's all bloody and so is Raptor.

There's only one conclusion I can draw from that.

I glance back to Striker's door. I guess it was inevitable that Striker would take Raptor on, but Striker wasn't due for his lesson for days, so he must have gone looking for the fight.

Sudden pain in my palms tells me my claws have shot out again and are cutting me. It took me the entire time in the shower to force my claws to retract. I'll have to be very careful not to reveal them in front of a teacher or a guard.

I'll also need to be very careful about getting hurt again—

physically, since I can't be more hurt emotionally than I am right now. My healing power was only triggered when I kissed Striker and I definitely can't rely on that option again.

I'm numb and it's protecting my heart, but I'm scared of how I'll feel when I thaw out again.

Squeezing my eyes closed, I focus on the present, my next move.

Making a decision, I stride down the corridor to the stairs, hurrying to the third floor. The compliance officers standing outside each of the bedrooms appear surprised to see me, which makes me think they're aware that Raptor hurt me this morning. Nobody will expect to see me walking around so healthy and unharmed right now.

I suddenly regret putting on a fresh shirt. Maybe I should have stayed a little bloody. But I couldn't very well get around in a shirt with no buttons.

I approach Lucinda's door carefully, finding her inside with Ashley and Bree, their heads together.

She jumps up when she sees me, rushing over to hug me and pull me inside.

"Peyton! You're okay." She quickly closes the door. "When Striker picked a fight with Raptor, we thought Raptor must have hurt you badly."

I'm a little stunned they'd think Striker would come to my defense. My focus quickly shifts to Ashley. Standing beside Lucinda, she's paler than I expected and when I look closely, a single green vein pulses at the side of her neck, her power showing through.

Her eyes are wider than normal, revealing her fear. "What did Raptor do to you?"

I wasn't prepared to give them details. I'm not used to having friends to confide in and it feels like brand new territory—a landscape I don't know how to journey across.

Maybe I should have just grabbed the bag of ice I intended to get for Striker and gone straight back to the attic. I'm afraid to talk about my power, but then... so were Lucinda and Ashley to begin with.

I consider the proximity of the officers outside the room—and the extent to which they can hear us—before I say, "I don't really want to talk about it but... I want you to know that I'm okay now."

They glance at the door and nod to let me know they understand my caution.

"Also..." I take a deep breath, glaring a little, willing them not to react suddenly as I hold up my hand, concentrate, and carefully extend my claws.

Lucinda slaps her hand over her mouth. Ashley's eyes widen and Bree bites her lip hard. None of them makes a sound.

Lucinda quickly gathers herself together, mouthing, *Holy hell.*

I give them all a lopsided smile. Lucinda and Ashley have both made themselves vulnerable to me by allowing me to know about their powers. Bree has spoken about hers, although we haven't figured it out yet. I need to be able to trust them with this.

Lucinda seems to make a decision. "You know... I think I heard there's an old library in the east wing on the fourth floor. We don't have classes there anymore, but Mr. Mallard is always telling us to do more research about the gods. We should check it out. I mean... it's not like we have anything else to do, right?"

"Except wait for Raptor to beat us up," Bree adds.

She gives me a shrug and angles her eyes at the door. She's right. We can't sound too keen about study right now, but Lucinda's suggestion is a good one. We need to start looking for clues about what we are and not only for Bree, but the other students too.

I ask Ashley a careful question before I turn to leave. "How was your walk this morning?"

Ashley smiles, her eyes lighting up with a satisfied glow as she tucks her hair behind her ear. "Riveting. Some might say the roses were so beautiful, they looked as if they were frozen in time."

I grin at her before I wipe my face clean, open the door, and head to the ice chest.

Scooping a large helping of ice cubes into a clean cloth, I tell myself it's not because I care about Striker. I've left him to his pain long enough to prove that.

I just don't want to stare at his swollen face in class.

Tying the ends of the cloth together, I carry the ice pack to the attic and drop it outside his door loudly enough that he'll hear it. Then I saunter away. Whether or not he retrieves it before it melts is up to him.

It's difficult sitting beside Striker in Magical Instruments class the next day.

The area around his eye is swollen and his face is more bruised than I've ever seen it. The ice pack was gone this morning, but I don't know if he took it inside before it melted.

Now Ms. Sparrow stalks into Magical Instruments class, her gaudy red hair even brighter, making me wonder if she's attempting beautification spells that keep backfiring. A bundle of wands float in the air behind her, quickly dispersing among the other students.

I wait for mine and so does Striker. They replaced his broken one a while ago, but today, Ms. Sparrow doesn't allocate the replacement to him.

A slight crease appears on his forehead when Ms. Sparrow starts giving instructions without handing either of us wands.

I stare at her, but she ignores us. Once she's ordered the class to attempt a spell that is supposed to move the crystal across the desk, she turns and heads in our direction.

She slowly pulls a wand from her belt and places it with a flourish across the space between our desks, its tip resting on my desk and its base on Striker's.

It's Kaitlyn's wand.

I cast my hatred at the damn thing. Raptor has to be behind this. He told me his job is to find out all our secrets and discover our weaknesses. He already seems to know everything about our pasts. He'd be sharing his knowledge with the other teachers, informing them of the best ways to get under our skin.

Without another word, Ms. Sparrow turns and saunters back to the front of the class, ignoring us again.

I stare at the wand, imagining all the things I want to do with it.

Snap it. Stomp on it. Or maybe... catch another glimpse of past Striker, the person he was before he became a complete asshole.

No. I have a better idea.

My hand darts out, grabbing the wand before Striker's palm lands on the table seconds after mine. His fist thuds my desk and his angry eyes meet mine for a second before he withdraws again, fixing his gaze on the front of the class.

I'm not sure what he intended to do with it, but I know exactly what I'm going to do.

My fist shakes. Memories assault me, but I fight them, all of Kaitlyn's cruel, manipulative thoughts. All of Striker's pain. I struggle to focus through the memories to concentrate on my forefinger as it rests on the wand.

With a deep breath, I allow the tiniest tip of my foreclaw to rise.

The small surge of power through my finger helps the assault on my mind to ease. I'm surprised. I assumed my ability to catch a glimpse of thoughts and feelings when I touch an object would be completely out of my control, but it seems I was wrong about that.

Maybe I can control this after all.

As much as I want this wand out of my hands as soon as possible, I also want to test my abilities. I draw on my power a little more. Kaitlyn's memories recede even further when I do.

Every small extension of my claw gives me greater control over the stream of memories until her cold thoughts are merely a tickle at the back of my mind, easily ignored.

With a growing smile, I dart a glance at Ms. Sparrow's back to make sure she isn't looking.

Striker's glare suddenly burns into me. I sense his gaze on my hand, drawn to my claw as if he can't look away.

I run my fingernail in quick, deft strokes across the wand, etching deeply into it before I place it, carefully balanced, between our two desks in the same position that Ms. Sparrow left it.

A sideways glance tells me Striker is reading what I scratched into the wand's surface.

Peyton woz here.

There's a pause.

Then a deep rumbling sound makes me glance up despite myself.

Is he laughing?

Not with humor. A bitter smile spreads across his face before he winces, his hand darting to his swollen lip as he looks away.

Yeah. I'm here, and no matter how much you hurt me—no matter how much I get hurt in this place—I'll fight back with everything I've got.

27. STRIKER DRAVEN

*P*eyton promised to tear out my heart and that's what she's doing, scratch by careful scratch.

I stare at Kaitlyn's wand, a bitter laugh at the back of my throat, taking in the way Peyton etched her own name into it like a brand, laying her own identity over the top of it.

It's Peyton's wand now and she'll do whatever the hell she wants with it.

Last night, she brought me ice. She dropped it at my door and I heard the message in the slap of cold against the floor. She has the power to leave me in pain. She has the power to end it. She'll choose whichever suits her.

She catches my eye before she faces forward again, the chill in her eyes telling me I'd better watch my step.

Damn. I love the way she hates me.

The more she pushes at me, the more I want to reach out and drag her chair across the distance.

But I won't. Not yet.

Somehow, I have to find a way to mend the broken bridge between us because, like it or not, my beast was right.

She's my match.

28. PEYTON PRICE

strange calm descends over the Academy over the next week.

The teachers are more subdued in the classroom, but I catch sight of them whispering to each other in the hallways, their gestures urgent before they wipe their faces clean again.

Lucinda is second to have her lesson with Raptor but she emerges unharmed and slightly perplexed.

"He asked me a bunch of questions," she tells me. "But it was nothing, really. Where did I go to school? Who were my friends? That one was easy—nobody and no one. He asked me about my parents, too. Where do they work? What supernatural species are they? Basic stuff."

"Did he offer you a weapon?"

Her forehead crinkles. "He put an apple on the table and left it there. He didn't talk about it or anything. I don't get it. He didn't hurt me. There must be something going on."

I force a laugh. "So we should freak out because he *didn't* hurt you."

She bumps my shoulder as we hurry to gym class. "You know what I mean."

"Yeah, I do." Before Raptor arrived, Striker told me that the teachers were going easy on us, but he didn't know why.

We received the gift of Raptor at the end of that lull. The quietness within the Academy halls feels the same now—the teachers are waiting for something.

"It's too quiet," I say.

Lucinda pushes on the back door and I follow her into the sunlight. "We should make the most of it. If we get cleaning duties, let's go to the library this afternoon."

We discovered that Maintenance class was the perfect time to scope out the fourth floor in the east wing. On the day we were told to clean the floors, we headed up there and found that Lucinda was right about the library. It's at the end of the hall, all four walls lined with bookshelves filled with old books. Lucinda and I took our sweet time scrubbing the floor while Ashley and Bree "dusted" the books under the watchful eye of our compliance officers. The girls quickly flipped through the books before we were ordered to finish up for the day. At dinner that night, they reported that there's a gold mine of information about rare supernaturals in those books.

Now, I give Lucinda a nod. "Good idea. We need all the information we can get."

I pull up short before I run into Striker, who's coming from the opposite direction. We've successfully avoided each other for the last few days, ignoring each other in class when we're forced to sit next to each other. The swelling around his eye is going down and his lip has healed.

The next day, Bree tells me that Raptor put a glass of water on the table while he questioned her. He asked her the same types of questions about her childhood that he asked Lucinda.

"I kept expecting him to throw the cup at me, but he didn't," she says.

Raptor's motivation is baffling, except for one thing that niggles at the back of my mind. Lucinda got an apple. Bree got a cup of water. Both of those objects are marginally connected to the nature of their power. I'm not sure what it says that I got a dagger.

Each of the other girls has their lesson with Raptor that week, followed by each of the guys. I don't hear much from the guys, but I hear stories that there was some new object on the table for each of the girls—never a weapon—and Raptor didn't hurt or threaten them.

I take advantage of the quiet to go to the library whenever I can—mostly only when we have cleaning duties.

Finding out as much as we can about our powers is the key not only to our survival, but also to our ability to fight back. We have the chance to return to the library three more times, stopping our cleaning for longer periods to study the books, a dusting cloth ready in our hands in case we're ordered back to work.

At first, I'm worried that the compliance officers will take action, but they seem more bored than anything else. I guess reading books is hardly rebellion in their eyes. They'd probably be more interested if we started tearing out pages.

Our visits to the library reveal all sorts of rare and unusual supernaturals who have a somewhat humanoid form—creatures like the draugr, which is an undead warrior with blue skin that was feared by the Vikings in ancient times, and the wendigo, which are flesh-eating monsters who roam forests.

Also in the flesh-eating, but not-so-humanoid, category are the so-called Mares of Diomedes—horses that like to snack on humans.

And in the weird and wonderful category is the enenra—a Japanese monster made of smoke and darkness, although it's unclear yet how it hurts anyone.

When my next lesson with Raptor arrives at the end of the week, I'm prepared for anything. He chose me for his special treatment and I'm already building protective layers around my mind, even if I can't protect my body.

I remind myself that he got the upper hand over me because the memories from his dagger overwhelmed me. Well, that, and he hit my head against the wall hard enough to make me pass out. I won't allow that to happen again.

As soon as I step into the room, I seek the table and whatever new object lies on it.

A thick, black rope rests coiled on the wooden surface, frayed at one end, a handle at the other, dotted with silver spikes.

It's a whip.

Great. Now we're into sex toys.

Raptor leans his elbows on his knees as he lounges in the chair. "Welcome back, Peyton."

I step up to the wall at the side of the room and press my back against it. It probably looks like a coward's move but this way he won't be able to circle around me.

He doesn't waste time inclining his head at the table. "Pick it up."

I laugh. "As if."

He lifts his hands into the air in a gesture of submission. "I promise I'll stay right here."

"Your promises aren't worth a thing, Professor."

"Oh, come on, Peyton. I haven't touched a single student this week. Why would I break my pattern with you?"

"Because I'm the beginning and end of the pattern. Starts with violence. Ends with violence."

"Maybe. But what can I do with a whip?"

Again, I laugh. "Strangle me. Lash me. Scare me."

His lips pull down as he nods in agreement. "True, if you crack a whip just right, it's pleasantly startling." He rises from his seat and closes the door, pressing his back against it, studying me from beneath the strands of his blond hair. "I really do want to see you crack it."

There's an air of expectancy around him that makes me shudder as he takes a step toward me. "What will it take to convince you to pick it up?"

It's hard to tell from this distance, but the whip looks like a serious weapon. Sharp silver tips catch the light as I shift to the side. I enunciate my words carefully. "There is no way in hell—"

"I'll do anything you want."

I blink at him in surprise. "What?"

"Anything that I can do right now in this room."

I narrow my eyes. "Can you go to hell?"

"One day. Not right now." His blithe response falls into the silence.

Fear creeps up my spine. I've kept him talking, but I'll run out of sass soon. He can keep me here as long as he likes and one way or another, he'll get what he wants. If I take him up on his offer, I can at least hope for some illusion of safety.

I point to the farthest corner of the room from the table. "Pull the chair to that corner of the room and sit in it. Don't get up until I put the whip down."

Wow, that sounded so wrong. I nearly expect him to reply with, "Yes, madam."

He gives me a snide smile but does what I ask, sitting his butt into the chair, folding his arms, and propping his legs out front in a casual position.

I calculate the steps to the table, assessing all the angles he can attack me from. I'll have a better chance if I grab the weapon fully prepared to fight with it. I approach from the end of the table so I don't stand with my back to him, keeping him in my sights at all times.

Several steps toward it, I pause to check his movements.

He arches an eyebrow at me. So far, he's stayed put, but I don't trust him at all.

Close up, I get a better look at the whip, taking glances at it while I try to keep an eye on Raptor. The weapon looks ancient. Hundreds of years old at least. It could be as long as six feet from handle to tips, but the rope part of it is made from a substance I don't recognize until I peer closer.

I quickly recoil.

It's hair.

But whose?

I shake myself. Just because it's hair doesn't mean the person the hair belonged to died. People cut their hair all the time. It could even be horse hair for all I know. It certainly looks like the strands are thick and course enough.

Sharp, silver points jut out all along the body of the whip, not just the lashes at the end—of which I count three. The handle is long and slender and made of silver metal. It looks light, but I won't know for sure until I pick it up.

Raptor leans forward as my hand hovers over the weapon, a gleam of anticipation entering his eyes. "It took me all week to procure this whip. The cost was astronomical. It had better be worth it."

The threat in his voice is clear: I'd better not disappoint him.

"So that's what you were doing all week," I say. "Waiting for this?"

No wonder he went easy on everyone. I've got to give it to him. He focuses his energy wisely. But if he was waiting for this moment, then that means he has something riding on it...

Something he wants.

The creeping fear in the back of my mind intensifies. I test the weapon by touching my finger to it, prepared to absorb whatever memories are attached to it.

An image fills my mind: a cabin in a forest with a shallow porch.

I take a quick breath before I sink into the memory...

I'm standing in the cabin door while the firelight from a

warm fireplace spills around me. Lamps light the porch, their light glowing in an arc across the clearing around the cabin.

I glide down the front steps as two stealthy figures emerge from the shadows of the surrounding trees—a man and a woman wearing black clothing that conforms to their muscles. The woman carries a katana and the man holds two gleaming daggers.

Whoever's eyes I'm seeing this through, these newcomers are not my friends.

They are both liars.

"Vulture Woman…" I whisper, addressing the woman in a voice that is not my own. "Why have you darkened my door this night?"

With a gasp, I wrench my finger from the whip and step away from it, jolting back to the present at the same time.

I take deep breaths as the image disappears. I can't be sure if I spoke aloud or only in my mind, but the connection with the owner of this whip is so strong…

Raptor leans so far forward that he nearly falls out of his chair. "Take it, Peyton. Pick it up."

I don't trust his motives. Not at all. But I need to know what happened to the woman this weapon belonged to…

My hand slips around the whip, grasping its silver handle. I was right, it's light but sturdy, the perfect weight.

The contact sucks me into the memory again.

The memory repeats and I hear myself ask, "Why have you darkened my door?"

The woman approaching the cabin holds her sword at an angle that tells me she knows how to use it, her footsteps light in the undergrowth.

Her green eyes are rimmed in silver. She doesn't have an aura but her power simmers beneath the surface, stronger than any I've ever felt before.

The man walking beside her is as large as Striker and just as chiseled. He carries his daggers with the confidence of someone who has killed many times before. His eyes are slightly wideset, a crisp and piercing blue, his expression unforgiving.

When the woman speaks again, pain strikes through my mind. I can't tell if it's her pain or mine. "You have something we want," she says.

My mouth opens and I whisper a response to her, forcing sound despite my agony. "What could you possibly want from me? I have nothing to give but pain and torment."

It only makes the silver-eyed woman smile. "Perhaps that's what we want."

Too many lies!

Agony explodes behind my eyes. I have to force the memory down, take control, or my mind is going to break.

Terrified that my claws will show, I grip the handle hard, clench my teeth, and concentrate on my fingers, curling my fingernails inward. My claws draw blood, but it eases the pain in my mind and the image quickly recedes.

With a flicker of movement, Raptor is suddenly beside me, gripping my arm in his big hand so hard, he'll leave bruises.

I raise my eyes to his with a barely human growl. "How did I know you wouldn't keep your word?"

He snarls. "Did you see them?"

I narrow my eyes at his hand. He hasn't made a grab for the whip yet, but it's only a matter of seconds.

"See who?" I ask.

"Don't play games with me, Peyton. Did you see the assassins?"

Assassins. Of course, it makes sense, the way the man and woman moved, the way they held their weapons, their focus pinpoint and remaining only on their target. But why does Raptor care? Why does he need to know?

Raptor shakes me. "Tell me what they look like! Did she have silver rings around her eyes?"

My jaw drops a little. I have no idea why the silver rings around the woman's eyes are important, but the urgency in his voice tells me he really wants to know the answer. In fact, he *needs* to know.

Hell, I'm not going to give him anything.

Except a little smile.

"Do what you will," I say.

His face darkens with anger a second before his fist arcs toward my face. I duck, the whip still gripped in my hand.

His punch sails through empty air.

I dance away from the table into clear space. He'll only beat me if he gets in close and pins me like he did before.

He spins to follow my movements as I back away. Not wasting a moment, he comes after me with deadly intent.

I leap back to narrowly avoid a punch to my stomach as well as his follow up kick. As my arms fly wide, the whip unfurls, lashing through the air, the momentum of my movement flicking it back and then forward.

It wails as it moves, a soft scream in the air.

The deadly tips lick forward, spreading out as they fly. The lowest tip bites his cheek, slicing cleanly through his face from his cheekbone to his ear. He's lucky all three didn't strike him at once.

With a loud curse, he stumbles away from me, grabbing at the bleeding cut, bumping into the table's edge.

I stare in amazement at the weapon.

Oh, this whip. It's like an extension of my arm, effortless, streamlined, deadly.

I've never held a whip before, but it feels… perfect.

His eyes widen as I swing my arm, testing the weapon's weight and speed. It curves above my head with a spine-chilling *whoosh* once, then twice before I extend my aim, crouching a little as I flick it forward.

The three tips scream through the air, a fierce shriek as they speed toward his head and torso fast enough to rip the flesh from his bones.

He ducks and rolls at the last moment. The tips tear through the surface of the table and the air cracks so loudly it sounds like gunshots. Wood splinters fly through the air behind him as Raptor dodges the shards.

To my horror, a smile breaks out across his face as he keeps moving, arcing around the room. "Well, at least I got one thing I wanted."

"What's that, Professor?"

He grins, wide and gleaming, a devilish glint in his eyes. "Confirmation."

Confirmation of what?

Sharp footsteps sound along the corridor. I hold the whip harder, my hand suddenly shaking. The self-satisfied way he stares at me is making me more afraid than if he'd threatened to beat me.

Headmistress Osprey rushes into the room, her fuchsia lacquered nails a garish contrast to the darkness of her curved wand. "Constrain!"

Her fashion sense might be off, but her magic is strong. Osprey's spell thuds into my body all the way from my toes to my head, propelling me back through the air and thumping me hard up against the wall.

I grip the whip in my outstretched hand, the only part of me that's still free, before the weapon succumbs to the spell too.

Osprey jumps out of the way just in time as its tips slice through the air with a whispered scream. The rope and tips thud into the wood, spraying paint chips as it plasters against the wall like some sort of deadly decoration immobilized beside me.

Ignoring me, Osprey strides to Raptor. "Well? Did Peyton see the Fury's final memory?"

He runs his fingertips across his bleeding cheek, checking

the blood on them. "I believe so, but she won't tell me what she saw."

Osprey practically stomps her foot. "Then make her! We need to know what we're dealing with before we can fight back."

Raptor laughs, flicking his hair out of his eyes. "Sure, but it won't be pretty. How badly do you want to keep Peyton alive?"

She throws her face into his, her permed curls flicking out of place with the sharp movement. "I am the Headmistress of this institution. Do whatever you need to do."

I'm struggling to make sense of their conversation. Raptor suspected that I have psychic abilities after I told him I knew that he killed innocent people.

Now, he's given me this whip, which apparently belonged to a Fury. It sounds like he was hoping I'd see her final memory of assassins who, judging by the way Osprey speaks about the Fury in the past tense, must have killed the Fury.

I don't know much about Furies, but I didn't think they could be killed. That either makes those two assassins incredibly powerful, or Osprey is mistaken. The only other thing I know about Furies is that, like gorgons, there are always three of them.

If this whip belonged to a Fury, then that would explain why it looks ancient. Its owner must be hundreds of years old. Or was, depending on whether I believe Osprey.

But what I don't understand is why Osprey and Raptor are so desperate to identify the female assassin. Why are they so afraid of her? Unless they think she's coming after them for some reason.

Now *that* doesn't surprise me. Now that I have this whip in my hands, I'd go after them too.

If I could.

If I wasn't pinned to this wall.

Osprey spins to me, looking me up and down as I glare back

at her. A faint crease appears in her forehead. She jumps when Raptor sidles up behind her, a full head taller than her. Funny how she always looks so tall around everyone else. Except Striker, that is.

"Magnificent, isn't she?" Raptor whispers, his gaze raking up and down my body. "It makes me sad to cut her up."

"Best to do it now," Osprey says. "Her physical strength increases every day. Other than the visions, has she shown any other signs of power? Do you have any idea what she is?"

Raptor is standing just behind Osprey so she doesn't see the sudden look of ridicule he gives her.

A cold chill runs down my spine.

The way he's looking at me... his constant glances at the Fury's whip...

It's like he thinks it's obvious what I am.

If I weren't immobilized, I would shudder.

Does he believe that I'm a Fury?

I don't know enough about them to understand whether it's possible. I struggle against Osprey's magic, suddenly desperate for answers.

Raptor's expression becomes perfectly blank when Osprey turns to him with annoyance. "Well?"

He gives her a shrug. "My guess at this stage is some sort of mage with clairvoyant abilities. A powerful fortuneteller, perhaps."

"Well, whatever she is, information about the assassins is more important to me right now. Get on with it."

She steps back, allowing Raptor to reach into his boot to retrieve the hated dagger. I can't do a damn thing to stop him as he cuts off my top two buttons with a sadistic smile.

Running footsteps make him pause.

Ms. Sparrow blows into the room, her red hair flying like bloody streaks across the air. She's moving so fast that her ankles wobble in her heels.

She snarls, out of breath. "Don't let Peyton scream."

Osprey's annoyance increases tenfold. "What's the problem?"

"We have visitors."

Osprey's brow furrows. "Who?"

"Draven's father and his men."

"They weren't due until tomorrow." Osprey huffs in annoyance. "It doesn't matter. Oliver Draven won't care what happens here. Carry on, Raptor."

Ms. Sparrow's gaze darts to me. "Zara Draven is with them."

"What?" Osprey's hand twitches beside her wand. "Oh, of course. It's her yearly visit with her brother."

Raptor's blade hovers above my chest, clearly impatient, taking glances between the two women. "Why should that stop us?"

Osprey rolls her eyes. "Zara Draven is a demon, but unfortunately, she has a significant soft spot for her brother. She could be a real thorn in our sides while she's here. We can't afford for her to become unhappy. This will have to wait until she's gone."

Raptor's blade presses against my chest, the tip breaking skin. "Can't you put a gag on Peyton? Let me get on with it in silence?"

Osprey scoffs. "How is she going to tell you about the assassin if she can't speak?"

"Well, what about soundproofing this room?"

"Zara goes wherever she wants. Fresh blood on the walls won't go down well."

Raptor curses. "How long will she be here?"

"However long she chooses. We'll have to pick this up after she leaves. In the meantime..." Osprey leans in to me, her washed out eyes conveying a dangerous threat. "Consider your options carefully, Peyton. It would be so much easier if you simply tell us what you saw, don't you think?"

She taps her wand against my wrist, forcing me to release

the whip. Raptor deftly catches it by the handle, testing its weight in his hands.

As Osprey reaches out to tap and release me too, he holds up his hand for her to stop. "Just a moment."

He steps forward, twisting the middle portion of the whip carefully around his hand, positioning it so that the sharp points along its edge face outward like a makeshift knuckleduster.

"The Furies crafted their whips from the tails of flesh-eating horses," he says. "Every part of this weapon is filled with malevolence."

He taps his injured cheek meaningfully with his free hand before he gathers up the handle and the loose tips.

"It's only fair," he says as he arcs his fist at my face.

A careful and deliberate punch.

It's a light enough hit not to cause any structural damage but the skin across my cheek splits painfully.

When I whimper, Osprey grabs Raptor. "No more for now," she says firmly. "I'm sure Peyton will change her mind. After all, why protect someone she doesn't know?"

Why, indeed. I certainly don't owe an assassin any favors. But the thought that someone—anyone—might be gunning for the teachers makes that someone my ally. I'm not going to help Osprey and Raptor evade her.

I drop to the floor when Osprey releases me, my gaze darting to the whip again. The pain in my cheek makes me angry and for the first time since I got here, it dawns on me that I don't cry when I'm in pain anymore.

Now, pain makes me mad.

My anger only intensifies my feelings. I can't explain why, but... I want that whip back. Badly.

"Get to your next class, Peyton," Raptor growls. "Gym, isn't it?"

I draw to my feet, wary of the way he holds the weapon. He doesn't care about Osprey's orders and his posture tells me he'll lash out at any second. A single cut to my cheek isn't enough for him. I'm better off getting the hell out of here and leaving the weapon behind.

Besides, the sooner I get through the day, the sooner I can find a reason to go to the library and find out more about Furies.

I need answers.

Hurrying down the corridor, I take a moment to catch my breath before I descend the stairs.

Movement and sound float up the staircase from the entrance area. The window facing outward at each staircase landing allows me to see the yard, not the front of the Academy, so when I glance out I can't see anything unusual. Just students practicing on the mat like usual.

I take the final flight of stairs carefully. Through the wide open front doors, I can finally see a large black truck and an SUV parked outside. The gate in the background is once again firmly closed.

Men traipse into the building, carrying crates labelled 'uniforms' and 'linen.' Ms. Vulture stands in the entrance directing them where to go, peering at them over her glasses.

I narrow my eyes at the truck outside. It's an awfully large vehicle to transport such small crates.

At the base of the stairs, staying out of the way, but too close to my location for comfort, a man stands waiting with a woman.

The man is tall and thin with olive eyes and sharp cheekbones, his dark hair graying at the temples. I know that not all children take after their parents, but he looks nothing like Striker.

I recognize the woman from the picture taped to the back of Striker's door. She looks like she's in her late twenties, probably three or four years older than Striker. Her tousled black hair is cut short below her ears, accentuating her graceful neck, dark-rimmed olive eyes, and perfect cheekbones. She's dressed casually in tight jeans with heeled boots and a crisp white shirt.

I lean back against the wall, trying to stay out of sight, but the woman turns at the sound of my footfalls. Her observant gaze follows the curve of the cut across my cheek and the bloody smears where I tried to wipe it before quickly descending to the missing buttons at the front of my shirt. The top of my bra is showing. I resist the urge to tug the material together.

I lift my chin. I have few choices in this place. I'll walk around like this for the rest of the day if I want to.

Osprey prances down the staircase behind me. "Out of the way, Price."

She focuses her disingenuous smile on the tall man. "Oliver! Zara! You're a day early. If I'd known, I would have prepared a welcome party."

She plants kisses on each of their cheeks. Despite her order for me to move, all three of them are now blocking the bottom of the staircase. I retreat up a step, considering whether I'll head back up to the attic and change after all.

Oliver Draven gives Osprey an equally insincere smile. "It's a pleasure to see you as always, Isadora."

Zara also nods her head, but her smile is firmly expectant. "Thank you, Isadora. Where is my brother?"

"He'll be here any moment, dear Zara. Why don't I fetch him for you?" Osprey asks.

"Thank you, yes. Bring him to me right away, please."

Osprey pauses, blinking rapidly. It's clear she didn't mean that she would personally get him. She clears her throat. "Well, then. I'll be right back."

I wait for Osprey to move away before I take a careful step.

Just then, one of the crates drops, cracking against the floor, and Oliver strides toward the man, who is trying to gather its contents together again, shouting orders as he goes. He has a big voice for someone so thin.

I focus on disappearing as fast as I can.

Zara's hand snags my arm as I pass by. My instincts kick in and I nearly punch her, but I force my arm to relax, unfurling my fist.

Her gaze darts to my fist and back to my face with an arched eyebrow. If she's a demon, she won't be intimidated.

"The cut on your face is going to scar." She rummages around in the large satchel she carries before she extends her hand. A small tube peeks from her fist. "Here, take this. Striker will have to make do without this one."

Her olive eyes glow a little as she speaks. It could be a trick of the light, but it could also be a sign that she's attempting to use her demonic power of persuasion on me.

For some reason, she really wants me to take her gift.

"That's healing gel," I say, refusing to move. It looks just like the tube from which Striker squeezed the last drops to heal my face that time he fell asleep in my room. "You're the one who brings the medical supplies for him."

She tugs her satchel close to her body again, but not before I spy multiple medical packages in the bag she carries.

I stare at the offered tube, a sense of anger growing inside me. Raising my eyes to her, I'm unable to keep the frost from my voice. "Do you have one of those for every student? We all get cut up on a daily basis, not just Striker."

It's obvious that she doesn't have enough medicine when she flushes pink. I don't care if she feels ashamed. She should.

"I thought not," I say, firmly dismissing her offering. I won't take a single thing from her.

Her hand closes tighter around my arm before I can pull away.

I narrow my eyes at her. She really should let me go or the fist I'm forming will fly at will.

She whispers, "We could be allies, you and I."

Again, her eyes glow, but her power of suggestion may as well be a breeze passing me by.

I step right into her space. Her quick inhale tells me she didn't expect me to become combative. I imagine she thought I'd be so downtrodden, I'd agree to any offer of help.

"You imprisoned your own brother in this place and choose to keep him caged," I say. "We will never be friends."

She has nothing of Striker's physical strength—or mine for that matter.

I easily pull out of her hold and stride away. She's lucky I didn't bloody up her face.

Whatever the hell kind of conscience she has, Zara Draven's money keeps this place going.

She keeps her brother captive inside these walls.

She may as well be Lady Tirelli.

29. STRIKER DRAVEN

I hit the practicing post as hard as I can, waiting for Ms. Hawk to call my name.

I heard the convoy arrive—the clang as the front gate opened—which means my sister's here.

But so is the truck. A day early. I guess Dear Daddy couldn't wait to bring the new beast for the pit.

Zara thinks that the truck contains food supplies, new uniforms, books, and linen. It does to an extent, but only enough that if she opens the back doors to look inside, she'll see crates of supplies piled high to the top.

What she won't see is the covered cage located at the back, inside which a tranquilized creature sleeps.

Last year, the truck contained a harpy to replace the Orthrus I killed. This year, who knows? My father is resourceful. It's definitely something they think I can't kill.

I'm surprised when Osprey herself shrieks my name. "Draven! Inside. Now."

The door slams as she strides away again.

I don't waste time, leaving my post and heading inside and down the corridor. Seeing Zara is like stepping outside the

Bloodwing world for a while, reminding me of what it was like out there.

Halfway down the corridor, I slow down as Peyton walks toward me, her steps purposeful, angry, her head high.

She's barefoot, as we often are here, her long legs strong and slender. I've lost track of her movements over the last week. She and the other girls disappear a lot, especially in the afternoons.

Now, her cheek is bleeding. She fixates on a point past me, but the missing buttons at the top of her shirt tell me everything.

My sister waits only twenty paces away, her expression lighting up when she sees me, but my instincts have already kicked in. I step directly into Peyton's path, forcing her to pull up.

Before I can stop myself, I reach for her face, calling her by her first name. "Peyton?"

"I'm not dying." She punches my hand away, her fist stronger than it ever was before. She told me that I only call her 'Peyton' when I think she's dying. Her eyes flash murder at me as she dares me to raise my hand in her direction again. I'll be the dead one if I try it again.

In the distance, my sister shifts, her smile fading, watching us carefully. I guess she didn't expect to see someone take me on. Or expect me to do more than ignore Peyton as she passed by.

Peyton glances back at Zara. She gives a sudden sigh, deflating a little, her gaze now firmly fixed on my shoulder. "Get out of my way, Striker."

I stay where I am. "You only call me 'Striker' when you want something from me."

Her gaze rises to my lips, but I know it's only because she's hurting more than she's letting on. The cut on her cheek looks vicious. The last time she was hurt, it took a kiss to heal her. How and why that happened is still a mystery to me.

She won't let me help her today. I know that. I just have to get my damn instincts under control.

I step out of Peyton's path, letting her pass, but I regret it straight away. There's only one teacher who likes to mess her up like that. Raptor has left most of the students alone this past week but with the arrival of the new beast, that's about to change.

Peyton is his number one target.

My beast has been very quiet since that day, distant, rarely waking up. He suddenly growls, *You gave up your chance to protect her.*

Ah, there he is, not so quiet after all.

I hate his truths.

I also have no choice but to let Peyton walk away right now. As I watch her go, Zara hurries toward me along the corridor.

I return her fierce hug, dragging my focus away from Peyton to give Zara my full attention. "It's good to see you."

"You, too, Striker." She stands a little below my height, nearly as tall as her father.

She presses a hand to my cheek like a mother would. She's only a few years older than me, but she took on the mothering role after Mom died like it was second nature to her. She supported me in all my decisions, even when she shouldn't have —although she definitely didn't approve of my cage fighting.

She seems satisfied to find me unharmed, but she arches an eyebrow at Peyton's disappearing back. "That's her, isn't it?"

"What are you talking about?"

"The other Unknown."

I start walking along the corridor, remaining casual. "What have you heard?"

"C'mon, Striker, you know Osprey gives Dad weekly updates."

"Right." I fix my gaze on my stepdad. "So you know about The Specialist then?"

She's quiet for a moment. "Yeah. I also heard you gave him a beating. That wasn't wise, Striker."

"Nothing is." I pull up as we reach my stepfather, who waits for us in the entrance. "Sir."

He gives me a disdainful nod. "Striker. You're still alive."

I give him a grin, stepping into his space. He stopped towering over me years ago. "I plan to live longer than you, Dad."

My stepfather has olive eyes like Zara's that glow an eerie green when he accesses his demonic power. He's a lesser demon, certainly not the most powerful, which means he can't possess another person, but he's very good at persuasion, manipulating people into doing what he wants.

It's always been a source of frustration for him that, for whatever reason, he can't manipulate me. Some clever supernaturals these days seek protective spells against demons or carry talismans so they aren't manipulated by demonic suggestion.

Over time, my stepfather's powers have become less useful. Still, he puts his callous heart to good use in the ruthless corporate world, making cutthroat deals that annihilate the competition. It seems to keep him happy.

His lips stretch into a cold smile. "I'm sure you'll appreciate all the supplies I've brought the Academy today."

He means the beast. "Thank you for your generosity, as always."

Zara steps between us. "Okay, then. Striker and I are going to take a walk."

She draws me through the doors into the front garden. I can't help noticing the way the workmen quickly shut the back of the truck.

They won't unload the beast until they have the cover of night. Zara will eat dinner in my room—the only night I'm allowed to eat in there—so she won't be any wiser.

To my surprise, she taps the side of the truck as we pass it. "I'm not stupid, Striker. I know what's inside this vehicle."

I don't often feel anger toward her. She may walk freely in the outside world but her life is primarily dictated by her father. Even so, it's much easier to forgive her if I believe she's ignorant about the way this academy operates.

I've never used an angry tone with her, but it slips out now. "Then you could have stopped them."

Her gaze flashes to mine, a quick assessment. "You're looking at me the same way she did."

"Who?"

"Peyton. When I offered her a tube of healing gel for her face, she told me where to shove it."

I give a short laugh. That sounds like Peyton. "She won't accept help."

"That's not what I mean, Striker. She was disappointed in me. Just like you are now."

I take a deep breath and exhale it out with a non-committal "hmm."

"You have every right to be," she says.

I'm wary of where this conversation is going. There are many topics she and I avoid talking about. Mom's death is number one on the list. My incarceration in this place is second.

We avoid facing truths because if we speak them aloud, our relationship will fall apart. She will become my enemy and I don't want that. My relationship with her is the only one I have that resembles something normal.

I trust her.

Even if I shouldn't.

I quickly change the subject as we approach the rose bushes. "Dad seems surlier than usual."

She runs her fingertips across the tops of the flowers, focusing on them, surprising me when her voice wobbles. "He's in trouble, Striker. Lady Tirelli hasn't been seen in months. Just yesterday, we confirmed that she's disappeared."

I jolt with surprise. "What?" I search her worried eyes. "Do you think something's happened to her?"

"Dad keeps saying she must be in hiding, but I don't believe him."

"Hiding from what?" I ask. "That woman isn't afraid of anything."

"She has something to be afraid of for the first time." Zara lowers her voice to a whisper. "The Assassin's Legion has a new Master."

"I don't see why that matters." I scoff. "Lady Tirelli's never been afraid of assassins before."

"This Legion Master is different. Some say it's a woman."

"Well, then the rumors can't be true. The Legion would never admit a woman to train with them, let alone appoint her as Master." The Legion is the one Faction that is completely male-dominated. The Dominion and the Horde both respect female assassins—welcome them, in fact. But the Legion is brutal. Equality means nothing there.

"I thought so, too, but there are whispers, Striker. I've been reaching out to my contacts in Boston and some say there is a very powerful female assassin living in that city now. More powerful than any before her. We're trying to identify her so that we can figure out..." She clears her throat. "So we can figure out if she's entirely human."

"Assassins are always human," I say.

"Usually."

I study my sister, the way she worries at her lip, the sharp dilation of her pupils that is associated with fear. "What has this got to do with us?"

"Whoever the new Master is, one thing is clear: they're coming after everyone associated with Lady Tirelli. And I mean *everyone*. Dad is Lady Tirelli's weapons supplier. Trucks carrying weapons are no longer making it to their destinations and the storage warehouses are being destroyed. Dad's bleeding money."

My eyes narrow to slits. "You mean *my company* is bleeding money."

She gives me a quick nod. "I'm afraid so."

"You think the assassins are doing it?" I ask.

"They're annihilating Lady Tirelli's organization. She's not around to protect anyone anymore. Dad is their next target."

Despite the damage to Draven Industries, I can't help but take some satisfaction from this information.

My stepfather has flown under the radar for a long time, living under the charade of a respectable businessman. He deals with humans and supernaturals alike and most of them don't know what he really does. "That feels like karma to me."

Her eyes glisten, but not with power. She's suddenly welling up. "I can't disagree with you about that, but… I'm a target too."

"Wait… why?"

She swipes at her eyes with shaking hands, cursing at herself. "My hands aren't clean, Striker. I could argue that I've done what I had to in order to survive. That Dad calls the shots and I have no choice but to go along with everything he does. I only manage the visible operations of the company—the legal operations. But I've stood at his side all this time. I haven't tried to stop him. I didn't try to stop him acquiring the monster in that truck. I didn't try to stop his deals with Lady Tirelli. I'm a *demon*, Striker."

She takes hold of my arm, her voice suddenly urgent. "I'm also a coward. My biggest shame is that I've let you down. Now I'll reap what I've sown."

"No." My voice is a whisper. "I won't let that happen."

She gives me a look like there's no saving me. "You've been a good brother to me. I have been nothing but a shit sister to you."

I open my mouth to argue, but she says, "There's no saving

me, Striker. I've destroyed innocent lives by knowingly placing weapons in the hands of violent criminals. If the assassins come for me, I'll be ready to answer for my crimes."

I'm cold inside. For the first time, I don't know what to say.

Zara may be everything she says she is—a willing accomplice—but I only know the sister who held my hand when I was a scared little boy without a mother, who dried my tears, told me I was strong, and convinced me I could get through it.

I should hate her, but I know deep down, her father controls everything she does.

She's just as trapped as I am.

30. PEYTON PRICE

The day passes with agonizing slowness.

No amount of ice can soothe the cut on my cheek and the pain is driving me crazy. I try extending my claws to see if that triggers my healing power, but I can't let it flow strongly enough to make a difference.

I won't have privacy until this evening when I can hide in my room. Until then, I have to put up with it.

All Lucinda has to do is glare at my face to make it clear she wants to know what happened. It's very difficult to tell her everything, but I snatch moments in gym class to give her the details as best I can: Raptor did it, I know something he wants to know, there's no way in hell I'm going to tell him, and I have a day's reprieve before I'm in for a world of pain.

When Maintenance class finally arrives and we're given the task of washing walls, I nudge Lucinda. "Library."

She gives me a rapid nod and we lug our buckets up four flights of stairs, our compliance officers traipsing after us.

Ms. Sparrow interrupts us on the third landing. "Where do you think you're going?"

We pull up sharply and I bump into Bree's back.

Damn. Ms. Sparrow is going to make us clean downstairs instead. The teachers don't care about keeping the neglected parts of the building clean.

The water in Bree's metal bucket splashes back and forth. Droplets fly upward and land on her hand where she firmly grips the wooden handle.

To my surprise, they disappear into her skin instead of rolling off again.

I quickly look away before I draw attention to it.

Bree clears her throat, her voice taking on a melodic tone. "Upstairs is very neglected, Ms. Sparrow. It needs cleaning too."

Ms. Sparrow cocks her head to the side as if she's thinking. "Upstairs *is* very neglected," she says, a thoughtful expression forming on her face. "It needs cleaning."

I stare at her. Did she just… mimic Bree?

Ms. Sparrow blinks at us as if we're stupid. "Well, what are you waiting for? Get on with it!"

We hurry past her and I try to keep up with Bree, but she seems more agitated than normal, putting her bucket on the floor as soon as we reach the library and quickly stepping away from it.

The compliance officers congregate outside the room. They don't bother coming in anymore.

Girls and books must seem harmless enough to them. They have no idea that knowledge can be more dangerous than fists, and girls who read books are the deadliest of all.

I murmur to Lucinda as she takes glances at Bree, too. "Cover us?"

She nods, and she and Ashley immediately plonk their buckets in the doorway, washing the doorframe and talking loudly about gym class.

I snatch Bree's hand, drawing her to the other side of the room. She's pale, but her aquamarine eyes are as calm as a still blue lake.

I whisper, "What did you just do?"

She shakes her head rapidly, speaking in a hushed voice. "I don't know. I really don't, Peyton."

As soon as she speaks, I see them.

Teeth.

Holy hell. Razor sharp, bite-a-chunk-out-of-your-neck, shark teeth.

She grabs my arms in a way that tells me I didn't hide my shocked reaction. "What?"

I speak carefully. "Do me a favor and, uh, touch your teeth. Do it carefully."

She raises a finger hesitantly, pressing it to her front teeth. They are all equal lengths, all ending in a very sharp point.

She snaps her mouth closed. "What the hell?" Sinking against the bookshelf, she asks, "What am I?"

"I was thinking demon when you persuaded Ms. Sparrow to let us come up here. But your power is definitely connected with water and you have—*ahem*—teeth like an aquatic predator so..."

Her eyes widen. She mouths, *Siren?*

She immediately checks her legs, but she hasn't developed a mermaid's tail. Other than her teeth, which are rapidly transforming back to their normal shape, she appears completely human.

I quickly pace to the bookshelf on the far side of the room, scanning the books for the one I want. It deals with supernaturals from the sea.

"Here. We could be wrong, but it's worth considering."

She prods her teeth, heaving a sigh of relief to find them back to their normal shape, before she flips through the book and buries her head in it.

I, too, quickly search for the book I want.

When Lucinda casts me a questioning glance, I give her a nod to let her know the danger has passed. She and Ashley relocate inside the room but remain as much of a visual barrier between us and the compliance officers as they can.

I finally find the information I need in a book dealing with supernaturals risen directly from hell and damnation itself.

Great. So if I'm a Fury, I'm going to be one of the bad guys.

An illustration fills the page on the righthand side showing three women, each holding a whip, wearing transparent clothing that hides nothing of their feminine curves. They have deep brown eyes, long legs, and identical features, but the color of their hair is different. One has red hair, another black, and the third golden blonde.

Snakes coil around their waists and torsos, the snakes' tails disappearing into the women's long hair. The image makes me shudder. I can't recall ever seeing a snake, but I don't think I'd let one roam around my body like that.

According to the book, their purpose is to carry out vengeance on the wicked by inflicting pain and disease. They were born of the primordial deity, Nyx, the mother of death. Their targets are wicked men and they especially hate liars.

With the power to see into someone's soul, to see every lie and every crime, they can discern a person's true nature.

I remember the Fury's rebuke to the assassin: *We have nothing to give but pain and torment.*

They're self-healing, just like I thought, and they can deflect any magic, which makes them the perfect executioners.

And they can levitate.

According to the book, their very breath can dull the senses of any victim, turning the most violent, brutal man into putty waiting for the Fury's revenge. No mints required, apparently.

Sinking into a chair in the corner of the room, I consider what I know about myself, ticking off characteristics as my mind slowly grows numb with shock.

No snakes or ability to make someone compliant, but I can tell when people are lying, see through flicker fits to the truth of other students' powers, and I can levitate—although I only did that once.

I can also literally see crimes when I pick up tainted objects —like Raptor's dagger and Kaitlyn's wand. And damn, I loved that whip.

Self-healing is another of my powers, but it seems to take a lot to trigger that power. Like a whole lot of Striker. Being with him, fighting with him, triggers all my powers. But… why?

I turn the page. The first line says:

A Fury is incapable of love.

I shut the book. Well, that's it then. I'm not a Fury because I—

Dear ancients.

No, that's not true.

I don't.

I hate Striker. He hurt my heart in a way that nobody ever has before. I hate him so much that I want to rage at him and tear him apart with my claws.

Taking deep breaths, I run my hands over the front cover. The book is embellished with gold text: *Hell and Damnation.* That part is certainly true of my life.

I jump when one of the compliance officers bangs on the doorframe with a barked order. "Time to finish up."

Bree grabs my hand as we leave the room lugging our buckets. She gives me a nod. She's pale. Scared. But she appears resolved.

"I'll get stronger," she says as we walk down the corridor. "Like Ashley and Lucinda. I'll control it. Then, when the time is right, I'll use it."

I meet her determined eyes.

The right time needs to be soon because I can't keep sleeping in a room beside Striker's, I can't keep pretending I'm okay with Raptor pushing me around, and I definitely can't accept that I'll die in this place.

After putting away the cleaning gear, we make our way to dinner. Bedtime can't come soon enough. I need privacy to extend my claws and hope that the wound on my face heals.

There's an edge of tension in the dining room and I soon see why—nearly thirty compliance officers line the walls, standing guard.

As I take my seat, Ms. Sparrow announces that we are on lockdown until further notice. It's the first lockdown since I arrived, but my curiosity is overtaken by impatience. I have longer to wait until I can try to heal myself.

When I look around, I discover that Striker isn't present. My annoyance quickly flips to worry. I might hate his face, but there's a certain comfort in knowing that he's around. If he's not here, it could mean there's trouble somewhere in the Academy.

Putting me more on edge, Ms. Sparrow spends the entire meal in the dining room. Usually, she departs after she's dispensed our meals. She stands close to my table, her gaze never roaming far from me, Lucinda, Bree, and Ashley.

When Osprey finally enters the room and gestures to Ms. Sparrow, the red-haired witch glides over to the door and the two women speak for a few moments.

At the end, Ms. Sparrow stares hard at me again before she announces that the lockdown is over.

More than a little unnerved, I murmur to my friends, "Be careful. Something's going on."

Lucinda grabs my hand, her expression urgent and afraid. "*You* be careful. Whatever they want to know, don't get killed over it."

I hurry up to the attic, meeting Zara Draven when I reach the third floor. She appears relaxed as she passes me, which must mean Striker is completely fine.

I don't like her much, but the hug she gave him this afternoon was genuine. I would hope that if he were in trouble, she wouldn't be so casual about it.

She gives me a formal nod. "Good evening, Peyton."

Maybe for you.

Taking deep breaths, I make my way to my room. The compliance twins peel off and head back down the stairs as soon as I reach Striker's room.

I slow my pace, casually glancing through his open door to make sure he's okay. He stands at his window, his arms folded across his chest. The curtains are open wide for the first time. He can see the front of the Academy from that side.

He's fine.

I can move on now.

"There's a new beast in the pit," he says, his voice halting me as I'm about to walk away. "They unloaded it this evening."

I miss my step, stopping at the side of his door. That would explain the lockdown, but it doesn't explain Ms. Sparrow's intense scrutiny during dinner. I keep my tone even. "What kind of creature is it?"

"The cage was covered when they took it inside." He half-turns. His hands lower to his sides, revealing his extended claws while one side of his face remains in shadow. "I'll soon find out."

I manage a laugh. "You or me. It'll be one of us."

I can't forget that Osprey and Raptor have promised me a world of pain if I don't tell them what I saw in my vision.

I've come to the conclusion that they are genuinely afraid of the assassins. Which means that the longer I hold out, the greater the likelihood that the assassins will catch them unawares.

I'd love for the woman I saw in the Fury's memory to creep out of the shadows one night and wreak havoc on this place.

Still, I consider how badly I want to piss Osprey and Raptor off. The reality is, no matter what I tell them, they'll hurt me. I'll be able to bear it if I can get a handle on my power to heal myself. Assuming I believe I can do it without Striker.

Striker suddenly turns and strides toward me, an oncoming mass of muscle and dangerous intent.

With a gasp, I backpedal as fast as I can, veering left so I don't crash into the windows.

I can't imagine what I've done to make him mad. Maybe his sister told him I was rude to her today.

He thuds into me before I can get far. I'm normally faster than this, but my instincts are dull, my reflexes sluggish. I put it down to dealing with the pain in my cheek all day.

Before I can slip his hold, he wraps his arms around me, drawing me upward in a fierce hug.

I'm so surprised, I don't fight back. Can't. Don't want to, but my arms hover around him, not hugging him back.

I've had group hugs with the girls, but this is a full-on, gather-me-up-against-him, hold-me-tightly, hug.

I don't know how to respond, where my arms are supposed to go, or where I'm supposed to rest my head. I was closer to him before when I was naked, but this feels different. Warm. Comforting.

His chest presses against mine as he inhales and buries his face in my hair. Just as I relax enough to venture to put my arms around him, he exhales carefully. "I'm sorry for what I did."

I freeze as he drops a kiss on my forehead and lets me go, turning and striding back into his room. He closes the door quietly behind him.

Staring at his closed door, I can't seem to find my feet. Up is suddenly down and my world is spinning. What just happened?

It's completely out of character for Striker to apologize for anything. One minute he was telling me about the new beast and the next he was hugging me. But... why?

I scowl at his door, completely thrown. I can't make sense of his actions, although his apology sounded genuine. I swallow a sarcastic laugh. No doubt, he's already regretting it.

What I know for sure is that the pain in my cheek has eased.

It certainly hasn't healed entirely, but just like before, physical contact with him has triggered my healing power.

I hurry to my room, trying to focus on what I need to do.

As soon as I close my door, I release my claws, taking deep breaths, trying to find the power inside me, whatever it is, whatever I really am.

I close my eyes, my head filling with the memory of holding the whip, how powerful it felt, the crack it made against the table. Especially the way it cut Raptor's cheek.

But his image is quickly replaced with Striker's, his furious amber eyes and the way he dragged me up against him in his room after we kissed, the heat in his gaze making me want more.

A tingle grows in my fingertips, the same shiver I always feel when I fight Striker, a rippling impact coursing up my arm, across my shoulder, and down my torso.

I feel... *angry*.

Justifiably angry.

Lifting my fingers, I slowly open my eyes and focus on my hands. My claws are fully extended, dark, blood-red, and razor sharp. The pain in my face is gone and the floor is now a full foot below me.

I've healed and I'm levitating again. My hair floats up beside me, giving me a sense of weightlessness. I wobble in the air, sucking in oxygen as fast as I can, forcing myself to breathe.

Panic seems like a rational emotion right now, but instead, a rush of rage flows through me. I curl my hands into my fists, not caring that I scrape my palms with my own claws.

Snapping my eyes closed again, I fight the fury, telling myself I need to regain control.

But... may the ancients help me... I don't want to calm down.

This feeling. It's like molten lava, powerful and indestructible, and I want more of it. I don't want to feel afraid anymore. I don't want to be vulnerable.

Rage flows fast inside me, filling my head, intensifying violently. It makes me want to grasp Osprey's neck in my hands and squeeze until she breathes her last. I want to take a knife to Raptor's heart and cut it out, one brutal stab at a time. I want to break every bone in Ms. Hawk's body the same way she breaks students...

I have nothing to give but pain and torment.

A moan tears out of me.

No. Oh, no.

They have made me furious.

I *am* fury.

I *don't* want this, but this is what I am.

I am vengeance, hell, and damnation.

With a gasp, I drop to the floor on my hands and knees, fighting the sudden hot tears burning my eyes. I don't want my sole purpose to be pain and torment. To be violence. I never wanted any of this.

I drop back against my door, wishing Striker would come in right now and hug me when I'm prepared for it.

I would return his embrace this time, cling to him as hard as I can, soak up the contact before it breaks, and accept his apology. I would ask him to kiss me, heal me, and I wouldn't dig into the power that's been concealed inside me all this time.

I crawl across the floor to his stolen blanket and pull it around my shoulders, curling up in a ball.

Now that I know what I am, I should feel powerful, but I don't.

For the first time in years, I cry myself to sleep.

31. STRIKER DRAVEN

The wall between us is too thin.

Peyton's muffled sobs permeate the partition, tearing out chunks of my heart. I've never heard her cry before, not even after Raptor hurt her.

Telling her I'm sorry was supposed to be the first step toward making things better between us. It wasn't supposed to make things worse.

Why the fuck can't I get this right?

I pace my room until her cries stop and the night's silence descends over me.

Far beneath the Academy, a beast waits for me. Peyton's right—one of us will meet it first. The only question is: her or me? Better me so I can find out what it is and discover its weaknesses.

When I finally fall asleep, my dreams are fitful, and I wake to a bright stream of sunlight. Peyton was right again—leaving my curtains open makes it much easier to wake up. A glance at my clock tells me it's not even four o'clock.

I beat her to the morning run, finishing up when she emerges with her compliance officers in tow. She's subdued, her face blotchy from crying, but there's something different about her eyes, even her hair.

I pause as she passes me by, trying to pinpoint what it is.

Her movements are smoother, impossibly graceful, and her hair has highlights of lighter brown in it that I never noticed before. I tell myself it's the early morning sun. I'm not used to the softer light bathing the Academy at this time of day.

Then I catch sight of her fingernails. Her claws are nowhere to be seen, but it looks like she's painted her nails blood-red this morning. She's lucky it's so early and nobody's around to see it yet.

She barely acknowledges me until she's a mere step away from passing me by completely. Then she glances up and the glint in her eyes freezes me to the spot.

They're full of pure, animalistic rage.

My beast roars to the surface and I can't stop his instant, guttural snarls. He's still not speaking to me, not even now that I've apologized to Peyton, but his response to the look in her eyes is intense.

He claws at my mind, tearing at the mental barriers with which I keep him caged, demanding to be let out, to get at her. To get close to her.

What the hell is she?

After her claws appeared, I wondered whether she was like me, even though my kind aren't normally female. But now I have no doubt that she's something else entirely, something that makes even my beast want to prowl around her, wary of her but drawn to her like hellfire.

I force myself to remain completely still, allowing her to pass me. I've done enough to hurt her. The last thing I want is to draw attention to her that could cause her more pain.

Using the spike in my power to run inside, I take all five flights of stairs two at a time. The physical exertion barely has an impact. I head to the shower, turning the water on full cold.

When I emerge into the corridor, she's walking toward me and her expression is hooded. She must be containing whatever flicker of power I saw before, but the edge of tension in her shoulders and the strain around her mouth remains.

I steer clear of her until the first class of the day—Magical History—when we need to sit together.

She keeps looking up, as if she's waiting for something to happen, flicking glances at the classroom door. I consider the classroom and everyone in it, uncertain about the cause of her wariness. She could be worried about the pit or it could be something else entirely.

Mr. Mallard drops his books on the table with a bang. He's the quietest of the teachers, the least violent, preferring to torture us with long lectures, but I've always been cautious around him, just waiting for the day when he shows his true colors.

He exhales into the silence, tapping his wand against his desk. Ripples of magic flow through the wooden surface before he raises his voice. "Today we're starting a new course of study. One we haven't touched on before because, quite frankly, I didn't consider it relevant." He leans forward with an unusual glint in his eyes. "However, it turns out we should have been studying this all along."

Rounding the table, he props his backside on it. It would be a casual gesture if not for the stern press of his lips.

"Supernatural monsters," he announces. "The creatures we like to hunt and kill." His voice lowers. "The creatures that like to hunt us."

Nobody moves. The room is as quiet as it usually is, but my senses suddenly go haywire. I don't often use my power to detect biological changes in others—mostly because I'm concerned about revealing my power when I do—but I take a chance to carefully allow my senses to open, inhaling the elevated stress levels around me.

Lucinda...

Ashley...

Bree...

All of Peyton's friends. Their heartbeats and adrenaline levels have suddenly spiked.

Peyton herself is like a flare of light in my senses, a wash of heightened emotions, fear at the forefront.

Mr. Mallard continues. "Supernatural monsters are not descended from the gods we have been studying. They were, in fact, originally created by the primordial deities who came before the gods; primordial deities such as Gaia, who gave birth to the titans, and Nyx, who is the mother of all death. Also Tartarus, from whom Hell itself was born." He folds his arms across his chest. "Who can tell me the difference between Class A, B, and C monsters?"

Peyton's anxiety levels spike again and then calm. Damn, she's good at controlling herself.

"I can," she says into the quiet.

Lucinda flinches, but Peyton's focus is firmly fixed on Mr. Mallard. For a second, the rage she hid before reappears but it's gone again so quickly, he would never see it.

"Go ahead, Peyton," he says.

Her tone is even and confident. "Class C monsters can only take animal form. Examples are griffins, winged stallions, and the deadly manticores. In contrast, Class B monsters are humanoid but have monstrous characteristics they can't hide. This forces them to live in forests and caves away from civilization. An example is the harpy I killed."

Mr. Mallard does well not to react to the reminder of what Peyton did. Much like my killing of the Orthrus, there are rumors about how she did it, but nobody will ever know for sure except her.

Peyton suddenly smiles. "And, then, as you well know, Mr. Mallard, Class A monsters are those that walk among us. They take human form at will and have no aura." Her smile broadens. "This is why they are the most deadly."

He clears his throat, his eyes narrowing momentarily. "Indeed, they are. Today, we're starting with the Valkyrie. Even though they're extinct, they're the archetype of a Class A monster. They have no aura and appear completely human; however, there is a theory that they can be identified by a subtle imperfection in their eyes. It's thought that they have silver—"

My heightened senses flare again. Peyton's adrenaline levels just shot sky high.

At the same time, Raptor strides into the room, interrupting Mallard.

I can't tell if Peyton's response is to what Mallard was saying about the Valkyrie's eyes or to Raptor's sudden appearance.

"Sorry to interrupt your class, Mr. Mallard," Raptor says, giving Mallard a cordial nod. "Lucinda Adams is due in my classroom."

Peyton's eyes widen. Her focus flicks to Lucinda who has frozen in her seat.

Mr. Mallard doesn't appear surprised. "Lucinda," he says. "Go with Professor Raptor. Everyone else, remain seated."

Peyton grips the edge of her desk. Lucinda twists in her seat, casting Peyton a fearful glance before she turns to the front again, slowly rising to her feet.

Raptor remains at the front of the class, a faint smile on his lips as he waits for Lucinda to step forward. His focus, however, is on Peyton, a cruel smile playing with his lips as he watches her reaction. A quiet scratching sound tells me Peyton is digging her claws into the underside of her desk, an angry, anxious movement.

As soon as Lucinda reaches him, Raptor's big fist darts out. He grabs her hair, digs his fingers into her braid, and yanks her head down.

Lucinda cries out, pain washing across her face. She's forced into a half-crouch so he doesn't rip her hair out.

Peyton shoots to her feet and so does Joseph, both their chairs scraping back—Peyton's topples and hits the floor with a *bang*. Raptor's gaze passes over Joseph before settling on Peyton.

"What's wrong, Peyton?" Raptor asks. He drags Lucinda back and forth at his side, making her cry out again. "If you don't want me to hurt your friend, just tell me what I want to know."

Now I'm certain I shouldn't have let Peyton walk away from me yesterday. I should have made her tell me what happened so I knew what was going on right now.

I tried to warn her about making friends, tried to make her see it's dangerous for whomever she befriends, but she didn't listen. Raptor is intensely observant. Even if he weren't, Ms. Sparrow has been eyeing the four girls for a while now.

The teachers know they can get to Peyton by threatening the people she cares about.

Joseph, too. He should know better than to reveal how much he cares about Lucinda.

But what does Peyton know? And how important is it that Raptor doesn't find out?

Peyton grips her desk, but Lucinda suddenly shouts, "Don't tell them anything, Peyton. I can handle it."

Her eyes leak tears as she thumps the nearest desk, her fingers curling around its leg. A gleam grows in her eyes that Raptor can't see with her face turned away. I saw Lucinda control whole trees. I know she's a dryad.

Give her one more second and she'll rip apart the desk with her mind and drive stakes through Raptor's heart.

If she does that, she's dead. The compliance officers will swarm and they will kill her slowly.

Peyton's shoulders begin to slump. I sense her giving in. She doesn't want to see Lucinda hurt or worse, killed.

As Peyton opens her mouth to speak, my instincts kick in. I don't know what she's about to say. It could be something completely harmless, like who broke the vase in the corridor the other day. Or it could be something catastrophic. Like the fact that I'm not Unknown.

I can't take that chance. Not when I can stop it.

Darting across the distance between us, I grip her throat tightly and run my thumb down the exact nerve I'm aiming for.

She gasps through her constricted vocal chords. "*Striker.*"

Shock and betrayal flicker across her face before her eyes turn blank, unconscious.

My heart thuds. The look in her eyes… the deepest distress.

As if I have the power to hurt her more than anyone else. Raptor told me the cuts I make are the ones that can't be seen.

Whatever apology I made last night is burned to ash now. The last time I used this move on her, she was out for nearly an entire day, a treachery she didn't quickly forget.

I let her go, allowing her body to fall. I can't afford to cushion her, can't be seen to care. I force myself to remain deadpan, uncaring, as her knees collapse and her shoulder hits the ground—luckily it takes the brunt of the impact instead of her head.

Lucinda's scream reaches my ears as Raptor shoves her away from him, ripping her hair at the same time. Joseph pulls her out of Raptor's path as Raptor rages toward me between the desks.

The other students rush to the front of the classroom—farthest from me and Raptor—while Bree and Ashley run for Lucinda, forming a protective shield around her.

I snarl. "Try making Peyton talk now."

He rapidly reaches behind his back as he moves, the glint of a blade flashing before he launches himself forward.

I feint left, grab his weapon hand, and crack my free fist

against his nose. Raptor may have trained with assassins, but he's never been in a cage fight. His weapon doesn't scare me.

What I don't count on is Mr. Mallard. Moving faster than I expected, he points his wand in my direction. "Cunning capture, control, and cut."

A glowing lash speeds from the tip of his wand toward my torso. Unlike the binding the compliance officers used on me after I fought Raptor the first time, this spell is not only effective at restraint. The cut part is real.

I flinch and dart backward, forced to release Raptor's weapon arm, but I can't escape the coiling rope. It twists toward me, snaking through the air in the exact spot I run to, looping around my arms and torso and pulling tightly.

I struggle, even though I shouldn't, every move I make causing the rope to sharpen until it forms a blade that cuts into my biceps. I fight my instinct to bare my claws and cut it apart as I thud against the back wall.

Raptor steps over Peyton's prone form, kicking her legs as he passes. His face is red with rage. "That's the last time you'll challenge me, Striker Draven."

The room quickly swarms with compliance officers.

Four of them use their magic to push me past the other students, my arms still bound, their power buffeting me along between the desks. Other officers stand guard with wands pointed both at me and the other students.

I catch Joseph's eye as I pass. He has no reason to trust me, but I give a quick tilt of my head back at Peyton. I'm not sure if he understands I need him to try to make sure she's safe. To the extent that he can, that is. I'm sure Lucinda will do her best too.

I'm not surprised to see Lachlan and Ryan standing protectively on either side of Ashley and Bree right now. Unlike me, they're good guys.

Osprey is already waiting for me in the corridor. She waves

her wand and her immobilization spell forces me against the wall. She slams the classroom door closed at the same time.

Raptor takes up position behind her and the compliance officers fan out behind him, wands pointed at me in case I try anything. Collin and Colby stand directly behind Raptor, never taking their eyes off me.

They were the ones who waited for me outside the pit the night I killed the Orthrus. They're cautious. As they should be.

Osprey snarls. "Defying the teachers is one thing, Striker, but your own sister needs the information that Peyton is keeping to herself. If anything happens to Zara, it's on your head now."

I grit my teeth against the sharp pain in my arms. The pressure of her spell is forcing the rope to cut farther into my skin. "What information could Peyton know that Zara needs?"

Osprey leans in close, lowering her voice. "Peyton can identify the assassins who are coming for your sister. She can also tell us whether they're more than human."

I keep my expression blank. Zara mentioned the same thing —that there are rumors that the new Legion Master is superhuman. I'm not sure how Peyton has come by this information, but a more important fact is that Osprey is scared. I've never seen such fear lurking in the back of her pale eyes.

Zara told me that the assassins are targeting all associates of Lady Tirelli. I guess I should have put two and two together before now. The teachers are running scared. Raptor is, too. As an excommunicated assassin he is perfect prey for his former colleagues.

I start to laugh, the pressure of my rumbling chest grating my skin against the rope. It's already cut through my clothing and blood seeps through the material. "They're coming for you, aren't they, Osprey?"

Her face flushes red, confirming my statement.

That would explain why Peyton withheld information—

however she came to acquire it. She doesn't know that the assassins are targeting Zara so she can't be blamed for staying quiet. After all, she *was* going to talk before I silenced her.

Osprey grits her teeth, pushing her wand against my neck, one hand gripping my other shoulder. Her breath stinks of an overdose of mints and a bad case of terror.

"You've done whatever you liked for too long, Striker. You terrorize the other students, yet you undermine my authority with every move you make. It's time for you to choose where your allegiances lie."

My laughter dies. "My allegiances?"

"You've done more damage to Peyton Price than I ever could have achieved on my own," she says. "You have the physical strength to subdue any student. You're built to cause pain. You're built as a predator."

She tips her chin. "Join us."

What?

"Become one of us. Help us. Help your sister. We can defend this academy from the attack that's coming."

For a second, I consider her offer. I could do a lot of damage from the inside if I were privy to all their conversations and plans, in a better position to manipulate their decisions. I'd have more power to affect my stepfather, too.

But at what cost? Would I have to stand by while they torture students like Lucinda, who is one of the most loyal people I know?

Would I have to pretend I don't care when they force students like sweet Ashley into the pit?

Osprey thinks I don't care.

I didn't. Not for a long time.

But *fuck it*. Sometime in the last five months, my heart started beating again. I vowed that Peyton wouldn't get to me, but she did. She reached in and grabbed my heart and squeezed until I had no choice but to care again.

It *is* time to pick a side.

It's time for me to be true to myself.

Taking my silence as willingness to consider her offer, Osprey prattles on. "In return, you can have whatever you want. Your father could be convinced to give you money. Your sister can visit whenever you want. We'll make Peyton sleep in your room if you want. She can be all yours. No limits. Do whatever you want."

Oh, lady.

Now she's done it.

An intense growl starts at the bottom of my lungs. It escapes my lips so suddenly that Osprey lurches backward in alarm.

"I will never join you." I snarl. "Lady Tirelli isn't here to protect you anymore." I wish I could move so I could threaten them physically, but for now all I have is my voice. "You're all going to die."

The blood drains from Osprey's old face until she's deathly pale. Her entire torso thrums as a scream roars up into her mouth. "Take him to the pit! If he won't join us, he can die there."

Her immobilization spell drops me back to my feet.

I consider fighting her and the compliance officers right now. I could bathe this corridor in blood, but there are too many officers still inside the classroom. I have to be smart. I need to catch them unawares, not when they're prepared for a fight.

It's better that I go to the pit first and kill whatever monster's waiting.

Then I'm coming back for every one of these witches and wizards and I'm going to end them like I should have a year ago.

I may have found my heart, but it's filled with fury and revenge.

Osprey may be afraid of the assassins now that Lady Tirelli's gone, but she *should* be afraid of me.

32. STRIKER DRAVEN

None of the compliance officers are brave enough to come within a few feet of me, not even Collin and Colby. They know I'll break their arms if they do. They use their magic to prod me along the corridor to the entry to the pit.

Osprey opens the hidden panel and I walk ahead of them as lamps come alive around me, lit by Osprey's magic.

She'll leave me in darkness soon, but I'm not afraid.

Osprey presses against the wall to avoid touching me when we reach the bottom. Her movements are suddenly furtive and quick. She peers cautiously into the dark corridor beyond the gate before she says to the compliance officers, "Be ready."

She hurriedly unlocks the gate. They use their power to shove me inside so fast, I hit the cave wall on the other side of the gate before Osprey locks it again. The rope around me disintegrates, leaving me with bloody cuts around my arms and chest, my shirt in ruins.

As the lights die, and the compliance officers' footsteps recede, Osprey whispers, "Don't expect to survive this one, Striker."

My torn shirt is a liability, something to catch my arms in, so I rip it off.

I wait for my eyes to adjust to the dark, listening carefully. There's no reason to hide my power here, so I let my senses expand to their full extent. I won't call on the beast until I need him, but for now I'll use everything at my disposal to prepare for the fight ahead.

I know every section of this pit well. The initial corridor opens up into a cavern supported by large rock pillars. The cavern itself stretches a hundred paces into the distance and splits into multiple tunnels, each long enough for a creature to hide in them. The safest place for me is inside the wide cavern directly ahead. It's exposed, but there are places to run if things go bad.

The Orthrus's bones lie farther ahead to the left as I edge out into the open.

My eyesight adjusts quickly, my ability to see in dark places an innate part of my power. There's a curious gap in the Orthrus's large ribcage. One of its ribs is missing.

I spy the bone lying next to a pillar in the center of the cavity. It would make a useful weapon if I need one. In fact… it makes me wonder if Peyton used it already. The dead harpy is long gone but that could be how she killed it.

Just as I take a step toward the bone, soft growls meet my ears coming from the tunnel farthest to the right.

Carefully, I back up, keeping my distance without working myself into a corner.

I need to know what I'm dealing with before I can make a game plan.

The beast slinks from the tunnel, its teeth already bared. I make out a short muzzle, a fierce mane, and four incredibly muscled legs with sharp claws at the end of each one. Its tail whips back and forth—solid and scaled with a stinger at the end. Saliva drips from multiple rows of sharp teeth—a shark's mouth.

Oh, hell… it's a manticore.

A creature with the head and body of a lion, the tail of a scorpion, and teeth like a shark. A bad mix of predatorial strengths. Some also have wings, but it looks like this is the wingless variety—which makes it more volatile.

Manticores are fiercer than an Orthrus and the scorpion tail can inject me with venom that will paralyze me.

I've never tested my strength against one, so I have no idea if I'll be immune to its poison.

Fear invades my mind as it prowls toward me, its snarls growing louder.

There's no avoiding the fight ahead.

Within a heartbeat, my beast roars to the surface. I sense my body shift, my shoulders and fists expand, my height increase, and the bones along my spine break from the surface, protecting my back. I've never seen what I look like, but hellfire crackles to the surface of my skin, streaming visibly through the veins along my arms and legs.

The beast's thoughts merge with my own.

I *am* the beast. I am more *me* like this than I am at any other time.

I snarl back at the manticore, baring my sharp teeth. If I get in close enough, I'll be able to rip its throat out. But then, he could rip mine out too.

The manticore leaps. I run at it, curling my fist, ducking, and punching it hard in the side of its head. It flies off course, hits the ground, scrambles to turn around, and leaps again. Like a cat, its claws are bared to dig into me, to latch onto my limbs and maul me.

I dart and land a kick to its side. I hit it so hard that I should have broken its ribs.

But the manticore finds its feet again, turning and running back at me.

This time I bare my claws and when it leaps, I duck, scraping my claws along its underbelly.

I don't make a mark.

Impossible.

A sickening fear grows inside my stomach for the first time since I got here. Manticores are difficult to kill, but I should have hurt it at least a little bit by now.

There are only a few possible reasons why I haven't, the worst being that Osprey has placed a protection spell around it. If that's the case, I'll have to break the spell to even make a mark on this beast.

If I can't, I'm a dead man.

The manticore whirls, rising up on its hind legs, its foreclaws slashing the air in front of my chest. I barely dance out of its reach in time.

A single claw rakes across my shoulder, making me roar as it slices through my bicep. I convince myself it's superficial, despite the splash of blood.

With a roar, I harness the fire inside my body and charge, taking the brunt of its claws across my chest and arms as I tackle the manticore to the ground.

It gnashes at me with its teeth, latching one set of claws into my right shoulder as I aim for its throat, managing to wrap my fingers around it.

Power screams through my arm into my hand, burning through my fingertips.

The creature's fur glows, the protective spell fighting back, shielding it, but I don't stop. I won't stop until I burn through it.

Hellfire streams down my arm like blood, pooling across the manticore's throat.

The protection spell sizzles… and *pops*.

The beast roars, finally vulnerable.

I've broken the spell, but I've made myself vulnerable. I roar in agony as its deeply embedded claw drags across my chest all the way from my right shoulder to my bottom left rib.

The cut opens wide and my brain has trouble processing it.

At the same time, pain pierces my side.

Oh... hell... no.

The creature's tail jabs deep into my waist, poisonous venom shrieking through me in a torturous rush.

With one hand still on its throat, I grab its tail with my other, digging in with my claws and ripping off its stinger.

Deep fury rushes through me. I have only minutes before I'll be paralyzed completely.

Claws bared, I rip at its throat, ramming the claws of my other hand deep into its chest, dragging at its body, tearing as hard as I can. Its bottom jaw rips off in my hand at the same time I pierce its heart.

The light in its eyes dies.

Its claws fall to the side.

But the blood gushing across my chest is not the manticore's. I struggle to stand, struggle to comprehend the damage to my body.

Patches of white tell me its claws ripped to the bone.

My legs buckle, but I need to put pressure on the wound. I need to stop the bleeding. If I don't, I'll bleed out.

I'll lose my life in this place.

I try to hobble to my shirt, determined to use it as a compress, my knees wobbling as I lose feeling in my feet, then my calves.

I thud onto my hands and knees, dragging myself through the dirt, screaming as my hips and stomach lose feeling.

The creeping paralysis spreads through my shoulders and down my arms.

I drag and drag, reaching for my shirt, my fingertips an inch away from it when the paralysis reaches my neck, and my body becomes nothing more than a dead weight. I can't feel, can only see the blood pooling beneath me, a growing puddle, my life leaving my body.

I can't stop it. Can't shout. Can't move. Can't heal myself.

My beast rages inside my mind, fighting the poison, the fire in my body trying to consume the venom—burn it up—but it's taking too long.

For the first time since I came to Bloodwing, I consider the possibility that I'm going to die here.

There isn't time to do the things I need to do. I need to make my stepfather pay for my mother's death. I need to free Zara from the shackles she's chained with.

More than anything, I need to see Peyton one last time. I need to tell her I'm sorry and make sure she knows it's true. That it was true the first time I said it.

I can't leave this world knowing that she thinks I betrayed her, that she believes she's not worthy of love.

She deserves so much more than me.

As the minutes pass, my beast grows weak. The fire inside me slowly consumes the poison, but my strength is also failing.

By the time feeling returns to my arms and legs, I'm numb for a different reason.

I've lost too much blood.

Trying to breathe, I force myself up on my hands and knees, crawling through the dirt, passing my ruined shirt—too late to be of any use—to reach the gate. One last surge of power heats up my palms enough to bend the bars apart.

I wedge myself through the gap, falling onto the rocky ground on the other side.

Breathe in. Breathe out.

I tell myself to get up. I have to see her.

That's all that matters.

I wasn't ready for this. I didn't think my time would be up today, but I guess fate's as monstrous as I am.

It's time to accept that I'm going to die.

33. PEYTON PRICE

"The time has come."

I wake to Osprey's voice, but when I ease open my eyes, she's nowhere near me. Confused, I try not to make any sudden movements.

I'm in my room, lying on my bed. My stomach turns as the poultice on the ceiling drags at me, but I force myself to lie still.

It isn't the only pain I feel. My shoulder aches as if it's been thumped and my legs feel bruised.

The changed sunlight tells me it's late morning, maybe even early afternoon. I try to remember what happened as my empty room stares back at me.

Lucinda's scream echoes in my memory. *Lucinda!* Raptor was hurting her and then Striker grabbed me, his fingertips stroking my neck...

He knocked me out before I could help her.

I can't even begin to understand his motive for silencing me. Trying to fathom Striker's thoughts makes my emotions go haywire. I believed his apology and then he went and hurt me again.

Worse, he endangered Lucinda.

I fight my panic, wondering what happened to her, hoping she wasn't harmed. Lying here isn't doing me any good. I have to get up and find her.

Just as I begin to move, Osprey speaks again, and this time I locate her voice, floating in from the corridor outside.

I stop very still, listening as she says, "Lady Tirelli's gone. We know that now. It's time to take action and protect ourselves. The students are a liability we don't need."

Ms. Sparrow responds, "They're all in the dining room on lockdown. We could send them to the pit one at a time."

"That will take too long."

"A death spell, then?"

Osprey's response is coldly clinical. "No, it can't appear premeditated. If we survive the assassins, we still have to answer to the Magnate. They tolerate flicker deaths—even one or two mortalities in the pit—but they won't be able to overlook a mass murder."

My stomach turns again and this time it's not the poultice.

I try to breathe, try to comprehend what they're saying. They're talking about killing everyone.

What the hell?

I smother my mouth with my hand before I scream.

Ms. Sparrow sounds annoyed now. "What then?"

"We should turn them out into the forest. The creature in the trees will finish them off before they make it half a mile."

Ms. Sparrow gives a delighted laugh. "Excellent. If anyone asks, we can say they tried to escape."

"First, we need to decide which students are useful to us. Peyton should be kept alive because she can tell us things we need to know. Lucinda, of course, is completely useless and will need to die. Along with Bree, although Ashley shows signs of useful power. Joseph, Lachlan, and Ryan have proven themselves to be good fighters. We should offer them a deal—"

"Because that worked so well with Striker." Ms. Sparrow's tone is more derisive than I've ever heard it.

"He was a fool to refuse to join us."

My heartbeat suddenly jumps. Striker turned them down. I picture the way he would have done it. Probably with a fist. That would have made Osprey furious.

Then Ms. Sparrow speaks again. "What will you do with him once he gets out of the pit?"

"Oh, he's not coming out," Osprey says. "That beast is like nothing before it. The pit is no longer a place of torture. Nobody's coming out of it ever again."

Fear strikes through me. I turn my head into the bare mattress, reminding myself that I don't care what happens to Striker. Can't care. Too scared to care. I want to thump my fist against the bed and wail.

I can't care!

Sudden tears burn the backs of my eyes.

I do care. I'm terrified that I won't see his brutal smile again, sense his gaze on me like a naked flame burning my skin. Terrified that I won't get to fight with him again.

Out in the corridor, Ms. Sparrow clears her throat. "We'll have to handle his sister carefully."

"Don't worry. I cleared it with his stepfather. He's more than happy to see the end of Striker. Oliver Draven will finally have complete control of the Draven fortune. He's promised to deal with Zara so there isn't any fallout."

Stepfather. That would explain why they don't look alike. Zara must be Striker's stepsister.

"What about Peyton right now?" Sparrow asks.

"There's nothing we can do until she wakes up. I'll send the compliance officers up here to watch over her."

"Okay, then," Ms. Sparrow says. "When will we order the students into the forest?"

"Tonight. The dark will make it harder for them to defend

themselves. Your job now is to get Vulture to agree—that old witch thinks all the students are worth saving." Osprey's sarcastic laugh fades and their voices recede along the corridor as they walk away, their heels tapping the floor.

I'm left cold and shaking. But not with fear.

Striker stopped me when I was about to tell Raptor about the assassins. I was going to tell him that the female assassin has silver rings around her eyes. That she could... possibly... be a monster too.

A monster like me.

Striker stopped me speaking in his Striker way—with brutality.

Then he told Osprey that he wouldn't join her.

Now he's in the pit, and he might not make it out.

Suddenly, all I can think about is the way he hugged me and apologized. He has claws. He must be a monster too. But when he hugged me... he was just Striker.

I may very well hate him until the end of my days, but I need him and want him too. He uses violence to work within the unbreakable lines that have been drawn around him. Lines that cage every student in this academy. He's learned how to survive and make sure others survive, and now I need to do the same.

Nobody is going to die as long as I have a say about it.

Making my decision, I swing my legs over the edge of the bed, focus on my claws, and extend them. It's easy while I'm sitting beneath the poultice that pulls at my power furiously.

I take a deep breath and let my lungs fill with darkness, let my power flow.

A desperate need for violence fills my head, but I rein it in as much as I can before my feet touch the floor, light as air. I can't afford to lose my head. I have to remain focused.

Striker has been training me for months now. It's time for me to believe in myself, to believe that I can fight back. I just hope the other students are ready to fight too.

But first, I'm getting Striker out of the pit.

I rip off my uniform and quickly pull on my gym gear, then I grab the roll of duct tape hidden in the bottom of my closet before I open the door and peer down the hallway to check whether anyone is there. Confirming that the way is clear, I stride down the corridor.

Osprey said she was going to send up compliance officers, so I pause at the corner of the stairs, crouching to push the tape against the wall.

Then I wait.

34. STRIKER DRAVEN

Collin and Colby startle as soon as I appear at the top of the stairs from the pit.

I drag myself through the opening, but their focus is on my chest, the bone-deep gash and the visible ribs.

I force sound from my throat. "Where's Peyton?"

Colby stares at me. He was always the more rational of the two men. "That's a bad wound," is all he says.

Collin, on the other hand, snickers. "Looks like you're a dead man, Draven."

I have enough fire left inside me to snarl. "Where is she?"

"In the attic. She's still asleep." Colby folds his arms across his chest, his snake skin tattoo visible with his sleeves rolled up. "Osprey's growing tired of waiting for her to wake up."

He doesn't try to stop me when I take a step to the side. Then another. The sunlight pouring through the windows above the plaque on the wall makes me squint after the darkness of the pit.

Collin takes a glance at Colby. "Should we stop him?"

Colby shakes his head at me. "You won't make it to the attic,

Striker," he calls out. "You'll be dead by the time you reach the top."

He's probably right. But I'm going to try.

Collin and Colby follow after me, their wands raised as I drag my feet. They won't kill me without a direct order from Osprey, so I'm guessing their orders were to watch the door, not end me on sight. Lucky me.

I press against the wall at the bottom of the first staircase.

There are no other compliance officers or students around. Their absence suggests they're on lockdown, most probably in the dining room, which leaves the hallways deserted. It's a small mercy that there's nobody here to see me stumble up the first step.

I ascend the staircase one step at a time, telling myself I only have to make it five flights. I ran up these steps this morning. The climb is nothing.

I collapse on the first landing but drag myself upright again, fighting the dull pain in every part of my body, only to find Osprey and Sparrow coming down the other side.

They don't look happy to see me, but Osprey's expression brightens when she sees my wounds. "It looks like your time is up, Striker."

I can barely form a fist, let alone make myself speak. "If you hurt Peyton… I will come back… from hell… and kill you."

Sparrow scoffs behind her and Osprey laughs, stepping into my space. "Finally found your heart, did you? Don't worry. Peyton's too useful to kill. Shame I can't say the same about the others."

She crowds me, pushing me back against the wall, reveling in the fact that I don't have the strength to crush her face.

"It's not like Peyton has anywhere to run, is it?" Osprey continues, her gloating face too close to mine. "That's what you don't understand, Striker. You don't *have* anywhere to go. Out there in the world, you would be hunted like the animals you are. We hurt you, but we keep you alive. You live because we let you live."

She pokes my shoulder hard enough to leave another bruise among the collection growing already. "You will die when we say you die. Which, in your case, is today."

Her face blurs and my head swims. To my horror, my knees buckle.

I slide down the wall, unable to stand, landing on my backside. My legs and arms won't respond. I try to put my hands out, but I slip to the side instead, the world tilting as my shoulder hits the floor before my head.

I can't make any part of my body work. Can't get up. Can't respond.

Osprey leans down to me, waving her wand across my face. "Fading life signs," she announces. "He'll be gone in a minute."

She rises again, towering over me, her hands planted on her hips.

Colby steps up to her side. "Should we take his body out to the forest?"

She purses her lips before shaking her head. "I need you and Collin to go upstairs and watch Peyton. Tell me the minute she wakes up."

He obeys her immediately, inclining his head at Collin before the two men disappear up the stairs without a backward glance.

Sparrow asks, "What of Striker's body?"

Osprey smiles, cruel to the end. "We'll dispose of it tonight. Leave it here for the other students to see. This is what happens if you disobey me. Even the unkillable Striker Draven is dead."

She and Sparrow turn on their heels and descend the staircase, leaving me where I lie.

I'm only aware of a few things, the strangest things: I'm not blinking; the floor isn't as smooth as it looks; and there's a patch of dirt on the next step.

Osprey's retreating back can't be the last thing I see.

Beast? I ask, my voice small inside my mind, a final plea. *Please?*

I just need my power for one more thing—to make it to Peyton's side. Even if all I can do is lay my head down beside her sleeping form.

The tiniest spark lights my chest.

After Osprey's footsteps fade into the distance, I drop my upper shoulder, plant my hands on the floor, and push upward, drawing my legs under me.

Just one more step.

35. PEYTON PRICE

Two sets of footsteps approach from below.

Both men are wearing boots. My heightened senses easily identify their tread as that of Colby and Collin—heavy, confident.

I count the steps as they draw closer, timing my attack. Like all witches and wizards, they have to speak spells to use their wands. They're so good at it—better even than the teachers because they've been trained in magical warfare—that they barely mutter anymore; even a bare whisper works for them.

I ready my fists and allow my rage to flow.

These men have hurt students, bullied them. They are liars and deserve to be punished. I haven't had time to practice at my power, but it's time to find out what I can do.

As soon as Collin turns the corner, I throat punch him, landing a brutal blow to the front of his neck that sends him flying backward.

One step down, Colby's eyes fly wide. He starts to speak, but my left hand darts out, grabbing him around the throat and squeezing.

Power flows through me and I rise up into the air, taking

him with me. He kicks the air as I crush his windpipe with my increased strength.

Collin darts back at me, his pale eyes glowing murder, but the moment he tries to rasp a sound, his voice fails him.

Yeah, I crushed his windpipe with that throat punch.

I kick high. My foot connects with his head so hard that he thuds back against the wall, dropping to the floor, unconscious.

Deprived of air, Colby slumps in my arms. I lower him to the ground, checking his breathing. I didn't break his neck despite the rage flowing through me.

Both men are still alive.

I move quickly, binding their hands behind their backs and trussing up their feet with duct tape. Then I wrap tape around their mouths so they can't shout when they wake up.

Osprey won't come looking for me until these two officers tell her I'm awake, which they won't do any time soon. What's more, the school is on lockdown, so all of the other guards will be in the dining room watching over the other students.

I have free rein over the upper levels.

Testing my strength, I'm surprised and pleased to discover that I can lift the men, one at a time.

Hoisting Collin over my shoulder first, I fly down the steps with him, heading to an abandoned room on the fourth floor east wing.

I'm completely graceless, wobbling wildly as I descend the stairs and along the corridor, but, hell, this isn't a beauty contest.

By the time I deposit Colby in a separate room—I'm not going to chance that they will help free each other somehow—and tape his arms to a desk for good measure, I'm slowly gaining some control over my movements in the air.

I'll need a lot more practice, but I can't help but feel happy with my progress already.

I return to the fourth floor landing, ready to glide silently down to the entrance area to the pit when I hear slow footsteps on the stairs beneath me.

There weren't supposed to be more compliance officers. I grit my teeth, determined to deal with them the same way I dealt with the first two.

I dart around the corner, ready to fight.

36. STRIKER DRAVEN

I don't know how many steps I still need to climb.

It doesn't seem to matter. There are always more. Too many. I could be two steps from the attic or a thousand. My legs won't obey me anymore. The tiny spark of power that has allowed me to continue moving is all but consumed and my beast is silent inside my mind.

Bumping the wall, I slide onto the step I'm standing on, one shoulder grazing the side as my feet slip out from under me.

I can't slow my fall, hitting the stairs with a thud, bumping down two of them before my legs catch at an awkward angle, stopping my downward momentum.

I sense movement above me. A pair of feet appear at my eye level and then gentle hands reach for me, wrapping around my face.

Peyton tilts her face to mine.

I must be gone already. She's supposed to be asleep. She can't be here right now.

Her eyes are the deepest chocolate brown, fiery flecks inside them the only indication of the blazing spirit she keeps tightly leashed.

I sigh at her touch. If only I'd let her love me when I had the chance.

Even if I'm only talking to an illusion, I have to tell her…

"Don't hate me, Peyton." I try to smile, but I don't know if I succeed. "Except in a good way."

Tears glisten in her serious eyes.

She whispers, "I will hate you always, Striker."

She only calls me Striker when she wants something from me.

She wants… me.

It's all I need. It's everything.

I close my eyes and finally… I let go.

37. PEYTON PRICE

I freeze as Striker appears before me, a shocking sight. His arms hang loosely at his sides. His shoulders are slumped and his amber eyes are dull and unfocused.

He doesn't see me. He takes another step, but his legs wobble.

A deadly gash stretches all the way from his right shoulder to his left ribs.

A cry grows on my lips when his knees buckle, but I force myself to swallow it. I barely make it to his side before he bumps the wall, slipping down a couple of steps until his legs catch under him to stop his slide.

Nothing is so intense as the fear rising inside me like a tidal wave. I whisper his name as I bend to him, but he doesn't respond, doesn't seem to hear me. The gash across his chest gapes open too wide and too deep.

He's already bled out.

How he made it up here is beyond me.

I take hold of his face in my hands, leaning into him.

He focuses on me, sees me, finally. His expression softens in a way it never has before when he looks at me.

"Don't hate me, Peyton." The corner of his mouth twitches up into a smile. "Except in a good way."

I can't stop the burn behind my eyes, trying to see him through the blur of tears. "I will hate you always, Striker."

That seems to be all he wants.

He closes his eyes.

My heart stops when his breathing ceases.

I press my hands against his cheeks. "Striker?"

He doesn't respond.

His chest is still.

No.

No, he can't die here. Not when he smiled at me for the first time. A real smile that made my heart crack.

He's not allowed to leave me that way.

I hoist my arms beneath his armpits. He's much heavier even than the compliance officers. Damn him for being so big. His body is a dead weight, but I can't let it stop me.

Forcing my power to flow, I rise up holding him, locking my fingers across his chest so he doesn't slip out of my grasp.

There has to be a way to save him. I could drag him to his room, to the medical kit, but it's too late for healing gels.

He has power. It makes him strong. I have to trigger it somehow. But... how?

My eyes fly wide.

The rune above my bed. It can drag out his power.

Panic makes me stronger. Pulling with all my strength and rising into the air, I scream at him inside my mind: *I hate you, Striker Draven. I hate you so much right now.*

A surge of power rushes through me with the spike in my emotions, making me stronger, allowing me to dart forward in the air.

I fly as fast as I can, up the next flight of stairs to the attic, down the corridor, and around the corner into my room.

I nudge the door closed and ignore the sickening pull of the rune above my bed, flying us directly under it and dropping down to the mattress in one swoop.

His body falls on top of mine, his back and thighs half covering my torso and legs. I don't care about the bruises I'll have tomorrow.

I lie still beneath him, the rune on the ceiling sucking at me, dragging my claws from my fingertips and—to my surprise—tugging at my hair this time. The strands around my face rise upward, waving and rippling in the air.

I turn my head to see Striker's face, praying for a sign of life.

My blood pounds too loudly in my ears as I wait for him to breathe.

"Striker!" My right arm is pinned beneath him, but my left is free. I thump my fist against the side of his chest, but he doesn't respond. "Striker!"

I'm beyond panicking. Every millisecond stretches out, pulling my heart too thin until I'm going to crack.

Moving him here gave me motion, movement, kept me from thinking or feeling. It was a distraction. A reprieve from facing the truth.

He isn't breathing. He's… gone.

"Striker!" A cry breaks from my chest. "Please, Striker. I don't hate you. I can't anymore. You have to come back and make me hate you again. You have to—"

My voice breaks. I can't anymore.

The silence is too much.

A keening wail breaks out of me.

A Fury is incapable of love.

I understand it now. *Love.* It hurts too much. Hate hurts too, but it makes me stronger. That's the way I'm built.

But love will kill me, tear me apart, destroy me. Striker will destroy me.

I dare to press my cheek to his, wishing I'd had the courage to do this while he was alive. "Striker. Please."

I close my eyes and count my heartbeats until I can't count anymore.

The seconds pass, quiet moments filled with constant denial and fading hope. Long moments of hurt and regret, of wanting to take back what I said and did, of wanting to do everything differently.

Moments of wanting him back. Moments of accepting that I would take the destruction of his love over losing him.

Long moments of stripping back all my defenses until I'm bare and vulnerable.

Until I'm Peyton and he's Striker and we are nothing more.

38. PEYTON PRICE

sudden sweat breaks out across my skin, heat prickling my torso and legs.

A *hot* sweat.

My eyes fly open.

A suddenly scorching heat burns through me.

Striker's hand resting against my side shifts and morphs. Claws elongate from his fingertips, sharper than mine. His palm grows before my eyes, turning into a fist twice its original size.

Bright fissures speed up his arm, starting at his fingers and rapidly spreading through his neck and torso. Fiery threads split his skin like cracks in brittle earth, each thread filling with molten flame as if fire is rising out of him.

The fissures spread, hitting his shoulders, which shift and expand next to me, broadening even more than they normally are. His entire body grows larger, maybe a foot taller, although it's hard to tell while he's lying on me.

A growl rumbles in his chest, a deep roar like a firestorm about to crash into me.

He roars upright, releasing me from where I was pinned beneath him.

I leap back, intending to jump off the bed, but he twists and pounces, pushing me back onto it, one fist landing on my left shoulder, the other resting beside my head.

His body pins mine again, pressed directly on top of me from the waist down.

He arches back, shaking out his shoulders, and when he lowers his torso again, I catch sight of sharp bones protruding from his back and shoulders.

I lie frozen as the molten cracks meander across his face, lighting up his skin. His eyes are no longer his own. They're filled with a fiery amber glow—the glow I've seen a hundred times, but never this intense. The shape of his eyes has also changed, tapering at the edges like a dangerous predator's.

The heat flowing from him should scare me, but I'm shocked to realize that I'm soaking it up, sucking it into my body with complete abandon.

Still, I don't dare to move as his gaze drags across my face, lingering on my lips and blazing down my chest with a blatant hunger he never revealed before.

Whatever he is now, he is definitely not a gentleman.

"Striker?"

When he opens his mouth to speak, two sharp incisors become visible behind his lips. "I know you."

A shiver runs to my toes, but my eyes widen with confusion. "It's me. Peyton."

He gives me a self-satisfied smile as his deadly teeth peek from between his lips. "Like I said, I know you."

He lowers his head, inch by slow inch, until his cheek nuzzles mine.

I gasp as his fiery skin brushes against my neck, my cheek, and my forehead. At the same time, the hand that grips my shoulder eases, his thumb drawing across my chest to my neck. It's a possessive gesture, raw and animalistic.

I remain very still, afraid to make any sudden moves, but the pure pleasure radiating from every touch of his hands and face is unbearable, demanding a response.

So help me, I want to nuzzle him back. He's alive and I want all of him, whatever form he takes.

I force myself to speak. "What are you?"

He growls. "I'm Striker."

A sudden laugh grows inside me. Striker only touched me like this once and afterward he pushed me away. The way I'm being touched now tells me that this… beast… whatever he is… won't back off. "You're really not."

"I really am." The corner of his mouth touches mine, the tiniest taste of my lower lip that strikes pleasure straight through to my center. "I'm the part of Striker that he controls and hides."

I close my eyes, trying to remain lucid as the heat and press of his body threatens to drive all rational thought from my head. At the back of my mind, one worry remains and it's not for my own safety: I can't see Striker's wound because he's lying too close to me.

I have to make sure he's healed.

Taking a chance to place both my hands on his chest, I attempt to push him away from me, testing that he'll do what I want. He lifts away from me a mere inch, but then he growls and fights me, pushing back against my palms to rub his cheek against mine again.

I shove harder and he gives an exasperated sigh. "Why do you push me away?"

I give him a stern look. "I need to see your body."

His incisors appear as his lips curve into a gleaming smile. "You can look all you want."

His arms straighten so his chest is visible to me, but his lower half remains resolutely pressed against mine. I'm not happy with what I see. The gash has remained as deep and raw as it was in the beginning—despite the power I sense flowing through him.

The edges of the wound glow hot, the dirt caught in the wound burned away, but the cut itself isn't healing.

An awful dread spikes through me.

He isn't healing. He's operating on remnant power. It must be one final burst.

"Do you have the power to heal yourself?" I demand to know.

He pauses for a beat, his expression hooded, before he shakes his head. "I don't."

My heart plummets. I stare into his serious eyes, trying to find hope, refusing to believe that there's nothing he can do. He's powerful and his power feels so much like mine, as if we're both forged from fire. "What are you saying? Are you saying… you're…"

Not coming back to me.

He drops his head to mine, brushing his lips in the lightest touch across my cheek. "I came back to say goodbye."

I shove him as hard as I can. "No, you didn't. You won't!" I grab his shoulders, attempting to push him away.

He barely budges, only lifting his head.

I snarl. "Don't you dare kiss me until you're healed!"

When he willfully brushes his lips to mine, I thump my fist against his shoulder. My claws shoot from my fingertips and I deliberately dig them hard around his upper arm, causing his eyes to narrow.

A sob rises into my throat. He can't have come back only to leave me. I don't care what he says. There has to be a way. "I'm ordering you to heal yourself or I will tear you to shreds." My voice rises. "Do it. *Now.*"

He gives me a perplexed look. "You love me."

Rage fills my head. "I hate you! I hate you more right now than I ever have. More than I've ever hated anyone."

A growl builds in his chest. His lips draw back in a threatening snarl. His teeth lower to my neck, but this time they brush against my veins, a threatening nip. "You don't want me to die."

I grit my teeth in the face of danger. "I'm not afraid of you, Striker."

"I know you aren't." His eyes burn me as he pushes up on his fists as far as he can go while still pinning me. The way his gaze rakes over me again is confusing. Does he hate me right now or lust after me? I can't tell which.

His shoulder heats beneath my palm, his power glowing where my claws rake his skin. Or maybe… it's my power glowing.

I sense my hair spread out across the bed as I press my other hand to his chest. Glistening strands of my hair rise up around my face and my claws appear on my left hand too, threatening to tear him to shreds.

"Listen to me carefully, Striker Draven. If you die today, I will follow you into hell itself and drag you back here."

His snarl becomes sharper, the predatorial glint in his eyes a deadly threat. "You can't win this, Peyton."

A frustrated scream rises to my lips. I told him I'd rip out his heart, but it turns out he's still ripping out mine, slowly and painfully.

The glow suddenly fades from his eyes. "It's time to let me go." He searches my eyes as he brushes the hair from my cheek with a sigh. "I'm tired of fighting."

I try to drag air into my lungs. "Then stop."

He's confused. "That's what I want to do. I want to give in."

"No… Striker… stop fighting *me*."

I never thought I'd meet someone who has built more defenses around their heart than I have. Striker protects his emotions with electric fences that have machine guns at the top to keep everyone at bay, slaying anyone who gets too close.

He needs me to stop fighting against him… and start fighting *for* him.

I've felt his power transfer to me when we fought each other and I've sensed mine transfer to him.

I've healed myself when he kissed me and, even though the power to heal is all mine, it was triggered by the emotions I felt when he was physically close to me. He makes me stronger. My hate for him makes me stronger.

I have to believe that I can make him stronger, too.

Retracting my claws, I slide my arms around him, drawing him down to me so his chest rests on mine. It's difficult—his body is so heavy—but I wriggle my legs out from under him and curve them around his hips, pulling him closer than he was before.

Refusing to close my eyes, levelling my gaze with his, I draw on every shred of power inside me, focusing on the rage I feel at losing him, focusing on hating him with all my heart and soul.

I speak with all the vehemence and fury that burns between us. "I will heal you and bring you back to me, Striker Draven. I want you, like you, love hating you, love fighting you… love kissing you… want to walk out of here with you… one day… together…"

The heat between our bodies increases. My skin prickles, my stomach hurts, but my heart hurts more.

The crease in his forehead deepens.

He starts to speak, but I continue. "I won't let you push me away. I won't believe you next time you tell me I don't mean anything to you. I'll hear what you really want to say—that you need me—and I'll wait as long as it takes for you to trust me. I won't give up on you. I'll protect you, and defend you, and I'll tear apart anyone who hurts you."

My power drains from me as I speak, flowing through my hands. I don't know if it's enough. I don't know if he'll let me heal him. I don't know if I even can. "Please… choose… me."

His gentle breath tickles my lips. "*You…* will defend *me?*"

"Yes," I say, squeezing my eyes shut now. "Always."

"You like me."

"Yes."

His touch is soft, a questioning kiss, the growl fading from his voice. "You want me."

"More than a little."

His body shifts above mine before his arms slide beneath me, lifting me up so that I sit straddling him. My hips settles against his as if we've sat like this a thousand times before. As if it's where I belong.

His arms tighten around me as I open my eyes, a question on my lips.

The fiery lines in his skin are fading, their glow sinking into his face, shoulders, torso, and arms again.

He rolls his shoulders a little as his back shifts, returning to its former shape, the bony protrusions jutting from his spine retracting. His hands soften against my back and his incisors withdraw behind his lips.

I hold my breath as a new glow spreads from my fingertips and passes across his chest. His wound begins to knit, flesh and skin slowly pulling together.

Pressing my hand firmly to his heart, I seek a beat beneath my palm. His wound will leave an awful scar and the flesh is vulnerable, not completely healed but…

Finally. Finally I sense a heartbeat.

I breathe out my relief.

He's okay. He's going to be okay. Tears flood my eyes and I can't stop them. I want to pull him close, kiss his lips, press my cheek to his…

"I do," he whispers, "I choose you."

Sheer terror fills his eyes as soon as he speaks but he doesn't look away.

I lean forward, very carefully, to kiss him. I don't know how

I did it, how I healed him. I don't know if I could ever do it again, but I know that I want him in my life, imperfections and all.

The warmth of his mouth is nearly my undoing, but I need to speak for my heart before I speak for my body. He's more open to me than he's ever been and I need him to know how much that means to me. All I want is truth between us.

"I will hate you furiously to the end of my days, Striker Draven. With all my heart and soul."

He strokes my hair, winding his fingers into my braid, a gentle caress against my neck as he lowers his mouth to mine, fitting our lips together perfectly.

I tip my head back and sigh. Wrapping my arms around his back, I trace his muscles, easing out the tension I find in them. I love the way he relaxes into my touch, closing his eyes and soaking it up.

"I'm a Fury," I whisper against his mouth.

He smiles. "I'm a Hellhound."

Of course he is. We're both creatures of violence and retribution.

He groans. "I want to stay right here with you, but we can't."

I stay close to him, stealing this moment, stretching it as long as I can before I say, "We have to fight now."

Stroking his cheek, I study his eyes. He's weary, still healing. He needs time that we don't have. It's mid-afternoon and the others have until the evening, but we can't leave it that late.

My promise to defend him was not an idle one. I'll have to watch his back closely in his weakened state.

"I'll fight with everything I've got," I say. "I won't hide my power anymore. I won't ask you to reveal what you are, but—"

"It's time to show them what I am," he says. "It's long past due."

He lifts me up off the bed, keeping me close, neither one of us wanting to part. With a sigh, I force my feet to the floor, but as he takes my hand, I catch sight of the ceiling.

"Wait," I say, harnessing my power to fly upward, release my claws, and drag them through the rune above the bed, scratching through it.

The awful sucking feeling fades and then disappears telling me that the magic has been destroyed. The hateful rune helped me, but I'm done putting up with it.

Striker's gaze follows me upward, his lips parting as he watches me move. I give him a smile as I float for a moment, relishing the sense of weightlessness I feel in the air while my hair rises around me.

He gives me a quizzical look when I return to his side. "Why did you do that? It's not like you'll be sleeping in here tonight."

I blush. "Where will I be sleeping, Striker?"

"Far away from here."

Oh. He means we're getting out of here, not that I'll be sleeping in *his* bed.

I shake my head at the way I feel disappointed by that, trying to laugh at myself. I guess I've really got my priorities straight.

His lips curve. He pulls me close, his eyes burning with an even brighter flame that tells me his power is regenerating quickly now. "What I mean to say is, far away from here in a bed that belongs to both of us." His gaze softens. "I should be afraid of you, Peyton Price. You see into the heart of lies. You see me as I am. You are fury and vengeance, but I want you in my life like I've never wanted anything."

"Then… will you fight at my side, Striker Draven?"

The flame in his eyes blazes. "Hell, yes."

39. PEYTON PRICE

e prepare ourselves quickly.

Our plan is simple: get the other students out of the dining hall and make it to the front gate. Whether we can pull it off is another question. We consider if it would be better to head for the back of the Academy instead—Striker will need to pull apart the iron bars either way—but we don't know anything about the supposed creature in the forest.

Given that trucks come in and out through the front, we have to assume there are barriers along the front entryway that will keep whatever is in the forest away from us.

"I'm not afraid of fighting it, whatever it is," I say.

He gives me a laugh. "You're rarely afraid. That's a Fury trait."

I wink. "I *am* the monster in the dark."

He rubs my arms, a tentative gesture. It will take time for us to figure out how to act around each other now, what kind of physical touch is acceptable.

"Even so," he says. "I don't expect our passage to the gate to be easy. If we make it there, we don't need to face another challenge so quickly."

We hurry down the corridor, but I keep Striker in my sights at all times, watching him for signs of fatigue.

The dining room will be full of compliance officers, so our first step is to ascertain which teachers are in there too. I'm guessing Ms. Sparrow, while Osprey is likely to be in the west wing somewhere. Ms. Hawk, Ms. Vulture, and Mr. Mallard are indeterminate. I've rarely seen them in the dining room, but this is an unusual situation.

Before we descend the stairs, Striker stops me. "The magic from their wands won't touch you when you release your power, but you have to fully transform. I will too. The compliance officers don't control instinctive magic, but we'll have to watch out for Osprey."

Instinctive magic is only controlled by a rare handful of very powerful witches who don't need wands to harness their power. I'd like to believe that Osprey's power is strictly contained to a wand but we can't underestimate her like she's underestimated us.

When we reach the first floor landing, moments away from gatecrashing the dining room party, Striker murmurs quietly, "They left me right here to die."

I grip his bicep, leveling my gaze with his, my voice a bare whisper. "That was their mistake."

He gives me a quick, firm nod.

Then he waits and I love the way he's willing to let me go first. I cast him a sideways glance from beneath my lashes that he returns with a sudden hint of heat.

As I glide down the last set of stairs, my feet are light and whisper-quiet. I haven't released my power much at all—I don't float—but what little I have released gives me buoyancy that allows me to tread without sound, one bare foot at a time.

I allow my senses to expand, listening carefully to all the sounds around me.

My hearing magnifies while my sight sharpens. I can

suddenly see, in detail, all the imperfections in the wooden doors opposite us, the grooves in the floorboards, and sense movements right and left.

Immediately to our right, the Founder's room is empty, but farther along the west wing, I sense the separate movements of three bodies. They're teachers, judging by their footfalls; one could be Ms. Hawk since she wears boots like the compliance officers.

Sounds higher up tell me someone is on the second floor in the west wing—another teacher not wearing boots.

"One teacher upstairs. Three in the west wing," I whisper. That's four teachers, including Osprey. "The only one I don't have a location on is Raptor."

Striker nods and I step carefully around the corner into the empty entrance. We'll have to hurry now. From here, we can be seen all the way down each straight corridor. This place is like one big rectangle. The only places to hide will be rooms along the way.

I'm done hiding. Myself. My power. My heart.

Striker's palm brushes between my shoulder blades, a quick affirmative touch. He has my back.

I break into a run, quiet as a panther, while Striker speeds behind me, his movements quiet and controlled.

Reaching the dining room, I slow down, approaching cautiously. I press my hand against the wooden door and listen.

There are so many bodies inside the room—compliance officers and students—that I can't distinguish them. I'll have to get better at using my power, but for now all I know is there are at least forty people inside.

"Time to make an entrance," Striker murmurs at my ear, causing heat to rush to parts of my body that shouldn't be engaged right now. We could be about to die. Kissing him should not be at the forefront of my thoughts.

He adds, "I'm looking forward to this. My beast has been dying to get some air."

His beast. My fury.

I give him a smile as I push on the door and stroll inside, casual as a summer breeze.

Ms. Sparrow stands at the head of the room, her back to us. Each student sits at their allocated tables, but unlike at dinnertime, they're bent forward across the table in front of them, their arms stretched forward and wrists shackled by glowing ropes that are anchored to the table's surface.

In that position, most of them rest their heads against the tabletop, their faces turned to the side. Compliance officers line the walls like usual for a lockdown, except that every one of them has their wand out.

The students must assume that we're teachers coming in because they don't look up when the door closes behind us.

The compliance officers tense and Ms. Sparrow whirls.

"Peyton Price," she hisses. "How did you get past your compliance officers...?"

Her voice trails off as her focus shifts to Striker walking behind me. Every student's head shoots up as far as they can. Lucinda's face is blotchy, but I don't misinterpret her tears as weakness. She's angry.

The blood drains from Ms. Sparrow's face, her red hair suddenly a garish contrast to her sickly pale skin. She backs up, gripping her wand so hard, her knuckles turn white. "Striker... you're supposed to be dead. I saw you die..."

We stop several paces away from her and I don't waste any time getting to the point.

"Ms. Sparrow, you have a choice," I say. "You can let us all go. Or *you* can die. Which do you choose?"

She scoffs, some of the color returning to her cheeks, an angry flush. "What are you going to kill me with, Peyton? You have no weapons. No wands. No powers. Nothing but a wishy-washy sometimes-useful clairvoyance—"

A shriek emits from her mouth when I hold up my hand and extend my claws in a rush. The blood-red tips gleam under the lights.

"I'll rip your heart out with these," I say, waiting a beat before I continue. "Now, which is it? Let us go or die?"

She screams at the compliance officers, her own wand outstretched. "Kill them!"

The air sizzles and hellish magic flies my way from every point around the room, every single compliance officer unleashing on me at once.

Power thuds through me, faster than I've ever harnessed it before. I jolt upright, shooting into the air mere milliseconds before the spells hit me.

Light bursts around me. Coiling magical ropes spear around my torso. Torture curses flicker up and down my body and it's all so bright that colors pop and flash in my vision.

My power isn't like having a shield; the spells don't rebound off me. Rather they sink in, all the hatred that comes with them feeding my fury. I tip my head back and soak it up, absorbing all the power they throw at me.

When I open my eyes again, a crimson haze has descended over my vision. Every person in the room has a glow. The students burn brightly, their forms flickering as they tug and struggle against their restraints. They look like angels without wings fluttering to be free.

In contrast, the compliance officers are dark shadows, silhouettes that suck the light from the room, and Ms. Sparrow is an inky dark figure like the deepest pit.

At the corner of my vision, the brightest flame is Striker.

He's morphed into his beast shape, his incisors gleaming white, flames burning across his skin, his true form dangerously predatorial.

I call out, "Lucinda! You know what to do."

The tears streaking down her cheeks run like liquid diamonds in my amplified vision. She raises her voice with a scream. "Disarm!"

Every wand is ripped from the hand of its owner, the compliance officers shouting as their weapons fly straight to the ceiling and stick there. The moment the connection is lost, the shackles around the students disappear.

Striker growls and I answer him with a smile.

I catch the way the corner of his mouth rises as he lunges forward, ripping into the nearest compliance officer. A thud tells me the man didn't have a chance. At the back of the room, another roar meets my ears, similar to Striker's, but more guttural.

My eyes widen with surprise when Joseph rises up from the table he was chained to. The brightness around him changes to a dark blue, blending with my crimson haze to a bloody purple.

His shoulders and fists expand like Striker's, his height increasing and his facial features becoming more chiseled, but less human.

My jaw drops. The only humanoid monster I've read about with blue skin and a larger-than-human physique is the undead warrior—the draugr.

He'll be able to change his height at will and being undead, well, no ordinary combat can kill him. The only way to kill a draugr is to chop off its head.

He doesn't waste a moment, plowing into the compliance officers behind him, ripping into them with his bare hands as they try to fight back. They don't have wands anymore, but they're well-trained in combat. It doesn't make a difference. There's nothing they can do to harm him.

The other students launch themselves to attack. I don't identify any other monsters among them and Bree is limited without water, but they've been training in hand-to-hand combat for months. More than one compliance officer drops to the floor, either unconscious or dead.

Closer to the front, away from the violence around the edges of the room, Ashley carefully removes her tie and wraps it around her eyes.

She steps up onto the table she was tied to, quickly surveying the room. She leaps from the table and races to the back corner where a compliance officer has grabbed Lachlan and holds him in a neck choke. Lachlan attempts to ram his elbow and feet into the man holding him, but he's quickly losing air, his knees buckling and his arms going limp.

Ashley screams as she runs. "Lachlan! Close your eyes!"

He immediately obeys her, squeezing his eyes closed.

She leaps from the nearest chair onto the tabletop, then jumps off it, her outstretched hands closing around the compliance officer's head. He jolts into the wall behind him as she claws his temples with her fingernails.

The moment she touches him, he freezes, thudding back against the wall.

Her hair rises into swirling, hissing clumps, snakes taking shape although not fully formed. She stops clawing him only long enough to drag the tie away from her eyes, her face close to his.

I can't see what she looks like. If the information I read is true, even a gorgon's power will roll off me like water. But I can see the effect on the compliance officer. His mouth opens wide in a final shout, his skin turning a pallid gray before he solidifies into a statue.

Ashley hurries to replace the tie around her eyes before she takes a step back, then swings a fist at the compliance officer's stone arm, shattering it into dust to release Lachlan from his hold.

Lachlan slides to the floor, coughing hard, his eyes still closed as Ashley reaches for him.

In front of me, Ms. Sparrow screams as she whirls back to me. Her terrified gaze flicks from Striker's hellish appearance to mine.

I have no idea what I look like now, but Ms. Sparrow backs away from me, wobbling in her heels. "What *are* you?"

"I'm pain and torment."

I reach for her, my claws extended, but a sudden whoosh makes me pause.

Ms. Sparrow gasps, freezing to the spot. Her gaze shoots to her chest, her hands fluttering over the wooden wand that protrudes right through the location of her heart.

Lucinda rises up behind her, her hands pressed forward in the air. Her teeth are gritted in barely controlled rage, tears still glistening on her cheeks. "She sent me to the pit to be mauled."

Years of fear and oppression can't be undone in one night, but this is a start.

Ms. Sparrow drops to the floor and I float over her, returning to the floor to pull Lucinda into a hug. It's the first I've offered her—she's always been the one offering hugs to me. She accepts it, dropping her head to my shoulder, a short moment of quiet in the chaos around us.

Within seconds, a compliance officer runs at us from the side. I release Lucinda to duck his right hook and smash a fist into his ribs, my power giving me more strength than I ever had before. With an *oomph*, he flies backward.

Lucinda flicks her wrist and the table behind him slides to the right just in time for him to hit his head on its edge and collapse unconscious.

Around the room, compliance officers either lie dead or unconscious. The final one falls when Striker knocks his head against a tabletop so hard it makes Lucinda wince.

A room full of students rise to their feet, but Lucinda has one more task to do.

"It hurts me to do this," she says before she raises her hands to the wands on the ceiling, closing her eyes moments before each one snaps in half and the broken ends clatter to the floor.

Joseph and Striker stride to the front of the room, both of them retaining their monstrous forms. Striker positions himself a step behind me. He doesn't seem at all perturbed about the fact that Joseph is as scary-ass looking as he is.

Ashley stays with Lachlan at the back of the room, her hair returned to normal, although she still wears the tie around her eyes. Bree joins Lucinda on my other side.

The other students are beaten up, but the fight in their eyes blazes as brightly as the flames in Striker's. Their focus travels over his massive form to me.

It takes me a moment to realize what they want. Striker leans in to whisper to me, "They're waiting for you."

I swallow, fidgeting so hard, I scrape myself with my claws. I'm not good with speeches. I'm better at telling people where they can shove it than asking them to work together.

"We don't have much time," I say. "Osprey is on her way here right now. She intends to kill you all tonight. But I'm here to tell you that's not going to happen." I take a deep breath. "This is my true form. I'm a monster. So is Striker—"

"Tell us something we don't already know," Ryan calls from the back next to Ashley and Lachlan. He's rubbing his jaw and it looks like a massive bruise is already growing across his face.

He breaks into a sudden grin. "I'll take a monster on my side any day."

I relax and give him a smile. "I don't know for sure yet, but I believe that every magically repressed person has rare and deadly powers. We just need a chance to discover what we are."

Lachlan steps forward. "I'm ready to fight. I might not know what I am yet, but I refuse to die before I find out."

I'm gratified when all of the students nod.

"Okay, then," I say. "Our plan is to get to the front gate. Striker can open it for us, but making it through is not going to be easy. Lucinda can disarm the witches, but we can't underestimate their determination to stop us."

"Why now, Peyton?" Bree asks quietly at my side. "They've caged us here for years. Why kill us now?"

We're running out of time. As we talk, Osprey will be gathering the other teachers and preparing for our rebellion. I'd be a fool if I didn't assume she heard the commotion in this room and knew something was amiss.

I don't fully understand the reasons why it's happening now, but the other students need the meager answers that I *can* give them.

"The Founder of this institution—Lady Tirelli—has gone missing. Osprey believes that a powerful group of assassins is coming after everyone associated with her. We're a liability, a drain on Osprey's resources. She's preparing for a war with the assassins and *we* are not the soldiers she wanted us to be."

"Let the assassins come," Lachlan says, openly squeezing Ashley's hand. She nods her agreement beside him.

"I agree," I say. "But they aren't here yet. It's up to us. We've been underestimated and pushed around, and we've been caged long enough." I level my gaze with theirs. "We will not die tonight."

I turn to Striker and Joseph. "I need you both to protect the students who can't manifest their powers yet. They're the most vulnerable."

"What about you, Peyton?" Joseph asks me.

I give him a deadly grin. "Apparently, when I harness my power, I can't be killed."

Striker suddenly grabs my hand and drags me to the side, away from the others, a demanding scowl descending over his beast face that makes him look terrifyingly ferocious. "Don't test it, Peyton."

I'm ready to snap back at him not to underestimate me, but then I catch the worry in the depths of his eyes, the tension around his mouth. I rein in my indignation but can't keep the bite out of my voice. "I promise not to do anything stupid."

He growls at me and his body heat suddenly intensifies. "I meant what I said."

I lean in to him, not afraid to close the gap, my eyes narrowed at him. "Which part?"

"The part about a bed."

My cheeks blaze. *Dear ancients.* Priorities again.

A nearby cough makes me whirl. Lucinda breezes past us with Joseph at her side. Her eyes are brighter and her skin has taken on a polished sheen, her dryad powers manifesting to a fuller extent. "If you two have finished raising the temperature in this room to sauna levels, let's go already."

I spin to follow her, but Striker grips my hand harder, pulling me back into his side, nuzzling my cheek for a moment. "Don't die, my Fury."

I brush my palm to his cheek. "I won't. I promise."

Satisfied with that, he lets go of my hand. I turn to the wide-eyed stares of half the students, who were evidently not anticipating any shows of affection between Striker and me.

Ashley wears a smile as she passes me by—she seems to see even better with her eyes closed—and I hurry to catch up with her. I was supposed to go first and be a protective barrier for all of them.

The corridor will be a death trap.

Thankfully, they all wait for me at the door. Many of the students carry broken wands, holding them like daggers. We haven't been trained to use weapons, but it's better than nothing.

I try to ignore the fear creeping through me. I've never sustained my power this long before and I'm worried about what will happen if it wanes. It's already been a difficult day. Osprey, Mallard, Hawk, and Raptor won't be as easy to subdue or disarm. I'm not so worried about Ms. Vulture, but she's an unknown element.

I don't kid myself that we'll have the element of surprise anymore. They'll be prepared.

I take a deep breath as Striker and Joseph take up position behind me, with Lucinda and Ashley at their backs. Striker growls at the other students to stay back until we know the coast is clear.

With my heart in my throat, I open the door.

40. STRIKER DRAVEN

*L*ight explodes right in front of Peyton's face.

In the split second before it ignites, I catch sight of a glass sphere floating in the air at head-height. It's a motion-triggered shard bomb waiting to go off.

My roar of warning is swallowed in the explosion. Hot, white light packed with shards of sharp stone cuts through Peyton's body in a single horrifying moment.

She turns with a scream, her hair flying around her face, her shocked eyes meeting mine. Her clothing is cut through but she pats herself, holding apart the material.

She shakes her head in disbelief. She isn't harmed. But her worried eyes travel to my chest.

A glance at my own body tells me I've taken the brunt of the explosion.

Joseph has, too. All down his left side. We are both peppered with glittering glass shards that would cut through a human.

Peyton's mouth drops. The shards must have shot straight through her without any damage.

"Looks like you're not going to be a shield after all," I say to Peyton with a grin, harnessing the boiling hellfire inside me to dissolve the tips embedded in my skin within seconds. The ends of the shards drop to the floor with a sound as pretty as the tinkling of glass.

Joseph gives me an annoyed glance, rapidly plucking shrapnel out of his chest and thighs.

"Well, this sucks," he says, huffing at his task.

Lucinda grabs his arm and takes charge, pulling out the hard-to-reach shards in his arm and side, her palm lingering over his rapidly healing skin.

He gives her a crooked smile as she lingers longer than she needs to.

Hell, he should just kiss her already. He might not get another chance.

Peyton's hand flies over her mouth. Holy hell, is she laughing right now? She is one of the most unpredictable women I've ever met. Mad at me when she wants to be, gentle when I don't expect it. It's going to take me a lifetime to get to know all her moods.

I just hope I have that long.

She gives me a sheepish smile. "Well, that was interesting," she says. "Should I scream again to make it sound like we're wounded?"

A glance back at the other students tells me that her humor is just what they needed. The rising tension in the room eases. The fact that we survived without any drama will make them all feel much safer.

"Okay, Shields," she says, addressing Joseph and me with our new function. "Stay close and let's go."

She rises off the ground by a foot and glides into the hallway, proceeding slowly and carefully. Joseph and I walk side by side while Ashley and Lucinda take up position behind us. I already knew about Lucinda's power, but Ashley's was a surprise. I'm not sure at this stage whether they have the same healing powers or ability to resist damage that Peyton and Joseph have, so I'm not going to take any chances.

Peyton pauses at the first door on the right. So far, none of the teachers has appeared. If I were them, I'd leave spells all along the corridor to be triggered by movement and wait for any survivors at both exits—the front door and the back. That means their forces will be divided. Knowing Osprey, she'll take the front.

Peyton continues along the corridor as the students file carefully behind us.

As soon as she passes the third door, a sudden click is the only warning we get. The air shifts at eye height and my heightened senses detect the power along the wall.

"Down!" I shout.

Peyton is the only one who doesn't obey me. Arrows appear out of nothing and shoot from wall to wall all along the length of the corridor. Joseph is so tall that one spears toward his shoulder before he can duck.

It stops midair.

Every arrow halts, many a hairsbreadth away from piercing the other students. The weapons clatter to the floor.

Lucinda turns to me with a bright smile, lowering her outstretched arms. "They're wooden," she explains.

I give her an acknowledging nod. "You have quick reflexes."

Lucinda gives me an unassuming shrug. "I sensed the arrows as soon as they formed. One day I'll be strong enough to stop them from materializing, but I'm still learning."

Peyton arches an eyebrow at me. Damn, she's sexy when she makes that I-told-you-so face. She turns in the air, a graceful arc, her hair floating around her, her eyes filled with pure violence. That's when I catch her scent. Wildflowers. Nothing like the sickly roses in the yard. This scent compels me to follow her, to do whatever she wishes…

I give myself an internal slap.

I don't know enough about Furies, but they have the power to compel even the fiercest warrior to do their bidding.

Her power is growing stronger.

Much stronger.

I didn't anticipate that her power of compulsion would affect me in my hellhound form, but I should have remembered that a Fury is built for vengeance on all creatures, human and supernatural. She is judge, jury, and executioner.

If I were smart, I'd fear her, but what I feel for her is much more intense.

I still can't believe how hard she fought to bring me back, that she's given me the second chance I never thought I'd get. I won't waste it. She's the most important person in my life now and I'll spend every day proving it to her.

She glances back at me, her lips curving. She promised to hate me always. She brought me back from the abyss. Even as the demons of hell gripped my ankles and pulled me under, she reached down and wouldn't let me go.

We reach the end of the corridor. The entrance area ahead of us is empty, but we can't see to either side. With a shiver, I realize that's why she smiled.

She raises her hand, palm up at me to *stop*.

I count my heartbeats. One. Two.

She darts forward, her arms outstretched, before she spins in the air. Glittering darts flood the space around her like deadly snow.

She whirls through them, dancing effortlessly until the flurry stops, at which she lands in the center of the floor, finding her feet, completely unharmed.

"I think that's it," she says with another laugh and again, the tension eases around me.

I don't think she realizes that it's not only her lighthearted speech, but her compulsion that is easing the minds of all of those around her. I'm glad for it. The last thing we need is for someone to panic and get themselves killed.

I stride up to her, expanding my senses. Contrary to what I thought, I count four bodies outside the front entrance and none at the back exit. "They're all out front."

She nods as if she already knew. "We should go outside first—just you and I—and kill them. I don't want to risk the other students."

She's so calm, talking about death so easily, it's scary.

My inner nature laps it up, but my human side is cautious. "The spells could have been tests."

Her eyes narrow. "You mean if we walk out of here alive, they'll know we have particular powers."

"Raptor's not stupid."

"You're right." She sighs. "I was worried he already figured out Bree and Lucinda's powers."

I'm curious. "Bree?"

She gives me a smile. "She's a siren."

That's news to me, but I stay focused. "I agree with your plan."

She raises an eyebrow. "You do?"

I grin at her, rolling my shoulders. "Why is that so surprising?"

Peyton shrugs. She leans in with a smile, but it fades, and she finally allows me to see the fear she's hiding, using me as a visual barrier so the others can't see her face. She lowers her voice. "They're ready for us this time. The dining room was child's play. The risk to the others is high now."

I contemplate the closed doors. I walked into this place through those doors. Strode in like I didn't care, willfully taking a knife to my sense of freedom.

Striding back to Lucinda and Joseph, I say to them, "We need you to stay here and protect the others. Peyton and I will let you know when the path is clear."

"I don't like it," Lucinda objects, but Joseph places a reassuring hand on her shoulder. "We can do that. We'll watch your backs in case anyone tries to come through here behind you."

Lucinda finally nods. "Okay, we *can* do that."

I return to Peyton. She turns her face up to mine. "I'm not afraid," she says.

She faced me down so many times, going head to head with me. Getting right back up again to challenge me again. "You rarely are."

"No, I mean…" She closes her eyes and takes a deep breath. "I'm not afraid of Osprey. But I *am* afraid… of…" She shakes her head. "It doesn't matter."

She leaves me wondering what she was going to say as she glides forward and presses against the door. The gleam in her eyes increases and her expression changes for a second, a shadow passing over it.

"It's time to cut some roses," she says.

41. PEYTON PRICE

I don't know how to tell Striker that I'm barely in control right now.

Somewhere between the dining room and the entrance, the rage inside me has escalated. I can't retract my claws. I had to force myself to return to the ground. My feet feel foreign on it.

I thought that if I threw myself into danger, I would regain my sense of self, but it only made things worse. A hundred glass shards passed through my body and I felt every one of them, heard myself scream a thousand times inside my mind, but even my own pain doesn't seem to matter.

I want blood. Just like the elegant plaque behind me announces: This is Bloodwing Academy.

Dusk has fallen outside, a gorgeous sunset glow bathing the front yard, turning the red roses crimson.

Mr. Mallard, Ms. Hawk, Raptor, and Osprey stand at intervals around the rose bushes, each fully contained within a large sphere of glowing power. Ms. Vulture isn't anywhere to be seen so I'm glad Lucinda and Joseph are watching our backs.

The spheres remind me of the poultice Osprey used on me when I first arrived, but without the sucking sensation. I won't know what the spheres do until I engage with them but I suspect they're some kind of defensive mechanism.

These teachers won't be so easily disarmed.

Osprey calls to us. "You can't touch us, Peyton. We're protected inside these shields. Our magic can get out but nothing can get in."

I stop at the bottom of the steps, Striker close at my side. "Let us go, Osprey. You said it yourself—we're a liability. Let us walk out of here and you'll never see us again."

She scoffs. "The location of this academy has been kept secret for years. The moment you walk out of here, you'll know where we are. Sorry, Peyton. I can't take the chance that you'll talk." She sounds anything but sorry. "Especially when the assassins come for you."

"They're coming for *you*, Headmistress. Not us."

She laughs. "That's where you're wrong. I wanted to give you quick deaths. The assassins will take their time."

She's lying through her teeth, but not about all of it. Assassins pride themselves on clean kills, but if they need information, well, Raptor's brutality is evidence of an assassin's interrogation skills.

I paste a smile on my face that quickly becomes genuine. "I was hoping you'd refuse."

Darting forward, I'm prepared to tear apart their magical shields with my claws if I have to.

The teachers shout in unison, "Cunning capture, control, and cut!"

Glowing magical ropes spear toward us as we run. Striker lopes ahead of me, taking the brunt of the ropes. He grabs two of them, twists, pulls them taut, and slices through them with his claws.

I follow his lead, grabbing the end of the final lash that flies toward me, my claws passing through it. As soon as I cut it, the lash disintegrates.

I reach Mallard's sphere first and Striker hits Hawk's.

Despite what Osprey said, the sphere's surface is like butter to me, my claws slicing right through it.

To my left, Striker has a harder time, ramming his claws into the sphere, molten lava flowing down his arm to his hand, sizzling across the sphere's surface. The magic keeping the sphere together pops and crackles, cracks appearing across its surface.

Ms. Hawk screams. Spells explode around Striker as she tries to fight back. Daggers appear out of nowhere and pierce his skin. A fireball hits his back, but he doesn't stop.

The sphere finally explodes outward. Ms. Hawk screams another spell, but Striker plucks a dagger from his chest and flings it into hers.

She falls to the ground and her scream stops.

I don't have nearly so much trouble with Mallard's sphere, slicing through it with a single downward cut and peeling it apart with my hands, stepping forward to join him inside it. Sounds outside the sphere are muffled from the inside, but Osprey's scream as Striker hits her sphere echoes around us, oddly amplified.

Mallard plasters himself against the back of the sphere, lowering his wand. "You weren't supposed to be able to do that."

"I wasn't supposed to live in this hellhole," I say. "What is it you think I'm supposed to do now?"

Other than the ropes, he hasn't tried to cast a spell on me. "I never hurt you, Peyton."

"You stood by while others did."

"True." He nods. "I came here for the research. I wanted to study the magically repressed. Find out what you are. You haven't disappointed. Not in the least."

I can't touch him unless he raises his wand. I want blood but I'm no better than Osprey if I have no honor.

Mallard lifts his left hand, palm up in surrender as he slowly places his wand on the ground and pushes it toward me. "You can kill me. It's your choice. But I'd like to live."

He steps away from his wand, pressing against the sphere.

Without taking my eyes off him, I bend to retrieve the magical weapon, hesitating before I touch it, wondering what I'll see.

My fingers close around it and an image assaults me: I'm looking at myself from a different perspective—Mallard's perspective. My body is lying on the floor of his classroom. Striker stands over the top of me, glaring back at Mallard. It must be moments after Striker knocked me out and stopped me telling Raptor about the assassins.

Raptor storms at him from the side, but Striker snarls, "Try making Peyton talk now."

Striker feints left as Raptor draws his blade and attacks, but then Mallard flings ropes at him, binding Striker. Striker thrashes so hard that the ropes turn to blades and shred his shirt. The sight of Striker's blood snaps me back to the present.

"I should kill you," I say, gripping the wand as I take a step forward amid a wash of perfume. Wildflowers. The scent swirls around us, intensified within the sphere and with it, my compulsion to control him increases.

Mallard nods. "You should." He drops to his knees and tips his head back, responding to my wish. "Will you, please?"

My hands shake. I fight the urge to claw his neck and end his miserable existence.

Snap. His wand separates into two, bringing me back to myself just in time. I grip both pieces hard and take them with me as I step from the sphere, leaving Mallard to slump within it. He can't hurt or stop us without his wand.

Outside, Osprey is fighting back with everything she's got. Every time Striker creates a crack in her sphere, she screams another spell, repairing it. He's bleeding across his neck, where she must have tried to slit his throat, but the wound is healing.

Raptor prowls within his own sphere, a dagger clutched in each hand. He has no magic to fight back with and can't come out to fight us. He flicks a glance at the front entrance, as if he's expecting something, but there's nobody there. Maybe he thinks Vulture is coming to help him?

As he turns, I catch sight of the weapon attached to his belt.

My whip.

I take a step toward him just as Striker breaks through Osprey's shield and everything explodes around us. A spell hits me from behind forcing me into Raptor's shield. My outstretched claws cut right through it so that I tumble inside to his waiting blades.

One slices through my shoulder, the other through my back, but my screams only sound in my mind. The wounds heal instantly.

He jolts backward, cursing loudly, driving the dagger into my neck and leaving it there.

I scowl at him, pulling it free and repositioning it in my hand. "That wasn't smart."

Keeping him within my sights, I tear an opening in the sphere and fling the dagger outside it. It doesn't bother me that he still holds one blade. He can't hurt me with it.

My only focus now is the whip.

Outside Raptor's shield, Osprey continues to fight back, keeping Striker at bay. I was afraid she might control instinctive magic and it looks like my fears are coming true.

He drops to his knees as a spell splashes against his heart. A blade forms before his face, arcing toward his eye. He grabs it with his hand, straining to keep it from descending, blood dripping down his arm as the sword cuts his palm.

He's not healing fast enough to hold on.

A smile crosses Osprey's face.

I scream at Raptor. "Give me the whip!"

The scent of wildflowers fills the space around us. He

shudders, shaking his head, trying to clear it, his hand inching toward the weapon.

His hesitation is all I need. I duck, roll, and snatch the whip from his belt. I run, one hand outward, claws slicing through the shield as I arc back, racing toward Osprey.

My power flows into the whip as I skid to a halt, raise my arm and swing. With a scream, the tips sail through the air, straight and true, wrapping around Osprey's face and neck twice before they crack against her cheeks.

I sense the moment of perfect tension in the whip, the moment that the *crack* splits the air.

Her startled scream is cut short as I retract my arm and the whip tears through sinew, muscle, and bone.

A clean kill.

Her body snaps to the side, rolling out of the whip as it unfurls and casts her through the air. She hits the ground, tumbles a couple of paces, and comes to a stop under a rose bush, lying on her side, her face turned away.

I should be horrified.

I should go into shock at what I just did.

But the blade at Striker's face disappears and I'm grateful because he's alive. I promised I'd defend him and I'll never break that promise.

He pulls to his feet, spits blood onto the ground, and then comes for me, taking my arms in his enormous hands as he searches my eyes. "Thank you."

I take a deep breath. "I'm not done."

He gives me a serious nod before he stands clear. "I won't stop you."

I turn, dragging the whip through the grass. I'll need to clean it later but its job isn't finished yet.

Raptor's shield disappeared the moment that Osprey died.

He flings his second blade straight and true into my heart, but I drag it right out, dropping it to the ground.

He backs up, his gaze flicking to the entrance again.

I adjust the whip as I advance on him, lifting it and preparing to swing.

"Stop!" The shout from the front door makes me pause.

Ms. Vulture descends down the front steps, her old lady legs hurrying as fast as she can. She's alone and isn't even carrying a wand. Striker advances on her, making her stop with a shriek as she takes in his appearance.

She pulls herself upright as he prowls around her, her head held high, smoothing her hair back and tugging her sweater into place. She eyes him over her glasses.

I keep Raptor in my sights as Vulture carefully raises her hand and flicks her wrist.

Both doors open and the students appear behind her. They shuffle together, Lucinda and Joseph at their head. Their bodies are wooden as they move, their eyes unfocused.

"What have you done to them?" I shout.

Ms. Vulture clears her throat. "I've used a compliance spell on them. You'll be pleased to know it was very difficult and won't last very long, but I didn't want anyone to get hurt. Joseph is already breaking free. Lucinda will be next. If you don't mind, Peyton, my intent is not to harm you. Only to delay you for a moment until—"

A loud clang rings out behind me.

"There," Ms. Vulture says, giving me a pleased smile.

I swing to the gate, stepping closer to Striker, both of us backing up so we can keep Vulture, Raptor, and the entrance in our sights.

Off to the side, Mallard has fallen to the ground, remaining on his knees as he, too, watches the gate.

It rattles as it opens.

42. PEYTON PRICE

The empty road stretches out before us, curving to the right and into the trees, the forest obscuring the rest of it.

It's the first time I've seen the gate open and the urge to race through it is so strong, I have to fight my instincts. I can't leave without everyone else and most of the students are still under Vulture's control.

The gate's iron bars slide open in both directions as two armored vehicles appear around the distant curve, both sleek and black, with tinted windows so no one can see who's inside them.

I brace, ready for anything as the first truck pulls to a halt in the entrance, not quite entering the grounds.

The passenger side door opens and an older man jumps from it, his movements sharp and controlled. He's wearing black body armor, with multiple weapon belts attached around his torso and hips. I lose count of the dagger hilts and guns, finally contemplating the tip of what appears to be a semi-automatic machine gun strapped to his back.

His hair is white-blond, his eyes striking blue, his jaw

chiseled in a perfect military way, and his clothing stretched over his muscled arms and legs. He looks mid-forties but carries himself like a twenty-year old.

As soon as his boots hit the ground, thirty other men dressed just like him pour from the back of the trucks, swarming into the yard and lining the fence line. One of them drags Mallard with him, gripping his arm and forcing him to his knees on the grass again.

Suddenly, we're surrounded and it's as if the nightmare is beginning all over again.

Striker growls beside me, reminding me that we can fight back this time. We just killed thirty compliance officers. We can kill these men too.

Maybe. We've fought magic, not guns. I'm certain I can withstand bullets, but I don't know about Striker. The students who are still in human form won't have a chance if bullets start flying. Tears of rage fill my eyes as I realize that I shouldn't have stopped fighting. I should have killed Raptor quickly, then Vulture, and been done with it.

I swing to Striker to see the same worry etched in his face. Our choices are limited now.

The newcomer lifts his hands, palms up, in a placating gesture, raising his voice at the same time. "My name is Adrian Hadrix. I'm not here to harm you."

Despite Hadrix's declaration, Striker remains tense beside me. "He's Lady Tirelli's man," he murmurs. "We can't trust him."

Hadrix stops at a distance that I calculate is just outside the reach of my whip. He's smart, I'll give him that.

He casts a sudden smile at someone behind me. Vulture hurries toward him, giving me a wide berth on her way to settle into the crook of his arm.

He kisses her forehead but raises his eyebrows at her. "Not your prettiest form, my love."

"Oh." She pouts. "You know you'll love me even when I'm old."

He gives her an intense smile. "Always."

She turns back to us before stepping out from within the circle of his arms. "Oops," she says. "Probably best to reveal myself."

She gives herself a shake, an extended shiver passing through her body.

As she moves, her face and hair change. So does her body shape. She grows half a foot in height, her glasses disappear, and her skin smooths to creamy white. Luxurious blonde hair falls down her back, accentuating her slender neck and narrow waist. Her clothes change, too, shifting into a pair of black leggings and a tight sweater. Like Hadrix, she appears in her forties as she smiles back at us with sparkling green eyes.

"Allow me to introduce my wife," Hadrix says. "So nobody gets confused, you may continue to call her 'Ms. Vulture.'"

Hadrix addresses his wife quietly. "I'm glad you warned me about Osprey's plans today, but it looks like things are under control."

He casts a satisfied glance at the two bodies lying on the grass: Osprey and Hawk, both dead.

Confusion grows inside me because it sounds like he's pleased that they're dead. Shouldn't they be his friends?

He makes an unhappy noise in his throat as his gaze passes over Mallard, who remains on the ground, the barrel of a gun pressed to his back.

"It wasn't easy getting my messages to you, darling," Vulture says to Hadrix. "I wasn't sure if you'd arrive in time. But Peyton and Striker performed beautifully."

"Of course they did," he replies. "I wouldn't expect anything less."

He takes a step toward me, glancing to the side at Raptor, who tips his chin at Hadrix as if they know each other well.

I narrow my eyes at both of them. By the sounds of things, Vulture has been communicating with her husband for some time. He and Raptor also appear chummy, particularly because Vulture stopped me from killing Raptor.

I don't know what's going on, but until I figure it out, I'm prepared for anything.

Hadrix dares to step within the reach of my whip. "I realize you have good reasons to kill Raptor—he can certainly go too far sometimes—but I guarantee he will be more useful to you alive."

A snarl grows in my throat. "I would rather he were dead."

Hadrix inclines his head. "I understand, but Raptor knows the inner workings of the assassin's world. He knows their magic. He can tell you how they operate. Most importantly, he can tell you their weaknesses."

"Why would I need to know that?" I snap.

"Because, Peyton, the assassins are coming for you."

Osprey said the same thing, but I didn't believe her. She lied so often that the words coming out of her mouth were a buzz inside my head.

Movement behind me tells me that the compulsion spell has broken and the other students are mobilizing rapidly, drawing close to Striker and me. The tension among them tells me they're prepared to fight if they have to.

Taking glances at the soldiers, Lucinda edges up to me. "What do you want to do, Peyton?"

"How much did you hear?"

"All of it. I just couldn't control my body."

Before I can answer, Hadrix turns in a circle, lifting his voice as he addresses all of the students. "The assassins are coming for all of you. If you don't believe me, just take a look at yourselves. Look at Peyton and Striker."

He points. I'm still floating above the ground, my claws

extended, and Striker remains in hellhound form, fissures of fire crackling across his body.

"You are deadly creatures," he continues, "every single one of you. You are a threat to everything they know and hold dear. You must be destroyed at all costs."

So far, he hasn't threatened me. The men surrounding us aren't pointing their guns at us, either. They stand watching but, other than the gun at Mallard's back, their hands are held behind their backs, at ease.

Now Hadrix is telling us what I don't want to hear: that the world outside these walls is more dangerous than the one within them.

"What do you want, Hadrix?" I demand to know. "You're not here out of the goodness of your heart."

He exhales. "I won't lie to you. All of Lady Tirelli's associates are being assassinated. The Assassin's Legion is wiping the slate clean. This academy is hidden from them. It exists in a place called a Realm that the assassins can neither find nor breach."

He lifts his hands, sweeping them across the air. In the fading light, it's almost impossible to see the sheen covering the sky.

Most of the students stare in confusion. Even Striker didn't see it until I pointed it out to him.

I remind myself that I'm a Fury. I can see the true nature of things. Most of the time. Frustration fills me that I'm still developing that power.

Right now, I really need to see Hadrix's true nature, but as hard as I try, it's hidden from me.

If what he's saying is true, then the cage around the Academy isn't to keep us in. It's there to keep others out.

"The only people who know where this academy is, are now standing within its walls," Hadrix continues. "If you leave this place, you will be vulnerable, a target. You're safe as long as you stay."

Striker growls beside me. "That's all well and good, but you didn't answer Peyton's question: What do you want?"

"I ask your permission to stay," he says. "I need safety for me and my men as much as you need shelter. Bloodwing is the only safe place left to us."

"Why would we agree?" I snap.

Hadrix inclines his head at Striker, stepping even closer. "The Dravens have provided Lady Tirelli with her weapons, but I trained her soldiers. Let me do the same for you. I can teach you weaponry and combat skills, and I can show you how to kill efficiently. Combined with your powers, I can make you better assassins than the assassins themselves."

His eyes gleam striking blue as he passes his charismatic gaze across all of us. "Then, when you choose to leave, you will be prepared for the fight ahead of you. They may call you 'monsters,' but I call you 'warriors.' I say *they* should be afraid of *you*."

It's a rousing speech, but it leaves me cold.

Now that he's standing closer to me, I sense Hadrix's power like a constrained rage, tightly leashed.

He's definitely not a wizard like his wife is a witch, but he *is* magical. *What* he is, I can't pinpoint.

He lowers his voice. "What do you say, Peyton? I know I'm asking a lot for you to leave Raptor alive. I can understand if it's difficult to trust someone who just appeared on your doorstep, but I promise you, I'm not here to cage you." He meets my eyes in a way that I'm certain is calculated to make me trust him. "You have a rare and beautiful power. I'm here to make you stronger."

Everything inside me screams at me to run, to take Striker's hand and get the hell out of here. The gate is open. We could run through it right now and face down the assassins together, but we'd be leaving behind students who aren't ready to defend themselves.

I carefully wind up my whip, glaring at Raptor, who stands with his arms folded across his chest, his expression hidden behind his messy hair.

I can't tell what he's thinking, but I will never forget what he did to me.

The blaze in Striker's eyes is dull now and I'm reminded that he's still recovering. I squeeze his arm as I lower myself to the ground and force my power to recede, hoping he'll see it as permission to return to his usual form.

If anything happens now, I will be his defender.

He shakes out his shoulders, carefully morphing back into human Striker. Joseph has already done the same and Lucinda's skin is smooth again. Ashley has also removed the tie from around her eyes.

They all look tired. The stress and fear have taken their toll. Not just from today, but from years of it piled on their shoulders.

"Is Hadrix telling the truth?" Striker asks. He doesn't bother lowering his voice. There's no point trying to conceal our conversation.

I nod reluctantly. "The threat is real. He's not lying about that. We're a target and we're not ready to defend ourselves against trained assassins. Only a handful of us know what we are. Those of us who do are still learning to control our powers."

What I don't say is that I watched those two assassins annihilate a fully-fledged Fury. The woman with the silver-ringed eyes is not to be messed with. Even at my strongest, even with this whip, it will take everything to kill her.

I reach for Striker, drawing him close. "You already started training us. Can you teach us the skills we need instead of Hadrix?"

He smooths the hair behind my ear. "I could try, but..." He glances at the soldiers and their guns, a dangerous glint returning to his eyes. "I don't actually believe we have a choice right now."

I turn to the others, picturing the bloodbath if things go wrong.

I've finally made friends, people I care about. The way Joseph is holding Lucinda's hand and Lachlan is holding Ashley's tells me they have a chance for happiness. All I can do right now is protect them within the new lines that are being drawn around us.

I choose my words carefully. "Striker and I will accept this new situation. We can learn from Hadrix and take the time we need to become stronger. We *will* fight anything that threatens us."

I hope the students hear my silent promise: If Hadrix threatens or hurts us, we will fight him too.

Nobody moves. Then, slowly, one by one, they give me silent nods. Striker is last, his agreement a single downward sweep of his head.

I can't read the expression behind his eyes. He promised me a faraway bed that belongs to both of us.

A dream that's fading fast.

"You've made the right choice," Hadrix says from behind me. He doesn't smile. Every move he makes is carried out with military efficiency.

I speak clearly. "We won't be treated like prisoners anymore. You will not threaten us with violence. If you or your men harm any one of us, you will answer to Striker and me."

He nods without hesitation. "You have my word, but please be warned, my training methods are not for the fainthearted."

I glare at him. "You have no idea how tough every student in this place is."

He grins. "I'm counting on it."

Vulture has remained quiet but now she exchanges a look with her husband. The silent communication between them makes me cautious again. I'm not sure I'm prepared to accept any more surprises.

"There's one more thing," Hadrix says. "But I'm sure it won't be a problem."

He waves at the first vehicle parked at the gate.

There's movement inside it, but I can't see beyond the tinted windows, especially now that my rage is diminished. I'm tired too. It's been a long day and all I want is a quiet place to mourn the loss of my freedom—the broken hope that Striker and I could start fresh today. I tell myself it won't be forever. I have a way out and a path to get there.

We will leave Bloodwing together. Just... not today.

The vehicle's door opens and a young woman steps down from it.

Her blonde hair is braided in a similar style to the other female students' hair, but she wears tight jeans and a sweater that hugs her slender curves. Her eyes are bright blue, but for a moment... I'm sure they switch to brown, then back again. Her hair shimmers too, rippling brown and then settling to blonde.

I blink, trying to decide if it's a trick of the light. Night will fall soon and visibility will only get worse. The sooner we settle this, the better.

A deep crease forms on Striker's forehead as he studies the approaching woman, his gaze passing from her hair to her eyes.

His confused expression suddenly clears and his claws snap out.

For a second, I think he's going to break away from me. A careful touch on his arm tells me that his beast is threatening to burst out at any moment, a new fire building inside him.

Hadrix places a protective arm around the woman's shoulders when she reaches him.

He pins Striker in his sights as he says, "I think you know my daughter, Kaitlyn."

I stare in shock. Silence falls over the yard. Lucinda bristles and so does Joseph, the tension rising around me a thousand percent.

Ignoring everyone else, Kaitlyn gives Striker a sweet smile that makes my blood run cold. "Hi, baby."

Oh, hell no.

I might have just made a deal with the bad guys, might have agreed to stay at Bloodwing when all I want is my freedom, but there's no way I'm letting this two-faced liar do whatever she wants.

Stepping directly in front of Kaitlyn, I turn myself into a visual barrier between her and Striker.

His rage is a comforting heat at my back, telling me he wants to tear her to shreds.

The Fury inside me practically purrs in response. Striker Draven is one scary-as-hell asshole, but his brutality is the mirror to my own.

"Hi, Kaitlyn," I say, matching her sweet tone. "We haven't met before. Allow me to introduce myself…"

She blinks at me, the faintest hint of annoyance that I'm in her way, but I don't let her irritation bother me.

This is my Academy now. I'll train and I'll fight, but I won't compromise my heart.

The assassins might be coming for us, the supernatural world might consider us disposable and worthless, but I know what I am and I'll only become stronger.

My smile doesn't reach my eyes. "I'm your worst nightmare."

~

Find out what happens next in Revenge.

REVENGE

(ASSASSIN'S MAGIC BOOK 6)

I am vengeance. A bringer of fury.

Love is a blade that could tear me apart.

My bond with Striker Draven has been forged in blood.

We fought for our freedom only to discover that our enemies are far more powerful than we thought.

The Assassin's Legion is hunting us like the monsters we are.

But the students are now my family and I would die to protect them.

Just as I would die to protect Striker.

He is strength and fury, a hellish beast whose touch ignites my dark soul.

And yet… the closer I get to him, the greater the danger grows.

Our enemies are weaving a web around us, spun with power and deceit, until I'm left with only one path to freedom.

A path that could break my heart.

Content information: Revenge is dark urban fantasy romance, the sixth in the Assassin's Magic series.

Recommended reading age is 17+ for sex scenes, mature themes, and violence. Ends on a cliffhanger.

ALSO BY EVERLY FROST

ASSASSIN'S MAGIC

(Dark Urban Fantasy Romance)

1. Assassin's Magic

2. Assassin's Mask

3. Assassin's Menace

4. Assassin's Maze

5. Rebels

6. Revenge

7. Rogue

8. Assassin's Match

SOUL BITTEN SHIFTER - COMPLETE

(Dark Urban Fantasy Romance)

1. This Dark Wolf

2. This Broken Wolf

3. This Caged Wolf

4. This Cruel Blood

SUPERNATURAL LEGACY - COMPLETE

(Angels and Dragon Shifters)

1. Hunt the Night

2. Chase the Shadows

3. Slay the Dawn

4. Claim the Light

DARK MAGIC SHIFTERS

(Dark Urban Fantasy Romance)

1. Wolf of Ashes

2. Bond of Flames

3. Crown of Fate

KINGDOM OF BETRAYAL

(Fantasy Romance)

1. A Sky Like Blood

2. A Sin Like Fire

3. A Storm Like Iron

4. A Soul Like Glass

BRIGHT WICKED - COMPLETE

(Fantasy Romance)

1. Bright Wicked

2. Radiant Fierce

3. Infernal Dark

STORM PRINCESS - COMPLETE

(Fantasy Romance)

1. Book 1

2. Book 2

3. Book 3

DEMON PACK - COMPLETE

(Dark Paranormal Romance)

1. Demon Pack

2. Demon Pack: Elimination

3. Demon Pack: Eternal

MORTALITY - COMPLETE

(Science-Fantasy Romance)

Mortality Complete Set: Books 1 to 4

1. Beyond the Ever Reach

2. Beneath the Guarding Stars

3. By the Icy Wild

4. Before the Raging Lion

<u>Stand-alone fiction - dark romance</u>

Corrupt Me: Immortal Vices and Virtues

ABOUT THE AUTHOR

Everly Frost is the USA Today Bestselling author of fantasy romance, urban fantasy and paranormal romance novels. She spent her childhood dreaming of other worlds and scribbling stories on the leftover blank pages at the back of school notebooks. She lives in Brisbane, Australia with her husband and two children.

- amazon.com/author/everlyfrost
- facebook.com/everlyfrost
- instagram.com/everlyfrost
- bookbub.com/authors/everly-frost
- goodreads.com/everlyfrost